THE
TREASURE
HUNT

With best wishes

Roger Barr

THE
TREASURE
HUNT

a novel by
Roger Barr

MEDALLION PRESS
St. Paul, Minnesota

The Treasure Hunt by Roger Barr

© 1992 by Roger Barr

Published by Medallion Press
P. O. Box 4204
St. Paul, MN 55104

Additional books may be ordered from the above address

ISBN: 0–9634408–0–2

For my treasures
Kate, Ellen, and Graham,

and

in memory of
Jan Schmitz,
who always understood
what a treasure life is.

A NOTE TO THE READER

The King Boreas Treasure Medallion Hunt has been sponsored for near-ly a half century by the *Saint Paul Pioneer Press*. The city's newspaper cre-ated the mystical event around the legendary Saint Paul Winter Carnival. My thanks to the newspaper for granting me permission to use the names *Saint Paul Pioneer Press* and "King Boreas Treasure Medallion Hunt." Thanks also to the Saint Paul Winter Carnival Association for giving me permission to use the name Saint Paul Winter Carnival. Special thanks go out to Terry O'Neill, Paul Zerby, Loren Taylor, Brenda Haines, Mary Byrne, Frank Schmidt, and David Farr for their support and guidance.

The Treasure Hunt is a work of fiction. The treasure hunt clues and the characters appearing in these pages (except for well-known local and national personalities) are the product of the author's imagination. Any resemblance between these characters and actual persons living or dead is entirely coincidental.

St. Paul geography, however, is another matter. Every effort has been made to re-create the present-day cityscape as authentically as possible. Astute readers familiar with St. Paul may notice that the dates of some historical events are inaccurate, and that buildings, events, and other details referenced in these pages are now different, or no longer exist. Credit these "errors" to the imperfect memories of the characters, and also to the endless changes that occurred in St. Paul during the writ-ing of this book.

R. B.

PROLOGUE

Winter OFTEN ARRIVES EARLY in the city of St. Paul. It may be a gentle snow, or a November blizzard of such fury that old-timers talk of their experiences in the great Armistice Day blizzard of 1940. Dressed up in holiday decorations and a blanket of fresh white snow, the city's fine old homes and snowy streets look like a Currier and Ives Christmas card come to life.

After the holidays, winter loses its freshness. The snow turns gray with dirt and grime. The biting cold creeps into the very soul of the city. The deep snow and brittle cold intensify people's reactions to everything around them—to life's big problems, to the daily routine. They start to hate their winter clothes. They grow sick of shoveling snow, sick of jump-starting cars. They even begin to grow sick of each other.

In late January, however, St. Paulites pull on their coats, boots, hats, and gloves and venture out into the snow and cold. They carry snow shovels and picks, ice choppers, and garden trowels. They are searching for the King Boreas treasure medallion, which lies hidden under the snow in one of the city's parks, waiting for whoever can decipher the cryptic clues published in the *Saint Paul Pioneer Press*. The people ignore the cold as they warm to their search. The days and nights melt together and the people keep searching, caught up in the treasure hunt.

SATURDAY

KEITH REYNOLDS SNAPPED THE TELEVISION SET off and watched the picture shrink into a tiny white dot and disappear in the center of the darkened picture tube. With the television off, he could hear the wind gusting around the corner of his basement apartment, rustling the stiff, lifeless rosebushes against the foundation, making the night sound even colder than it was. He checked the thermometer in the kitchen. Eight below already, headed for twenty below according to the ten o'clock news. It was going to be a cold one tonight.

Ten-thirty was too early to go to bed on a Saturday night. He looked at his briefcase sitting on the corner of his desk, next to his computer. No way was he going to work tonight. He had already put in a brutally long week on Gopher State Products's computer program. There would be enough time early next week to get the rest of the program written and dumped into Gopher State's mainframe computer by Friday. This was Saturday night, for crying out loud.

Not that he had anything else to do. He *could* get an early start on the King Boreas Treasure Medallion Hunt. The annual treasure hunt officially started tomorrow with the publication of the first clue in the Sunday edition of the *Saint Paul Pioneer Press,* but early copies of the paper were available in convenience stores on Saturday night. The SuperAmerica down on the corner of East Seventh Street and Johnson Parkway should have the paper by now.

He was ready. This was going to be his year. This year, he was going to find the treasure medallion. He'd taken the week off to have his days free for deciphering clues and for bundling up and going out into the city to search. Three days ago, he had purchased and registered his Saint Paul Winter Carnival button, which doubled his prize money if—no, *when*—he found it. His snow shovel and two-cell flashlight were already in the trunk of the Nova. He had dug his coffee thermos out of the cupboard. His treasure hunt files were on his desk.

He was ready.

Last year he had just missed finding the medallion and collecting four thousand dollars. When he saw in the paper the picture of the people who had found it, he recognized them as people he had seen searching through the snow nearby. That meant that he had been in the right place at the same time as the finders were. And in '87, he had been searching in Mounds Park and actually saw a couple of guys find it.

Going down to the SA to get the Sunday paper would mean dressing up and going out in the cold. It was not a very appealing idea, but you could let winter push you around only so far. This last cold snap had just about done him in, a whole week with the temperature never making it above zero. The apartment was giving him a severe case of cabin fever. According to legend, cabin fever drove people to do crazy things, like commit suicide or murder.

He had no intention of committing suicide, but lately murder seemed like a definite possibility. He should keep the cabin fever defense in mind for his boss. Down at the office, General Jerry had been ragging on him and the other programmers for weeks about the most piddling, asinine details. Last week it had been office tidiness. This week it had been a ten-minute lecture about the importance of keeping their logbooks up-to-date—as if a group of professionals really needed to be told something as elementary as that. Next week it would probably be bathroom privileges. A vacation from programming work and General Jerry's orders couldn't have come at a better time.

On a decent night, he would have walked the mile or so down to the SA, but tonight walking was out of the question unless the Nova wouldn't start. He heard a gust of wind sweep around the corner of the house and rattle the rosebushes. He decided to wear his blue parka, even though he was sick of the very weight of it. He shoved his stockinged feet into his Sorels and tied the laces. He slipped into the parka and zipped it up to his chin. From the deep pockets, he pulled out gloves and a red stocking cap, and put them on as he headed out into the cold.

The Nova, its windshield frosted over, sat in the driveway next to the exterior stairwell that led down into his apartment. More than ten years old, the gold Nova was on its last legs. To be safe, he plugged in the tank heater on the engine block anytime the temperature hit zero. On the coldest nights, he pulled the battery out and kept it in the apartment on a blanket inside the front door. He would be lucky to get through the winter without having to break down and buy a new battery.

He disconnected the tank heater and swung the stiff extension cord up against the side of the house. As he unlocked the driver's door and climbed into the Nova, he heard a muffled bark from inside the house. Glancing up, he saw a hand part the sheer curtains of the window above his stairway. Mrs. Wright, the landlady, was at her usual post, keeping tabs on his comings and goings. Maybe the cabin fever defense would work on her, too, and especially on her miserable little poodle Tiffany. He could picture himself on the witness stand. *It was the weather, Your Honor. That cold spell in the last half of January—it just got to be too much. It kept snowing and she kept pushing the snow off her steps in front of my living room window so that I couldn't even see. And her dog kept barking at me every time I went out to try to start my car. I couldn't help myself.* A poodle. Any fair-minded judge would let him off for killing a poodle. It would be a public service.

The cold of the plastic seat ate through the layers of clothes, making his ass goose-bump. He sat light in the seat. "Okay." He pushed the key into the ignition. The engine turned over without firing. "Come on, damn it, start." He pumped the accelerator twice, and turned the key again, holding his breath. The engine caught and sputtered. He accelerated slowly until it ran evenly at high speed, then raced the engine a few times. The instant he let the engine fall to an idle, it coughed and died. Pumping the accelerator once, he turned the key again. The engine started on the second turn and settled into an even idle. If anything, the Nova was predictable when it came to starting—it always had to die once before it would go.

Gunning the engine, he backed into the street, bouncing over the little ridge of snow left earlier in the week by the snowplow. He had made a study of this: no matter if he shoveled the driveway early or late, the snowplow always seemed to come *after* he shoveled. Murphy's Law or something. But he was lucky that Ivy was a snow emergency route. Half of the residential streets in St. Paul were nearly impassable during the winter, growing narrower with each snowfall.

The Nova clunked along on square tires, unsure of itself. Where Ivy, Barclay, and Prosperity came together, he turned left and headed south on Prosperity toward Maryland Avenue, straining to see through the frosty windshield, wishing he had scraped it before starting out. The wind seemed to push the Nova along. Little snakelike currents of snow slithered in front of the car.

Through the frost, he saw the Maryland traffic light turn red. The brake pedal was stiff from the cold under the toe of his boot. Prosperity followed Maryland for a few feet before zigging off to the left again, winding through Phalen Center, where it ran into Johnson Parkway. Making a left on Prosperity allowed him to miss the lights at Clarence and Johnson.

With the exception of a movie theater, Phalen Center had just about everything he needed to get by: a grocery store, hardware store, Laundromat, and nearly every kind of fast food, including a couple of burger shops, a taco joint, an ice cream place, and for Sunday, a steak house.

No one was out tonight. The huge parking lot was empty except for a few snowbirds. A couple of cars huddled against the front of the taco joint, as if they were trying to get out of the wind.

He swung off Johnson Parkway into the SuperAmerica parking lot and stopped in front of the door. Even the SA looked cold, its windows frosted over, the interior a white blur. He left the Nova's engine running. The warmth of the store enveloped him, making his glasses fog over.

The Sunday papers were stacked on the floor in front of the magazine rack. As usual, the top paper was dirty and torn. Pulling one out of the middle of the stack, he checked the front page to make sure the clue was there. There was no sense buying the paper for nothing. "Treasure hunt underway," read the headline in the lower half of the page. After a paragraph of introduction came Clue 1: *Somewhere on the ground in Ramsey County, King Boreas has hidden his royal bounty.* It was a typical first clue—didn't say much. He skimmed through the rest of the article.

Out of the corner of his eye, he was aware that the woman at the checkout counter was staring at him, watching his every move, trying to be casual about it. Her eyes followed him as he walked up to the counter. She smiled at him, something more than the automatic, artificial smile clerks always wore, but exactly what the smile meant, he couldn't tell.

"Hi. Will there be anything else?"

He shook his head, ducking under her gaze. His change rang on the counter. Tucking the paper under his arm, he turned toward the door, aware that she was still staring at him. He had better get out of here quick before she called the cops.

"Excuse me." Her voice, tentative and urgent at the same time, stopped him in his tracks. "Aren't you Keith Reynolds?"

He swung around to face her. She didn't look familiar. Blond, out of a bottle, not bad-looking. Leaning toward the heavy side. She looked a little nervous.

"Yeah," he answered hesitantly.

The woman smiled again—the real thing this time. Her face flooded with a look of relief. "I thought it was you. You don't recognize me, do you? Toni Benson. Well, I'm Toni Benson now. I used to be Toni Stoltz. You were a year ahead of me in high school. I didn't know you lived in the Cities."

Toni Stoltz. A vague memory of a slender, dark-haired girl flickered through his mind.

"You sat behind me in study hall," he struggled. "You used to borrow paper from me all the time. I'm sorry, I didn't recognize you. Hi."

"Well, I've changed, I guess. Dyed my hair. Got fat. But you look just the same."

"I wouldn't go that far," he said, thankful that his stocking cap covered up his thinning hair.

"This is incredible. Meeting you after all these years. Do you live around here?"

"Up by Lake Phalen. I was on my way home from a friend's. Thought I'd stop and pick up a paper."

"How long have you lived here? In the Cities?"

"I came down in '73 to go to the U. Just sort of stayed." He groped for something to say. "How about you?"

"We came down in '83. With the mines closing down, my husband—my ex-husband now—couldn't find a job. We thought it would be better down here."

"Was it?"

"What?"

"Better. Was it better?"

"Not really. We split up anyway. Three years ago. Are you married?"

The question made him feel awkward. Why did she want to know? Was she making a play for him, acting on some long-smoldering crush?

"Not married exactly."

"Living with someone?"

"I guess you could say that." At last, a use for Mrs. Wright and her miserable poodle.

"I don't suppose you have any kids then. I got two, a boy thirteen and a girl eleven. Lance and Sarah. Here—" She pointed to two pictures in small gold frames sitting next to the cash register. "Having their pictures here makes the time go faster." She laughed nervously. "I suppose you think that's funny."

"No, not at all. I know what you mean. They look like nice kids."

"Do you stay in touch with anybody? From school, I mean?"

"Not really. I get home once in a while to see my parents. It's all changed. There isn't much to go back to anymore."

"I'm still a Silver Bay girl at heart. I don't really like it here, but there's just no jobs at home. Not that I'm setting the world on fire here." She snorted.

"How long have you worked here?"

"I started on Thanksgiving Day. They needed somebody and I told 'em I was their somebody. What do you do?"

"I work with computers."

"Do you, like, run them?"

"I'm a programmer."

"That sounds really interesting. Really." She laughed again. "I guess you could say I work with computers, too." She pointed at the electronic cash register.

"Well, that's not a true computer," he said. "It doesn't require any real programming."

A flicker of discomfort flashed across her face. "I meant it as a joke," she said.

An awkward silence grew between them, amplified by the sounds of the store: the drone of the coolers along the far wall, the low electronic hum of the cash register. The Sunday paper suddenly felt heavy under his arm.

"I'm sorry," Keith said. "I didn't mean it like it sounded."

"It's my fault. Mickey—my ex—used to correct me all the time. I guess I'm overly sensitive about stuff like that."

"It *is* a computer in the sense that it adds numbers together, I guess. What I meant was it's not a computer in the sense of one that you program to carry out certain functions, like organize spread sheets or turn equipment on and off."

"Like the kind you work with?"

"Right. Like that."

"Well, it suits my needs," she said, swiping his change off the counter. In a single motion, she rang up the sale, dropped the coins into the appropriate compartments, and pushed the drawer shut.

"I guess I better be going," he said. "I left my car running."

"Well, I'm really glad to see you, Keith. Maybe I'll see you again sometime. I put in a lot of hours here."

"I don't stop here very often. Just stopped by to pick up a paper."

"Well, I wouldn't want you to go to any trouble—"

"No, I didn't mean it like that. I don't usually come here because there's a store closer to where I live. It might be—would be—nice to see you again."

Toni ripped off a length of cash register tape and jotted a note on the back of it. "Here's my phone number at home. If I'm not here, I'm usually home. If a kid answers, don't hang up."

He folded the paper and stuffed it into his coat pocket. "It was nice to see you, Toni. I'll give you a call sometime."

"Bye."

"Bye." A blast of arctic air chilled his face as he pushed the frost-covered glass door open and stepped out into the black winter night.

The rules of the King Boreas Treasure Medallion Hunt, as he read them over a cup of bitter, reheated coffee, were about the same as they had been in years past. The contest was open to everyone except employees of the *Saint Paul Pioneer Press,* their immediate families, and members of their households. The finder would receive two thousand dollars from the paper, and an additional two thousand dollars from the Saint Paul Winter Carnival Association if the finder or finders had registered a Winter Carnival button two days before the start of the contest.

The medallion was hidden on public property on the ground. It could be wrapped in something or otherwise disguised, but it was unnecessary to destroy any property in order to find it.

The clue in the Sunday edition was the first of twelve clues. Starting Monday and continuing through Friday, two clues would be published each day, one in the morning edition of the paper, and one in the afternoon edition. The twelfth and final clue would be published in the paper on Saturday morning. If the medallion was not found by midnight Saturday, the *Pioneer Press* reserved the right to terminate the hunt and donate the money to charity.

That, he thought as he took a sip of coffee, wouldn't be necessary. He was going to find it. This year charity began right here on Ivy Avenue.

He went to his desk at the end of the room. Over the years, he had built up an extensive collection of treasure hunt materials. His bookshelf held a dozen or so books on St. Paul, including Upham's *Minnesota Geographic Names,* Empson's *The Street Where You Live,* and a couple of picture histories of the city.

On a detailed street map of St. Paul and its suburbs, he had circled with a red marker all medallion locations from 1952 to last year. He had crossed off two places on the map—Irvine Park, just outside of downtown, and the entire city of Maplewood. In 1977, the medallion had been hidden in a cigar box in Irvine Park, and the park had been torn up by all the jackass treasure hunters who didn't bother to read the rules. The park had since been restored to someone's idea of its nineteenth-century appearance. It was unlikely that the organizers would hide the medallion there again and risk damage to the park, or complaints from the neighboring residents who had sunk a ton of money into their homes.

The medallion had been hidden in Maplewood's Wakefield Park in 1971. The treasure hunters had torn that park to pieces, and Maplewood's city council had passed a resolution that year declaring that the medallion should never be hidden in Maplewood again. In spite of the council's action, the medallion had been hidden in Wakefield Park in 1982. Maplewood had raised hell all over again. It stood to reason that the medallion would not be hidden there this year. On the other hand, it also was possible that Wakefield Park was *exactly* the place officials would hide it. If they waited eleven years between 1971 and 1982, then 1993 might be the year to concentrate on Wakefield Park.

In addition to his map and books, he had a manila folder stuffed full of newspaper clippings that related to the treasure hunt. The file contained everything the *Pioneer Press* had published about the treasure hunt in the past several years—including clues, stories about the finders, stories of treasure hunts past, and letters to the editor complaining about how bad the clues were.

His pride and joy, however, was his computer file. Last summer, enduring hot nights at the main branch of the St. Paul Public Library, he had researched old microfilm copies of the St. Paul papers and made copies of the treasure hunt clues, their explanations, and the location of the medallion for each year—all the way back to the first treasure hunt in 1952. Through the late fall, he had entered all of the information into his computer, creating separate files for the first of the twelve clues, the second, and so on. This way, he could call up all first clues ever written, along with their explanations, and study them together; all third clues; or whatever clue he desired. In a separate file, he had entered the clues by year, so that he could study all twelve clues and their explanations for any given year. If there were any patterns in the clues, any twists of phrases that the clue writers used to mean certain things, he'd find them.

Keith switched on his computer and waited for the system to boot up. When the main menu appeared on the monitor screen, he called up the file "Clue 1," which contained all the first clues from the past. For the hundredth time, he read each first clue and its explanation, looking for some kind of pattern. The first clues were pretty much stiffs. About all they said was that the medallion was hidden in Ramsey County. At the end of the file, he typed in the year and then this year's first clue: *Somewhere on the ground in Ramsey County, King Boreas has hidden his royal bounty.* He sat back in his chair, clasped his hands behind his head, and stared at the screen.

The treasure hunt clues were always pretty worthless until about Wednesday. By Wednesday afternoon there were seven clues to read and interrelate. Some educated guesses could be made about where to look. The statistics, according to an old clipping in his file, were against finding the medallion before Thursday. According to the clipping, the medallion had been found on the last day, Saturday, ten times; on Friday, nine times; and six times each on Wednesday and Thursday. Twice it had been found on Tuesday, and never earlier. Again he read through the first clues on his screen, concentrating on the white type against the black background. The flashing cursor hypnotized him.

It was odd running into Toni Stoltz again after so many years. With the exception of a couple of kids who had come down to the U with him, he had never run into any Silver Bay people down here, and he hadn't seen his U classmates in years. Seeing her had been a surprise, all right. She looked so different, the dark hair and skinny body replaced by a bleached blond shag and an attractive plumpness—the kind of woman he felt himself drawn to physically. Sandy had been that type of woman.

The familiar, bitter memory slipped out—himself standing outside Sandy's front door, the locked screen door between them. "You can't just lock me out of your life," he had yelled at her through the screen. But she had. And it had hurt. He had been careful about women since Sandy. Now Toni had practically thrown herself at him, asking if he was married, giving him her home phone number. Alarmed, he had protected himself the only way he knew how, by holding back, massaging the truth a little.

It would be nice to have someone in his life—he wasn't a hermit, after all. But why lay himself open again? Why did relationships have such risks attached to them? That was the trouble with people; they were unpredictable. With computers, you wrote a program and you knew exactly what results to expect. And if something did go wrong, there were procedures to follow that would find and fix the malfunction. People malfunctioned without warning, and there was no set procedure for fixing things. He had never been able to fix things with Sandy, anyway.

One thing he could be sure of—he wasn't getting anywhere with these first clues. There just wasn't enough to go on. He saved the Clue 1 file and cleared the computer's screen.

Toni had two strikes against her already—her kids. What were they, thirteen and eleven—just at the age where kids were impossible to deal with. Sandy's kids had been about that age, and they had hated him from the beginning, Jason especially. If it hadn't been for the kids, he and Sandy probably would have gotten married.

The cursor flashed at him, waiting for instructions. He might as well open a new file for this year's clues. The white characters appeared on the screen one by one, turning into words, a sentence. Alone on the screen, the clue looked insignificant and useless to him, white type in a sea of black. On Monday he would add the second and third clues and, hopefully, have something more to go on.

Maybe he should call Toni up, get together with her, and see what she was like now. Until he talked to her again, he really wouldn't have a clue as to what to do about her. From his parka he retrieved the slip of cash register tape with her phone number, and looked at it for the first time. It was a 774 number, somewhere east of here, maybe in Maplewood. She wouldn't be there now, of course; maybe he would try calling

Sunday night or Monday. He smoothed the piece of paper and carefully placed it under the corner of the blotter on his desk.

The digital clock on his desk read 12:30, red numbers with a blinking colon between them. It was time to hit the sack. He labeled the file on the screen and hit the keys to save it. Pushing the switch on his computer, he watched the white type on the black background implode into a tiny dot in the center of the monitor screen and disappear as the screen went black.

SUNDAY

ONE

SHARON PRESCOTT USED A FORK TO TURN the strips of bacon frying in the electric skillet. A hiss of steam came out of the waffle iron, and she opened it to check the color of the waffles. Another minute or so and they would be the same golden brown as the waffles pictured on the label of the plastic syrup bottle. She smothered a yawn and reached for her Boston University coffee mug on the counter. An extra hour of sleep would have been welcome, but the Prescott Family Sunday Breakfast was a tradition that dated all the way back to their lazy, carefree Sundays at Boston U, before she and Phil were even married, and long before the boys were born. In the Old Days, as the boys so cruelly put it, Sunday morning breakfast had consisted of whatever Phil could stuff into his pockets at the dorm cafeteria and smuggle back upstairs to his room, where she waited for the code knock, ravenous and in violation of dormitory rules. These days, breakfast meant a properly set table, coffee, orange juice—the works, a scene right out of "Father Knows Best" or "Leave It To Beaver." It was the one meal each week that Phil made a point not to miss. Consequently, she made a point to get up to prepare it. She opened the waffle iron again and flipped the golden waffle onto a waiting plate, noticing that the corner was missing because she had not poured in quite enough batter. This one would never have made the label on the syrup bottle.

She heard Phil trooping down the front stairs, on his way to the porch to get the Sunday paper. The front door opened, banged shut, opened, and banged shut again. Sunday morning sounds. Phil came into the kitchen, paper in hand, wearing a T-shirt and sweat pants.

"Ooh, bare feet," she said. "How can you stand to go outside in the cold like that?"

19

"It's not that bad."

"Eighteen below zero is not that bad?"

"Paper says it's supposed to warm up." He held up the front page and pointed to the kicker above the masthead. "Twenties by the middle of the week. That's almost spring." He glanced into the skillet. "Smells good."

"Temperatures in the twenties are *not* my idea of spring," Sharon said. "I wish you'd stop that."

"Stop what?" She looked up from the skillet, fork poised in midair, a strip of bacon hanging from it, dripping grease.

"Taking every opportunity to complain about the cold, which is another way of reminding me that you didn't want to move out here in the first place. You know, I miss Boston, too. But this is where the opportunity was." Phil poured himself a cup of coffee and sat down at the kitchen table with the paper to separate the news sections from the advertising supplements.

Sharon stared at her husband across the kitchen peninsula. She felt the heat from the skillet on her face, and inside her she felt the heat of her anger bubbling up through her sudden hurt. He was always jumping on her about that. Their relocation two years ago from Boston to St. Paul was the only major sore point in their eighteen-year marriage, festering in innocent comments that one made and the other took the wrong way. It was an old argument without resolution or concession, a series of chess matches ending in stalemate after stalemate. Except for the first match, which Phil had won when he had decided to take the phone company's promotion, uprooting them, bringing them here. Boston vs. St. Paul could ruin any day, if she let it. But not today. Not on Sunday morning.

"Phil, I didn't mean it that way. I'm sorry." And then a little bubble of anger burst to the surface, and she heard herself go on, although she didn't want to: "You know, *you* never miss an opportunity to tell me how 'invigorating' the weather is here. I get just as tired of you defending the weather all the time."

Phil dropped a Dayton's supplement onto the stack of advertising. The stacks of news and advertising were about the same height. "Well, it *is* invigorating."

"Tell me, Mr. T-shirt-and-Bare-Feet: how invigorating was it out there on the front steps?"

"Invigorating as hell." Phil shivered violently in exaggerated agony, hugging his arms to his chest, doubling over in his chair. "Brrrrrr."

Sharon laughed and felt her anger slip away. "Well, at least you admit it's cold."

"Babe, I'm sorry, too. I didn't mean to jump on you so hard. It's just that . . . oh, hell. You know what I'm trying to say. How many times have we been over this?"

"Two thousand one hundred and twelve."

"That many?"

"That few. Call the boys again. Breakfast will be ready by the time they get down. Tell them we're having waffles. Maybe that'll hurry them up."

"Waffles. Hot damn." Phil scurried out of the kitchen. His voice, wound up like a morning disk jockey's, made her smile as he called from the foot of the staircase, "Jeff! Chris! Hey, boys. Let's hit the floor. Your mother's got breakfast ready. Waffles and bacon." The Deejay, as Jeff sometimes called him. And when no immediate answer came from upstairs, she heard his feet pounding up the stairs, as he headed up to shake each boy awake and marshal them downstairs to the table. He approached everything this same way, flat out, with equal parts of energy and impatience. That combination had carried him (and them, too, she knew) a long way; no doubt it was what made him the successful salesman he was. But sometimes—like now—that relentless energy irritated her. Giving them five minutes wouldn't hurt.

Over breakfast, Sharon felt her irritation float away. Across the table from her, the boys, still wearing their bathrobes, were packing away the last of their third helping of waffles and bacon. Sometimes, as she looked at the two of them these past few weeks, it seemed as though she were looking at someone else's grown-up children. Jeff was sixteen already, filling out through the shoulders and chest. A serious boy, more adult than child, spending as much time with the front page of the paper as he did with the sports and the funnies.

And Chris, doing better in the seventh grade than he had done last year just after the move, had pulled his grades up from Cs to Bs, and even a stray A here and there. At thirteen, he was still all boy, but already full of the same restless energy and impatience as Phil, and totally consumed by ice hockey.

" . . . bet you that the North Stars beat the Bruins," he was telling Phil. "They've beat 'em every time this year."

"The North Stars used to get creamed by Boston all the time," Phil said. "Back about ten years ago they couldn't beat the Bruins to save their life. Once I saw this brawl between them, and like Rodney Dangerfield used to say, a hockey game broke out. What a fight. They set the all-time NHL record for penalty minutes in a single game."

"Who won?"

"North Stars. Their first-ever win in Boston Garden."

"So who do you think is going to win tonight?" Chris asked.

"Well, the North Stars, of course," Phil said, feigning disbelief at the question. "Is there any doubt?"

"Dad, do you know anything about the Winter Carnival?" Jeff asked from behind the front page of the paper.

"It's an annual city festival here," Phil said. "It's supposed to get people out of their houses and into the invigorating—" he glanced swiftly at Sharon "—cold weather, instead of holing up for the winter in front of the tube. Why?"

"They have some kind of contest," Jeff said. "You find a treasure and win a bunch of money. There's a clue here."

"Oh, yeah," Phil said. "I think I remember something like that from last year. So what's the clue?"

Jeff spread the front page over the table, the edge dipping into the leftover syrup on his plate. *"Somewhere on the ground in Ramsey County, King Boreas has hidden his royal bounty."*

"Piece of cake," Phil said. "It's in Ramsey County."

"Where in Ramsey County?" Sharon said. "I think you have to be a little more specific than that."

"Read it again."

"Somewhere on the ground in Ramsey County, King Boreas has hidden his royal bounty."

"On the *ground,* in Ramsey County."

"So run out and pick it up." Sharon propped her elbows on the table and rested her chin on her clasped hands. "I'll make out a shopping list to spend the money. Let's see . . . we could redo the kitchen, or—"

"Well, I need a few more clues before I know *where* on the ground." Phil turned to Jeff. "When's the next clue?"

"Tomorrow."

"Do you think we could look for it, Dad?" Chris's face wore the same look of ambition and impatience as his father's.

"Look for it? We'll not only look for it, we'll find it, too!"

"Do you think we have a chance?" Jeff looked skeptical, his dark eyes deep pools of doubt. "We don't know much about the city. There are people who have lived here all their lives."

"Come on, Jeff." Phil leaned back in his chair and crossed his arms over his chest, his usual sign of disgust. "You gotta think positive. The golden rule of sales. Hasn't living around your old dad rubbed off at all? If you assume you can't find it, you won't. On the other hand, you think you can and you just might. Remember the Little Engine That Could.

"We need a little optimism here," Phil continued. He placed his open palms on the table and leaned toward them. "Okay. Memo: Effective immediately, the Prescott family of Cambridge Avenue, Tangletown, St. Paul, in the shadow of Macalester College, will devote all its spare time to searching for and finding the Winter Carnival treasure. The prize money from the aforementioned treasure hunt find will be used tooooooo . . ."

Sharon watched as he held onto the last word, drawing it out until he had everyone's attention. He fell silent for a moment, then gave her a wink from across the table.

" . . . finance a trip to Boston or the Bahamas, your mother's choice."

"All right!" Chris clapped his hands and raised his arms over his head as if he had just scored a goal. "Where we goin', Ma?"

"Well, maybe neither place." She looked across the table at Phil. "I'm thinking of something a little more exotic . . . the South Seas, Africa, Australia. But first we have to find the treasure."

"Now let's get this organized." Phil spoke in what Sharon thought of as his supervisor's voice—the tone she imagined he used when he handed out assignments to his sales staff at work. He turned to Jeff. "What are the rules here, Tiger?"

"Sounds pretty cut and dried," Phil said when Jeff had finished. "Anybody got any ideas? A lot of times they'll give it away in the very first clue if you just crack their code. You've got to think in terms of double or triple meanings. Somebody should take notes. Chris, get a tablet or something to write on and a pen."

Chris disappeared into the living room. She heard his quick feet taking the stairs two at a time. In a moment, he returned with a school notebook and a ball point pen, which he dropped in front of her.

"Here, Ma."

"How come I got elected secretary?"

"'Cuz you can write pretty. Mrs. Addison makes me rewrite stuff all the time in English because she can't read it." He dropped into his chair, out of breath.

"Well, you want notes, Mister, you just take them yourself. Practice your penmanship." She pushed the notebook over to him.

"Geez."

"No 'geez.' Do it."

"Okay," Phil said, "what's the first really important word? Read the clue, Jeff."

"Somewhere on the ground—"

"There," Phil interrupted. "Ground. What does the word *ground* mean?"

"What you walk on. You know, dirt."

"That's the obvious meaning," Phil said. "What else could it mean?"

"Coffee grounds," Chris offered. "Hey, Ma, did you look in the coffee pot this morning?"

"Come on, guys," Phil said. "What else? Coffee grounds is the right idea. What else can it mean?"

"It's what parents do to kids when their kids do something they don't like." Jeff spoke softly, not looking at either of them.

"Yeah!" Chris jeered, "you should know. Two weeks for staying out late."

"Shut up, Squirrel Face," Jeff said.

"I don't shut up, I grow up," Chris fired back. "When I see you, I throw up. When I throw up, I—"

"Chris, that's enough," Sharon interrupted. She glanced across the corner of the table at Jeff. "That's old business." And troubling business, too. She had imposed the two-week sentence more for his being evasive about where he was and with whom, than for being late. He was sliding into those scary, uncommunicative years when he was developing ideas—a life—of his own. The line between being a concerned parent who set limits, and a permissive parent who allowed him to make his own decisions seemed to keep moving beneath her feet.

Phil looked around the table. "Can we get on with this treasure hunt, if everyone is through? We were talking about what ground could mean besides the stuff you walk on."

She gave Jeff a final look. "How about to anchor an object so that it won't electrocute you?" she said.

"Hey, that's good," Phil said. "It could mean a power plant or power station of some kind. Write that down. Now that's the right idea. Ground relates to something about the city, suggesting a place." He turned to Chris. "What have we got so far, Slapshot?"

"Coffee grounds, being grounded, not getting zapped by electricity."

"What else? *Ground.* To ground." Phil was on a roll, she could tell, absolutely in his element. Ideas came spinning out in a steady monologue. "Let's see, what other grounds are there? Grounds for divorce. That's not related to the city. Grounding out. Grounders, could indicate baseball diamonds. Feet on the ground . . . ground round. Ground Round—that restaurant we went to once. Where was that?"

"Har Mar Mall."

"Somewhere near there. Run aground, as in boats running aground."

"That could be near the river," Jeff said.

"Right. What do the rules say? Hidden on public property? That means parks along the river. Where's our map of the city?"

"Out in the car," Sharon said. "You want it, you go get it. The weather's invigorating."

Phil shot her a glance. "Let's move on. What other important words are there? Read the clue again, Jeff."

"Somewhere on the ground in Ramsey County, King Boreas has hidden his royal bounty."

"I'd say royal and bounty are the only other words that could have double meanings," Phil said.

"Not necessarily. Ramsey could mean something," she said. "There's a Ramsey Street. It veers off from Summit Avenue. I took it by accident one day. What a hill. Maybe there's a park near the street. Or even a Ramsey Park somewhere. Royal could refer to something connected to royalty. Kings, queens, princes, like that. Maybe there's a King Street or King Park. Queen Street."

"I like that," Phil said. "You got all that down, Chris?" He watched as Chris scribbled down big, jerky words that each took up half a line. "Any other ideas? Anybody? You know what I think? I think it's on the ground somewhere in Ramsey County. I think we need another clue."

"Boy, Dad, brilliant deduction," Jeff snorted. "I said that earlier."

"You did," Phil acknowledged. "But you said that instead of trying to figure out what the clue meant. I said it *after* we tried. There's a big difference."

To Phil every instance, every situation offered an opportunity to teach. He spoke in lessons. Sharon watched as Jeff searched through the paper and selected the funnies, his quest for knowledge of the world's news apparently satisfied. Like herself, he seemed to take his father's daily lessons in stride.

"All right," Phil said. "Enough for today. Everybody back here tomorrow morning for the second clue. You guys better get dressed."

"Put your plates in the sink," she said. "And see to it that the dishes are done by dinner time."

Phil leaned forward and pointed a finger at Chris's slim chest. "I want to see some attention to homework today, Buster. Get a few more of those Bs up to As." Reaching out, he landed a light, fatherly swat across Chris's rear as he passed by.

After the boys had gone, she looked across the table at her husband. "You didn't need to say that," she said.

"Say what?" Phil looked at her, his deep blue eyes even, unblinking.

"About Boston or the Bahamas."

A smile spread across his unshaven face. "Well, I think it would be good for you. Good for all of us. I know I could use a break. Keeping Flannary happy has about worn me out. You've put in a lot of hours getting your bookstore off the ground. Elaine, too. So tell me, Babe," he said, reaching across the table to catch her hand, "which should I pack, my winter clothes for Boston or my swimming trunks and golf clubs for Nassau?"

"Well, you don't mind if I don't make reservations just yet?"

"You're as pessimistic as Jeff."

"Or as practical. What are you going to do for the rest of the day?"

"Down to the office for a while. Flannary has some kind of meeting scheduled for tomorrow and I want to look everything over, just in case I need to make a report. It won't take long. How about you?"

"It's my Sunday to work," she reminded him. "Did you forget?"

He held his forearms in front of his face as if to shield himself from her.

"Guilty," he confessed.

She stood up. How could he always remember when it was Elaine's weekend to run the bookstore, but never when it was hers?

"It will be interesting to see what we get for traffic on a cold Sunday." She poked him in the ribs as she passed his chair. "See how many locals come out in this invigorating weather."

Phil grimaced and clasped his hands to his heart. "Uhhh! Shot through the heart with my own word." He slumped in his chair, his head lolling to one side, feigning death.

TWO

"Now to use a jigsaw you got to have a strong hand and a good eye . . . . Take your time with the saw . . . . Don't try to saw it all off in one stroke . . . . Be careful to follow the line we drew . . . . That's great, Alfred. Darned if that don't look just like a cat . . . ."

"Do you really think so, Rudy?"

"You bet. Now we'll paint it all black, then paint the lines of the face in with white, and we'll have us a black cat. Then we nail this wedge on the back and we'll have a doorstop. People'll see it by the door and think it's a real cat—"

"Alfred? Alfred?"

It was Genevieve's voice, urgent and questioning, that floated down the basement steps to where Alfred sat alone on a carpenter's sawhorse. Where was Rudy? Wasn't he just here? Where did he go? In the damp basement chill, he felt tears burning down the sides of his face. Above him, he heard his wife's feet moving across the kitchen floor toward the basement door.

"Alfred Krause! Are you there?" A note of alarm had crept into her voice. He was aware, suddenly, of sharp pain in his hands, and looked down to see that he was clutching the wooden cat doorstop so tightly that, had it been alive, he would have smothered the life out of it. Quickly he dropped the doorstop on the workbench and pulled his handkerchief from his hip pocket to wipe his eyes and try to pull himself together, to throw off the stone weight of grief that was crushing him.

"Alfred!" Genevieve's tone was sharp. Before he could find his voice to answer, he heard her feet heavy on the old wooden steps as she made her way down the narrow staircase. A moment later, her sturdy, indignant profile appeared in the doorway of his workshop.

"Why didn't you answer me? Are you going deaf? I was half—Alfred! What's wrong?" She took a step toward him. "Did you hurt yourself?"

He turned away from her, stared hard at the wall filled with neatly hanging tools. He blinked back his tears. The shame at being caught like this, blubbering like some two-year-old who had skinned his knee, flooded over his grief. But then his eyes fell again on the wooden cat. Its rich black color and face of white lines, once so bright, had faded over the fifty-odd years since he had painted it. And in his mind he saw again that recent, awful scene, the coffee mug lying on its side on the faded, thinning carpet, a large brown stain spreading away from it, the newspaper crumpled under the prostrate body; and the face, Rudy's face, cheek pressed into the carpet, puffy like rising bread dough, discolored. Inside himself he felt the ground shifting, earth giving way. It was no use. This weight he had been carrying was too much, too heavy. Rudy. His only brother. Gone.

He felt Genevieve's hand on his shoulder. "It's all right, Alfred," she said in a near whisper. "Let it go. You've held it in too long. It's all right to cry." It was not so much Genevieve's words as her tone of voice that tore down the last bricks in the wall of his resistance. His grief came crashing down on him, doubling him over at the middle. He covered his face with his hands and wept into them. Great, choking sobs shook his shoulders, cutting off his breath. In the chilly silence, his sobs echoed around him. Blood pulsed through his ears. A parade of images flashed through his mind—Rudy's body lying on his living room floor, the oak casket surrounded by flowers, the cold grave hacked into the frozen, snowy earth, the flowers wilted and brown with frost.

At last, he straightened up. He reached for his handkerchief and wiped his eyes, stared at a red-handled pipe wrench hanging on the wall, and tried to pull himself back together. He blew his nose hard into his handkerchief.

"You were down here so quiet, for so long, I thought something had happened to you," Genevieve said.

"I ran across this today while I was cleaning at Rudy's house." He picked up the wooden cat and turned it over in his hands, scratching at the grime with a fingernail. He looked up at Genevieve. Behind her glasses, her eyes were wet. Tears streaked the sides of her lined face. Like the wooden cat he held in his hands, she suddenly seemed old, faded. Everything—himself especially—seemed old and faded today.

"Rudy helped me make this when I was eleven. I was sick with rheumatic fever and couldn't go outside all winter. He spent every afternoon after school with me. I cut it out with a jigsaw and he helped me paint it. It was the first thing I ever made with my own hands." His hands caressed the wooden cat as though it were real. "It got me started blubbering and I couldn't make myself stop."

"You Krause men," Genevieve clucked. "Holding your feelings in. It's not good for you."

"Takes a man not to cry. Rudy said that once."

"Well, he was wrong. I don't care if he was your brother. It's a natural thing. You don't lose a brother and just get over it like a case of the flu. We should hurry up and finish cleaning that house out and get it sold. It's not good for you to sit in there day after day looking at all those old things." She patted his shoulder to take the harshness out of her words. "Come upstairs. It's too cold down here."

"In a minute."

Genevieve pulled her sweater around her. "Well, I'm going up." She stood next to him for a moment and then silently went upstairs.

Slowly he stood up. His arms and legs seemed as heavy as cement, yet he felt lightheaded. His eyes burned. Out the basement window, the snow in the backyard was pink with the glow of the setting sun, the graying shadows bending toward the east. The end of the day, when everything seemed just slightly larger than life. He picked up the wooden cat and traced a finger along the wavy edge of one of the cat's ears. That long-ago afternoon when they made this doorstop had been a bone-chilling day like this one, thirty below in the days before wind chill was invented, and you just looked at the thermometer to see how cold it was. Yet it seemed like yesterday. *To use a jigsaw you got to have a strong hand and a good eye.* He had used both hands to make the jigsaw eat its way through the white wood. How his arms had ached from the tiny, rapid strokes of the jigsaw as he labored his way around the outline of the cat pattern, with its tricky curves and sharp points. *Be careful to follow the line we drew.* Here and there he could still see where he had strayed off the line and then looked to Rudy in shame and frustration for help. But Rudy, standing over him, offered advice instead of help. *Don't try to saw it all off in one stroke.* And painting in the face, when his hand had trembled with uncertainty, making the white nose a little off center and the whiskers a little too thick, Rudy had pretended not to notice, heaping praise on him for a job well done. *Darned if that don't look just like a cat. People'll see it by the door and think it's a real cat.* The words had made him swell with pride. And now . . .

He carried the doorstop upstairs. At the top of the stairs, he paused to push its wedge under the bottom of the basement door. Two steps away he turned around to look. No one, either now or back then, could possibly mistake it for a real cat sitting in front of the door.

Genevieve was in the living room, settled into her chair, her feet up on the ottoman. A section of the Sunday paper was spread out on her abundant lap. In the halo of light cast by the reading lamp, she looked as old and misshapen as the chair she sat in—so much so that she and the chair looked like part of the same object. There had been a time when both she and the chair had looked better. Settling into his own chair, he felt old and misshapen himself, his insides yanked and twisted around. His burning eyes had ignited a crackling headache.

Genevieve looked up from the paper. "Remember Janet's friend Melody who used to play here sometimes when they were kids? Her mother died. She still lived over on Michigan. Seventy-two."

Seventy-two. The same age as Rudy. Alfred picked up the A section of the paper and paged through it, trying to read, to form the letters into words, into sentences. He found it especially hard to read these past few weeks—to concentrate on much of anything. Though his eyes followed the words, his mind often strayed away from the business at hand, wandering aimlessly through the years to recall old times and conversations with people long since gone. Always, it seemed, these pleasant journeys brought him back to the same place, back to the same task: adjusting his life to fit the present.

Genevieve folded her section of the paper and dropped it onto the stack on the floor beside her.

"Are you reading the treasure hunt clue?"

He shook his head.

"Well, it didn't say much."

He turned back to the front page and found the headline near the bottom. *Somewhere on the ground in Ramsey County, King Boreas has hidden his royal bounty.*

"Are you going to look this year?" Genevieve asked.

Another adjustment to make, hitting him full in the face without warning. He and Rudy had searched for the medallion for years, without ever finding it, of course. Good luck like that always seemed to happen to somebody else. But it was fun, the two of them banging around the city, like in the old days when they were kids. They'd actually come close to finding it one year, seeing a man and woman find it stuffed inside a tobacco pouch that was wedged between the slats of a bench in old Smith Park in downtown. Looking for the treasure without Rudy wouldn't be the same.

"Too cold," he said.

"But you always look. You and Rudy always—" From the kitchen the harsh ring of the telephone startled them, mercifully interrupting her. "Now who is *that*?" Genevieve drew herself up from her chair and hurried off toward the kitchen.

He counted the rings until Genevieve answered. Six. She used to answer in three or four. He didn't know who it was, but he knew who it wasn't. Until last Thanksgiving weekend, Rudy often called about this time of day—just before dinner—and the two of them would make plans to go fishing the next day or to hit the garage sales.

"It's Janet!" Genevieve called from the kitchen. He folded his newspaper and laid it on the end table. He knew this call from his daughter had been coming. Slowly he pushed himself to his feet and shuffled through the little dining room into the kitchen.

" . . . Well, it's cold today, I'll tell you," Genevieve was saying. "Twenty-three below this morning on our thermometer. WCCO said eighteen below . . . . I can't wait myself." She cupped a hand over the receiver. "She wants to know when we're coming."

He sat down heavily at the kitchen table. He didn't look at Genevieve, looking instead out the window into the wintry side yard.

"I don't know if we should go."

"Not go?" Genevieve was astonished. "We've been planning to go ever since they moved down there. Why don't you want to go?"

He looked at the basement door, at the cat doorstop. "You know," he said.

"Well here, you tell her, then." Genevieve held out the receiver to him.

He waved it away. "Just tell her we'll have to call her back on this."

"You tell her." Genevieve laid the receiver on the counter and walked out of the kitchen.

He watched her go. He rubbed his throbbing temples with the tips of his fingers and dug at his burning eyes. How would he explain it? How could he tell them?

"Mom? Mom?" From the receiver his daughter's voice, thin and far away, was barely audible. "Hello? Mom!"

He picked up the receiver and slowly raised it to his ear. It felt as heavy as lead.

"This is your dad."

"Daddy?" Janet's voice was shrill with surprise. "What's going on? Where's Mom?"

"She went in the other room. She wanted me to talk to you."

"About what?"

"About the trip."

"What about it? Daddy, what's going on?"

"We'll have to call you back on this."

"Why?"

"We're not sure we're coming."

"Not coming? Why?"

"It's just not a good idea to come right now."

"But you haven't been here since we moved. I thought you were looking forward to coming down to Houston."

"It ain't a very good time. Maybe we can come later."

"Is something wrong?"

"No," he said quickly. "Nothing's wrong. It's just . . . not a very good time."

"The kids will be disappointed. So will Dan. I'm disappointed, too."

"We'll see about coming some other time," he said.

"Well, I suppose I better get supper going," Janet said. "Dan and the kids will be home pretty soon. They went to see the Rockets play this afternoon." Her voice was tight with disappointment. "Tell Mom good-bye."

"I will."

"Bye, Daddy."

"Bye."

He hung up the phone. Rudy was gone, and now both Genevieve and Janet were mad at him. He stared again out the kitchen window into the side yard. The sun had disappeared, and the sky had turned a deep red over the bare lilac hedge. The snowbanks that the wind had swept up against the lilacs had turned gray. The world no longer seemed larger than life as it had at sunset. It seemed diminished somehow, darker and more lonely and frightening, as if some unknown thing were outside in the cold, waiting for him.

Genevieve came silently into the kitchen. She leaned against the door casing, her arms folded over her chest. Her face was set like stone. Behind her glasses, her eyes were as hard and cold as sapphires. Her mouth was drawn into a straight line.

"Now don't start on me," he said.

"What's the matter with you?" she demanded. "Why don't you want to go? They've lived down there for two years and we haven't been yet."

"I said not to start on me," he snapped.

But Genevieve was insistent. "Well, I'd like to know. We planned to go this year. And now you say no."

"Leave me alone on this," he said angrily, turning away from her. He could feel her sapphire eyes boring a hole in the back of his head.

"I'm going upstairs," she said. "You can just make your own supper."

He sat alone at the kitchen table, feeling as diminished as the fallen day. He crossed his arms on the table and rested his head on them, wishing that the unknown thing lurking about outside in the darkness could find him.

THREE

BRUCE MITCHELL AWOKE WITH A START, a clanging sound in his ears. Automatically he reached for the alarm clock on the nightstand, groping in the darkness for the button on the back. The clanging came again in a hard, shattering burst that sent a current of fright through him even as he recognized it as the sound of the phone. He rolled over and, reaching out with one hand into the cold, fumbled around on the floor beside the bed. The night chill pricked his bare shoulder as he snapped up the receiver.

"Hullo."

"So you know where that treasure's hid?"

"Hey, Butch." Bruce rolled over onto his back, pulling the phone under the covers with him. He should have known it would be St. John. He yawned and shook the cobwebs out of his head. "Sure. I thought I'd run out tomorrow morning and pick it up."

"So where is it?" St. John demanded.

"Beats the shit out of me."

"Me, too. So how you doing there, Sundance?"

"Well, I was studying the insides of my eyelids. What time is it, anyway?"

"Little after midnight."

"Midnight! Christ, Butch, don't you ever go to bed? Haven't you got anything better to do than call me in the middle of the night?"

"Your lady friend there?"

"No, she's at her place."

"I almost didn't call. I figured she'd be there."

"Ah, she was afraid her car wouldn't start tomorrow, so she went back to her place where she could put it in the garage. So what do you want?"

"You sure as hell don't have it."

"No, and I wouldn't give it to you if I had it to give."

St. John's staccato laugh filled his ear. The laugh ended in a raspy cough.

"*Ewe* would have to say that," St. John said. "Somebody say go. One-two-three go. I'll bet you really went out on a *lamb* for that one."

Pun derby. Bruce sat up in the darkness, the covers falling away from him. Ewe. Lamb. Things related to sheep. His mind spun like a roulette wheel, a blur of red and black. The little pea rattled around inside his head, unable to land on anything. Sheep. Sheep.

"That was only two-thirds of a pun—pee-yew!" he said. If all else failed, put the enemy on the defensive.

"Still, I bet it made you feel *sheepish*." St. John was rolling. "I'll bet it really got your *goat*. Come on, man, I'm creamin' you."

"Shit," Bruce protested, "What do you expect? Wake me up out of a dead sleep and expect me to be quick-witted."

"Not quick-witted. Half-witted, maybe."

"I'd give a *buck* to come up with a decent pun." Finally, a hit. And it even made sense in respect to the rest of the conversation, and by all rights should count for extra points.

"You're just trying to pull the *wool* over my eyes."

"That's *shear* nonsense. But I am trying to *clip* you. I'm trying to *ram* these puns down your throat."

"Well, it's about to get my *goat.*"

"Uh-uh! You already said that one," Bruce said, fully awake now. "Game's over."

"Don't try to *kid* me."

"Doesn't count. Game's over."

"So how many'd you get there, Sundance?"

He went through his list. Buck, shear, clip, ram. "Four." A respectable showing, considering he was dead asleep forty-five seconds ago. St. John wouldn't even remember to breathe forty-five seconds after he woke up if it wasn't natural. "How about you?"

"Let's see . . . ewe, lamb, sheepish, goat, . . . wool . . . . Five, I guess."

"Cheap win. You had the advantage. You were awake." Shivering, Bruce snuggled back into the warmth of the heavy covers, pulling them up to his chin. In the few seconds that he had been uncovered, his body had turned to ice.

"So how's it going, Butch?" he asked. "Did you hear today if you were going back to work tomorrow?"

On the other end of the line, he heard St. John take a deep breath as though he were about to dive into a swimming pool and swim to the other end without coming up for air.

"Nope. Probably won't go back this week. Man, I'll be glad when they get that sucker roughed in and we can get some heaters in there."

"That's one thing I don't miss about construction work," Bruce said. "In the winter you have to freeze if you want to eat."

He heard St. John take another deep breath. "So guess who called me just a little while ago."

"Your ex-wife."

"Wrong. My ex-wife. How did you guess?"

"Only two people would call you this late. I'm one of them, and I was sawing logs. So what did Old-What's-Her-Face want?"

"Ah, Christ, I don't know. She calls me up and just starts talking to me like nothing ever happened. Tells me all about how she's doing, tells about this ski trip she's taking. I thought she was going to invite herself over for the night, she was so friendly. Then she starts telling me about some doorknob she's been going out with, and how wonderful he is and everything. All of a sudden she just cuts loose and starts yelling at me, telling me what a son of a bitch I am, and how I ruined her life. Then she calls me an asshole and hangs up on me."

"Well," Bruce drawled into the receiver, "you are an asshole." The two of them laughed. It was an old, familiar joke of long-forgotten origin, but it made them laugh every time.

"Thanks, I needed that," St. John said. "I'll tell you, Sundance, I don't know what I'm going to do with her." St. John fell silent. Bruce heard the snap of a match, a deep drag on a cigarette, and a long exhale. In his mind, he could picture St. John pacing his kitchen floor, his stiletto exhale of smoke dissipating under the glare of the kitchen's fluorescent light. The line hummed with a jumble of noise, a snatch of metallic conversation from crossed wires. ". . . tell him he can't see the kids unless he pays his support," a woman's indignant voice was saying. "But Mom, that's not fair to the kids." "Do you think what he's doing to you and the kids is fair?" He waited for St. John to go on. Often their late-night phone calls had as much silence as conversation, as if they were sitting together in the same room, pulling their thoughts together. Lying there in the darkness, he could imagine simultaneous telephone conversations going on across the country, people coming off a bad weekend of dealing with ex-husbands and ex-wives, calling up friends or relatives to unload their frustrations.

"You still there, Butch?"

"Yeah. God, she pisses me off." Another silence. The voices of the mother and daughter were gone. Bruce heard the sound of water running.

"You doing dishes?"

"Just a couple of pans. You watch the North Stars tonight?"

"Hell, no. Sunday nights are depressing enough as it is. Who won?"

"Boston shelled 'em 8-2. They played most of the game in the Stars' end zone."

"What's that, three losses in a row?"

"Four. They won't even make the playoffs if they keep playing like this. God, they suck. Just like the Vikings did this season." He heard a burst of running water as St. John rinsed off a pan. "What is it about our professional sports teams that they're so bad? God damn it, anyway."

Over the years, he had observed that St. John's mood often could be predicted by checking the sports page for the standings of the local pro teams. If the team was hot, St. John could be counted on to point out the silver lining behind every cloud. But with the Vikings missing the playoffs again, the Timberwolves getting slaughtered night after night, and the North Stars struggling through the middle of another mediocre season, St. John had taken to looking at the cloud in front of the silver lining. Since hockey and basketball season overlapped with baseball season, there was every reason to fear that St. John's funk would continue through the spring and summer, and right into football season, when the cycle would start all over again. What he really needed in life right now was for the North Stars to get hot.

"So what do you think I should do about her?" St. John asked. The sound of another burst of water came over the receiver, followed by a heavy, dull clunk of cast iron on stainless steel.

"Tell her to go fuck herself and hang up," he said. He switched the receiver to his other ear. "Why take that kind of shit? If you put the brakes on her and don't put up with that shit, she'll probably lay off."

"She catches me by surprise," St.John said. "Lays all that nice stuff on me, and I think this time she's going to be nice. Then all of a sudden, she goes for my throat."

"That's her thing. Shoot the breeze for a while, and then let fly. You ought to know that by now."

"I know. Shit." A final clatter of pans came over the receiver, followed by the sound of water gurgling down the drain.

A pair of pale rectangles of light from a passing car headed out South Robert Street appeared on the bedroom wall and slid around the room, briefly illuminating the walls, the furniture. Above the bedroom door, the rectangles broke across the ceiling in odd, geometric patterns and suddenly disappeared as though yanked out of the room through the window.

The long silence was broken by the snap of a match as St. John lit another cigarette. "So where do you figure they planted that medallion this year?"

"I say Como Park."

"You say that every year."

"So one of these years I'll be right. I didn't even read the clue today. They never say anything the first day except that it's buried on the ground somewhere."

St. John took a drag off his cigarette. "I think they hid it in one of those dinky little parks in the suburbs that nobody's ever heard of. The only way you can find it is to wait until the last clue on Saturday and they tell you right where to look. Then you got to fight off about two million people."

"We ought to show up with a couple of flamethrowers and roast everybody the hell out of there."

They laughed. "Yeah," St. John said, "and then use the flamethrowers to melt the snow. I like that. Beats shoveling."

"Probably melt the medallion, too," Bruce said.

"You know, some year some kid is gonna find it and not know what it is. Wouldn't that be a pisser? Search all week and the damn thing isn't even there?"

"I heard once they hide it the night before, so nobody can accidentally find it early."

"I remember reading or hearing that they hide it early, like in the fall."

"They never say in the paper."

"They probably hid it months ago, and some kid probably found it and stuck it in his coin collection," St. John said. "Or else we'll look for it all week, and some plowhead will have found it early in the week and sat on it. Probably my ex-wife and her doorknob boyfriend will find it."

"You all right?"

"Yeah, shit. I just don't know what to do."

"I know how you feel. Michelle did the same thing to me. Just try not to let her get to you. That's what she wants. Just try to slough it off. We already know you're a son of a bitch and an asshole, so don't sweat it."

"What a jerk."

"Hey, that's what friends are for." Bruce yawned and adjusted the covers around him. Under their comfortable weight, he suddenly felt his exhaustion tugging at him, pulling him under the surface of consciousness, like a trout rising up from the dark depths to take a fly.

"God, I'm about to fall asleep on you here," he said. "I got classes in the morning."

"Yeah, well, I better let you go. Maybe I'll give you a buzz tomorrow."

"You sure you're okay?"

"Yeah. I'm all right. Thanks for listening there, Sundance."

"Well, hang in there. It gets better. Boy, does it get better . . . . Every time she and I do it, it gets better—"

"Well, don't let your eyelids slam shut," St. John said.

"Later, Butch."

Lying alone in the darkness, the covers smothering him with a pleasant warmth, he felt a sadness creep over him. St. John was wound up. Karen could sure push his buttons. He would be up most of the night wandering around his apartment, listening to the blues on his stereo, working his way through a pack of cigarettes. A flicker of guilt passed through him for cutting St. John a little short. It took St. John awhile to open up, to get around to saying what was on his mind. He probably should have given him a little more time. That, after all, was what friends were really for.

Three years ago, St. John certainly had been there for him when he had split up with Michelle, sitting up with him into the wee hours when he wanted to talk, walking around and around Como Lake when he couldn't stand to sit—their record was seven laps in a single evening—and finally, in exasperation, kicking him in the ass, forcing him to get his life started again. In those strange, discordant days, their friendship, which stretched back over ten years, had turned from gold to platinum, taking its place among the great friendships of all time. Lennon and McCartney cranking out hit after hit, Laurel and Hardy lugging the piano up an endless staircase, and of course, Butch and Sundance, swearing they would never be taken alive.

Dennis St. John and Bruce Mitchell. Butch Cassidy and the Sundance Kid. They'd seen that movie together a dozen or more times, laughing at the same lines every time, repeating them just ahead of Newman and Redford, incorporating them into daily life to illustrate a point or explain themselves when other words failed them. . . . *Think you used enough dynamite there, Butch? . . . What are the rules? Rules? There are no rules in a knife fight! KICK. Somebody say go. One-two-three—go . . . . Hell, the fall will probably kill ya . . . .*

St. John's fall had damn near killed him: a long, screaming plunge through a year-long, stormy marriage, culminating in a deep splash and a tumbling ride through the emotional currents of separation, with him popping to the surface every so often for a breath of sanity.

Only St. John hadn't told him that he couldn't swim.

Another car passed by on the street below. The rectangles of light slid around the room and were jerked out the window. He rolled over to look at the clock. It was nearly one, too late to call Joanna. He wished, desperately, that she had stayed over, so he could have drifted off to sleep with her nestled, spoonlike, against him. He could almost feel her warmth in the bed with him. And in a sudden moan of the winter wind, he could almost hear St. John's coarse, haunting cry as he sang another verse in his endless song of the blues.

MONDAY

ONE

MORNING WILL NEVER COME, thought Steven Carpenter as he pulled the single blanket tighter about him and curled into a ball to try to stay warm. The streetlight glowed through the frosty living room window, telling him it was still very early. Unused to sleeping naked on the couch with just a single, scratchy blanket for warmth, he was sure that he had been awake most of the night, thinking black thoughts about Debi. She probably didn't even know that he never came back to bed after stalking out of the bedroom and slamming the door behind him.

He threw back the blanket, rolled off the couch, and stood up. His bare skin goose-bumped and he knew that Fitzgerald had turned down the heat again. The dead of winter and the caretaker turns the heat down like it was the Fourth of July. Shivering, he slipped into the dark kitchen and fumbled on the wall for the light switch. The fluorescent circle hummed and glowed a dim pink, then blinded him with its sudden flash. He squinted to see the clock on the wall. Six o'clock, a full half hour before the alarm would go off. He snapped off the light and groped his way back to the couch. Wrapping the blanket around himself Indian-fashion, he stood for a moment in the bay of the living room window, staring out into the street below. In the streetlight's icy blue circle lay the same old dirty piles of snow, the same icy sidewalks and rutted street. A St. Paul police car drove by headed west, thick exhaust rolling behind it like tumbleweeds in the wind. Their own car, a Honda Civic, huddled forlornly against the curb, dead now for nearly a week, at the mercy of the snowplow if there were another snow emergency. It was a depressing sight for any Monday morning, let alone one after you had a big fight with your wife the night before. He sat down on the couch, pulled his feet up and under the edge of the blanket so that just his head was exposed, and tried to sort things out.

In the months since he, Steven James Carpenter, had taken Deborah Ann Bradley for better or for worse, he was beginning to believe that the times for the worse far outnumbered those for the better. Certainly last night had been one of their worst; their argument had erupted at bedtime and quickly spread out of control—a fire sweeping over dry prairie.

It wasn't his fault. She'd started it. By tradition, they spent Sunday nights quietly, watching rented movies or reading and listening to music—nothing too heavy. As the weekend receded before them like the outgoing tide, they went to bed late, trying to put off as long as possible the approach of Monday morning. Usually they had sex and finally drifted off to sleep as the new week came washing in.

But last night had been different. As he had lain in bed watching Debi undress, she had broken with tradition, dredging up an issue they had discussed at least a dozen times already.

"We have to decide this week on the couch and chair. The sale ends next Saturday."

"Let's talk about it tomorrow," he had said, reaching out and pulling her into bed with him. His intention had been to kiss her, but she had pulled away from him and propped herself against the headboard, her eyes hot with anger and her bare breasts heaving with indignation.

"Let's talk about it now. You've been stalling for two weeks."

"Stalling? How can you say that? I said two weeks ago that I didn't think we could afford a thousand bucks for furniture. The couch and chair we got from my mom and dad are perfectly good. What's wrong with them, anyway?"

"Nothing's wrong with them. I'd just like to have something that's ours. Do you want to spend your whole life living with other people's hand-me-downs?"

Hand-me-downs. The term had stung, like they were being given Goodwill clothing. The couch and chair looked brand-new. In fact, they were only two years old.

"You've hated that couch and chair from day one. Just because they're the wrong color. We don't have enough money in our savings account to pay for new furniture."

"We could charge it, Steven. We do have a charge card, you know."

"Then we'd have to pay all that interest."

"So you pay a little more so you don't have to pay for all of it at once. Everybody does it."

"That's no reason to go into debt, just because everybody else does it. Would you shoot somebody just because everybody else does it?"

"Don't be a jerk. That's not the same and you know it. Why can't you just decide?"

"Christ, you never give up, do you? You only listen for what you want to hear. All right! I don't want to buy it! We can't afford it! There, I've decided. Is that plain enough for you? Jesus Christ, anyway."

A tense, brittle silence had followed, and when Debi finally spoke, her voice had been bitter with resentment.

"How come we can afford everything you want? How come we can afford records and tapes . . . and *compact discs* and . . . and a new guitar, and sheet music that you can't even *read,* for godssake? You never even ask about stuff like that. You just go and get it."

Always, always, when she had nothing else to throw at him, she went after his music.

"That's different."

"How is it different?"

"It's an investment."

"An investment? Give me a break!"

He had sensed the tone of accusation in her voice, overreacted to it, feeling the need to justify, to say something—anything—to defend himself.

"The chords are on the sheet music. They help me learn the songs. If I get a club date we can charge off all this stuff as business expenses."

"A club date?" Debi had snorted her contempt, twisting away from him and throwing herself into a position of sleep. And then, with her naked back to him, came her most cutting remark of all, her famous 'how can you expect' question, a question with its own answer built right in.

"Steven, how can you ever expect to be a professional musician if you won't even play for me?"

"Go buy the goddamn couch," he had yelled, flinging the covers back and vaulting out of bed. "Go buy a whole house full of furniture if you want to. Buy the stinking house, too. Put it on your fucking charge card. It's the only thing getting fucked around here."

With that, he had stomped out of the room, slamming the bedroom door behind him so hard that the framed Dylan poster on the bedroom wall—the one she had given him for his twenty-first birthday—bounced on its wire hanger.

"Up yours, Carpenter!" Debi had yelled after him through the closed door.

From the apartment below, Fitzgerald had beat on the ceiling with a broom handle.

And now, clutching the blanket around him, he felt shitty about the argument and at least half responsible for it. It seemed to him that he and Debi argued about everything these days, yet at the same time it was all over nothing. Maybe it was just the winter getting to them, or their jobs, or the fact that it was Sunday night.

Lately, he had found himself wondering why he had married her. What had he seen in her, anyway? In their first meeting, on the steps outside the student center, she had been lost and asked him directions to Bridgeman Hall. His first impression of her, this pretty, small-town girl from just south of Mankato, was that she needed his help. He'd asked her out on the spot, and she had accepted. They spent all four years of college together, maintaining the fiction of separate dorm rooms, but in truth, snuggling nightly in the single bed in his room. They had been married last June, a month after graduation, in a country church a mile from her parents' acreage. But being married was far different from sharing a dorm room for the night. Those nights when they had slept snugly in his single bed had given way to too many nights like last night, when one or the other of them lay in their double bed stiff with anger and resentment. And in these last seven months, he had revised his early impression of her: she didn't need him. She didn't really need anybody. Even their original meeting, when she had asked directions, he now saw differently. If he hadn't happened by, she would have simply asked somebody else and gone on about her business.

The buzz of the alarm clock, distant but still obnoxious through the closed bedroom door, startled him. It buzzed for a very long time, until Debi finally realized he wasn't there and rolled over to hit the snooze button. Debi could sleep until noon, missing work altogether if he let her, and this morning he was sorely tempted.

Wearing the blanket, he padded into the bathroom, closing the door behind him. He took a leak. Turning on the shower, he adjusted the temperature of the water to as hot as he could stand it and climbed in. The hot water hit him across the neck and shoulders, running down his front and back, down his legs. After a chilly, scratchy night on the couch, the scalding rush of water felt good.

As he was toweling off, the alarm clock buzzed again for what seemed like a full minute before Debi shut it off. He brushed his teeth, shaved, and dried his hair, dreading the thought of going into the bedroom to get dressed.

When he finally tried to open the bedroom door, he found that it was locked. Apparently, Debi had thrown the lock on the door after he had slammed it. He tapped on the door lightly.

"Deb?"

A moment later, he heard the sound of the lock turning and the door opened. Debi was wearing a long T-shirt.

"I'm sorry," he said.

He waited for her to say that she, too, was sorry. Instead, she walked right past him into the bathroom, closing the door a little too hard behind her. He heard the sound of the toilet flushing and then the roar of the shower.

He dressed for work and left the apartment before Debi came out of the bathroom.

Hunching his back to the biting north wind, Steve stood at the Selby Avenue bus stop with a handful of other shivering riders. He turned his collar up and jammed his gloved hands deep into his pockets. So he and Debi had had a fight. It certainly wasn't their first fight, and almost as certainly, it would not be their last. As usual, he had made his apologies, but Debi had not even spoken to him, let alone apologized. Who did she think she was, anyway, ignoring him like that?

As the minutes passed, the group swelled to about ten people. It was a mixed group, whites, blacks, and Hmong. The Hmong talked among themselves. They wore outdated clothing and coats that were too light for weather like this. Occasionally one of the group stepped out into the middle of the street and looked hopefully to the west in search of the bus. He felt sorry for them. He knew very little about the Hmong, but he admired them for coming to America and starting over. He could hardly imagine moving to a foreign country where the weather, the customs, and the language were completely different. The Twin Cities had seemed foreign enough after growing up on the North Dakota plains.

Finally, the bus arrived. One by one, the riders stepped on, dropping their change into the slot or showing their passes. Steven settled into the last empty seat on the right side. The bus pulled out and continued east on Selby Avenue toward downtown—the Real World, as Debi called it. Far down the street, past the green dome of the Cathedral, he could see the tops of the downtown skyscrapers.

As the bus filled up with passengers, he felt his spirits sink. A year ago, he had looked forward to graduation, to leaving academics behind and joining the excitement of the Real World. But after weeks and weeks of job hunting, he had finally concluded that the Real World did not hold sociology majors in high regard. In near desperation, he had taken a clerical job in the library and officially had become a card-carrying member of the nine-to-five world. The Real World, he soon realized, was not all it was cracked up to be. He could no longer sleep late on weekday mornings or skip work altogether, like he skipped classes. There was never time to practice his guitar and work on his songs. The ultimate realization that he was grown up came at Christmas, when, for the first time in his life, there was no Christmas vacation. In retrospect, college seemed like the perfect life. He wished he could go back.

The bus lurched to a stop at the Dale Street light. The seats were filled and riders stood in the aisle, clinging to the overhead handrail. Out the window, he watched the buildings go by. The Selby Avenue neighborhood was as diverse as the passengers who rode the bus. Boarded up shells of houses stood next to newly restored homes that glowed in the pink sunrise. Empty storefronts gaped at him. Red and blue neon signs lit the windows of trendy coffee shops and restaurants opened to catch the breakfast trade. Vacant lots had been converted to dumping areas for snow cleared off the city's streets and sidewalks. Block-long row houses and condos loomed over the sidewalk.

Who did she think she was, anyway? Debi had embraced the Real World with an all-consuming passion. Speech and theater major in hand, she had hit the streets immediately after they returned from their Black Hills wedding trip. Within three weeks, she had accepted an entry-level job in a stock brokerage firm. Almost overnight, she underwent a complete metamorphosis, shedding her funky college clothes like an old skin in favor of what she referred to as "big people clothes." Every night she sat in front of the television set with an issue of *Glamour* or *Mademoiselle* in her lap. Her side of the closet soon bulged with dresses, blazers, blouses, skirts, and suits. She subscribed to *Money* magazine and quoted articles out of the *Wall Street Journal*. Every weekend she went shopping and came home with something new for the apartment that they didn't really need.

Normally, Debi rode the bus with him. Right now, she was probably standing at their stop, waiting for the next bus. She was going to be late. Maybe she needed him for something after all.

The bus ground to a stop at Mackubin to pick up a man in a dark brown overcoat carrying a leather briefcase. The riders in the aisle shifted one position toward the back to make room. By the time the bus reached the Cathedral, the aisle was packed. Staring through the dirty bus window into the triangular parking lot, he watched a woman running toward the bus in high-heeled boots slip on the ice and fall. She was still picking herself up when the bus lumbered around the corner onto John Ireland Boulevard. At the traffic light, the driver swung wide to turn right onto Kellogg Boulevard. They crossed over the I-35E Parkway and followed Kellogg around the Civic Center, which always looked to him like the great round saucer of the Starship Enterprise after it had traveled back through time and crash-landed on the edge of downtown. The wreckage of the rest of the ship—the center cylinder and the twin pods housing Scotty's beloved matter/antimatter engines—was probably scattered across the West Side.

He got off the bus near the library building. The clock in the Landmark Center tower showed four minutes to eight. He darted up the steps. He had exactly four minutes to be in his spot and escape the wrath of the Overseer. Knickerson had hung that nickname on their supervisor, who was a stickler for—and Knickerson's deadpan imitation was a dead ringer for the supervisor's endless monotone—"punctuality, accuracy, and reliability."

Knickerson was already at his desk, his face buried in the newspaper, when Steven slid into his own chair. A new cart of paperbacks had already been wheeled up next to his desk. Not books to read and enjoy—"Mr. Carpenter, pleasure reading is not allowed; it consumes too much time"—but books to process: type the title of the book and its author on a little pocket envelope, tuck it inside the back cover, and pass it on to Knickerson, who glued the envelope to the inside back cover and passed it on to Lorraine for labeling. Type, tuck, pass. There were other tasks, equally as boring, that filled up his day. Factory work, he and Knickerson called it; they were assemblymen in the book factory.

He tucked an envelope into his IBM typewriter. He wondered what his own name would look like on the cover of one of these paperbacks. Or better yet, on one of the compact discs or cassette tapes he sometimes processed. He even had a title all picked out for his first album: *The American Dreamer.*

Type, tuck, pass. Type, tuck, pass. On and on, over and over.

Knickerson's face was still buried in the paper. He had already let five books pile up. "Hey, Knick, get the lead out," Steven said.

"Just a second," Knickerson mumbled. *"'I think I can, I think I can,' might be a clue that has just the right meaning for you."*

"What's so damn interesting? Somebody declare war on us this morning? Psst," Steven motioned with a nod of his head toward the Overseer's desk.

Knickerson quickly folded the paper and stuffed it under his desk. He grabbed a paperback and reached for the glue gun.

"It's gotta mean something about trains," he said.

"What does?"

"The clue."

"What clue?"

"What clue? What clue? Earth to Stevie! Come in, please. The clue to the treasure hunt. You know, St. Paul, the Winter Carnival? Stevie Boy, where you *been* for the past two weeks? Rice Park is *full* of ice sculptures. The Vulcans have been *terrorizing* downtown in their fire engine—which, incidentally, I think is some kind of secret phallic symbol. There was a big *parade* last Saturday. You been on drugs or what?"

"Or what." He felt slightly annoyed. Knickerson was a lifelong resident of St. Paul, an East Sider, while he was just a kid from North Dakota who had come to the big city to go to college and stayed because there was nowhere else to go. How was he supposed to know all this local color shit?

"Cheez, I can't *believe* you went to college here for four years and never got into the treasure hunt." Knickerson ran the glue gun over the back of the envelope as though he were decorating a cake.

"So sue me! Are you gonna explain this or rag on me some more about it?"

"Mr. Knickerson. Mr. Carpenter." The Overseer suddenly stood between their desks. "How are you this morning?"

"Later, man," Knickerson muttered.

TWO

THE WHITE CHARACTERS APPEARED SLOWLY as the flashing cursor traveled from left to right across the black screen: Clue 2: *"I think I can, I think I can" might be a clue that has just the right meaning for you.* Keith folded up the A section of the *Pioneer Press* and tossed it over to the coffee table. It missed, hit the edge, and fell to the floor. He leaned back in his chair, clasped his hands behind his head and stared at the newly entered clue on his computer screen. It followed Clue 1, which he had entered Saturday night. Together, the two clues looked and read like a short poem, something a grade school student would write— singsong rhythm and forced rhymes.

He took a careful sip from his coffee—his second cup of the morning—and cradled his hands around the warm cup. His breakfast, Grape Nuts and whole-wheat toast, sat half-finished at the corner of his desk. Outside, a garbage truck groaned to a stop at the end of the driveway. On the floor above him, Tiffany broke into a chorus of yapping. Old Tiffany. The poodle from hell.

He read the new clue again. *"I think I can, I think I can,"* was what the Little Engine That Could puffed in the children's story. The clue must have something to do with trains or things associated with trains. The phrase was set off in quotation marks. From studying the clues and their explanations from previous years, he knew the early clues sometimes contained obscure references to the treasure site that were a stretch to the imagination, even when the clues were interpreted in the newspaper at the end of the week. Given that, what did the quote marks mean? Quotes were used to identify the exact words of someone, or to call attention to and give special meaning to words. Maybe the clue was simply quoting the Little Engine. And the phrase was used twice. Did that mean anything?

Sipping his coffee, he read the clue over and over: *"I think I can, I think I can, I think I can, I think I can,"* conscious of the driving rhythm. Like a train. His mother had read it to him like that when he was a kid. She used to read to him all the time. An old memory popped into mind. He was four, maybe five, wearing his pajamas and sitting in her lap. She was reading *Millions of Cats* to him. The old man came in the back door. His grease-stained clothes smelled of smoke, which meant that he had stopped at the King of Clubs on his way home. "Let's eat!" he demanded. "In a minute," she had said as she turned the last page of the book. The old man had leaned in close to them, his breath stale with liquor, as though he were going to give them each a kiss. Instead, he'd grabbed the book and flung it across the living room. "How about now?"

A real prince, his old man.

He reached for a piece of toast, took a bite, and chewed slowly as he stared at the clue again. Trains seemed like a disarmingly simple solution, unless there was a catch to it, something so obvious that he was missing it. Perhaps the clue was actually engine, which could refer to train engines, fire engines, or some other type of engine, for that matter. Fire engines didn't seem very likely. The fire stations he was aware of were in the wrong places, on busy streets instead of near public parks. It had to refer to trains in some way. Something about trains and a public park; that was the message of the two clues so far. Now all he had to do was figure out *what* about trains, and *which* public park. What, he felt certain, was railroad tracks. But the second part of Clue 2— *"might be a clue that has just the right meaning for you"*—hinted at some special meaning, as though the first impression was incorrect. Or maybe he was trying to read too much into it.

He unfolded his city map and searched for railroad tracks. As he feared, there were dozens of them crisscrossing the city and its suburbs, each track a thin line on the map dissected by little cross hairs. On the map, the tracks looked like scars left by surgery. That was fitting. In a way, the real tracks that cut up the city were scars.

He took a pink highlighter from his desk drawer and started to highlight all of the railroads that he could locate. The highlighter squeaked against the paper as he traced over each railroad track. Its heavy, chemical smell filled his nose. When he finally finished, pink lines ran all over, anchored at the edge of the map, converging on the downtown St. Paul area. It looked like the beginnings of a spider web woven in a broken window by some giant spider overdosed on Pepto Bismol.

If this was the right interpretation of the clues, it still wasn't going to be easy. On his map, public parks were represented by the color green. Green clung to the blue line of the Mississippi River, which arced through the city like a gigantic sine curve. Green filled in the great city parks—Phalen, Mounds, Highland, Como, Cherokee—and the parks were all connected by thin green lines showing the parkways: Lexington, Summit Avenue, Wheelock, Johnson Parkway, Como Avenue. Scattered across the city were dozens of little green blocks: parks and playgrounds, some too small to have names. There were a dismaying number of places where the freshly pinked railroad lines ran through or close to a patch of green. Those railroad lines in Maplewood and around Irvine Park he felt he could ignore. The rest of the places where pink met green were possible treasure sites—many of which he would be able to eliminate with succeeding clues until, hopefully, he had eliminated all of them but the right one. At this time, it probably wouldn't be worthwhile to make a list of candidates to begin a physical search.

He studied the map, tracing his finger along familiar routes, trying to picture the real places in his mind, hoping to receive a sign or inspiration of some kind. He wondered if psychics would have any better luck with this than he did—he didn't believe in that shit himself—but if they did, it would be an unfair advantage, worse even than metal detectors had been before the medallion was changed to plastic.

Reaching for his coffee, he found it had gone cold while he was weaving his pink railroad spider web across the city. He got up, taking his unfinished breakfast with him. The apartment's tiny kitchen was still cold, the gray tile icy under his bare feet. Setting his cereal bowl and plate in the sink, he poured the cold coffee down the drain and refilled the cup from the Mr. Coffee machine on the counter. He switched on the oven and pulled the door open until it caught itself. Mrs. Wright controlled the thermostat upstairs, and no matter how often he complained, she kept the heat at a chilly sixty-five degrees upstairs, which left his apartment a frigid sixty-two. Often on winter mornings he ran the oven with the door open for a few minutes to take the chill out of the air.

Back at his desk he caught sight of the strip of cash register tape with Toni Stoltz's home phone number on it. Sunday had slipped by as he had debated the pros and cons of calling her. He picked up the scrap of tape and read the name and number for the twentieth time. The note *looked* like it had been written by her: large, rounded letters, the "i" in Toni dotted with a circle, the "t's" in her last name crossed with a flourish. *I'm really glad to see you Keith. Maybe I'll see you again sometime.* She had seemed glad to see him. Friendly, nice. *I wouldn't want you to go to any trouble.* She'd also completely misunderstood him, half lashed out at him, emphasizing that word *trouble.* Without doing anything wrong, he had been forced to apologize, to correct her misunderstanding. It was a poor start.

Carefully, he pulled a pushpin from the cork bulletin board above his desk and pinned the slip of tape to the board.

Clues 1 and 2 were not going to betray enough information for him to find the treasure this morning. Maybe the file of second clues would give him a hint. He typed in the commands to save the file and hit the return. The computer hummed and groaned and then fell silent, the little cursor flashing, waiting. He called up the Clue 2 file, where all the second clues ever written were stored. The file flashed on the screen. Starting with the year 1952, he read the clues one by one, scrolling through the file until he reached its end. He typed in the current year and the newest second clue. The white letters slowly appeared on the field of black as the cursor moved across the screen.

There was no discernible pattern. Some of the clues read like mere extensions of the first clue, giving only the broadest of details—in a public park, or within the city limits. Other second clues were teasers, containing obviously important pieces of information about the location, like near picnic tables or tennis courts, information that would be useless until later in the week, when a future clue—probably on Thursday or Friday—narrowed the location down to one or two places. Clues like this were like the first big Oscar presentation on the Academy Awards show—both of them gave you something that seemed important, teasing you into staying with it, enduring boring awards and lots of commercials—or frustrating clues—until the really big payoffs came at the end. A few of the second clues didn't seem to make much sense at all. They seemed to have no direction in either the micro or macro sense; no specifics, no broad hints—just bad poetry.

This analysis of clues for insight into the clue writer's psyche didn't seem to be leading him anywhere so far. But there had to be some kind of pattern, some repetition of phrases or concepts. You couldn't write more than 350 clues over the years without developing some kind of pattern.

Scrolling back to the beginning of the file, he read all of the second clues again. Nothing. He punched in the commands to save the file. The computer hummed and clicked. The cursor flashed, waiting . . . .

The Academy Awards. Sandy had been a big fan of them. Every year she had thrown an Oscar party—come as your favorite movie star, popcorn, that awful movie candy, and pop served in huge paper cups.

And how about Toni? Was she a big Oscar fan, too? There was only one way to find out. He glanced up at the phone number pinned to the cork bulletin board. He'd find out later.

He saved the Clue 2 file and snapped off the computer. The screen went dark.

THREE

SITTING IN HER OWN BOOKSTORE, Sharon felt a bit guilty reading the morning paper instead of one of the books on the shelves. She knew it was bad advertising for customers to come in and see one of the owners reading a newspaper instead of a book, but sometimes she just didn't feel like reading a book.

She opened the paper to the editorial pages to see if Ellen Goodman's column was running today. Finding Ellen Goodman in the St. Paul paper had been both a surprise and a bit of a relief. The *Pioneer Press* was not the *Boston Globe*, but having Ellen Goodman to read once or twice a week was almost like having a neighbor from Boston visit her. The only problem was that she had never quite figured out exactly which days the column ran. Opening the paper each day was almost like calling Ellen Goodman on the telephone without knowing if she was home.

Ellen was not home today. She turned back to the front page and scanned the headlines. In the lower lefthand corner was the second treasure hunt clue, which they had discussed over breakfast. *"I think I can, I think I can," might be a clue that has just the right meaning for you.* Phil had already forgotten yesterday's pronouncement about finding the treasure, but Chris had brought the paper to the breakfast table. They'd decided almost immediately that the clue had something to do with trains, but before they could go any farther, they'd run out of time. Phil had promised to spend time on it tonight.

The little bell above the door tinkled. She looked up from her newspaper and groaned. The Queen of Hearts was approaching the counter, carrying a grocery bag filled with books. Elaine, her partner, had named the obese young woman the Queen of Hearts for her choice of reading material—nothing but romances. Once a month she stopped in at the store, lugging a bag filled with well-thumbed Harlequins and Regencies. In the year that the store had been open, Elaine and Sharon estimated that the woman had read nearly a hundred romances. She seemed to favor the ones with the raciest covers—raven-haired heroines in gowns with plunging necklines and open backs, swooning in the muscular arms of bare-chested, square-jawed Prince Charmings.

The young woman set the grocery bag on the desk, smiled almost apologetically, and without speaking, headed straight toward the romance section. There was a heavy sadness in the young woman's movement. Her face was slack with a look of resignation. Her shoulder-length blond hair was straight and limp. She wore her pink coat unzipped, like an expectant mother would, though she clearly was not pregnant. The coat was gray with dirt around the pockets, the white fake fur around the hood ratty.

Sharon dumped the books on the desk and started to tally up the credit. In among the well-thumbed romances was the copy of Margaret Atwood's *The Handmaid's Tale* that she had given the woman on her last visit. After watching the woman read bags of romances, she had tried to nudge her on to something more substantial, something that counteracted all the fantasy. Spying Atwood's book on the counter, she had impulsively picked it up.

"I just finished this recently," she had told the woman, although she actually had read it in hardcover shortly after it was published. "It's very good."

"What's it about?"

"Well . . ." She had paused, choosing her words carefully to make the book sound less intimidating. "It's about women and how they are in the future."

"Science fiction? I don't like science fiction much."

"You might call it science fiction, I guess. But not in the sense of monsters or outer space. It's very believable. It's more futuristic."

The young woman's eyes had shifted away. "I don't think I have enough money for it today."

"Well, you've bought a lot of books here. I tell you what. I'll throw it in as a bonus." The Queen of Hearts had shrugged her acceptance.

And now, holding *The Handmaid's Tale* in her hands, she saw that her efforts were all for naught. The Queen of Hearts was hard on paperbacks, bending the bindings backward, dog-earing the corners of pages to mark her place. Often her books came back in such poor condition that they were not fit to put back on the shelf for resale. *The Handmaid's Tale* was in perfect condition.

As she finished totaling the credit on the adding machine, the woman came up to the counter with a new load of books. More racy covers—heroines and heros locked in passionate embraces.

She pushed the returned books aside. *The Handmaid's Tale* was on the top of the stack.

"That book," the woman said, pointing at it. "It was good."

"I'm glad you liked it. Will there be anything else?"

She sorted through the books that the Queen of Hearts had brought in. Two of them were damaged so badly she shouldn't have accepted them. She tossed them in the wastebasket. The rest she put in the bin for reshelving later. Putting the unread Atwood novel in the bin gave her an empty feeling.

When she and Elaine had opened the Paperback Library, she had harbored visions of making good books available to people who could not afford hardcovers, or even first-sale paperback prices. She had imagined impoverished students coming in to buy the great literary classics. They had stocked the shelves with used paperbacks of the great authors: Dickens, Shakespeare, Tolstoy, Dostoevski, Melville, Twain, Fitzgerald, Hemingway, Faulkner, and all the rest.

But the customers came in wanting not *Moby Dick, Huckleberry Finn,* or *War and Peace,* but the newest James Michener, Stephen King, or Barbara Cartland. Their sparse shelves quickly filled up with popular novels and genre fiction: suspense, mysteries, horror, science fiction, westerns, and, of course, romances.

Of all the genre fiction they stocked, she disliked romances the most. To her, they were the woman's equivalent of pornography. Pornography was an exaggeration, a lie about relationships between men and women. Men who drooled over pictures of nude, large-breasted women spread-eagled across beds, tied to chairs, or whatever, had no idea at all about

the relationship between sex and love. They merely looked at their partners, and wondered why they didn't look and perform like the women
in the girlie magazines. Romances, as far as she could see, exaggerated
and lied about relationships just as much, if in a different way. Romance-
reading women, she was sure, looked at their partners and wondered where
their white horses were, or if they had sent their shining armor out for
a polish and never picked it up. No one, it seemed, addressed love. Love
wasn't whips and chains or multiple orgasms. It wasn't all passionate embraces and knights in shining armor. Love was compromise. Love was
. . . leaving Boston.

One day last fall, she and Elaine had both been in the store when
the Queen of Hearts had wandered in with her grocery bag of books.
After she had left, Sharon had restated her desire to expose people to real
literature, to real knowledge. Elaine had merely laughed at her.

"If you want to be a teacher, get a job in the school system,"
Elaine had said. "We're here to sell books. And popular and genre are
what sell."

And sell they did. A Judith Kranz disappeared almost the same day
it was put on the shelf. Newer Stephen Kings moved well. Louis
L'Amour came and went by the shelfful. Dickens, Shakespeare, and their
peers gathered dust.

But business was good enough in this store for them to consider opening a second. It was Phil who had suggested that they look into expansion.
He was helping them identify areas to research to see if there was a large
enough market to sustain a second store without cutting into the business they already had. It was, Phil said, the sort of research the fast food
franchises did all the time to make sure they didn't put their restaurants
too close together. If such research could sell more hamburgers or
tacos, it should sell more Barbara Cartlands.

She wasn't sure she wanted to sell more Barbara Cartlands, but if
it would work for Barbara Cartland, why wouldn't it work for Dickens
or Fitzgerald or the rest of the classics? She was toying with the idea of
trying to develop a paperback shop that sold educational books, college
books, how-tos, literary classics. There had to be a way to market such
a store, to find poorer people who read to educate themselves instead
of to escape. This wasn't a poor city. There were no slums like those on
the East Coast. There had to be enough Horatio Alger types around town

to offset the Queen of Hearts types who had already given up while still in their twenties.

The phone rang. She glanced at her watch. It was almost eleven-thirty, time for Elaine to call, as she often did just before noon, to say she would be a few minutes late. Sharon reached under the counter for the phone.

"Paperback Library."

"Hi, Babe, how's it going?" Phil's deejay voice, charged with excitement and a little too loud, filled her ear.

"Okay. The Queen of Hearts just stopped in for her monthly load of romantic porno. You sound excited. Did we just win the *Reader's Digest* Sweepstakes?"

"Remember yesterday after breakfast when I said that Flannary had some kind of meeting planned? Well, we just had it and I still can't believe it. I'm still just knocked right on my ass. You know what happened?"

"He hit you?"

"Very funny. You won't believe this. I was just offered a promotion! My own district! Can you believe that? Flannary called me into his office first thing this morning. One of the company vice presidents from Boston was sitting there with him. The veep told me they had two openings and they had decided to look within the company first. Flannary had suggested me a couple of weeks ago. They'd checked me out, liked what they saw, and wanted to talk to me. The guy grilled me all morning. I just got out. The promotion is mine if I want it."

"That's great, Phil."

"There's two spots open." She heard Phil clear his throat, take a deep breath. "There's just one catch."

"Wait, a minute," she said. "Did you say your own district?"

"That's the catch."

She felt a sharp pain cut though her, a fencer's lunge. Don't say it. Don't say it.

He said it.

"If I accept, we have to relocate."

"Relocate? Oh, no!"

"Sharon, it's at least ten thousand a year more, just in salary. That's after taxes. There's benefits on top of that. The company will pay relocation expenses. Ten thousand is almost equal to a year's worth of college. Jeff'll be old enough in three years."

The question came to her lips slowly, pointlessly, for she already knew its answer.

"I don't suppose Boston is one of the choices?"

"No."

"What are they?"

"Denver or San Diego."

"We don't know a soul in either place."

"Babe, we didn't know anyone here either, and everything turned out okay."

"So you've decided already?"

"No, of course not. I can't just rip off a decision as big as this. There's a lot at stake here."

"When do you have to decide?"

"A week. I told them I wanted time to really think about it. Are you all right?"

"I'm fine. I'm just stunned, that's all."

"So am I. I never in my wildest dreams expected something like this when I walked into Flannary's office this morning."

She took her time in asking the inevitable question, pulling the words together, taking care to keep her voice level, under control.

"Do you think you'll take it?" To her, her voice sounded almost inaudible, like a radio on its lowest volume.

"We'll talk about it tonight. Let's look at it from all sides. We've got all week and over the weekend to decide."

"What time will you be home?"

"By six. I promised the boys this morning we'd work on the treasure hunt tonight."

"I may be late. If you get home first, start dinner." She hung up the phone. She felt tired, suddenly, cold inside and out. She paged through the paper, read the comics, "Dear Abby," the old standbys. She turned to her horoscope, fully expecting to learn she was going on a journey. "A family conflict can be resolved with tact and diplomacy. This is a time to consider new business ventures. Don't give in to impulses."

She closed the newspaper. It wasn't in her horoscope, but still she could feel a trip coming on. She may as well go home tonight and start packing. But she wouldn't be packing for Boston or the Bahamas. She would be packing for Denver or San Diego.

FOUR

ALFRED KRAUSE STOOD AT THE KITCHEN STOVE trying to fry bacon. The sizzle and pop of the hot grease nearly drowned out WCCO's noon news on the kitchen radio. He wasn't accustomed to making his own meals, but it was clear that if he wanted to eat, he would have to fend for himself. Genevieve hadn't spoken to him since last night, when she had declared he could make his own supper and then marched upstairs. She had come down briefly at midmorning, made a breakfast for herself, and gone wordlessly back upstairs. He had taken the hint.

Her march up the stairs last night had reminded him of something that had happened long ago, in this very house, during their courting days. The house belonged to Genevieve's folks then. One Saturday night he had sat uncomfortably in a stiff-backed parlor chair, hands resting in his lap, waiting for Ma and Pa Martin to shut off the radio and go to bed. Finally, they had said their good-nights, reminding Genny about Mass in the morning.

After the old folks went upstairs, he had turned off the lights so he and Genevieve could sit together on the overstuffed mohair couch. Sitting next to her in the dark, his heart thumping under his ribs, he had felt himself swelling in his trousers. He had let his hands wander, inching away from her slim shoulders toward—

Genevieve had moved swiftly, catching his hands in her own, dumping them back in his lap.

"You stop," she had ordered.

"Stop what?" he had asked, feigning complete innocence.

"You know what!" she said, delivering a sharp elbow into his ribs. "I'm not that kind of girl."

"What kind of girl are you?" he teased.

"I'm the kind of girl who goes to Mass on Sunday morning with a clear conscience."

After a polite interlude, his hands had found her shoulders again and he pulled her toward him. And she had come willingly. Their lips found each other's in the darkness, and Genevieve returned his kiss with a sudden passion that both surprised and delighted him.

"What kind of girl are you?" he had murmured teasingly as his hands slipped away from her shoulders.

Swoop. His hands were in his lap again. He heard a squeak of springs and felt the swift motion as Genevieve lurched to her feet.

"I'm the type of girl who waits until she's married, Mr. Hot Britches. If you're going to behave like that, you can just sit down here in the dark by yourself. I'm going upstairs."

And she had marched up the same steps as she had last night. There had been nothing left for him to do but slip out the door as quietly as he could and go home.

The grease in the skillet hissed and popped. The strips of bacon curled up in the pan, then turned hard as wood shavings. He fished out the charred pieces with a fork and dropped them onto his plate. He cracked two eggs on the sharp edge of the stove, and dropped them one by one into the hot skillet. One of the yokes broke. The clear egg whites turned brown in the bubbling grease. The other yoke broke as he tried to flip the eggs over. He wished he had scrambled them. He never could fry eggs right, the way Genevieve could.

He managed to get the mangled eggs onto the plate next to the too-crisp bacon. He sat down at the kitchen table and realized he had forgotten to make toast. He put bread in the toaster.

Genevieve's long-ago march up the stairs had been his first taste of her resolute stubbornness. They had, indeed, waited until after they were married. Over the years, she had marched up the steps many times. He had learned that her icy moods sometimes melted slowly, and the best thing to do was to go on about his business until they did.

She would get over this trip business in a few days, and things would get back to normal. She just didn't understand, that was all. With Rudy gone, he was the last of the Krauses. Janet was a Peterson now, and so were his grandsons Mike and David. They were nice boys, but history would remember them as Petersons, not Krauses. When he was gone, there would be no more Krauses. He just couldn't go anywhere right now. Not so soon. Why couldn't she understand that? To climb into an airplane and fly high into the sky, held aloft by some unseen force, by the hand of God. What if God were distracted? He'd seen on television what could happen. The unidentifiable hunks of charred and twisted steel spread across a hillside. Searchers, with masks over their noses to cut the stench of burned flesh, picking through the wreckage for pieces of arms and legs. They said that flying was safer than driving, that it could never happen here. Well, it could. A plane had crashed in Highland Park some years back. He wasn't going to end up that way, no sir. That was no way for the Krauses to come to an end.

His toast popped up. He got up to get the butter from the cupboard. He buttered each piece and sat down again to eat.

What to do with his afternoon? He had spent the morning waiting for Genevieve to come downstairs. The days passed slowly now that he was home all the time. The golden years of retirement, forced upon him. Once he had actually looked forward to retiring someday, to walking out of the Schmidt brewery for the last time, full of retirement cake and coffee, a fishing tackle box under his arm as a gift from the fellas. Someday. But the company, not himself, had picked the day, shutting the plant down last summer because it was unprofitable. It was just dollars and cents to them, but to himself and a couple hundred others it had been more than dollars and cents. It had been a routine, a reason to get up in the morning. A life.

He had looked around for something else, but no one wanted to hire a man within sight of retirement. So for better or worse, he was now retired. Free.

Free to take the trips with Genevieve that they had never taken when they were younger. The two of them had discussed several trips, agreeing on none of them. Genevieve wanted nothing more than to fly to Houston to stay with Janet and the grandkids. He had talked of a driving trip to Yellowstone or the Grand Canyon.

Free to go fishing with Rudy, already retired from the railroad. They had planned to put an ice fishing shack on Bald Eagle Lake this winter. But before the shack was even finished, Rudy's heart had blown out like a tire, flooding his chest with blood. And in those few seconds between heartbeats, his fishing partner, his best friend, was suddenly gone.

His freedom now entrapped him. With Genevieve and himself unable to agree on where they should go, travel no longer held the appeal it once had. The ice fishing shack remained unfinished in the tiny garage out back. He found himself welcoming the heavy snowfalls of this winter, which at least gave him something to do.

The wooden cat doorstop sat patiently against the basement door, as if waiting for a wooden mouse to creep by. There was no real doubt about what he should do for the rest of today. He should go down to

Rudy's house and work for the afternoon. As hard as it was to sort through Rudy's things, the job had to be finished sometime. Genevieve was after him to list the house with a real estate agent.

He finished up his eggs and bacon, stacked the dishes in the sink, then snapped off the kitchen radio. In the back room he scraped frost off the north window to see the thermometer. An even zero, the warmest it had been in several days. The warming trend that the weather forecasters had predicted—if you could call zero warm—was on its way.

Grunting with the strain, he pulled on his overshoes, a job that seemed harder every winter as his arthritis settled deeper into his bones and his middle expanded. He lifted his heavy winter coat off the hook and shrugged into it. Carrying his cap and mittens, he trudged through the house to the bottom of the stairs and called up to Genevieve.

"Going down to the house to work."

There was no answer.

Outside, the wind howled around the corner of the house, nearly knocking him to the snowy ground. The pickup started on the first try, like he knew it would. Chevrolet made a good pickup. This one was not as good as his first Chevrolet pickup, which had lasted twenty years, but it had lasted seven years so far, longer than most things lasted these days.

He let the engine warm up a couple of minutes, then backed down the driveway into the street and headed east on Goodrich. At the corner, he made a right and headed out West Seventh Street. Had the pickup been a horse, he could have let it go its own way, for over the years he had made more trips down this street than he could count. Trips to work, trips down to Rudy's. He had lived his whole life in the West End, making trips back and forth on this street between the only two houses he had ever lived in. Driving away from the downtown end of West Seventh, he was leaving the house that had belonged to Genevieve's folks, where he and Genevieve had moved the day they were married to take care of Genevieve's father. He was driving toward the house where he was born, owned by his parents, who had been killed in a streetcar accident near downtown when he was only nine. Rudy had lived his entire life in the house.

Topping the crest of the railroad overpass, he had a clear view of the West End, nestled between the bluffs to the north and the banks of the great Mississippi just to the south. Off toward the north, curls of chimney smoke rose above the roofs and bare trees. On pale, cold days like this, when the thick haze of chimney smoke hung over the steeply pitched roofs, the scene always looked and felt very Old World to him, like some German town nestled in a valley of the mountains. Although he had never been to Germany and seen the villages of his ancestors, he felt a connection to them every time he crested this overpass.

Beyond the little houses, beyond the recently completed I-35E Parkway that cut like an open wound across the West End, he could see atop the distant bluff the tall chimneys of the great mansions of Summit Avenue and Crocus Hill. St. Paulites loved to brag about their mansions, driving their out-of-town guests down Summit, pointing out the houses where big-shot millionaires like James J. Hill lived out their days attended by their servants. But this distant, silhouette view of the city's mansions was the view that he was most familiar and most comfortable with. On those infrequent drives down Summit Avenue past the great brick and stone houses, he felt uncomfortable, out of place, as if he were in Minneapolis or some other unfamiliar city. No, he didn't belong up there; he belonged down here at the bottom of the hill, with the rest of the little people in their little houses, scratching out a living.

Just ahead on the left, the Schmidt brewery towered over West Seventh Street like a medieval castle. Such a familiar sight—the tall smokestack, the red brick tower, and the gray concrete elevator connected to each other high above the ground by the enclosed catwalk. And the famous red neon Schmidt sign—old-world script a dozen feet high. Even though the plant was closed, the sign still blinked away in the night, advertising Schmidt beer brewed in some other city. He was surprised that no one had vandalized the sign. As he passed under the great tower, he felt the same dull ache in his heart as he felt years ago when he had walked by his old school just before it was torn down.

Waiting for the traffic light at Randolph, he felt the familiar sense of coming home, although the strength of the feeling had faded over the years. Instead of old friends, he now saw only strangers hurrying along the sidewalks, their shoulders hunched against the cold. The old stores that he had grown up with had closed one by one until only a bare handful were left. Machovec's Food Market was still open, and so was Pilney's just down the block, each one somehow hanging on against the supermarkets and convenience stores. There was still a hardware store, though Mr. Bauer was long since gone. Too many changes.

Three blocks past Randolph, he pulled over to the curb and stopped in front of the house. This house, the house where he was born, where he had last seen his parents alive so many years ago, where Rudy had lived his entire life and died. It had changed little over the years. Every ten years, Rudy had repainted the outside the same light brown color so that the change was hardly noticeable. Not at all like he and Genevieve, who had jumped on the remodeling bandwagon when Janet was little, and were now stuck with wide, pinkish siding that never needed paint, but looked horribly out of date, as though it were hiding something. Their house looked like an old woman wearing too much makeup. This house looked like an old woman with no makeup.

Standing just inside the front door, staring at the clutter of boxes, at furniture pulled away from the wall, drawers open and half-empty, he still felt the electric shock of the discovery, the panic that had swept over him as he had rolled Rudy over onto his back, found his flesh cold, limbs bent and stiff. The coffee stain in the living room carpet was still faintly visible, despite Genevieve's diligent efforts to scrub it out.

He unzipped his coat and sat down in the same squeaky rocking chair as he had on that terrible day, numb with shock, after calling Genevieve and the police. The squeak of the chair as he rocked and waited for the coroner to arrive had echoed deafeningly in the absolute stillness of the house. He caressed the smooth, hard wood of the rocker's arms, his heart heavy with despair. This chair was Rudy's favorite. It had been in the house ever since he could remember. Mother had probably rocked both of them in it when they were babies. He had no idea where it had come from, who had first sat in it, back in the days when the century was young. Rudy would know the history of this chair if only he were here to ask.

He sighed deeply and watched his smoky breath hang in the air. The furnace was turned down low, keeping just enough heat in the place to keep the pipes from freezing.

There was no sense putting it off any longer. He moved across the room to sit at the old secretary, where he had been working yesterday afternoon. The fold-down desk top was covered with newspaper clippings from a large shoe box found in the secretary's bottom drawer. He had started sorting the clippings, reading them one by one, putting them into piles. Obituaries. History articles. Wedding write-ups. Articles saved for no reason that he could determine. The things that people saved. How could you know why they viewed something as important enough to save? It was hard to decide what should be saved and what could safely be thrown away.

Closing out a life. This sorting and cleaning, saving and throwing, was like nearing the end of a book, knowing the final page lay just ahead, with "The End" at the close of the last paragraph. When the house was clean, it would be put up for sale. Once the realtor's sign went up, it would be over. Rudy would be gone, living only in his heart.

He unfolded a clipping that surprised him. A write-up about the couple that they had watched find the Winter Carnival treasure medallion in Smith Park. A twist of fate, a few seconds here or there, and it could have been Rudy and himself in this picture instead of this man and woman. This clipping—he knew why Rudy had saved it. He felt tears sting his eyes as he refolded the clipping and placed it in a pile to be kept.

FIVE

BRUCE MITCHELL SCANNED the Tech school cafeteria for Joanna, gave up, and sat down at the first empty table he found. He tested the temperature of his coffee and surveyed his lunch—a bowl of chili, a pair of hot dogs, and a package of corn chips. He opened the bag of chips and dumped them into the chili, feeling more disappointed than hungry. Lunch with Jo had become a part of his day that he looked forward to from the moment he opened his eyes in the morning. Sometimes as the lunch hour approached and the lecture droned on, he couldn't tell if it was hunger or anticipation that gnawed at his belly.

The chili was too hot to eat. He tore the corner from a foil package of ketchup and squeezed its contents onto one of the hot dogs. It was unlike Jo not to be here. She never skipped classes. Maybe her car hadn't started after all, or something was wrong. Or maybe he simply had missed her. He half stood up and scanned the sea of heads again, looking for that shimmering cascade of blue-black hair.

At moments like these, he marveled at how Jo had become a major part of his life in such a short time. Just the other night, he had been telling St. John how damn lucky he felt. A couple of months ago, he was just a former construction worker taking printing classes at Tech during the day and chasing around St. Paul at night and on weekends with St. John, halfheartedly looking for love. And then one day, quite by accident, he had found it, here in the Tech cafeteria. It began innocently enough—a near collision between them at the cash register. She had smiled at him, then in a measured voice spoke a single word of apology: "Sorry." In an instant, she had passed in flying colors what St. John referred to as the eye test. She was small, her shape hidden by a bulky sweater. The fluorescent light had danced off her hair like moonlight off a northern lake. Her brown eyes had remained fixed on him for just a moment before she turned away. The next day he had smiled at her and said hello, receiving a smile in return. After that, he had started to watch for her. It was several days before he spotted her again in the hallway after classes let out. Before he had even thought about it, he swallowed the lump that suddenly appeared in his throat, fell in step beside her, and invited her to have coffee with him. Over their coffee, he sat captivated by those expressive eyes as they exchanged backgrounds. She was twenty-six, four years younger than he, and lived up in the Midway area. She was tired of being a waitress and was studying graphics. "Well, maybe I'll print something you design someday," he had said, intertwining their futures.

She had insisted on paying for her own coffee, an act he interpreted as a show of independence. When he had asked for her phone number, she refused, taking his instead. "I'll call you," she had said. *I'll call you.* He gave up, knowing what the line meant.

He was still pouting when she actually called two days later. Did he like Mexican food? They went to dinner at Boca Chica. The talk had come easily, the different pieces of their lives fitting snugly together. On their fourth date, their bodies had fit snugly together, too, at her place after dinner and a movie. Her skin had glowed in the light of the candles that burned on the nightstand beside them. His own skin had jumped and quivered under her butterfly touch. He still felt the magic of her caresses hours later.

But it wasn't all magic. As the days passed, he discovered there was a part of Jo that was as mysterious as the dark side of the moon. One night at his place, right in the middle of their lovemaking, she had suddenly pushed him away and, sobbing, fled naked into the bathroom, slamming the door behind her. Alarmed, he had followed, tapping lightly on the door, only to be ordered away.

When she came out, she had tried her best to explain. He hadn't done anything wrong. It was not his fault. It was old baggage. She would tell him about it someday. His heart had moved violently in a way he had never felt before. He wanted to know everything about her. He had cradled her against his chest and tucked her head under his chin. "Tell me," he coaxed.

She had been engaged once, four years ago. The wedding was all planned, the invitations already printed, when she decided to call it off. Her fiance had been accepted by a law school in California, and she knew she couldn't move there. Her mother had told her she was blowing her one big chance, then threw the engraved invitations in the trash. The relationship between herself and her parents—especially her mother— had deteriorated ever since.

She was sorry it had come up. He had said something in the middle of their lovemaking that her fiance used to say. It had brought the whole incident back, fixed her mother's disapproving face in her mind, and spoiled everything.

"What did I say?" he had asked. "I don't want to say it again if it hurts you."

"So fine," she had whispered.

So fine. She was, in so many ways, old baggage and all. His eyes moved around the cafeteria in search of her as he finished the first hot dog. He stirred the chili again and held a spoonful up to his mouth. It was still too hot. He pushed it away. He opened a second package of ketchup and applied it to the remaining hot dog.

What made some relationships work and some not? He had asked St. John that the other night over beer and deep-dish pizza. St. John had grinned and leaned over the table toward him.

"First you got to find the ideal woman. Someone who's three feet tall, has a flat head and no teeth."

"I'm serious, you asshole."

"You're asking me—a guy who walked in on his wife while she was humping some other dude? How the hell should I know?"

But some relationships did work while others didn't. It had never really worked between Michelle and himself. He had sensed from the start that something that needed to be there for him wasn't, but had ignored his misgivings and moved in with her after only a month. From the minute the two of them started living together, it had started to go sour. Whenever he mentioned how much he hated construction work, she had given him a lecture instead of sympathy. If he hated his job, why didn't he get a new one? When he talked about doing something else, she had asked him what he wanted to do, and then rolled her eyes when he couldn't answer. It put some kind of pressure on him that made him strike back in the only way he knew how: he dragged his feet. She wanted to set the date; he stalled. She wanted to buy a house; he balked at meeting with an agent. She wanted to save more money; he went out and bought the Camaro. The harder she pressed for commitments, the more he dragged his feet, and the worse their fights became. Their Frogtown duplex turned into World War III.

St. John had stood by him right through to the very end, when he finally decided to break up with her.

"Look, if you ask me, you'd be doing the right thing by breaking it off," St. John had said on the night he finally admitted he wanted out. "So you don't love her. That's not your fault. In the long run you'd be doing both of you a favor by breaking up."

"I shouldn't have let it go this far," he had said. "It was a mistake."

"You learn from your mistakes," St. John had said. "I mean, in the movie, the baggage car guy saw how easy Butch and Sundance blew up the first safe, so he put better locks on it. Butch and Sundance had to use a little more dynamite the next time."

"Yeah, and they blew the whole damn baggage car to smithereens, money and all," he said.

St. John had shrugged and flashed his lopsided grin. "Well, at least the baggage car guy didn't repeat his mistake."

"So, Dr. Freud, what were my mistakes?" he had asked. "I don't want to repeat mine either."

"Well, let's see . . . your first mistake was being born," St. John had begun. "Your second was—"

"Wake me up when you get to Michelle," he had interrupted, faking a snore.

He pushed the last bite of hot dog into his mouth. He stirred the chili a final time. The corn chips had started to turn soft and mushy. He ate about half of it, pushed it aside, and reached for his coffee.

Months later, he privately decided that he had made two mistakes. The first, as he had confessed to St. John, was letting things drag along for nearly a year once he realized he wanted out. The second mistake—something he had been too ashamed of to even tell St. John—was breaking up in a way that made Michelle think it was her fault. He had been driving down Grand Avenue when he saw her coming out of a restaurant with some guy he didn't know. When she got home, he had confronted her, shouting down her explanation that the guy was an old classmate from Central High, although he had no doubt that she was telling him the truth. *If this is your idea of making a commitment, then you can just forget the whole damn thing.* He had packed his bags the next day, and St. John had helped him move into the upstairs apartment on South Robert that he had already rented. He remembered the relief he had felt that it was finally over.

The guilt had come later.

St. John had verbally kicked him in the ass one night after he finally told him how he had ended it with Michelle.

"Look, you can't sit around here forever, feeling sorry for yourself. So you treated her pretty shitty. You did the right thing in the wrong way. You can't let something like this take over your whole life. You got to learn from your mistakes and move on. Use more dynamite next time, or less. But quit moping, for chrissake! It's time to get your ass back in the ball game, Sundance."

You got to learn from your mistakes. St. John had been right about that. What he had learned was not to let himself get involved with someone just for something to do. He had learned—too late for it to do any good—that there were two sides to every relationship.

What he had learned, after months and months of mulling it over in the back of his mind, was that what was missing in his relationship with Michelle was really missing in himself.

He had slowly put himself back in the ball game, finally quitting construction work and enrolling here at Tech. Now if only he didn't mess this up with Jo. What made some relationships work and some not? He knew it worked with Jo, so far, and maybe that was all he needed to know. To dissect it, to learn why, risked destroying it, like killing the goose that laid the golden eggs.

To his right, he heard the scrape of a chair sliding back. A black man wearing a purple Vikings sweatshirt was vacating the table next to him, leaving his newspaper behind.

He pushed his tray aside and leaned over to retrieve the abandoned paper. He found the treasure hunt story at the bottom of the page. Clue 2: *"I think I can, I think I can," might be a clue that has just the right meaning for you.* The Little Engine said "I think I can." That meant something to do with engines or trains. Railroad tracks, maybe, but that seemed so obvious. Were there any railroad tracks up in Como Park? He tried to remember if St. John had mentioned buying and registering a Winter Carnival button. All he could remember was that St. John had been bummed out by a call from Karen. So now here they were with the tables turned—St. John was deep in the dumps just when he was nicely hooked up with someone new. Would the day ever come when they were both hooked up at the same time?

SIX

THE PARKING LOT OF THE SUPERAMERICA was empty. Keith Reynolds parked the Nova near the door, and left its engine running. Although the temperature had crept up during the morning, the wind still clawed as he skated over the icy sidewalk. The store's windows were still white with frost, and he was unable to see who was at the cash register until he opened the door. The attendant was a heavy, bearded man, wearing a shapeless gray cardigan over his store uniform, the sleeves pushed up to his elbows. He leaned over a newspaper spread out on the counter, supporting his bulk on his forearms.

Keith went to the magazine rack and pulled a copy of the afternoon *Pioneer Press* from the middle of the stack. He looked at the bottom of the front page to read the new clue. Clue 3: *Enter with a queen, leave via river, this little clue may make you shiver.* He read the clue again, letting the words soak in. This looked like a good clue, full of nouns and verbs.

"That it?" asked the attendant as he dropped the paper on the counter. "Two bits."

He gave the attendant a dollar bill. The two gold-framed pictures of Toni's children were missing from their place next to the cash register.

"You a treasure hunter?" the attendant asked, handing him back three quarters.

"Sort of."

"What do you make of this new clue?"

"Looks like a hard one. What do you make of it?"

"Well, I think it's got something to do with where the ice palace was at Lake Phalen a few years ago."

"What makes you think that?"

The attendant leaned over the counter toward him in a confidential manner and pointed at the newspaper spread out before him. He tapped the clue with a blunt index finger.

"Queen. I figure that the Winter Carnival queen was probably there. And this word, shiver, refers to something cold. That must mean the castle. What do you think? Should I quit my job here and run over to Phalen and start digging?"

"What about river—how does that fit in?" Other people's interpretations of the clues, no matter how stupid they were, fascinated him. You never knew when you might pick up something useful.

"I don't know. Maybe it means the stream or whatever it was that runs by where the palace was. Remember you had to walk over this little bridge? What do you think?"

"It's possible, I guess."

"So how about you? What do you think it means?"

"I'm not very good at figuring out the clues, I just like to follow them." He straightened up and tucked the newspaper under his arm.

"Have a good one." The attendant bent over his newspaper again.

Go ahead, Keith told himself. *Ask him.* He adjusted his newspaper under his arm. "Uh . . . Excuse me . . . ."

The attendant looked up.

"Do you know Toni Stoltz by any chance? She works here."

"No. Never heard of her. Just started here myself a week ago."

"She brings in pictures of her kids and keeps them by the cash register."

"Oh, her. She chewed me out first afternoon I worked here. Said I hassled a customer. Acted like she owned the frigging place. You know her?"

"Just a friend. Is there any schedule you could check to see when she's working?"

"Probably," the attendant said. "But I wouldn't know where to look for it. I can barely find the can in this place. Know what I mean?"

"Well, thanks anyway."

"Hey, no problem."

Keith pulled onto Johnson Parkway and headed north toward home. As soon as he got home, he would jump on this new clue. The attendant in the store didn't know what the hell he was talking about. Queen and river—those were the real clues. Obviously, queen and river referred to street names, and shiver had nothing to do with it— that was just a phrase to round out the verse. Queen was probably a street that led into the park, and river one that led out. All he had to do was go over his city map and look around each park for street names that were related to queen or river. Then he could mark those parks that he found and see if they had any pinked-in railroad tracks near them. And he might learn something by comparing this Clue 3 with third clues from previous years in his computer file. Maybe he'd find this on Tuesday, if the Tuesday clues were any good. Just like that, four thousand dollars would be in his pocket. Found money, so to speak. And he would tie the record for the earliest day the medallion was found to boot. Four thousand dollars. He could use that money to start his own computer programming business someday.

A battered Plymouth flashed past him, driven by a woman wearing her hair in a blond shag. In the fleeting moment he saw her, she looked like Toni. It was the sort of car, anyway, that he pictured her in. He'd been half disappointed that Toni hadn't been there. But this bossiness that the SA attendant had mentioned concerned him. *Acted like she owned the frigging place.* One thing he did not need was one more person bossing him around, telling him what to do. It was bad enough at work. He'd have to think about calling her up.

Driving through Phalen Center, he slowed the Nova to a crawl, looking at the fast-food marquees. Which would it be? A burger, roast beef, or tacos? A horn blared behind him.

"Yeah, buzz off." He swung the Nova into the parking lot of one of the burger shops, heading for the drive-up window. Like the old commercial said, he deserved a break today.

SEVEN

STEVEN CARPENTER SAT on the living room couch, his Martin guitar in his lap. On the seat cushion next to him was his little cassette tape recorder. He pushed the record button, strummed the opening chords to a song he was working on, and leaned toward the little microphone. He took a deep breath, and on the beat started to sing:

> I used to get lost in your eyes,
> Used to go wild at your touch, and
> Oh, how I loved you so much.
> But something's gone wrong,
> Somehow, something's changed, and
> Lovin' you doesn't thrill me anymore.
> Now I don't know why,
> It makes me want to cry, but
> Love's not the same anymore
> Just not the same anymore
> Just not the same anymore
> Just not the same.

He played a break, tapping the beat with his right foot, concentrating on making the chords clean and clear. He swallowed, took a breath, and started the next verse, putting a harder edge in his voice:

> We used to make our sweet plans,
> We thought that we had it all, and
> Oh, I thought life was a ball.
> But something's gone wrong,
> Somehow, something's changed, and
> Life doesn't thrill me anymore.
> Now I don't know why,

It makes me want to cry, but
Life's not the same anymore
Just not the same anymore
Just not the same anymore
Just not the same.

He played the break again, harder than the first time, trying to imagine what the passage would sound like if played by a full band; a bass note here, a cymbal crash there, rhythm complementing melody.

Something's gone wrong,
Somehow, something's changed,
Nothing can thrill me anymore.
Now I don't know why,
It makes me want to cry, but
It's not the same anymore
Just not the same anymore
Just not the same anymore
Just not the same.

He sang this chorus one more time, beating out the chords, pushing his voice to the limit. Then he played the break a third time, slowing the tempo down to its original pace. Dropping his voice to a near whisper, he sang four final lines, softly, slowly, trying to fill his voice with melancholy and regret.

Oh, I wish I knew why,
It makes me want to cry,
But it's not the same anymore
It's just not the same.

He fingered the closing notes to the song, holding each note a beat or two longer, hitting the final chord softly, cleanly. Quickly he reached over, hit the stop button, and leaned against the back of the couch to stare at the ceiling for a moment. He rested his guitar against the arm of the couch, rewound the tape, and punched the play button.

His opening chords sounded hollow and tinny coming from the tiny speaker. The sound of his voice, thin and bleating, made him wince, and he hit the stop button. God, he sounded like shit. On tape, his voice never sounded like it did inside his head, and no matter what he did, he could never turn what he heard into what he wanted to hear. For this song, he wanted the wispy voice of Dan Fogelberg in his earlier days. In his other songs, when he was reaching for the blues shout of B. B. King, or the tuneless voice of Dylan, he always ended up sounding like this— like some asshole singing in the shower at the top of his lungs.

He rewound the tape and started it again, this time checking his watch.

I used to get lost in your eyes . . .

The first verse actually sounded fair, but the break was too messy. He could hear his fingers making little shadow sounds as they moved along the strings to make the next chord.

We used to make our sweet plans . . .

The second verse sounded too flat, too much like the first verse in tone. It needed to sound wearier, sadder. The second break was a total mess, too loud and too harsh.

Something's gone wrong . . .

The first repeat of the chorus didn't sound right; the tone of his voice was colored wrong. The second repeat was all wrong.

Now I wish I knew why . . .

There. He wasn't getting his voice up high enough, where he wanted it to be. Each word in that line should get stronger, until the word *knew*, where he wanted to go right through the ozone into the stratosphere. And the word *why* should start out high and fall into a hush at the end. The closing four lines seemed pretty good, just the right amount of regret and sadness in them.

He shut off the tape recorder and glanced quickly at his watch. Two minutes and thirty seconds. Pretty short. It needed something. Some part seemed to be missing, a third verse maybe. That would stretch it out to nearly three minutes. But what was there to write about after you said life had lost its thrill? Maybe he could write a new first verse and use the two verses he already had as the second and third verses. The new verse could be something from his childhood, like the price of M&Ms.

He picked up his guitar again and strummed meaningless chords. He wondered what this song would sound like if someone like Dylan sang it. Maybe he should send it to him. God, what a kick that would be, having someone like that record his song. It wouldn't matter if he never made a cent off it; just hearing Dylan or even Fogelberg sing it would be payment enough.

The living room was growing dark. Debi would be home from work in a few minutes. He had just enough time to run through the song again. He pushed the record button on the tape recorder again and strummed the opening chords, slowing the tempo just a bit from the first time. He closed his eyes as he sang, seeing himself in a dark club, a blue spotlight thrown on him.

When he opened his eyes at the break, Debi was standing in front of him, still wearing her coat and gloves, holding the afternoon paper. Abruptly he stopped.

"That's really nice," Debi said. "Whose song is it?"

"It's an old Fogelberg song," he said, hitting the stop button on the tape recorder. He laid the guitar down in its case and closed the lid.

"You don't have to quit."

"I'm tired of playing." Snapping the latches of the guitar case shut, he carried the case into the bedroom, standing it in the corner next to his side of the bed. He dropped down onto the bed, staring up at the dark ceiling. Deep in his belly, he felt his anger from last night and this morning rekindling itself.

The ceiling light flashed on, half blinding him, as Debi came into the bedroom. She opened the closet door and started to undress, pulling her bright blue dress up over her head. He watched her undress, a sight that normally turned him on.

"So how was your day?" She pulled off her slip and hung it on a hook on the inside of the closet door. Her pantyhose came off next. She wadded them up and dropped them in the dirty clothes hamper. Wearing only her bra and panties, she came over to the bed and sat down next to him.

"So how was your day?"

He stared at the Dylan poster on the bedroom wall. "How come you're so friendly all of a sudden?" He heard his voice crack with anger. "You wouldn't even *speak* to me this morning."

"Come on. Let's not fight, okay?" She reached out and touched his shoulder.

He twisted away from her and stared out the window. The streetlights were on, halos of amber light casting a warm glow onto the snowbanks that lined the street.

"You could at least say you were sorry. I apologized to you this morning."

"Okay, I'm sorry."

He snorted. "You could also *mean* it."

Debi lurched to her feet. She whirled around to face him, planting her hands on her hips. In the split second before she spoke, he noticed that she was gaining weight.

"Steven, what *is* it with you? Why are you so hostile? I come home, give you a compliment about the song you were playing, and you just quit and walk out of the room. I come in here and you jump down my throat. I can't win. I swear I can't."

He stared at the ceiling again, tracing the cracks from one end of the room to the other.

"The song I was playing was mine. Only you don't have enough *respect* for me to even consider the fact that it could be mine. You just *assumed* that because it was 'nice' it had to be someone else's. You never—"

"Steven, I just *asked* you whose song it was! Why did you lie? You could have said it was yours."

"I told you what you wanted to hear. Shit, you never give me the benefit of the doubt."

"Steven—"

He swung off the bed to his feet too quickly and felt his head go light, bloodless.

"You *never* support me." His accusation hung in the room, turning the air foul.

Debi turned away from him, turned back. She sat down on the edge of the bed, hugging her breasts.

"Steven, look." Her voice was low, spiritless. "If you want to be a musician, then be a musician. I'll support you, I promise. But *do* something about it, for godssake. That's all I'm saying. Don't just sit around here and talk about it. Go and do something about it. All right?"

As abruptly as it had flared up, he felt his anger flicker and die. Why did they always fight? He sat down on the edge of the bed with her.

"Look," he said. "I'm sorry. I just had a bad day. The Overseer got on my case first thing this morning. Then every little mistake I made for the rest of the day was like some big deal."

Debi got up and went to the dresser and pulled out a pair of jeans.

"Well, you don't have to take your bad days out on me." She pulled the jeans on and zipped them. She rummaged in the drawer for a sweatshirt, pushed her arms through the sleeves, and pulled it down over her head. "I'm going to start supper."

"That was good." Steven propped his elbows on the table. "I think spaghetti's the best thing you make."

"Don't forget it's your turn to do the dishes," Debi said. "Throwing compliments at me won't get you out of doing them."

A friendly barb tossed at him. Over supper, the tension between them had slowly evaporated into the air, like so much spilled milk, leaving behind the stain of accepting responsibility, of setting things right. Final apologies were in order, a last pass with the cloth to wipe things clean.

"Deb, I'm sorry I yelled at you. I really am."

"Don't worry about it." Debi picked at the remains of her pasta. "Are we friends?"

"We're married. I'm stuck with you." She pushed her plate away.

The remark cut. She never returned an apology or a compliment. Did she do it on purpose, or was it just her nature to dismiss his efforts at restoring the peace? It was a subject he did not feel like pursuing, at least not tonight. They'd fought enough for one night. He pushed himself out of his chair.

"Where did you put the paper? I'll do the dishes later."

"It's in the big chair."

In the living room he switched on the floor lamp and slouched into the overstuffed chair. Knickerson never had finished telling him about the treasure hunt after the Overseer had interrupted them. He found the headline on the front page and skimmed through the story.

Debi came in and flopped onto the couch.

"Throw me the business section."

He pitched the section across the room to her. "Don't ruin your eyes on all the little print."

She unfolded the section. "Mr. Savage said they might have an opening for a broker trainee in a couple of months, especially if Joe Lindgren leaves. I've got a shot at it."

"Terrific. Today, St. Paul, tomorrow, New York! I can just see you standing on the floor of the New York Stock Exchange, screaming your lungs out."

"Up yours, Carpenter." Her face disappeared behind the paper.

Another clue had been published since the morning. He read it, then read it again. "Deb, listen to this: *Enter with a queen, leave via river, this little clue may make you shiver.* What does that make you think of?"

"What is it?"

"A clue to the treasure hunt."

"The what?"

"The what? Earth to Debi. Come in, please. You know, the Winter Carnival. The Vulcans? Where have you *been* for the past two weeks?"

"I know what it is, jerk, I just didn't *hear* you, that's all. Read it again."

"There's three of them." He read the clues one at a time.

"Well, the first one sure isn't much of a clue," Debi said. "So it's in Ramsey County, big deal."

"Knickerson thought that the second clue had something to do with trains," he said.

"'I think I can' is what the Little Engine said," Debi nodded. "That makes sense. It probably means train tracks. So it's in Ramsey County near some train tracks. Read the third one again."

He read the clue again, conscious of the rhythm and rhyme of the words. It wasn't bad—it was terrible.

"Well, the river must mean the Mississippi," Debi said. "And isn't there a riverboat that is the *Something Queen? Mississippi Queen?*"

"*Delta Queen,*" he corrected her. "But it's not a local boat. It's from down South. It only comes up here once or twice a year."

"Well, if you *enter with a queen,* then you'd have to come from downstream where the riverboat comes from. So it's got to be somewhere in Ramsey County, near train tracks, where the riverboat comes from."

He got up and went to the stereo. Flipping through his old albums, he pulled out a Steve Goodman record from the early seventies, dropped it on the turntable, and cued up "Turnpike Tom." The song was about a hitchhiker who got his kicks out of giving false treasure maps to gullible, greedy people he rode with. It seemed like the perfect song to play. If he could only write a story song as good as this one someday.

"What you're saying doesn't make literal sense," he said as he collapsed back into his chair. "How can you *enter with a queen* and *leave via river* when the boat runs on the river? That doesn't make sense to me. They're both the river."

"So what do you think it means, Mr. Know-It-All?"

He listened to Goodman's guitar work. It was sharp, clear, and very smooth. He wished he could play that well.

"I don't know," he conceded. "Maybe it does have something to do with the river."

"Maybe it means it's only accessible by water. Like on an island." Debi tucked her legs under her. "I know—it's on that island under the Wabasha Bridge. I can see it out the window in Mr. Savage's office."

"That's too easy. The hunt is supposed to run until the end of the week. They wouldn't give it away this early. Besides, if it's hidden on an island, how is everyone going to get there to look?"

"Let me see the paper."

Wordlessly, he folded the paper and tossed it across the room. The act gave him a feeling of passing control of something over to her.

"Hey, this article says if we found it, we could win up to four thousand dollars. God." Debi looked up from the paper. "What I could do with four thousand bucks." She folded the paper and dropped it on the floor. "What would you do if someone handed you four thousand dollars? After taxes, of course."

"I don't know. Save it, I guess."

"No, don't be practical," Debi said. "I mean four thousand that you could just blow. Spend any way you wanted to. What would you do?"

"I don't know. What would you do?"

"I'd go out and buy a new couch, for one thing. Or I'd spend it on a vacation. Or I'd get rid of the Honda and buy a new car. I'd use it to put a down payment on a house."

"It's going to take a little more than four thousand to do all that. More like forty thousand."

"Well, it doesn't hurt to have plans."

That was the thing about her. A shopping list as long as your arm, spending money that they would never see. She always seemed to know what she wanted, where she was going.

"Speaking of the Honda," Debi said, "are you ever going to get it started again? It's been dead since last week."

"Why is it always me that gets stuck with getting it started?"

"You're a man; you know those things."

"What a double standard. I'm supposed to help you with the dishes and the housework, and you just wash your hands of the *man's* work? Go wash your own dishes, woman."

"Steven, don't you know that a double standard only works one way?"

"It seems that way."

"So when are you going to get the car started?"

He took his time to answer. "It's supposed to warm up. I'm going to try and start it tomorrow."

Debi disappeared into the bedroom and returned with a bottle of red fingernail polish. "I might as well make double use of my time," she said.

"Don't stink the place up with that stuff," he groaned. The harsh odor of polish filled the living room. With tiny, precise strokes, Debi turned her thumbnail from pink to red.

"Turnpike Tom" ended with the singer suckered into driving hundreds of miles out of his way with the key the hitchhiker had given him, only to open a condom machine in a gas station and find not the promised treasure map, but a sign that said he'd just been had in a sanitary way by Turnpike Tom, the outlaw with the fastest sense of humor. The turntable shut itself off.

"So," Debi said, "you didn't tell me what you would spend the money on."

"You really want to know?" He watched her paint a nail pink to red, debating whether to tell her the truth. He decided to.

"Well, I'd quit my job, live off the money, and bum across the country. I'd write some songs about what I saw, put an album or tape together, and call it *The American Dreamer*."

Debi rolled her eyes.

"I knew you'd do that," he said. "It's no more impractical than buying a couch we don't really need."

"Up yours, Carpenter." Debi bent over her nails again. "Go do the dishes."

EIGHT

—※—

"DAD, I'M DONE!"

Sharon Prescott looked up from her *Inc.* magazine article on business start-ups. Chris stood before his father, wearing an impatient look. Phil's head bobbed up from his issue of *Corporate Report.* Father and son face to face, almost as if they were squared off against each other. Just like his father at thirteen, she thought, looking at the two of them. God help the world when that boy grows up.

"That was quick," Phil said. "Book report, too?"

"Yep. Can we?—"

"Let's see if you know your stuff." Phil pitched the magazine onto the coffee table. "Let's hear it. Title, author, and plot summary."

"You mean right now?"

"Right now. You know the rule: no television, stereo, VCR, or treasure hunting until all homework is finished and approved."

Phil's rule, invoked after Chris's grades had plunged when he first started at Ramsey Junior High. Phil's close supervision had produced results, all right—Cs and Ds up to Bs and Cs—but still a far cry from his straight-A days. Or had Chris simply adjusted to his new home like the rest of them, relocating his center of gravity, finding his balance again? How could you be sure which way it was?

"The Adventures of Tom Sawyer," Chris began nervously. "By Mark Twain. It starts out with this kid named Tom Sawyer, who . . ."

Tom Sawyer. A classic, she thought, as Chris rambled through the plot. Good for him. And good news for her used/educational-bookstore idea: the classics held on. As she listened to Chris's rambling plot summary, she began to wonder if he had actually read the book or was simply bluffing his way through it. She hadn't seen it lying around the house, his usual sign of reading a book.

"Good report," Phil said when Chris had graphically documented Injun Joe's pitiful demise in the cave, and the glories of Tom's and Huck's wealth (though wasn't it twelve thousand dollars, instead of twenty?).

"Let's work on the treasure hunt clues. You said."

"I said." Phil jumped to his feet, bringing his hands together with a loud clap, rubbing them in anticipation.

"Everybody to the dining room table," he said in his deejay voice. He motioned with great exaggeration toward the dining room, throwing his whole body into the gesture. She laid her magazine aside. A far cry from this morning, when he had forgotten all about it. All evening Phil had been exceptionally breezy. He had dinner—his famous chili, always too spicy for her tastes—on the table when she got home. Over dinner the conversation had centered around the boys, around last night's humiliating North Stars' loss to the Boston Bruins. The promotion had not been mentioned. If the phrase "waiting for the other shoe to drop" hadn't already been invented, it would have to be to explain the way she felt right now.

"Where's Jeff?" Phil asked as they gathered around the dining room table.

"He's upstairs talking on the phone," Chris said.

"Go holler at him."

"I'll go," she said.

At the top of the stairs, she found the door to the master bedroom closed, sealing off the outside world from the serious business of adolescence. She tapped once on her own bedroom door, then pushed it open. Jeff lay on his back on the floor, his feet propped on the edge of the bed. He was in the middle of a laugh.

"You're wanted downstairs."

He jerked his feet off the bed and rolled to a standing position in one movement, phone in hand.

"Listen, I gotta go. I'll talk to you tomorrow at school, okay? Bye." The receiver banged into its cradle.

She knew she shouldn't ask, shouldn't commit the parental sin of prying into a teenager's private life, but she asked anyway.

"Who were you talking to?"

"Nobody."

"How do you talk to nobody on the phone?"

"It was just a friend."

"Was it a girl?" A pause; flickers of guilt and embarrassment flashed across Jeff's face.

"Sorta."

"Sorta?"

"Yeah, sorta."

"Somebody you like?" A stupid question, she decided immediately. Why would he waste time talking to a girl he didn't like?

"Mom, give me a break, will ya?" His face, flushed crimson, said it all. Why was this subject such a difficult one between generations? Was it the kids or the parents who made it so hard? These same probing questions from her own parents years ago had made her feel equally uncomfortable.

"Come on, Romeo, let's go downstairs," she said, trying to sound lighthearted. She failed. Jeff gave her a look and slipped around her into the hallway. She followed his broad shoulders down the stairs, shaking her head. Good luck, son. I'd help you if I knew how.

"Got our notes?" Phil turned to Chris as they settled themselves at the dining room table. Chris held up his notebook.

"So where did we leave off this morning?" Phil began.

"That it had something to do with trains." Chris drummed his hands on the table impatiently, a steady beat that called to mind about half of the rock-and-roll songs ever written.

"And why was that?"

"'I think I can' is what the Little Engine That Could said." Chris rapped out his answer without a moment's hesitation.

She sighed. If only he were this sharp in school. *Has the capacity to do better, but not the interest,* one of his report cards had said at the quarter's end. *Slow to adjust to new situations.*

"What specifically did we decide the clue said about trains?" Phil sounded more like a lawyer cross-examining a witness than a salesman.

"Nothin'," Chris said, "we ran out of time. That's what we was going to do tonight."

"Were," she corrected him.

"Were."

"So what do you think it means?" Phil asked.

"Train tracks," Chris said.

"But what about train tracks?" Phil leaned back in his chair, crossing his arms over his chest. He looked squarely at the boys, his face set with challenge, and the boys looked at the tabletop.

The Challenge look irritated her. He was famous for it at the company. He had told her that last spring, an unmistakable note of pride in his voice, after catching a leaf of gossip that had fallen off the company grapevine. You challenge people with a look, he had told her then. And if they don't deliver, you put the question to them again.

"What about train tracks?"

"It's hidden near train tracks?" Chris's voice was suddenly colored with doubt.

"Maybe. How about you, Jeff? What do you think it means?"

"Huh? I don't know. Near railroad tracks, I guess." A distant voice to match his distant look. Slouched deep in his chair, his hands shoved into his jean pockets, it was clear that his mind was still upstairs, talking on the telephone, not down here with the old folks and his kid brother.

"It could be train tracks, but it could be something else," Phil said. "Look at the second part of the clue: . . . *that has just the right meaning for you.* Maybe train tracks is too easy. The second part of the clue might mean that it is something other than tracks. Something that 'I think I can' tips us off to."

"Yeah, I'll bet." Chris pulled at the spiral wire of his notebook.

She could see the wheels turning inside his head as he struggled to think of an alternative and solve the problem straightaway, to rise to The Challenge.

"Let's move on to tonight's new clue," she said. "Maybe this one will mean something more to us later on."

Phil motioned for the notebook and studied it for a moment. "Let's do move on. And let's hope that the next clue has a little more to go on. They can't expect us to solve this without a little meat in these clues." He pushed the paper at his elder son. "Jeff, read us the next clue."

In slow motion, Jeff pulled his hands from his pockets and straightened up in his chair. He reached for the paper. *"Enter with a queen, leave via river, this little clue may make you shiver."*

"Read it again," Phil said when he had finished. "Slower."

Jeff's words came out distinctly, tonelessly, as if delivered by a computer.

Phil passed his hands through his salt-and-pepper hair and let out a low whistle.

"Now that's what I call a real clue. There's all kinds of hints in there. Trouble is, what do they mean?" He looked around the table at each of them. "Ideas?"

The silence felt like the silences in high school and college classes when no one had read the assignment and the teacher's question hung in the air, unanswered.

"It could mean a lot of things," she heard herself say.

"Near the Mississippi River?" Chris suggested doubtfully.

"What makes you think that?" Phil looked across the table at him.

"It's the only river here."

"Didn't yesterday's clue mention something about royalty?" Jeff ventured. He looked at the paper again. "Royal bounty. That could tie into queen somehow."

"That's the idea," Phil said. "Now we're getting somewhere. Relate the clues to each other. Just get ideas out on the table. Sooner or later something's going to match up and make sense."

"The Mississippi River runs through parks, I'll bet," Chris said.

She reached for the paper and read the clue to herself. "I think the key words here aren't queen and river. Enter with a queen, leave via river. Enter and leave. I think those are the key words. I think they'll help tell what queen and river mean."

"Now we're cooking." Phil clapped his hands together and rubbed them back and forth. "Enter and leave what?"

"A park?" Jeff looked to his father for confirmation.

"Obviously," Phil agreed.

"You would enter a park on a street," Jeff reasoned.

"Or maybe you drive by something," she added. "Something related to a queen, or named after a queen."

"What queen things can we think of?" Phil said in his supervisor's voice. "Let's list them. Jeff, you start."

"The queen in a deck of cards."

"Chris?"

Chris's eyes fell toward the table. She felt herself frowning. Did Phil secretly enjoy putting people on the spot? Did he even know he was doing it?

"Nothing?" Phil's eyebrows were raised in question. "Okay, we'll come back to you. I'll say queen bee. How about—"

"I got one," Chris interrupted. "Queen Elizabeth."

She searched her memory for more names. "I'll add the names of other queens: Queen Victoria; Queen Isabella; Queen Mary; Mary, Queen of Scots." Those dry, dusty classes in European history back at Boston U were finally good for something.

"Chris . . ." Phil pointed at the notebook. "Write 'em down. Come on, what else?"

"Something named queen or with queen in it," Jeff ventured.

"The band Queen." Chris pounded the table in a heavy beat. "We will, we will ROCK YOU."

"Thank you, Elvis," she said. "We get the point. More than get the point."

Phil leaned back in his chair again and crossed his arms over his chest. He was frowning. "None of these are things that can be found in the city. We must be missing something. Jeff, get the telephone book. Check under Queen."

Jeff disappeared into the kitchen and returned a moment later carrying the St. Paul white pages. They looked so thin, nothing at all like the three-inch-thick Boston directory.

"Queen Fashions, Queen's Court Studio of Dance, Queen's Crown of Design." He stopped and looked up from the page.

"None of those sound very promising," Phil said. "Go on."

"That's all there is."

"That's *all?*" Phil shook his head in disbelief. "Geez, Boston would have had a whole page of listings. So much for that idea."

"How about Dairy Queen?" she suggested.

"Bingo." Phil slapped the table with an open palm. "I'll bet that's it. You could drive by a Dairy Queen on the way into a park. Look under Dairy Queen, Jeff."

"There's a whole bunch of them."

"There can't be that many. We could go through them one at a time."

Jeff's finger moved slowly down the page. "There's thirty listed here." He looked up from the page. "We could check the locations on a map and see how close they were to a park."

"Where's our street map?" Phil said.

"It's still out in the car, where it was yesterday." She kicked at him under the table. "And it's still cold out. If you want it, you know where it's at."

"Zero isn't that cold," Phil protested. A mischievous look brightened his eyes. "It's invigorating."

"I'll go get it," Jeff volunteered. "You know, this is kind of neat, like playing *Clue*. Everybody gets the same clues, and the same chance to find out whodunit."

"Or, in this case, whereisit," she amended. "Let's save that for tomorrow. I know a thirteen-year-old who needs his beauty sleep."

"Ma, it ain't even ten o'clock yet."

"No, but it takes you nearly an hour to get to bed. So get going, Mister." She thumbed over her shoulder.

"Geez." Chris slammed the notebook shut and pushed his chair back in preparation to stand up.

"Just a minute." Phil motioned him back into place. "Let's talk about something else for a minute." He clasped his hands together and rested them on the tabletop. There was a different air about him, a shift to a minor key.

She felt her stomach lurch as though she were a passenger in a free-falling elevator. Here it comes. The other shoe, about to drop.

With a long index finger, Phil traced the oak grain of the tabletop. He looked up at her briefly, struggled for a smile.

"I've always told you boys that if you work hard you'll be rewarded, haven't I?" He looked gravely, first at Jeff, then at Chris. "That's what brought us here two years ago. Because I worked hard and did a good job, the company promoted me and sent me—us—here to St. Paul."

He laid one hand on the back of the other and leaned slightly forward. "Well, I've been rewarded again. The company has offered me a big promotion to district sales manager."

"Wow, that's neat." Chris pounded the table and raised his hands above his head in triumph. A goal scored.

"Hey, Dad, that's great," Jeff chimed in.

"The promotion would make me one of the most powerful men in the company. And it means a big raise in pay. At least ten thousand dollars a year. That's an important consideration. I don't want you two to have to work all through high school and college, like I did."

"He started out washing dishes at the country club in Quincy when he was in junior high," Jeff began in a narrator's voice.

"Then he switched to caddying because he could collect tips," Chris continued.

"The bigger the cigar, the bigger the tip," they said in unison, wagging a knowing finger at each other. They erupted with laughter.

"All right, have your fun," Phil said, holding up a hand in surrender. "So you've heard me tell my sad tale a few times." He leaned back until his chair squeaked in protest, then snapped forward. "Well, you left out a couple of parts that I still remember. Like stealing food from the club kitchen to take home so we could eat the next day. And what you feel like when the man with the biggest cigar in the whole club tells you to take off your jacket and cover his golf clubs when it starts to rain." His voice was laced with bitterness.

The boys looked at each other and then sideways at her. Phil's grim, fatherless childhood in Roxbury was usually played for laughs, or mined for an occasional bootstraps anecdote to illustrate one of his frequent lessons.

"I worked hard to get where I am," Phil continued. "A little hard work is good for the soul. But I don't want either of you to go through the hard times like I did. That's why this promotion, if I accept it, is so important."

Like I did. Her own childhood in South Boston had been almost as hard, but it was his anecdotes that had somehow been woven into family mythology.

"Why wouldn't you take it?" Jeff's voice was tight.

She looked across the corner of the table at him. His eyes told her that he had suddenly guessed what Phil was about to say.

"There's one catch." Phil locked his fingers together. "The job that's open isn't here in St. Paul. Mr. Flannary is district manager here. To accept the job, I—we—would have to relocate. Move to either San Diego or Denver. There's a position open in both cities."

He was in gear again, off and rolling, and his voice picked up, gaining speed. "That would mean a change again for you boys. There're some things we'd have to give up. We'd have to give up the North Stars, the Vikings, the Twins, and the Wolves. But we'd get the opportunity to see a new part of the country, and there are new teams to root for. In San Diego there's the Chargers and the Padres. In Denver we'd have the Broncos and the Nuggets."

His typical sales approach; she knew it well. Sell the hell out of the good points, he'd told her once, hammer away at them. Gloss over the weak points. She herself had been charmed and disarmed by this strategy many times.

"Relocating means—"

"It means," she broke in, "you would have to start all over in school. You'd have to leave all of your friends again."

Phil's eyes shifted toward her, turned from gray to black. He turned back toward the boys.

"That's true, but you've done that before when you came out here, and you've done really well. I'm proud of you. Both of you.

"Of course, this isn't set in stone. I don't have to give an answer to Mr. Flannary until next Monday. We've got time to think about it. Think about what it means to you, and we'll talk about it later in the week." He slapped the table with his open palm. "Now both of you head for bed."

The three of them got up in a bumping commotion of chairs scraping across the hard oak floor. Their voices trailed off, floating on the dry heat thrown off by the old cast iron radiators clanking away in the corner of every room. She heard footsteps trudge up the carpeted stairs. The door to the den opened and clicked shut.

The refrigerator in the kitchen kicked on and settled into a steady hum. Damn him. Dumping a responsibility like that on the two of them. *I'm proud of you.* And now make me proud again. Make the sacrifice.

Someone dropped into the chair across from her. She looked up into Jeff's eyes, high beams of blue light.

"I thought you were on your way upstairs."

"In a minute." His eyes fell to low beam. It was clear he had something to say, but had no idea where to begin.

"Her name is Lisa." His voice cracked with self-consciousness. "She lives on Summit Avenue down by the law school."

The girl. She was not expecting this at all. Don't pry, she warned herself. Show interest, open the door, but don't try to drag him through it. Let him come through on his own, when he wants to.

"That's a nice name."

"She's neat." The beams switched to high. "I'm going out to the car to get the map." With that, he was gone. She heard the door to the hall closet open and slam shut as he got his coat.

A life of his own. Was it fair to him, to any of them, to pull them away from what they had built? The front door opened and banged closed. A moment later, she felt a chill moving across the floor.

NINE

LYING ON HIS BACK, HANDS FOLDED behind his head, Bruce Mitchell let himself drift through the cozy darkness. The soft rushes of Joanna's breath felt warm across his chest as she dozed, her head on his shoulder. Under the press of covers, he felt weightless, his heart floating under his ribs. Every time was as magical as the first. Time and space had just been altered; he'd seen stars; all the old cliches that people dragged out at times like these were true. And then everything had gradually floated away and disappeared, even himself—his body—until nothing remained in all the world but this *feeling*. This incredible feeling. He spun out a little fantasy: down the line, a new job in the printing industry, a wedding, maybe a house of their own, and a couple of kids. Anything, whatever it took to keep this feeling alive, to keep it going on forever.

He heard the sound of a car outside and opened his eyes. Pale rectangles of light slid around the room, then broke across the ceiling as the car passed by on the street below. The world was perfect, except for one thing.

"You awake?" he whispered, touching Joanna on the shoulder.

"No, I think I died and went to heaven."

"You want anything to drink?"

"What do you have?" She rolled to the adjoining pillow, pulling the covers around her.

"Well, we got your Coors, we got your basic two percent milk, your typical West Side water—"

"Got any Diet Coke?"

"And your basic Diet Coke. I just happened to have picked up a twelve-pack today."

"What a guy. Got any crackers?"

"You serious?"

"Sure. I want to see if you kick me out of bed for eating crackers."

"Not a chance." He pressed his lips against the hollow of her neck, then flipped back the covers and sat up. Cold air hit his body as he groped around on the floor for his underwear.

"What time is it?" Jo asked.

"Eleven-thirty."

"I should go."

"It's not as cold as last night." He stood up, pulling his underwear up around his waist. "If your car won't start in the morning, I'll jump-start you."

"You already did."

"I love it when you talk dirty," he said.

He moved easily in the familiar darkness through the living room and into the kitchen. The twelve-pack of Diet Coke was still on the counter. He opened it and pulled out a can. How could she drink the stuff? From the looks of her, she drank a lot of it. A dancer's body, compact and firm.

He took a tray of ice cubes out of the freezer and banged it into the sink. The dry chill of the ice cubes as he scooped up a handful and dropped them into a glass sent shivers running over his body. He'd be glad to slip back under the covers. He got a Coors from the fridge for himself, popped the top, and took a swig. There were no crackers in the cupboard. Next time there would be. Instead, he took down a new package of Oreos. He loaded everything on a Schmidt beer serving tray that he had stolen from a bar years ago, then draped the dish towel over his arm. A waiter serving junk food in his underwear.

"Lights," he warned as he came into the bedroom and switched on the lamp on the nightstand. Joanna was sitting up in the bed, her back against the headboard.

"Madam, your Diet Coke. The kitchen says we are out of crackers, but we do have . . ." He lowered the plate so she could see.

"Oreos! My favorite."

He tossed aside the dish towel and crawled under the covers again. The wooden headboard was cool against his back. "The cook said they go great with Diet Coke."

"And beer? Yech."

"Hey, they go great with beer. Watch." He opened the bag, popped a cookie into his mouth, and took a long pull off the Coors. The oily sweetness of chocolate cookie and white filling made the beer sharply bitter.

"So?"

"They're great. Terrific." He made an exaggerated face. "They're terrible."

They worked their way through half a package of cookies before Joanna pushed them away.

"Get these out of here before I make myself sick."

He leaned over the side of the bed to set the tray and their empty cans on the floor. As he straightened up against the headboard again, he caught her looking at his right arm. She looked away. His past catching up with him again. Sooner or later, it always had to be explained.

"She was my girlfriend in high school," he said.

"What?"

"Anita." He pointed to the crude, homemade tattoo that stretched across his upper arm. His skin was pale behind the blue-black ink. "She was my high school girlfriend."

"You don't have to tell me. It's none of my business."

"Because you'd never ask is the reason why I want to tell you. There's not much to tell, actually. It was just a stupid thing high school kids do. We started going together in January of our senior year. One night a couple weeks before graduation, we got stoned and decided to make tattoos. Symbols of our undying love for each other, she called them. We cut the names into our skin with an Exacto knife—Bruce for her, Anita for me. Then we rubbed the ink in. We were too stoned to do a good job. That's why the letters are so crooked and uneven. She put that curlicue thing underneath trying to even it out a little. It only made it look worse." He rubbed the name. "It was a stupid thing to do. Our undying love for each other died about the time the infection from the ink cleared up."

"And you were left with broken memories and a tattoo?"

"Broken ribs, mostly. Her brothers didn't like a gringo hanging around their sister. The night before graduation, they caught me in a parking lot and kicked the shit out of me. I ended up in the emergency room at Ramsey. Missed graduation the next day."

"Ooohhh. That must have hurt." She touched his ribs and he shivered under her touch, felt his blood rushing in his veins.

"I hated the damn thing after her brothers broke us up. I used to cover it with a Band-Aid. Michelle—my old girl friend—*really* hated it, so I kept it covered for her. I don't pay much attention to it anymore. Now it's sort of a symbol, a reminder that things change. You can't always expect things to stay the same. Gotta move with the flow, you know." He motioned with his hand, a fish swimming through water.

"Mr. Philosopher." Joanna stroked his chest. "You're funny," she said.

"Why?"

"You just are."

"I'm not sure I want to be funny."

"It's a nice kind of funny."

"Well, you're kind of funny yourself. Can't decide if you're going to stay over or not."

"I'll stay, if you promise me my car will start in the morning."

"It'll start."

He switched off the light and they slid down into the covers, burrowing in.

"So, how about dessert?" he said.

"What are you serving, waiter?"

"Satisfaction."

"I hear it's the house specialty. I'll have some."

"Self-service," he said.

Her hands touched his face, traced his Fu Manchu, traveled down to his chest, his belly, fire and ice on his quivering skin. Her weight, pleasant and warm, pressed against the length of his body, and once again he felt himself whirling through space and time, past the bright lights of the stars out into the far reaches of the universe toward—

It was not his ears that were ringing, but the telephone. *Damn, not tonight. Not with Joanna here. Let the son of a bitch ring.* The phone rang a second time, a third, the rings echoing through the darkness. Joanna rolled away.

"Go ahead," she said. "Answer it."

He rolled over and fumbled around in the dark for the telephone. He felt like telling St. John to go fuck himself and then hanging up.

"Yup."

"So Sundance, did you run out and pick up that medallion today?" St. John's voice boomed in his ear. In the background, the Charlie Daniels Band was smoking its way through "No Potion for the Pain," a blues song about a man out to even the score against his wife and her lover.

He felt his anger fall away. "No Potion" was a song that St. John played whenever he was in a particularly ugly mood. He tried to remember if he had promised last night to call him during the day and then welshed, but all he could remember for sure was that St. John had been bummed out after Karen had called him.

"Nope," he said, pulling the phone under the covers with him. "I plan to run out there tomorrow."

"So where is it?"

"Told you. It's in Como Park."

"What makes you think so?"

"Hold on a minute." He felt in the darkness for Joanna. "I'm sorry," he whispered. "Can you hang this up in a minute?" He rolled out of bed and slipped into his jeans.

Out in the kitchen he switched on the light, squinting in its bright flash, and picked up the receiver.

"So you were saying?" A heavy click filled their ears as Joanna hung up the bedroom extension.

"Your lady friend there?"

"Yeah. I'm out in the kitchen. Your timing really sucks."

"Were you . . . uh . . ."

"Yeah. For the second time tonight. She was just about to—"

"Maybe I better call you tomorrow."

"It's too late now. The big man left town the minute the phone rang, if you know what I mean."

"Hey, I'm sorry," St. John began. "Look—"

"It's okay. I meant to call you today anyway. How you doing?"

"Horseshit. This sitting around this winter is fucking driving me crazy."

"Any news today about when you go back to work?"

"Nada. Probably won't go back this week. Hell, it may be spring, the way the weather's been." The snap of a match came through the receiver as St. John lit up a cigarette.

"So maybe it's time to get into a new line of work," he suggested.

"Sure, I could be a *printing press operator.*" There was an edge beneath St. John's breezy tone.

"Well, working in a nice warm printing plant sure beats sitting around half the winter with your thumb up your ass because it's too cold to work outside."

"What a wuss. Let a little cold weather scare you off."

"Yeah, and who was bitching at me last week because the company had you out there working in the cold? I'll tell you, I sure as hell don't miss it." He paused. "You ought to sign up for some classes next quarter."

"Yeah, one of these days." St. John fell silent on the other end. In the background, the Charlie Daniels Band was evening up the score out on Highway 65. St. John's raspy growl suddenly joined in on his favorite line. "I took *back* what they *owed* me, left no one there aliiiiive."

"You missed your calling, Butch. Charlie would be downright proud to have you join his band. So have you heard any more out of old What's-Her-Name?"

"Nope."

He heard St. John take a long hit off the cigarette, and half expected to get an earful of smoke.

"So what makes you think the medallion is in Como Park?" St. John asked.

A swift change of subject. Karen was off-limits tonight.

"Well," Bruce said, "did you see the clues today in the paper? The second clue sounds like it has something to do with trains. I figure that regular train tracks is too easy. It's gotta be something else. Remember that—"

"That little train ride up there by the zoo where them little kids' rides are!" St. John broke in.

"Right. Fits in perfect with the kids' rhyme in Clue 2."

"I was thinking the same thing. There's a big locomotive, too, that sits up there in the park somewhere. Remember you could pull a cord and ring the bell?"

"Hey, that's right. I forgot about that." He warmed the bottom of his bare foot against his pant leg. "God, I ain't been up around the zoo for years."

"So how does this crap about the queen and the river fit in? The stuff that was in the last clue?" St. John blew another lungful of smoke into the receiver.

"I dunno. Maybe there's a Queen or a River Street or something. Maybe it means one of the animals. If lions are the king of the jungle, maybe there's a queen of the jungle. What do you think?"

"I think you're just *lion* to me. Somebody say go. One-two-three— go."

"Ah, shit. You asshole! You always hit me with this late at night." Animals. He thought quickly. "I can't *bear* to go through with this."

"That was a pretty *fowl* pun."

"Well, that one doesn't get my *seal* of approval, so don't *monkey* around with me or I'll go *ape* on you. How do you like that?"

"Don't try to *buffalo* me," St. John shot back.

"I'm just trying to go for your *jaguar* vein." A pretty bad one; he'd be surprised if St. John let him get by with that one.

"You do, and I'll treat you like a *leopard.*"

"I'm *bewildebeest* by what you're saying."

"No way, Jose," St. John said. "That's stretching it too far."

"Bullshit!"

"Bullshit, nothing. Game's over. How many? I got four."

He counted them up. "Six. That makes up for my narrow defeat last night."

"I gave it to you," St. John said. "Consider it charity. Listen, I think we ought to drive up to Como Park tomorrow and take a look around. Maybe we can figure out what queen and river mean."

"I got classes until midafternoon."

"Skip 'em."

"Nah, I can't do that. Why don't I meet you after class?"

"Ya wanna meet at The Dive? I hear it's a ritzy place."

An old joke. Long ago, they'd nicknamed their favorite bar The Dive. One night while they were sitting there having a beer, they overheard a couple of kids sitting behind them talking about how ritzy the place looked. St. John never again referred to the place by its real name. To St. John, the official name of the place was The Dive, I Hear It's a Ritzy Place.

"Sure. I can probably be there by five."

"We'll go looking for love."

Another old joke. He wasn't interested in doing much looking these days. He felt suddenly tired of old jokes, and wanted to be back in bed. He studied his reflection in the dark kitchen window. God, he was starting to get a gut on him. He sucked in his stomach, filled his chest with air, and flexed his muscles as best he could. No more Coors. He'd have to start drinking Diet Coke with Joanna. He stepped close to the kitchen window and peered out. The air felt noticeably cooler against his bare chest. A car was heading out South Robert Street.

"Listen," he said, "I hate to be a party pooper, but I'm freezing my ass off out here with no shirt on, and there's somebody all soft and cuddly keeping my spot warm back in bed."

Silence.

"Yeah, well, I'll see you tomorrow, Sundance, if you can make it out of bed by then." The snap of a match punctuated St. John's sentence.

In the bedroom he found the lights off. The smooth rhythm of Jo's breathing told him that she was asleep. He stripped off his jeans and underwear and slid into bed, trying not to wake her. *If you can make it out of bed by then.* What a horseshit thing for St. John to say.

TUESDAY

ONE

W̲ITH A SHAKING HAND, Alfred Krause poured another shot of brandy and looked up at the clock. Three A.M. A half hour had passed since he had awakened on the couch in a cold sweat, his heart racing in his chest. The sweat had dried on his body, but the dream was still very fresh in his mind. The brandy warmed its way down, tugging at the tight knot of fear in his stomach.

It had all seemed so real, unwinding like a color movie, as he had watched himself from a distance arrive late for a family gathering of some kind, held in a place familiar to him, somewhere he had not been for many years. His family was seated at a table. Rudy was there, dressed in the suit in which he was buried. Opposite Rudy sat his parents, Frederick and Gretchen, young and handsome—never grown old. Seated with them were assorted aunts and uncles, cousins he had known as a boy, all long since dead. And there was a tiny baby there; no, it wasn't really a baby yet, but the beginnings of a baby, a little boy.

At the other tables, he saw familiar neighborhood faces, faces that had disappeared from this earth, this time. The red-haired Treniery boy from the sledding accident on Ricketty Hill. There was old Mr. Bauer from the hardware store, and the postmaster who had sold him penny stamps.

Standing in the doorway, facing the roomful of people, he'd absorbed all this in just an instant. And then Rudy had looked up, spotted him, and risen to his feet. He turned to everyone and called out, "He's here! He's here!" Then Rudy had turned to face him again, a broad smile on his face, his hand extended in welcome.

"Alfred, where have you been? We've been waiting for you. Come and sit down."

"No! No, I don't want to. It's too early!" And he had backed through the doorway as flames shot up from the floor, engulfing the room.

Terrifying. He drained the last of his brandy, and waited for it to do its work. And yet somehow wonderful at the same time, those familiar old faces.

The flames shooting up in that familiar room. Now he knew what it was. It was the basement of St. Stanislaus Catholic Church. Not the present St. Stan's, but the one that had burned down in 1934 one Sunday right after Mass. From across the street, he and Rudy had stood with the crowd, their faces red with heat, watching the flames lick through the roof while flying embers floated over their heads, igniting the roofs of nearby houses on Goodhue and Banfil Streets.

"We were just in there," Rudy had said over and over. "It could have killed us all."

But it hadn't killed any of them. Their time had not yet come. In the nearly sixty years since that spectacular fire, the time had come for most of the people who had attended Mass while the fire smoldered deep in the belly of the church. Rudy's time had come. And his own?

He poured himself another shot. The heavy liquid slid warmly down his throat. There had been something else in the dream. He'd backed out of the doorway into the wintry outdoors. He was now wearing his heavy winter clothes. Rudy was there, in his familiar green parka and the engineer's cap he always wore. They carried shovels. They were searching for something, digging through the frozen snowdrifts. Something glittered in the dirty snow. Rudy stooped to pick it up. The picture of the two of them standing there in a snowy field, which he saw from a distance even while he *felt* himself standing next to Rudy, turned into a newspaper photograph, black-and-white, grainy.

The medallion. He'd look after all. Maybe he could find it as a memorial to Rudy. It would be something to do, anyway, something to get him out of the house and away from Genevieve's wrath.

Genevieve. The evening had ended on an even more sour note than the morning had begun. He had come home at dark from working at Rudy's, hoping to find her busy with supper in the kitchen. Instead, the kitchen was dark.

"I'm home!" he had called from the back room as he kicked off his overshoes and hung up his coat.

"Genevieve?"

No answer.

He had found her in the living room, sitting in her chair reading the afternoon paper. She had not looked up at him when he came in.

"You going to fix any supper? I'm half-starved."

She had ignored him. For a few minutes, he had stood at the living room window watching the young neighbors across the street trying to jump-start their rusty green Dodge. An unfamiliar foreign car was parked headlight-to-headlight with the Dodge, the hoods up. The kids appeared to be arguing as they tried to sort out the jumble of cables.

"Got a lot done this afternoon," he said. "Sorted through all the drawers in the secretary by the front door."

No answer.

Outside, the kids' Dodge finally sputtered to life. The headlights brightened briefly as the girl raced the engine. He heard the bang as the hoods were slammed shut. The foreign car pulled away.

"You just going to ignore me for the rest of your life? I've had about enough of this silent treatment. What's eatin' you so bad?"

"*You've* had enough?" Genevieve's tone was deadly. She threw the newspaper to the floor and lurched to her feet. "You've had enough! Well, let me tell you something. *I'm* the one who's had enough! I'll tell you what's eating me. For forty years I've put up with you and your whims, and I'm sick of it. We've been talking about this trip for two years. And now all of a sudden you dig in your heels and won't go."

"You know why I—" he'd begun, but she had cut him off.

"Well, I don't know what's got into you, but I won't stand for it. I'm gonna call Janet tonight after the rates go down and tell her I'm coming down to Houston. You can stay here if you want to, but I'm going to visit my daughter and my grandsons."

And with that, Genevieve had marched upstairs, leaving him to fend for himself once again. She had come down after the ten o'clock news to use the telephone; he'd overheard her end of the conversation. *I'm coming down,* she had told Janet, not mentioning him at all. *Just tell me when it's okay to come.*

He swallowed the last of the brandy, and looked at the notes she had left on the kitchen table. Leave the last Saturday in February. Stay two weeks. Home second Saturday in March.

So let her go.

He rinsed out his shot glass in the sink, put the pint away in the cupboard. There was little use in trying to go to bed. He turned out the kitchen light and shuffled through the dark dining room toward the living room, where the afternoon newspaper still lay on the floor.

TWO

"YOU WANT TOAST?"

"Just coffee. I've got an early meeting this morning. I'll grab a donut later."

Sharon set her coffee mug on the counter and pulled the little cover off the toaster. Weekday breakfasts were hurried affairs: orange juice, a couple pieces of toast, maybe a bowl of cereal. And, of course, coffee. That first life-saving sip in the morning made it possible to face the rest of the day.

"What's the meeting about?" she asked as she dropped two slices of whole wheat bread into the toaster for herself.

"We're under projections so far for the quarter. I'm going to light a fire under the sales staff this morning."

She sipped at her coffee and watched the waves of heat shimmer out of the toaster, felt the waves of resentment emanating from her. Could he feel them washing over the patterned linoleum to engulf him as he sat at the kitchen table? If so, he certainly didn't show it as he slurped his own coffee. As for her, functional, civil conversation was about all she was capable of this morning.

The boys shuffled into the kitchen. Jeff carried the morning paper and the city map. Chris clutched the treasure hunt notebook against his chest.

Phil turned his attention toward them. "So what's it say? What's the clue? The suspense is killing me." Though it was barely seven o'clock, he was already dressed for the day, looking as crisp and clean as a new ten-dollar bill in his dark blue three-piece suit and maroon tie. The IBM look. She and the boys were still in their bathrobes, barely awake, rubbing the sleep out of their eyes.

"Who wants toast?" Sharon asked. Chris's hand shot up. Jeff wordlessly held up two fingers as he plunked himself down at the table. He opened the A section of the paper.

"So? So?" Phil leaned forward in his chair, his face alive—almost too alive—with anticipation. Chris, she noted, leaned forward in exactly the same manner, wearing the same expression.

"It says . . ." Jeff pulled himself up into a news anchor's pose, a young Dan Rather in a bathrobe. "It says . . ." He paused for dramatic effect, looking around the kitchen at each of them.

"Come on already," Phil prodded in mock irritation. "Read it."

"Clue 4: *Watch planes come and watch them go, leaving far behind all this ice and snow.*"

The words came out in a silky falsetto, like one of the singing chipmunks. The three of them erupted in laughter. Phil had always been good at initiating this kind of horseplay between himself and the boys. Standing at the counter buttering her toast, she felt left out.

"Read it again."

Jeff read the clue again, this time sounding like a sixteen-year-old version of John Wayne. More laughter.

"Well, I see we're back to the old worthless clue routine." Phil leaned back in his chair. "One decent clue last night and then back to the same old stuff. Sheez."

All fun and games this morning, as though last night had never happened. That was his way. Once it was over, it was over. She, on the other hand, carried such things too long, particularly their arguments. She hated to fight, and last night after going to bed they had fought over the transfer. In the darkness, she had felt Phil's anger hit her like a blast of hot air when she had suggested he was trying to manipulate the boys.

"It was a simple statement of fact," he had hissed at her. "I *am* proud of them. Don't read your own feelings into what I said."

"But don't you realize what kind of responsibility you're putting on them? 'You made me proud once, now do it again.'"

"That's baloney. I told them to think about what the transfer meant to them and we'd talk about it later. Or do you choose not to remember that?"

And there the argument had stalled. As she had rolled away to face the wall, her unspoken answer chugged around and around in her mind like a toy train on a track. *No, I didn't forget. I just don't know if I believe you.* The time had dragged along as she lay in bed, feeling defeated and infuriated, listening to the easy rush of Phil's breathing. Sometime deep in the ticking hours of the night as she lay awake, it had made a perverse kind of sense. He probably was proud of them. After all, their pictures hung on the wall of his office among the cluster of framed awards for salesmanship.

Now, however, on this blustery Tuesday morning, as she buttered toast for the boys and watched Phil as he hunched over the newest clue with them, the same heavy feeling of defeat, of doubt in herself, settled over her. She had lost an argument when she knew she was right. The old saying talked about losing a battle to win the war, but it didn't go into what you do when you are losing both the battle and the war. Or was there a war being fought at all?

She set a plate of toast in front of each of the boys. Refilling her coffee mug, she carried her own toast to her seat at the table.

". . . planes in the sky," Jeff was saying. "That's the clue, obviously. Maybe—"

"It could be planes, but it could be something else," Chris interrupted, echoing his father's exact words and tone of voice from the night before.

"Like what else?" Jeff challenged.

Chris shifted in his chair, avoiding everyone's eyes. He drew a little square in the margin of a page in his notebook and colored it in.

"*Leaving far behind all this ice and snow* could mean some *particular* place with ice and snow," he said finally.

Jeff made a sound somewhere between a snort and a laugh. "That's stupid. Take a look around outside. Which particular place with ice and snow did you have in mind?"

"Don't call me *stupid.* You've got to keep yourself open to other things. Dad says."

"That's right." Phil spoke firmly in his supervisor's voice. "But," he said, turning to face Chris, "I think planes is probably the clue."

"I'm not stupid." Chris's mouth flattened into a thin, pouting line.

"No, you're not, but you aren't acting like part of the team, either. Let's just throw out some ideas here and not take things so personally. And," he said, turning to Jeff, "let's not make unnecessary judgments about ideas. Never criticize in brainstorming sessions. That's the rule."

"So," he continued, "what does this clue tell us about airplanes? Let's hear some ideas."

She took a bite from the corner of her toast. Phil's shift of gears from team leader to referee back to team leader was done so artfully, so smoothly, that the boys had been jerked back into line without even feeling the tug. He did have a talent for managing people, moving them along. *We've got time to think about it. Think about what it means to you, and we'll talk about it later in the week.* Maybe he hadn't already made his decision. Maybe she was just being paranoid, reading her own feelings into it. She should give him the benefit of the doubt. At least for today.

". . . must mean the treasure's in a park near the airport," Jeff was saying as he opened the city map. The map nearly covered the table when he finally got it unfolded. He studied the patchwork of fine lines and cramped words. "Highland Park, Ft. Snelling Park, and Minnehaha Park. No, wait—that one's in Minneapolis. It could be in Highland or Ft. Snelling."

"That's good. Let's get those written down."

"Maybe that's too easy," she said. "What about a park where you can see planes fly overhead? I hear planes fly over the house all the time."

"And," she added, suddenly remembering the image of small planes descending over downtown St. Paul, "there are two airports, don't forget. There's that little airport by downtown."

"Good point." Phil rubbed his jaw. "That doubles the possibilities. What parks are near the downtown airport?"

Jeff studied the map, marking downtown St. Paul with his finger. "Mounds Park is just across the river from the airport," he said, looking up.

"Okay. Mounds Park. Let's get that one down."

"I bet it's something else about planes. Not the ones that fly in the sky." Chris stuck out his chin. "I'm writing it down, at least."

"That's the idea," Phil said. "Never rule out an idea. You never know on this type of thing what will come of it. Remember all those murder mysteries on television where they go over the same clues again and again, and then someone suddenly makes a connection no one made before and they nab the bad guys. That's what we need to do here.

"So what have we got? Let's get the possibilities written down." Phil glanced at Chris, nodded at the notebook. He counted the possibilities off on his fingers. "One, it could be in a park near the big airport where we flew into St. Paul. Two, it could be near the little airport near downtown. Three, it could be in any park where planes fly overhead—landing patterns for the airports, probably."

"Or it could mean a different kind of planes," Chris said. "I already got that down."

Phil nodded. "It could be a different kind of planes." He looked across the table at her, a blank expression on his face. He seemed to be miles away even as he spoke.

"So, Mr. Detective," she said, "how does this relate to the rest of the clues? By the way, last night we didn't talk about what river could mean, only queen. I was thinking—is there a Charles Street near any park? As in Boston's own Charles River?"

Phil glared at her. "That will have to wait until tonight. At least for me." He swallowed the last of his coffee and set the mug down with a thump. "I've got to get moving."

And he was up and away, planting a kiss on her cheek as he passed her on his way toward the dining room. They heard the closet door in the front hall open and close as he got his coat. A moment later he passed through the kitchen again. A shudder went through the house as he slammed the back door behind him.

She looked at the microwave clock. Seven-fifteen. Time to push the boys along toward getting ready for school and get ready to go to the bookstore herself. She watched Jeff struggle to get the folds of the street map right. He finally gave up, pushing the half-folded map into the center of the table. Chris doodled in the notebook, drawing little squares, filling them in. They looked like patients in a doctor's waiting room, listening for the sound of their names. She felt the issue hanging in the air around them, mingling with the faint odor of toast and the acidic smell of coffee grown too strong.

"Well, what do you think about your father's news? About the promotion offer?"

Was that a change of expression that she saw flicker over Jeff's face, a quick pulling on of a mask? Or merely wishful thinking on her part?

"He must be really good at his job to get such a good offer," he said. "I guess it's kind of neat."

"Yeah, it's really neat." Chris colored in a square, drew another.

Basic, noncommittal reactions. Words chosen to test the waters. She wanted to go on, to break into that tightly secured and heavily guarded keep, where boys—kids in general, she guessed—stored their real thoughts, sneaking them out in privacy for examination, casting off what they thought their parents wanted them to think, to recite upon command. But she held herself back. To make them commit now, so early in the week, was unproductive, even dangerous. She took a last sip from her mug, got up, and poured the bitter liquid into the sink. Dangerous for whom?

"Your father told you to think about it, and decide what it meant to you," she said. "You'll have to tell us what you think about it. We can't do that for you. You'll have to be honest with us. And with yourselves, too. Now hurry and get ready for school."

THREE

WRAPPED IN A TOWEL AND STILL DRIPPING from the shower, Steven Carpenter stood beside the bed and looked down at his sleeping wife. In the gathering daylight she looked almost like a little girl, or a teenager, hair falling in dark strands across her face. But she wasn't a little girl; she was a big girl, a clerk in a brokerage firm who was going to be late for work if she didn't haul her ass out of bed pretty quick.

"Deb." He tapped her gently on the shoulder. "Come on! It's twenty after seven. You'll be late for work. I'm out of the bathroom already."

"I'm very happy for you." Her voice was thick with sleep. She opened her eyes and fixed him with a hollow stare. "I'll put you in for a medal." Her eyes fell shut again.

He tugged at the covers.

"Buzz off." Debi pushed at his hand, turned her head away from him. "I'm never getting up."

He switched on the bedside light, watching with delight as Debi squinted and covered her eyes with her hands.

"Come on! Get up! Wall Street is waiting for you. What would you do if you didn't have me around in the morning?"

"Sleep late." Clutching the covers, she threw herself away from him into the middle of the bed, curling into a ball, returning to the womb.

The usual getting-up routine. He would be dressed and headed for the kitchen to eat breakfast by the time she dragged herself out of bed. And while he sat at the kitchen table eating his Rice Krispies, he would hear her as she clattered through her bathroom routine and rushed furiously around the bedroom, banging dresser drawers open and closed, slamming the closet door a half-dozen times. Miraculously, she would appear in the living room dressed for work just as he was about to head out the door.

He pulled the towel from around his waist and vigorously dried his hair with it, then threw it out into the hallway by the bathroom door. He slipped into clean underwear and socks.

"Deb!" He grabbed the covers and flipped them back. He missed the sheet. Debi's hand shot out from underneath the sheet and clutched the top so he couldn't pull it off her.

"I died during the night," she whined. She rolled onto her back and pulled the sheet around her tightly, at the same time throwing it over her head. She lay perfectly still, hands lifeless along her sides, a cadaver on a slab in the morgue.

"I'm just like the Honda," she said, her voice muffled by the sheet. "Dead until spring."

The sheet outlined the mounds of her breasts, the sweeping curves of her hips, her long legs, toes pointing up. They had missed their usual late Sunday nighter, and last night they had been too tentative around each other to think seriously of lovemaking. For a fleeting moment, he wanted to shuck off his underwear and socks and crawl back into bed.

"You know what this country needs?" He sat down on the edge of the bed and pulled the covers back to expose her face. "This country needs a good set of human jumper cables, to jump-start people in the morning. I think I'll invent them, get rich, and never have to work again. We'll have to have two places to attach them, of course. I know, we could attach them to your—"

"Don't you dare say it," she said reaching out to slap at him.

"—thumbs."

She laughed, her first real laugh since Sunday. "Let's be late for work," she said. She gave him an exaggerated, obscene wink.

"Oh, right. And what will I tell everyone at work? 'Gee, I'm sorry I'm late, but I was home screwing my wife.'"

"Steven, where's your sense of adventure? Sometimes you have to ignore what people are going to say about you, and just do what you want."

"Tonight," he said.

"Tonight I may not feel like it." She flipped back the sheet, stretched, and sat up. "I wish we took the morning paper."

"Why?"

"Shouldn't there be a new treasure hunt clue this morning?"

"Since when did you get to be such a treasure hunter?"

"Since I read last night we could win four thousand dollars by finding it. That's a lot of money."

"You know how many people are looking for it? Thousands. Maybe millions. What chance have we got?"

"Well, somebody has to find it. It may as well be us. Honestly, Steven, don't you *ever* think positively? About what could be?" She padded naked toward the bathroom.

"Shit, I must be late already," he called after her, jumping up. "You're up and I'm still in my underwear."

"Funny." She stopped in the hallway, bending over to pick up his towel. Turning around, she shook it at him in accusation.

"Would you please not throw your towel on the floor?"

"Give me a break. I was gonna pick it up on the way out."

The bathroom door closed behind her. The toilet soon flushed and a moment later he heard the roar of the shower. Falling into the morning routine. He pulled on a pair of jeans and a blue pullover sweater. One thing the library had going for it—he didn't need to wear a frigging tie. His tennis shoes were . . . where? He had kicked them off out in the living room last night while watching television.

The bathroom door opened and Debi poked her wet head around it. "Fitzgerald gets the morning paper. Go sneak down and get it." The empty shower roared behind her.

"We can't do that."

"Sure we can."

"What if he misses it?"

"He's nuts. He's so forgetful, he'll never know the difference. He probably doesn't even remember that he gets the paper."

"No. I'm not going to steal an old man's paper." He was never quite sure if Fitzgerald's chronic forgetfulness was a shrewd act designed to cover up his incompetence as a landlord, or if he really did forget from one complaint to the next that they lived in the apartment above him.

"We'll just read it and put it back afterwards. He won't even know the difference."

"Forget it. And you're dripping on the floor." He slipped past her out into the living room to look for his tennis shoes.

As he laced up his shoes, he heard the front door lock being thrown open, footsteps descending the carpeted stairs. Debi had slipped through the back bedroom door that led into the front hall and was sneaking down to steal Fitzgerald's paper. A moment later he heard returning footsteps, the sound of the front door again. She came out of the front hallway into the living room, wearing her bathrobe, wet hair hanging limp around her face. She held up the paper.

"Do you want to hear it, or are you too goody-two-shoes?" Without waiting for an answer, she opened the paper, scanned the front page. "Clue 4: *Watch planes come and watch them go, leaving far behind all this ice and snow.*"

"You had to do it, didn't you? Well, let's at least write it down and I'll take the paper back downstairs. And you better get ready for work." He took the paper from her and pushed her toward the bathroom. Opening the little secretary that had come with the apartment, he jotted the clue down on the back of a Dayton's envelope.

He slipped out the front door and down the dark flight of stairs to drop the paper in front of Fitzgerald's door. As he turned to head back up the stairs, he heard the shuffle of footsteps behind the landlord's door.

Back in the apartment, he went to the kitchen and fixed himself a bowl of Rice Krispies and carried it toward the bathroom, pausing at the secretary to pick up the Dayton's envelope with the clue written on it.

The bathroom was foggy with clouds of steam. Debi was back in the shower.

"Well, it has something to do with planes, obviously," she said over the sound of the rushing water.

"Obviously." He sat down on the john to eat his cereal.

"I still think it's on that island under the Wabasha Bridge." She shut off the shower and threw back the curtain, her skin glistening with water, hair shining wet. Catching the towel he tossed at her, she dried her face.

"That's it, I tell you. You can see planes come and go at the downtown airport. Let's drive down there tonight and look around."

"It could be something else." He watched as she dried her arms and legs, then wrapped the towel around her, tucking it in between her breasts. "Maybe we're on the wrong track. There's another airport, you know." He thought for a moment, arranging and rearranging his meager knowledge of the city in his mind. "And the river runs close to there, too. And there's an island, just below Ft. Snelling, remember? We hiked there last summer. And some of the paddle-wheelers go up that far on the river. Or almost that far—we saw them.

"Besides," he continued, "the queen and river clue might be something else entirely. We could be on the wrong track completely."

Debi reached for the hair drier, clicked it on, and passed it over the mirror a few times to evaporate the condensed steam that had clouded the surface.

"Don't be so negative," she said over the whine of the hair drier. "We won't find it unless we look. And I didn't hear you come up with any better ideas about queen and river last night."

He watched Debi style her hair. She moved the drier and the comb around her head with the skill of a surgeon, turning the straight, limp strands of hair into long flowing waves. He set his empty cereal bowl on the toilet tank.

"It's there," she said, shutting off the hair drier and hanging it on its hook. "Under the Wabasha Bridge. I feel it. Trust me." From the medicine cabinet she took out a handful of little bottles and cases, stacking them on the back of the sink. She leaned toward the mirror to apply her base makeup, working in quick, precise strokes.

He watched her as she applied blush to accent her cheekbones. Eye shadow, eyeliner, lipstick. So sure of herself. He admired and hated her at the same time for it. How did she do it? There was so little in the world of which he was completely, confidently sure. It was the big difference between them; she was sure of everything, right or wrong, and he was sure of nothing.

"It won't hurt to drive around tonight and look," she said. "That is, if you get the car started."

"Maybe we could. There'll be a new clue out tonight and maybe that will help."

Debi put her makeup clutter away. "There," she said, giving herself a final inspection in the mirror. "Eat your heart out, Julia Roberts."

He followed Debi into the bedroom and watched her as she dressed. Her power clothes, she called them. In a bright blue suit with a blue and red scarf tied loosely around her neck, she looked like one of the horde of hungry young professional women he saw during lunch break whenever he ventured into the downtown skyways. He felt self-conscious in his jeans and sweater. He glanced at the clock. He was due at work in ten minutes. No chance.

"Well, I'm ready," Debi said. "Let's go."

"Shit, I'm going to be late." A sinking feeling came over him. He desperately wished the workday over and the two of them back here, struggling to get the car started so they could go out driving in the city, looking for the treasure.

Buried treasure. Greed. Dreams of striking it rich. There was a song in this somewhere, maybe a story song like "Turnpike Tom," or Harry Chapin's "Taxi"; but he wouldn't have time to work on it now because he was going to work, to the book factory, for another day of watching other people's books and records go by. Why did he get up and go to this lousy job day after day? What was it Deb had said? *Sometimes you have to ignore what people are going to say about you, and just do what you want.* He should do it. He should just quit this dead-end job and start playing and singing. Come out of the closet and be a musician. Play a few open stages to get some experience, and then look for a club gig.

He glanced at his guitar case standing in the corner of the bedroom, then hurried to catch up with Debi, who was already out in the front hallway putting on her coat.

FOUR

Damn it, no paper, Keith thought, as he opened his front door and looked out onto the empty welcome mat that lay at the bottom of the stairwell. He slipped up the steps in his stockinged feet and spotted the paper lying on the sidewalk near the front of the house. Basement apartments. No one but him, it seemed, ever came down these stairs—certainly not whoever delivered his paper.

He was up much later than he had planned. He had planned to be working on the treasure hunt long before nine o'clock. For someone planning to find the medallion on Tuesday and tie the record for the earliest find, he wasn't off to a very fast start.

According to the announcer on his clock radio, it had warmed up slightly during the night; but the wind still clawed, whipping under the tail of his flannel shirt as he stooped to pick up the paper. Without waiting until he was inside, he opened the paper and quickly read the clue. Planes. Something to do with planes.

A gust of wind from the north rattled the rosebushes against the foundation and pushed him down the cold cement steps.

Back inside, he dropped the paper on his desk and went out into the kitchen to make coffee. The kitchen felt cold, as it always did in the morning. He switched on the oven and opened the oven door. He set the timer to remind him to shut the oven off later.

He used the last of the coffee. He tossed the empty coffee can toward the wastebasket in a high, arching set shot. It bounced off the rim onto the gray tile floor and rolled under the table in a metallic clatter. Upstairs, Tiffany barked, protecting her mistress from the evil coffee can. It would be fun to attack Tiffany with a coffee can. The little mutt would just about fit into a two-pound can. He could just snap the plastic lid on quick and drop it into the middle of Lake Phalen.

At his desk, he opened the paper and read the clue again. *Watch planes come and watch them go, leaving far behind all this ice and snow.* It must mean a treasure site near the airport, or one where you could see planes land and take off. There were two airports. That cut the city into two main parts: one near the international airport, and the other near the downtown airport. Not much help.

Of the four clues so far, the first, which said the medallion was on the ground, was of no real help at all. The second hinted that the treasure was near something to do with trains, which according to all the pink lines he had drawn on his map yesterday morning, could be almost anywhere in the city. The third clue said to enter with a queen and leave via river. And now the fourth clue tied in planes, which, like trains, could be just about anywhere in the city. Of the four clues, the third clue, queen and river, seemed to be the clue that offered the most information. Queen and river most likely referred to streets.

Yesterday afternoon, he had made a list of street names related to queen and river, jotting the names down as he read the street name index on his city map from A to Z. Every name he saw that could even be remotely perceived as the name of a queen, he had written down. Any one of these unfamiliar names could be one of those obscure queens that filled European history—unfortunate women who sat on the throne for a few weeks or months, and then were sent off to exile in some convent or had their heads chopped off.

He picked up the list, and read down the names for the tenth time: Ann Street, Ann Arbor, Annapolis Street, Carroll Avenue, Charlotte Street, Dale Street, Eleanor Avenue, Elizabeth Street, Emma Street, Eva Street, Florence Avenue, Grace Lane, Grace Street, Hazel Street, Hazelwood Avenue, Heather Drive, Heather Place, Isabel Street, Janet Street, Jayne Street, Jessamine Avenue, Josephine Place, Juliet Avenue, Margaret Street, Maria Avenue, Maryland Avenue, Mary Lane, Myrtle Avenue, Nina Street, Priscilla Street, Theresa Place, Victoria Street, Virginia Street, Wanda Street. He'd have to investigate each of these names one by one to determine if there was ever a queen by that name. Then he would locate each street that bore the name of a queen on the map and see if it ran into any parks.

The procedure would be the same for his river list, which, thankfully, was shorter than the list of potential queens. He had put down any street name that struck him as the possible name of a river: Albany Avenue, Avon Street, Buffalo Street, Cayuga Street, Cedar Street, Charles Avenue, Chippewa Avenue, Cottonwood Avenue, Delaware Avenue, Elk Street, Iowa Avenue, Minnesota Avenue, Minnesota Street, Mississippi River Boulevard, Missouri Street, Mohawk Avenue, Ohio Street, Old Hudson Road, Riverview Avenue, Riverwood Place, Saratoga Street, Sycamore Street, Wabash Avenue.

He put the two lists side by side on his desk. Out of these names, two streets should surface that would identify the park where the medallion was hidden. Based on the third clue, his guess was that you drove into the park on the queen street and out of the park on the river street.

For good measure, throw in the fact that the park was near railroad tracks and one of the two airports, or you could see planes land and take off from the treasure site.

He switched on his computer and booted up the file of this year's treasure hunt clues. When the file flashed onto the screen, he scrolled to the bottom and began to type Clue 4 underneath the third clue. The cursor moved across the screen. Just as he finished and hit the save command, he heard the slam of Mrs. Wright's back door upstairs. A few moments later, he heard careful footsteps descending the cement stairs outside. A shadow passed across his living room window. Then came the familiar knock at his door, a rendition of "shave and a hair cut—two bits." He groaned and held his head in his hands. The knock came again, louder.

He crossed the room and yanked the door open. Mrs. Wright, an unbuttoned coat thrown over her housedress and sweater, was still on her tiptoes, trying to peer through the high, slotted windows in the heavy wooden door. Her left hand was balled up into a fist, poised for a third knock. Tiffany the poodle peered out from under her right arm. In her right hand, she was clutching a small package wrapped in aluminum foil.

"Mrs. Wright."

"Hello, Keith," his landlady said as she dropped onto her heels again. "Tiffy and I came for a quick visit to bring you these." She held out the aluminum foil package as far as she could without dropping the dog. "We were hungry for brownies, so we baked early this morning. We heard you moving around here all day yesterday, and then when you didn't leave for work this morning, we thought maybe you were sick. I told Tiffy that we would just bring you some brownies and make sure you were all right."

"Thanks," he said, taking the package from her. "I'm fine." When she made no move to leave, he motioned into the living room. "Do you want to come in?"

"Well, maybe for just a minute." She shifted Tiffany to her other arm and brushed past him. He prayed that she would not take off her coat. If she did, she would be here for an hour. He set the package on the arm of the big chair.

"They have nuts in them, the way you like them," Mrs. Wright said. "I have to get them out of the house, or I'll eat every one of them. Or worse yet, I'll share them with Tiffy. Her doctor says she must avoid sweets, although she loves chocolate so. Don't you, sweetheart?" She pursed her lips at the dog and made a kissing sound.

Tiffany licked at her cheek. "Yes, you *do*, don't you, sweety?" She leaned over and Tiffany hopped to the floor. The poodle circled behind her mistress's thick legs, stuck out her gray nose, and sniffed at him. Then she showed her teeth and let loose a chorus of high-pitched barks. The sound made him think of someone stepping with a bare foot on the sharp point of a nail protruding from a board.

"Tiffy, bad girl," Mrs Wright said. She leaned over and picked up the poodle again. "You stop that now. That's Keith. You see him all the time."

All the time, he thought. Every day for the past five years, and you bark at me every time, you little mutt.

"She's so protective of me," Mrs. Wright explained. "Aren't you, baby?" She held the poodle up to her cheek so that Tiffany could lick her face. "You don't want anyone to hurt Momma, do you?"

"I'm working at home a lot this week," he said. "I was just getting started." He pointed toward his computer. "Big project. I've been working on it for days."

"Your work sounds so interesting." Mrs. Wright started across the living room toward his desk. "I don't understand any of this computer stuff." He stepped around her and quickly cleared the treasure hunt file from the computer screen.

"I can't let you see that," he said. "The company has to keep information about its clients confidential."

"Oh, of course," Mrs. Wright said. She gave him a devilish smile. "Tiffany might sell secret information to the enemy."

"I'll be in and out all week, working on this project," he said. "So if you hear me, don't worry. I'm not sick or anything."

"You mustn't work so hard, Keith," she said. "You'll work yourself into an early grave, like my Maynard did." She noticed the *Pioneer Press* lying on his desk. "They've got the Winter Carnival treasure hunt going again, I see."

He nodded.

"My Maynard looked for the treasure every year, you know, before he died. I don't follow it much myself anymore. I was never any good at figuring out what those clues meant. Whoever writes them is much too smart for me. My Maynard almost found it one year. He actually saw someone pick it up. He just missed, didn't he, Tiffy?" She bent over and let the poodle hop to the floor again.

Tiffany wandered into the narrow hallway that led toward the bathroom and his bedroom.

"Tiffany, no no," Mrs. Wright said. "We mustn't pry."

Go ahead, you little shit, he thought. I'll flush you down the toilet. Or come out in the kitchen and I'll show you my empty coffee can.

"I like the Winter Carnival parade myself," the landlady said. "Course, I don't go down and stand in the cold anymore, but I always watch on television."

The aroma of brewing coffee floated on the cool air. Mrs. Wright drew in a long breath. "Isn't fresh coffee the most wonderful smell? It makes me want a cup every time. Do you drink regular or decaffeinated?"

"Regular," he said. "I'd ask you to stay, but I really must get to work."

"If it's regular, we would have to decline anyway. We only drink decaffeinated now, don't we, Tiffy? My doctor says I must avoid caffeine. We're a pair, aren't we, old girl? You can't have brownies and I can't have real coffee."

The timer on the stove suddenly went off. Tiffany let loose a string of barks and scurried between Mrs. Wright's legs.

"Are you baking?" Mrs. Wright raised her voice to be heard over the buzzer.

He shook his head. "I run the oven sometimes if the kitchen is cool."

"Well, you should call me and I'll turn the heat up for you. Tiffany, we must get back upstairs. Our shows are coming on before long." She bent over and patted her leg. Tiffany jumped into her arms.

"Keith, you must come up and have supper with us some night. We get so lonesome for company. I'll fix Swiss steak if you do. I know it's your favorite. You told me so yourself."

"I'll do that, Mrs. Wright," he promised as he escorted her toward the door.

He shut the door behind her and hurried to the kitchen to shut off the buzzer. The nosy old biddy. The only reason she had come down here was because she couldn't stand not knowing why he wasn't at work.

He poured himself a cup of coffee and returned to the living room. He picked up the aluminum foil package from the arm of the chair on his way to his desk. He sat down and booted his treasure hunt file up again.

She was an old biddy, all right, but she made great brownies. He peeled back the aluminum foil, selected one, and bit into the corner. The brownie was so moist with chocolate that it was almost liquid in its center. He sipped at his coffee. The coffee and chocolate made a tasty combination. He finished the brownie in one bite and reached for another.

Beside him, the telephone rang, and he jumped at the sudden noise. As he reached out to pick up the receiver, he wondered who it was. He seldom got calls. His eyes flicked up to his bulletin board, where the little strip of cash register tape with Toni's phone number was pinned.

"Hullo."

"Keith?" It was not a woman's voice on the other end of the line, but the too-familiar voice of General Jerry from work.

"Hi, Jerry. What's up? Can't stand it there without me?"

"We're fine," Jerry said. "I'm calling about you. Are you all right?"

"Yeah, I'm okay."

"Well, we were wondering. You weren't in all day yesterday and didn't call in. Then when you didn't show up this morning, we got concerned."

He laughed. "Jerry, when you're on vacation you usually don't come in or call. Did you think a mass murderer got me or something?"

"Vacation?" Jerry's voice was sharp with surprise.

"Yeah, I took the week off."

The line hummed blank for a moment. When he spoke, Jerry's voice was businesslike, flat.

"You didn't tell anybody."

"I did, too. I told you."

"Keith, you're not on the vacation schedule. I checked myself yesterday to see."

"Well, we talked about it. We stood right in the door to your office and talked about it. Two weeks ago."

"You told me you were thinking about taking a week off. And that was the last I heard about it."

"But I said . . ." he began, frustrated. "I thought—"

"Did you fill out a vacation request and file it?" Jerry's voice was smug.

He paused a long moment before answering. "I must have forgotten."

"You know the policy—if you're not on the schedule, you're not on vacation." Jerry cleared his throat. "We need you in here at least for today, and maybe tomorrow."

"But I've made plans. I've—"

"Listen, Keith. I'm pretty steamed about this. You've done this kind of thing before. We're jammed up and we need you in here. Today. I expect you in the office before noon."

"But I—"

"I'm not going to talk about this on the telephone. We'll talk about it when you get in. Before noon."

Keith slammed the receiver into its cradle. There went his Tuesday afternoon searching. Everyone would have the jump on him now for sure. He hadn't even had a chance to add this year's Clue 4 to his file of previous fourth clues. He looked at the digital clock on the corner of his desk. Nine-thirty. He punched in the commands to call up the Clue 4 file. He had two-and-a-half hours before noon.

FIVE

BRUCE MITCHELL SCANNED THE SCHOOL'S half-filled cafeteria, and spotted Joanna sitting alone at a table in front of the windows. Her tray was pushed aside. A newspaper lay open in front of her, and she was sipping coffee from a Styrofoam cup. Carrying his own tray, Bruce slipped up behind her.

"This seat taken?" he asked in his best barroom pick-up voice.

"My boyfriend is going to sit here, and he's the jealous type," Joanna replied with icy indifference, picking up on the game. The unapproachable woman to his macho man. She turned the page of the newspaper without looking up.

He sat down across from her. "I feel pretty tough today. I'll take my chances." He lowered his voice to a husky whisper. "Do you come here often?"

She didn't answer. Adjusting the paper slightly, she threw him a look of exaggerated disgust.

"What's a nice girl like you doing in a place like this?" he asked.

"Trying to read the paper. But these *jerks* keep interrupting me."

"An intellectual type. I like that. Are you a student here? What's your sign? Want to go home with me?"

Joanna looked up from the paper at last, noticed his loaded tray, and rolled her dark eyes.

"I never go home with a man who loads his tray up like he's going through a soup line." Her eyes narrowed as she took a sip of her coffee. "You're lucky you didn't use lines like that the first time you talked to me."

He laughed and bit into one of his hamburgers. "I didn't have the guts. I was afraid you wouldn't talk to me as it was." He popped a couple of fries into his mouth.

"How could I resist a line like 'The coffee around here tastes like swamp water, but at least it's cheap. Can I buy you a cup?'"

"I didn't say that!"

"You did, too. Those were your exact words."

"Well, they must have worked. I better write them down for future use." He slapped at his pockets as though in search of a pen or pencil, then stopped short when he realized the implication of what he had said. "I didn't mean that quite the way it sounded. I don't want there to be a next time."

Joanna smiled, her eyes deepening, and reached out to stroke his hand. "Neither do I. Aren't you glad you're not out there hitting the bars? With all the diseases and everything floating around?"

"Looking for love is what St. John and I always called it. We never found it." He went back to his hamburger.

"Two hamburgers, fries, coffee, and dessert? You must be hungry."

"I'm starved. Haven't eaten anything since those Oreo cookies last night."

"And whose fault is that?" Joanna teased, her eyebrows arched mischievously. "Who slept too late this morning to eat breakfast?"

"I'm never any good in the morning," he said around a mouthful of fries. "It takes me awhile to get started."

"I wouldn't say that."

"Well, I'm better at some things in the morning than others. That today's paper?"

"Somebody left it here. That's why I picked this table. So how were your classes this morning?"

"Exciting. We went over inks and how to get them to stay on the paper. Give me the front section if you're through with it."

Joanna pushed the paper across the table to him. He dropped his half-eaten burger on his tray and pushed it to one side to make room. Spreading the paper out in front of him, he rubbed a column of print with his thumb, and looked up at Joanna. "Special ink," he said. "Designed not to rub off. We talked about it this morning.

"But this," he said, pointing to the treasure hunt clue at the bottom of the page, "this is why you read the paper this week: Clue 4: *Watch planes come and watch them go, leaving far behind all this ice and snow.*"

"I can never figure out those clues," Joanna said. "I think it means something, and then after it's found and they explain what the clues meant, I'm completely wrong. And their explanations make so much sense that I feel like an idiot because I didn't figure it out myself."

"That's the fun of it. Have you ever gone out and searched?"

"My uncle took me once when I was about seven or eight. About all I remember is being so cold I thought my hands and feet were going to fall off."

"Oh, but you were too young to take along a little antifreeze to keep you warm. That's what St. John and I do. We look every year. Have since high school."

"You never found it, I take it?"

"We were close a couple of years ago. This year, we're gonna find that little sucker." He picked up his hamburger again.

"Where do you think it is?" Joanna leaned back in her chair, swept her hair back from her face with her hands.

"Well, it's still too early to really have enough clues to make a decent guess. About tomorrow we'll really get serious. St. John and I decided it might be in Como Park. We talked about it last night."

"I remember," she said.

Last night. He covered his eyes with his hand, then opened his fingers wide enough to peek through them.

"I'm sorry about that," he said. Damn St. John anyway for interrupting them. And damn *himself*, for not cutting the bastard off.

Jo smiled. "Don't worry about it. It happens once in a while. Tell me. How did you come up with Como Park? I read those clues and I couldn't come up with anything."

He turned inside the paper to the other clues. "This one," he said, pointing at Clue 1, "says it's on the ground. Big deal. The second one has something to do with trains—*'I think I can'* we figure means the Little Engine That Could. St. John and I figure that the big trains that run on railroad tracks are too obvious. There used to be a little train up there next to the zoo—a kiddie ride—and we think it might be that. We don't really know what the third one refers to—*enter with a queen, leave via river*—we didn't really talk much about it last night."

"So what does the new one mean to you? How do you fit that in?"

He flipped back to the front page and read the fourth clue again. "*Watch planes come and watch them go, leaving far behind all this ice and snow.* Planes, obviously. Planes that fly overhead, or planes landing or taking off. Maybe there's a kiddie airplane ride up by the zoo. St. John and I are going to drive around Como Park tonight. Why don't you come with us?"

A small frown came over Joanna's face. Her eyes narrowed. "No, I better not."

"Come on."

"I don't know if I should. I know he's your friend and everything, and I like him—a lot, but . . . I get . . . sometimes I think I make him uncomfortable."

"Nah, it's not you. He's just been down in the dumps for the last month or so."

"What about?" Joanna broke a piece out of the rim of her Sytrofoam cup and dropped it inside her empty cup, then broke off another.

"He's been off work for a while because of the weather. And his wife called him up the other day."

"Wife?" Joanna looked up from the cup. Her face showed her surprise, dark eyes widening, a set of lines appearing on her forehead. "I thought he was divorced. He's only referred to her once or twice, but he called her his ex-wife. I'm sure he did." She broke another piece off the rim of the cup and dropped it inside.

"He calls her his ex-wife, but officially, she's still his wife. It's a long story. Haven't I ever told you?"

"Just bits and pieces."

He set his own coffee cup on top of the newspaper. "About three years ago, St. John met this woman, Karen—stopped to change a flat tire for her. And they really hit it off. They got married almost right away—four months or so after they met. I stood up for him. St. John was like on cloud nine—floated down the sidewalk without even touching the ground. That was on the outside. From what he's told me since they split up, it was bad news from the beginning: fights, stuff like that. To me, something always seemed kind of—you know—different about her. Like when I was pretending I was trying to pick you up just now when I sat down? She got off on that, loved to play games like that."

He leaned forward, looking into Joanna's dark eyes, and lowered his voice slightly. "I never told St. John this, but she even came on to me once. Made this big deal out of the fact that he was gone for the afternoon, and why didn't I come over. I was pretty embarrassed—I thought I had done something to encourage her."

He blew on his coffee, took a small sip. It *did* taste like hot swamp water.

"Anyway, about a year ago, St. John slipped and fell at work—fell about ten feet. I saw him fall. He landed flat on his back. He wasn't really hurt, just got his bell rung pretty good. The foreman sent him home for the rest of the day anyway. All of us on the crew razzed him about falling on purpose so he could get the rest of the day off. Anyway, he goes home, walks into the apartment and—"

Joanna's hands left her cup and covered her face. She shook her head behind them. "Don't tell me."

"You guessed it. He found Karen in bed screwing some guy. Some old guy, about fifteen years older than she was. St. John went crazy. Told the guy he'd kill him if he ever went near Karen again. Then he literally threw the guy out—threw him out the front door in his birthday suit. Locked him out in the hallway. Karen had to take his clothes out to him, and he got dressed down in the laundry room and split."

He looked around the cafeteria. It was almost completely filled, men and women between job and school, or school and job, grabbing a quick bite to eat. People reaching for a second chance. He leaned forward so that he could be heard over the cafeteria noise.

"He fell just before lunch. He walked in on them early in the afternoon. He was sitting on the steps to my back door when I got home from work about five. I was surprised to see him, I figured he'd be home sacked out. He was, like . . . trembling all over so bad he had to try three times to light up a cigarette. I don't know how he drove across town without killing himself. At first I thought it was the effects of the fall, but then he starts telling me what happened. He got so . . . so *tight,* that I thought he was going to explode. To be honest, I think that guy was lucky to get out of there alive."

"So what happened?" Joanna had worked her way all around the rim of the cup and was starting a second pass. One by one, little pieces of Styrofoam went into the cup.

"This is the part where it gets stinky. Karen packed up and moved out on him that night. They had this screaming, knock-down-drag-out fight while she was packing. Turns out that she had been seein' this guy for the last year or so while St. John was at work. The guy was rolling in dough and he'd made all these promises that he'd leave his wife and kids and marry her after he got divorced and all that shit—real 'Dear Abby' stuff." He cradled his hands around his coffee cup, felt its warmth on his palms.

"Well, that turned out to be a lot of smoke. The guy probably just told her that to keep things going. He split on Karen immediately—I guess he was afraid that St. John really would kill him if he ever got hold of him again. And that's kind of where it sits. They're still legally married. Every now and then Karen calls St. John up and strings him along a little and then blasts him for screwing up her life. I guess she figured this guy was her ticket to the big time and she blames St. John for wrecking it."

"Why doesn't he divorce her?"

"You tell me." Bruce shrugged deeply. "He still loves her, I guess. He *must*, to put up with that kind of shit. If she'd done that to me, I wouldn't hesitate to deep-six her. Sometimes I think he still believes, or hopes, anyway, that they'll get back together. Sounds pretty corny, doesn't it?"

"Sounds unhealthy to me," Joanna said. Little pieces kept falling into the cup.

"What really bothers me is that he's just sort of spun his wheels ever since. Can't seem to get over the whole thing. We were going to go to Tech together, but he's just let that slide. I've talked about it to him and he just blows it off."

"Maybe he needs to find someone new," Joanna suggested. "Find someone who'll take his mind off her. It doesn't sound like it would be hard to find somebody better than her."

"I shouldn't say this, but he's had trouble with women since. Having her step out on him like that really messed him up. A couple of times he's hooked up with somebody, and when they got down to business, he couldn't . . . you know . . ." He searched for a gentle term, gave up and used the familiar one. "He couldn't get it up. Don't ever let on I told you this. He'd *die* if he knew I told you."

A classmate he didn't know by name was passing by them, a bowl of chili steaming on his tray. They exchanged polite nods.

"I don't know what to do," he continued. "St. John's kind of a drag to be around right now. It hasn't been fun like the old days."

The remains of Joanna's cup was full of little pieces. She set it on her abandoned tray.

"Maybe it's time to let go of things a little."

"Let go?"

"You know, like you said last night—you can't always expect things to stay the same. Got to go with the flow. Maybe you're growing apart."

He looked out the window. Somewhere behind the clutter of buildings and freeway bridges, the tree-lined bluffs of the East Side huddled together under the raw winter clouds. He and St. John had scoured Mounds Park over there a few years ago in search of the medallion. Back then he had been floundering himself, his own heart as solid and heavy as lead, his nerves rubbed raw. And St. John had hung in there with him, pulling him through. No; what Joanna had just said, that couldn't be.

"This is different," he said, looking into her steady eyes. "The guy's my best friend."

"What's different about it?"

"I don't know. It just *is*. He's Butch and I'm Sundance." He looked away, out the window again, surprised by the sharpness in his voice. A hard gust of wind was moving south across the city, bending the little plumes of chimney smoke.

Joanna stood up and pulled her coat off the back of her chair. "Well, Mr. Sundance Kid, I have to get going."

"Wait," he said. "I'm sorry. I didn't mean to sound mad."

"It's all right. I have things to do this afternoon if I'm going to go traipsing around in the snow and cold with you two tonight." She picked up her tray.

"You mean you'll go?"

"I must be crazy, but I'll give it a try."

"I'll pick you up, then," he said. "You'll be at your place?"

She nodded.

"See you tonight, Etta."

"What?" She stopped, one arm pushed into the sleeve of her lavender coat.

"Etta Place—the Sundance Kid's girlfriend in the movie. Katherine Ross played her. I think you're prettier."

Joanna rolled her eyes. "Puh-leease," she said with a half smile and turned away.

SIX

ALFRED SAT AT THE KITCHEN TABLE with the morning paper opened to the treasure hunt clues, his mind fuzzy and soft. He yawned and rubbed the aching muscles in the back of his neck, worked his stiff shoulders. He had stayed up after the dream rather than going upstairs to bed. In the creeping hours of the night, his nerves still raw and the brandy still warming his belly, he had picked up the newspaper off the floor where Genevieve had thrown it, and sat in the living room reading the treasure hunt clues—getting nowhere with them—and thinking about Rudy. Early this morning as the gray daylight had crept in, he had gone out to buy the morning paper to get the newest clue, stopping in a cafe for breakfast.

The morning had passed slowly. He had tried to take a nap on the couch, but found he could not sleep because of Genevieve. She had stayed upstairs all morning, but he had felt the heat of her silent anger all the way downstairs. Her anger, he had learned through many years of experience, was impenetrable. The best thing to do was to fight silence with silence. Today, however, he didn't even feel up to that. If she was going to Houston, he wished she would hurry up and go, and leave him alone in peace.

One more time, he told himself, turning back to the clues. Clue 1: *Somewhere on the ground in Ramsey County, King Boreas has hidden his royal bounty.* That meant it was on the ground, just like it always was. Maybe Ramsey County meant it was not in St. Paul, but hidden in one of the suburbs. Clue 2: *"I think I can, I think I can," might be a clue, that has just the right meaning for you.* "I think I can" was what the Little Engine said—he remembered reading the book to Janet over and over when she was little. That meant something to do with trains or train tracks. Train tracks ran all over the city, though it was nothing like the old days after World War II, when he heard trains chugging up the incline from downtown every few minutes, and saw the sooty plume of engine smoke moving through the neighborhood.

Clue 3: *Enter with a queen, leave via river, this little clue may make you shiver.* He had no idea what this meant, unless it had something to do with the Mississippi. That could mean Harriet Island or Mounds Park, or maybe Cherokee Park across the river on the West Side. Clue 4: *Watch planes come and watch them go, leaving far behind all this ice and snow.* That had something to do with planes, planes landing or taking off. Or maybe planes flying overhead. It could mean almost anywhere.

He wished that Rudy were here to ask; Rudy had loved the treasure hunt, had looked forward to it as the hard days of winter settled in around them. He had always bought and registered their Winter Carnival button early every year. This year, Alfred suddenly realized, he didn't have a button; if he found the medallion, he would get only two thousand dollars, according to the paper, instead of four thousand.

He closed the paper and folded it, feeling defeated by the cryptic, meaningless little verses. Rudy had always been good at figuring out the clues, spinning out ideas, connecting and reconnecting different interpretations of each clue until something finally clicked. He'd probably have known right off what this queen and river referred to.

Genevieve came silently into the kitchen. Ignoring him, she opened the refrigerator door. Out of the corner of his eye, he watched her set a plate of ham, the bread, lettuce, and the jar of mustard on the counter. She cut slices of ham for herself, spread the bread with mustard. The smell of mustard ignited his appetite, but he knew better than to ask her to make a sandwich for him. Genevieve had not spoken to him since last night, when she had thrown the evening paper to the floor and told him she was going to Houston alone.

A fine way for a wife to act, making her husband fend for himself, he thought, as he heard the clink of a plate on the counter top. The refrigerator door opened and closed. Carrying her plate, Genevieve disappeared into the dining room.

He got up from the table and went into the back room to put on his coat and cap. He slammed the back door behind him hard enough for Genevieve to hear it and know he was gone. The wind did not seem as biting as it had at dawn. He started the pickup, backed into the street, and headed toward West Seventh, not knowing where he was going—

he was just going, anywhere to get out of the house and be alone, away from Genevieve's silence.

He drove out West Seventh, up and over the railroad overpass, past the brewery, past Machovec's and Pilney's. He pulled up in front of Rudy's house, but did not shut off the engine. No, not here. It was too sad and depressing inside. He pulled away from the curb, threading himself into the midday traffic.

At Montreal, he veered right and headed up the long hill, leaving the West End behind. He crossed under the arched bridge and climbed the hill into Highland Park. The treasure medallion had been hidden here in the park near the abandoned pool a few years ago. He and Rudy had figured out the clues and rushed to the park only to find searchers swarming so thick over the area that they could hardly find room to dig. Today, however, the park and golf course were deserted. A lone cross-country skier moved slowly across the golf course, a dot against the expanse of white.

He stopped at the intersection of Montreal and Snelling Avenues, and waited behind a van for the traffic light to change. Down Snelling to his left, he could see the one-room Mattocks schoolhouse, dwarfed by the smooth white brick and glass walls of the senior high school that had been built behind it. Different schools for different times. He had been in the Mattocks school once many years ago before it was moved here from farther up Snelling, long before the junior and senior high schools were built—indeed, before much of the neighborhood even existed.

The Highland Park neighborhood had been mostly undeveloped when he was young. Rudy had always claimed he could remember when cows had grazed in open fields west of the park. He himself could remember driving with Rudy through the area after the war, seeing the yellow wooden frames of houses going up. Through the forties and fifties the neighborhood had filled up with neat little bungalows and ramblers, so different from the tall, narrow houses of his own neighborhood. There was money here in this neighborhood, you could tell, but comfortable money that you could live with; not like Summit Avenue, where there was too much money. He and Genevieve had talked once of moving up here when Janet was young. Genevieve had been all for it. It was a much better neighborhood, she had claimed; the new junior high school going up would be better for Janet. But he had found that he could not leave his cramped, familiar old neighborhood behind. He had decided on new siding for their old house instead, and was rewarded with several weeks of stony silence.

He turned north on Snelling Avenue, drove past the stone water tower that he had always wanted to climb but never had; past neighborhood shops and neat little homes; past funeral homes—there were several along this stretch of Snelling, clustered together like the fast-food restaurants along South Robert Street on the West Side. The perfect place to get hit by a truck, Rudy had said the night the treasure medallion was found in Highland Park—the undertakers would be out before the police even got there, bidding for your carcass. He passed Macalester College's sports stadium. Janet had started college at Macalester, but after a year she had transferred to the University of Minnesota because it was cheaper.

As the pickup chugged along, he realized that he had not decided where he was going. Farther north up Snelling lay the clutter of Interstate 94 and University Avenue—a jungle of traffic lights, where exhaust fumes hung like fog over the street on cold days. He had no business—no interests up there. He signaled a right-hand turn and headed east on Grand Avenue, driving past comfortable two-story houses, neighborhood shops, and rows of apartment buildings. He crossed over the Short Line Road, the cramped, narrow highway that started nowhere and went nowhere. Ayd Mill Road, they called it now, for God-knew-what reason.

At Lexington Parkway and Grand, he impulsively signaled a right turn and cut onto Lexington from the inside lane, causing the driver behind him to lay on the horn. A block later, he pulled over to the curb in front of an ordinary-looking brick apartment building, and shut off the pickup's engine. The building hadn't changed much over the years. It had looked newer back in 1934, when he, at age nine, and Rudy, then in his teens, had stood on the front lawn in the chilly March wind with scores of excited onlookers, staring, speculating. Probably no one driving by today knew that on a long-ago Saturday morning, this building, in a rattling burst of machine gun fire, had instantly become the most famous, most notorious building in St. Paul.

Looking up at the third floor, he located the correct windows. There. From that third-floor apartment, John Dillinger had shot his way out of a police raid and escaped. The news had swept over the city that Saturday morning, passed from one person to the next in excited shouts. Rudy had bundled him up, and they had hurried down West Seventh and up Lexington Parkway to stand in front of the building with the rest of the crowd that had gathered. They had pressed as close as they could get to Dillinger's Ford coupe, straining to see where the cops had shot out the tires so it couldn't be used as a getaway car. Pushing and jostling their way into the crowded alley, they had stared at the blood spots in the snow— Rudy had held him on his shoulders so he could see. They had milled around the yard, talking to other excited bystanders and listening for scraps of new information until the cops had sent them all home. And as they had walked back down Lexington Parkway toward home, chilled from being outside so long, he had felt disappointed that Dillinger had escaped, yet oddly relieved at the same time. Later that summer when Dillinger was shot down in front of a movie theater in Chicago, he had felt more disappointment than relief. Sure, Dillinger was a gangster, a killer, but he had been exciting to read about in the newspapers during a time when little that happened was truly exciting.

He started the pickup and slowly pulled away from the curb. Where should he go now? He thought of driving to the cemetery where Rudy was buried next to their parents, but gave up the idea almost immediately. Some people, he knew, got something out of going to cemeteries and sitting next to the graves of their loved ones, but he wasn't one of them. He felt closer to those lost to him by being in the places where he had watched them go about their everyday routine.

At St. Clair Avenue, he turned left again and headed east. St. Clair would eventually cross West Seventh, and a right on West Seventh would take him back to Rudy's, completing a large triangle around the part of St. Paul that was home to him.

The rest of the city held little interest for him. His whole life was in the West End, not in neat little bungalows and ramblers, nor in the massive Crocus Hill houses that loomed up ahead on the left. He stopped at a stop sign that hadn't been there before, debated whether to swing into the little park that looked over the West End, and decided against it. On the way to Rudy's, he'd stop at the burger place on West Seventh and buy a hamburger and some coffee. Fast food. The world slowed you down in one place and sped you up somewhere else.

A few minutes later, he pulled up in front of Rudy's house and shut off the pickup's engine. Bittersweet memories flooded over him. Carrying the bag containing his hamburger and coffee, he trudged up the walk and climbed the steps. Crossing the porch to the front door, an odd little memory slipped out. In the days following the Dillinger shootout, he had played gangsters with the neighborhood boys, shooting it out with the G-men on this very porch, bursting through this very door with a stick for a machine gun. He unlocked the door and went inside. His breath rolled in a ghostly swirl in front of him. He turned up the heat. In the dining room he sat down at the table where he had eaten so many of Rudy's simple meals and opened the bag. Without really tasting it, he ate his hamburger, drank the black coffee.

Enough, he told himself. He should get to work. Instead, he went into Rudy's bedroom and lay down on the bare mattress, using his coat to cover himself. For a while he lay restlessly, aware of the emptiness in his heart. But there came into his mind the image of a little boy shooting it out with the G-men, while an older boy looked on approvingly. He fell deeply and calmly to sleep.

SEVEN

SHARON WATCHED AS HER PARTNER, Elaine, slammed the lid on the gray metal cashbox, jerked the zipper shut on the green zipper bag, and shoved it into her purse.

"Well, that's quite the little bombshell, isn't it?" Elaine said. "So when do you make the big decision?"

"Sometime this week." She dropped into the shelving bin the last of a stack of science fiction she had just priced, grateful that the news was out at last. It had taken all morning and half the afternoon to find a moment when the store was empty and her nerve was up. She looked up into Elaine's oval face. Behind her heavy tortoiseshell glasses, her partner's eyes were fixed on some distant, invisible point.

"I wasn't going to tell you until we decided," she continued, "but I needed to talk to somebody about it."

"Well, I'm real glad you picked on me," Elaine said coldly. "This just makes my day." Elaine pulled on her coat, grabbed her purse off the counter. "I'm taking this deposit to the bank. And while I'm there, I'll just tell them that the Paperback Library is going down the tubes."

"Elaine—"

"God damn it, Sharon, why the hell did you tell me this?"

An ugly silence hung in the air between them. She had not counted on this kind of reaction from Elaine at all. Panic rising in her throat, she struggled to say something, to right what she had suddenly knocked astray.

"I told you," she said with effort, "because I thought you'd understand."

"Understand? You bet I understand! Dean has been transferred three times in eight years. Each time I had to drop whatever I was doing and spend a year getting moved and then resettled. Now I finally get something put together for me to do, something that's mine, and *your* husband comes along and *screws it up* by jumping at some big job like a dog jumps a bone."

"Elaine, this . . . you're not being fair. We haven't left yet."

"Oh, but you will," Elaine said bitterly. "Just like you did last time. Just like I did three times. I'll bet my half of the store on it." She turned away.

"Wait." She reached across the counter to snare Elaine's arm, but missed. Elaine turned around to face her.

"Look, I'm sorry. I shouldn't have brought it up. I should have waited until we knew for sure." She felt tears forming in her eyes, blinked them back.

Elaine fixed her with a solid stare, then suddenly looked down at the floor and shook her head. She laid her purse on the counter, then ran her hands through her sleek gray hair.

"No," she said tonelessly, "I'm the one who should be sorry. The last thing you need is me throwing a tantrum." She sighed and moved around the counter to the empty chair.

Overcome, Sharon looked away, concentrating on the shelves of flashy romances. Fantasies filled with trials and tribulations, happy endings. She felt Elaine's mothering hand on her shoulder.

"I do understand," Elaine said. "That's the whole trouble. I know exactly how you feel."

Elaine lightly massaged her shoulder. She felt tears sliding down her cheeks, hot, oily drops. She pulled a Kleenex from the box under the counter and wiped her eyes. The world suddenly felt as if it were spinning backwards, toward another time in another place.

"I feel so powerless," she said. "And angry. I don't remember feeling angry last time, just sad and resigned."

"It gets worse each time," Elaine said, "because you know how awful it is. I was angry for a year after we moved here."

"What did you do?"

"I got over it. Well, maybe I should say I just got so I could live with it. Starting this store helped."

Over their heads, the electric heater kicked in, settling into a rattling hum. A wave of warm air engulfed them. Elaine unzipped her coat.

"It still bothers me," she continued. She pulled off her glasses to rub her eyes. "You know what bothers me the most? The house we live in. I just *hate* it. Dean flew out here and bought it himself. There's no closet space, the basement is like a cave, and the kitchen! Well, you've seen it." She pushed her glasses on and adjusted them on the bridge of her nose. "He buys the house and I'm the one who has to live with it. I still miss our house in Connecticut, and it's been eight years since we left." She sniffed away tears.

"But," she said, catching herself up, "that's the risk you run when you're married to a corporate migrant worker."

Sharon laughed. "Corporate migrant worker. I like that."

"Well, it's true. They follow the big jobs around the country, just like migrant workers follow the crops."

"And what's that make us?"

"If you need to ask," Elaine replied, "there's a copy of the *The Grapes of Wrath* over in the Literature section. I think it's been here since we opened."

"I just dread the thought of packing everything up and moving again," Sharon said. "I haven't even unpacked some boxes yet."

"Well, you've got the rest of the week to work on him. Maybe a miracle will happen."

"For all I know, he's already decided." She looked around the room. When the two of them had opened this store together a year ago, the unpainted shelves had been nearly empty. Now they were running over full, books crammed sideways on top of the books standing on the shelves. Comfortably messy, the way a library should look.

"If we go," she said, turning to Elaine, "we'll work out something that lets you keep the store."

"If it happens, it happens. There's no sense in worrying about it until the time comes. Not much you can do about it right now." Elaine pushed herself out of the chair and zipped her coat again.

"I better get to the bank before it closes. You want me to come back today?"

"No, go on home. I'll close up." She watched Elaine gather up her purse. "Elaine . . ." The words came slowly and difficultly, fighting against a wave of emotion, a sudden sense of loss. What, oh what, would she do in Denver or San Diego without Elaine? ". . . thanks for listening."

Elaine smiled, a sad, slow smile. "What are friends for, except to listen and then give advice you don't want?"

"Well, you've listened; now what's your advice?"

"Do what you think is right."

"Elaine, that's a cop-out."

"You bet it is, honey," Elaine said over her shoulder as she started toward the shop door. "I can't pretend to know what to tell you." She stopped by the door and lifted her gray knit scarf and matching hat off their hook. She wound the scarf three times around her neck and pulled the hat down over her ears.

"If you really want my advice—go, if for no other reason than to get away from these miserable winters."

"We had long winters back East."

"Back East." Elaine snorted in amusement. "I never heard that term until we came out here."

The rest of Sharon's afternoon dragged, as Tuesdays often did. To keep busy, she dusted shelves. What *would* she do without Elaine, she wondered, as she moved her way through the Mystery section. Practical, outspoken Elaine, the business-minded one of their partnership, still privately mourning, of all things, the loss of a house in Connecticut; angry that she had been left out of the hunt for a new house here in St. Paul.

House hunting. She and Phil had flown from Boston to the Twin Cities, bought a home, and caught the redeye back to Boston, all in one hellish day. As the plane had banked around, she had looked out the window to glimpse for the first time the neat, compact downtowns of St. Paul and Minneapolis, the great Mississippi—not all that great here—essing its way between them. From the sky, downtown Minneapolis and St. Paul had looked ridiculously small-town, a few skyscrapers rising up out of the trees.

An overeager and overweight real estate agent wearing a gold blazer had picked them up at the airport, and driven them around the Twin

Cities on a whirlwind tour: Edina, St. Louis Park, downtown Minneapolis, South Minneapolis, Summit Avenue, downtown St. Paul.

Over a Kentucky Fried Chicken lunch, the agent showed them the list he had compiled of twenty houses in their price range.

"What are these names in parentheses?" she had asked the agent.

"They're names of the communities the houses are in, Mrs. Prescott," the agent had said lightly. "New developments. I know you'll like them."

"We told you no suburbs," she had said, crossing them off the list. She needed the stability of old, established neighborhoods around her, not some dreary suburb where the houses all looked the same.

But she had been surprised and heartsick to discover that old in St. Paul referred to anything built before 1900. "Boston's suburbs are older than St. Paul," she had whispered to Phil in the back seat as the agent drove them to the first house.

Phil had asked all the questions—neighborhood value, resale value, taxes, assessments, financing. The bottom-line man. Blocking out the agent's endless monologue of statistics, she had tried to concentrate on each house itself, whether she could feel at least comfortable, if not at home, in it. They went on to the next house and the next and then the next. Halfway through the list, her mind a blur of living rooms, bathrooms, and kitchens, she gave up, ready to submit to a two-bedroom apartment in some high rise.

They were driving west on Grand Avenue when she looked out the car window and saw what appeared to be a college campus. Georgian buildings of dark red brick built around a grass court. Very eastern. She had felt a twinge of recognition, a vague connection.

"Is this a college?" she had asked the agent.

"Macalester College." The answer drifted over the front seat to where she and Phil sat in the back. "Fine college. Some claim it's the Harvard of Minnesota."

A classification that caused her to smile. "Anything listed in this neighborhood?"

"In Tangletown? Well, let's see," the agent said, pulling over to the curb.

There had been one house, a three-bedroom Victorian on Cambridge Street. Cambridge Street. The name had floated over her like the silver notes of a favorite song. The house itself had narrow rooms, uneven hardwood floors, tall ceilings. It was filled with contemporary furniture, the walls papered with patterns that clashed brutally with the carved woodwork. But beyond the decor, the house looked comfortable, at least Victorian, if not colonial old.

"It's this house or nothing," she had told Phil. He signed the purchase agreement on the kitchen table.

And so, a little pocket of St. Paul, with its crooked streets bearing familiar eastern names—she later discovered Amherst Street and Princeton Avenues nearby—became home. Not the kind of home where the heart lived, but at least Tangletown was a neighborhood that looked and felt familiar enough to substitute for home. Tangletown. The name had a sort of Boston ring to it.

The house, it turned out, had its inadequacies. It was short a bathroom, and its narrow living room was too small. The wiring and plumbing needed frequent repairs. Every redecorating project that started out cheap gradually became expensive. Phil had paid the bills without comment, his recognition of her sacrifice.

Now here they were, set to go though it all again: the quick trip into town to buy a new house, the packing, the unpacking. The loneliness. Her first year here, there had been no one but Ellen Goodman to keep her company. If she had to choose between San Diego and Denver, she'd check to see which paper carried her column. But what would she do without Elaine?

EIGHT

ANOTHER DAY AT THE BOOK FACTORY behind him, Steven thought as he felt his way up the dark stairs toward the apartment. One more day, added to all the other days, that he was a library clerk instead of a musician. The bricks of his life moving from the pile to be lived to the pile already lived. Insignificant bricks. Someday, all of his bricks would be in the same pile again, and what would he have built? He needed more time to devote to his music. If only he didn't have this stupid job hanging around his neck like a millstone. If only he didn't have Debi around at night so that he could practice. *Sometimes you have to ignore what people are going to say about you and just do what you want.* God damn it, he'd just make time—the hell with everyone and everything else. Starting tomorrow—no, *tonight*—he'd play two hours every day, no matter what.

The apartment door was unlocked. He found Debi in the bedroom standing in her underwear next to the open closet door, hanging her blue power suit on a hanger.

"The new clue is kind of a bummer," she greeted him. "Did you read it yet? Paper's on the couch." Reaching into the closet, she shoved hangers aside in both directions and hung the dress in the empty space.

"Hello yourself," he said. "How was my day? Oh, lousy, like always. And how was your day?"

"Oh, all right. Hello," she said, brushing her lips across his cheek. "Go look at the clue. I want to see what you think it means."

"So look who's standing here in just her underwear. I could be in just my underwear in a second or two." He peeled off his coat and tossed it on the bed. He reached out to pull her into his arms, but Debi slipped beyond his grasp.

"You had your chance this morning," she said, moving across the room toward her dresser. "I told you I might not be in the mood tonight."

"You're never in the mood anymore," he mumbled.

"That's not true. I was in the mood this morning, only you weren't."

"I was too in the mood. We didn't have time. It was time to go to work. We've got time now."

"Steven, let's not get into a big fight about it. Maybe later, okay?" She pulled a pair of stone-washed jeans out of the bottom dresser drawer and threw them onto the bed. "Go look at the new clue. And hang up your coat." A pink sweatshirt sailed through the air toward the bed. She sat down on the edge of the bed, her white back to him, and started to pull on a pair of striped socks.

Maybe later. A door closed politely but firmly in his face, a promise beckoning from the other side. In protest, he ignored her order to hang up his coat. He glanced at his guitar case standing in the corner of the room. Two hours, he reminded himself. You are going to play for two hours tonight.

Debi followed him into the living room, carrying her jeans and sweatshirt. He felt her eagerness like heat flowing from a radiator as he picked up the paper and scanned the front page for the new clue. *In a distant place they're running races, from the treasure site you can't see the runners' faces.* He sat down on the couch and propped his legs up on the scarred coffee table.

"So what do you think it means?" She plopped down on the couch and pulled her jeans on over her legs.

"I don't know," he said. "It's pretty vague." Running races. Runners' faces. The words had a lyrical, songlike quality about them.

"I think it means steamboat races," Debi said, standing up and pulling her jeans up over her behind. "Didn't they used to have steamboat races here in the old days? That would fit in with the other clues." She pulled up the zipper with a quick movement of her hand. "Under the Wabasha Bridge. That's the place."

Steven read the clue again. "No, not steamboats. It says runners' faces. That must mean people, not steamboats."

"It could mean the faces of the people on the boats." The edge in her voice was muffled as she pulled her sweatshirt over her head and shoved her arms through the sleeves.

"No way," he said. "There's no reference to the past in the clue. It says *they're running races—they are* running races. There aren't any steamboat races nowadays."

Debi jerked her sweatshirt down over her breasts. "Well, I don't hear you coming up with any hot ideas. So far all you've done is pick apart someone else's."

"I wasn't picking apart your ideas. I was just analyzing the clue. I can't help it if I don't interpret it the same way that you do." The paper was snatched out of his hands.

"Hey, do you mind?" He grabbed at the paper, missing it. "I happened to be looking at that."

Debi collapsed into the overstuffed chair across the room from him, and disappeared behind the paper.

"Maybe it means the joggers running over the Wabasha Bridge during their lunch hours," she said from behind the paper. "Some of those fools run all year long."

"I'm only relying on memory because somebody just grabbed the paper right out of my hands . . ." He jerked his legs off the coffee table. ". . . but didn't it say they were running races? Joggers aren't really running races; they're just jogging."

The paper crumpled into Debi's lap, revealing her indignant face, like a curtain dropped from a portrait. Her lips were a tight line, her eyes blazing. The Mona Lisa she wasn't.

"Maybe they are racing *each other*. Steven, we're never going to find this thing if we don't work together. All you're doing is picking and finding fault."

"And all you're doing is defending yourself. You're not trying to figure out the real meaning of the clue at all. You're just trying to be right."

The paper came flying across the room at him, landing on the edge of the coffee table.

"Then you figure it out, smartass." The paper slid off the coffee table and dropped to the floor. Debi swung her legs over the arm of the chair with angry, jerky movements.

He picked up the paper from the floor and smoothed the crumpled front page. The room was growing dark. Already the streetlights were winking on along Portland Avenue, amber halos glowing through the bay windows. He snapped on the floor lamp next to the couch. He reread the clue, letting the words sink in slowly: nouns, verbs, and adjectives. *In a distant place they're running races, from the treasure site you can't see the runners' faces.*

"Well, Sherlock Holmes, what does it mean?"

He glared at her over the top of the newspaper. Her face was etched with frustration and impatience, the same look that she had worn in front of the Student Center the day he met her, a look he had come to know so well. Phrase by phrase, he read through the clue, interpreting aloud. "*In a distant place.* Distant place must mean a particular spot. *They're running races.* They—people. Who are they? Whoever they are, they're running races. *From the treasure site you can't see the runners' faces.* That must mean it's too far away to see their faces—a distant place, like it says in the first line of the clue.

"It's in sight of a distant place where they're running races," he concluded, looking at Debi again over the top of the newspaper, "and from the treasure site you can't see the faces of the runners."

Debi pulled a small pillow from behind her back and fired it across the room at him. "Steven, you're such a jerk. That's no help at all. All you did was read the clue out loud. Who's running races where?"

"If we knew that, we'd know where the treasure is."

Debi swung her legs to the floor. "Well, this clue has got to connect somehow to the other clues. And we decided this morning that the treasure was under the Wabasha Bridge," she added decisively, as though it were an unalterable fact. She popped to her feet, paced around the living room. "We must be missing something pretty obvious."

He leaned over to pick up the pillow Debi had thrown. With a flick of his wrist, he tossed it spinning like a frisbee into the chair across the room. He laid the newspaper on the coffee table.

"Look," he said, "we're going about this the wrong way. All we're doing is picking a solution and then trying to make the clues fit it. Let's look at what the clues actually tell us. It says, *In a distant place they're running races.* Who runs races?"

"That's a stupid question." She stopped in front of him, hands on her hips, a questioning look spreading across her face.

"Well, if it's stupid, it should be easy to answer. Who runs races?"

"Runners, obviously." She backed into the big chair, tucking her legs under her.

"And who are runners?"

"Athletes. Track runners."

"All right. Now where do these runners, these 'they' people, run races?" He felt like Perry Mason questioning a hostile witness on the stand. Any moment he expected to hear a voice from a dark corner of the courtroom shout "I did it. I killed him. I had to."

But it was Debi who spoke, her attention fully turned to him. "On running tracks."

"Right," he said. "Now where are the running tracks?"

"High schools, colleges."

"Right. And you have to be able to see one of these tracks from the treasure site because it says so in the clue. Now—"

"So all we need to do," Debi interrupted, jumping to her feet, "is figure out where these running tracks are around town, and we know the treasure is near one of them. Then we use the other clues to eliminate some of the locations."

"By George, I think she's got it."

"We could eliminate some of the tracks if there's no park near them. Eliminating from both ends. I like that. We need to make a list." She went to the secretary and opened the fold-down lid. Rummaging through the piles of bills and papers, she found a green spiral notebook and a pen. "A list of high schools and colleges is what we need," she said. Settling back into the big chair, she opened the notebook.

"Okay, there's Central High School," she began, jotting it down in the book. "On Lexington Parkway." Central, located a few blocks away, was the only high school either of them really knew. Out-of-towners both of them, they had no school loyalties, knew nothing of the old school rivalries.

"What are the other high schools?" She looked up at him from the notebook. She was in control of the project again, brimming with enthusiasm, the defeat of her solution already put behind her and forgotten. He admired that ability in her and hated it at the same time.

"There's Johnson High," he said, thinking of Knickerson at work. A Johnson grad, Knickerson was fiercely loyal to his alma mater, always checking the paper for the basketball and hockey scores, gloating over wins, mourning the losses.

Debi scribbled the name into the notebook. "Okay," she said. "What else? There's some big school down by Highland Park—what's that one?"

"Check the phone book." He suddenly felt tired of treasure hunting, of Debi's self-absorbed enthusiasm, of sitting in this room, for chrissake. He knew what he wanted to be doing, what he *should* be doing for the next two hours. *Sometimes you have to ignore what people are going to say about you, and just do what you want.*

While Debi was getting the phone book, he slipped into the bedroom, closing the door softly behind him. Moving across the dark room, he closed the other bedroom door that led into the front hallway so Debi couldn't hear. He switched on the lamp on the night table.

The Martin caught the reflection from the lamp as he lifted it from its case, flashing golden patterns of light off its shiny body up against the dark ceiling, like a mirror reflecting sunlight. He dug into the red felt along the rounded bottom of the open guitar case in search of a pick. Tuning up was a torturous procedure, thanks to Johnny Williamson, a punk-haired guitar player who had lived down the hall in his dorm and played in a Top Forty band. One night while he was playing alone in his dorm room, Johnny had suddenly opened the door without knocking and stuck his head inside. "Hey, Carpenter, your low E is flat," he had said, and shut the door. After that, his formerly brief tune-up had evolved into endless chording. Tightening and loosening the keys to put the strings in tune. Sometimes he actually gave up and started all over again. He had had nightmares about playing horribly out of tune in a smoky club and Johnny standing up in the audience shouting, "Hey, Carpenter, your low E is flat."

He warmed up on "Fire and Rain," an old James Taylor favorite, singing the lyrics silently in his head as he played the verses and chorus. On the last verse, the bedroom door opened. Debi slumped casually against the door casing, notebook in hand.

Shit, what's she doing here? he thought. But he kept playing, pushing himself through the final chorus, strumming out an ending that faintly resembled the fade-out on the record. Ending songs that faded out on record was always hard.

"That was nice," Debi said.

"Thanks." He strummed a few nervous chords, trying to decide what to play next. Maybe a Fogelberg song.

"Okay, I got these high schools: Central at 275 North Lexington; Como Park at 740 Rose Avenue; Harding at 154 East Sixth; Highland Junior and Senior High at 1015 South Snelling; Humboldt on 30 East Baker Street; and Johnson at 1349 Arcade. And something called Jefferson Alternative on 90 Western Avenue South. And colleges: Hamline, of course; Macalester; St. Thomas; St. Catherine; Concordia; the University of Minnesota, St. Paul campus. Let's drive by some of these places tonight, okay?"

He fingered the opening notes of "Run for the Roses," one of his all-time favorite Fogelberg songs. A go-for-it song.

"Steven, it's almost dark." Debi dropped onto the bed next to him.

"So?" He stopped playing, looked up at her.

"If we're going to drive around, you have to get the car started first."

"I'm practicing now."

"Steven, it's supposed to snow tomorrow."

"Thanks for the weather report." He fingered the opening notes to the song again.

"If we don't get it started, they'll tow it away if there's a snow emergency."

"I'll do it later. I'm busy now."

"Steven—"

Incensed, he struck a brutal chord. The metallic, sour notes echoed through the room, notes that would have frightened even Jimi Hendrix.

"I can't believe you. Last night, you gave me this big lecture on being a musician. 'If you want to be a musician, be a musician; I'll support you.' That's what you said. So here I am trying to practice and I get through one song—*one fucking song*—and you're after me to quit and go start the goddamn car. Some support."

"Steven, I just—"

"Go start it yourself, if you're in such an all-fired hurry. Shit."

"Don't yell at me!" she shouted.

"Then quit nagging and acting like a bitch," he snarled. "Jesus."

Debi leaned toward him, bringing her face very close to his. Her eyes were as hard and cold as flint.

"Stuff it, Carpenter," she said in a low, deadly voice. She pushed herself to her feet. "Stuff it where the sun don't shine." The bedroom door slammed behind her. The Dylan poster bounced on its hangers.

He sat for a long moment in the sudden, unpleasant silence, hugging the Martin against his chest. Then he laid it back in its case, closed the lid, and snapped the latches. He stood the case up in its place in the corner of the room. The music had left him, as quickly and completely as if a radio had been shut off, the Run for the Roses lost.

He went to the window and pressed his burning forehead against the cold glass pane, cupping his hands around his eyes to block out the lamplight. Down Portland Avenue, lights glowed from kitchen windows, from living rooms and upstairs bedrooms. People slipping into the routine of another evening. Why couldn't she understand? Why couldn't she give him the support she had promised? An old Pontiac passed by below the window, sliding to a stop at the stop sign. Pulling away, the car got hung up on a rut and its engine stalled. He heard the whine of the starter and saw the headlights dim. That's just the way he felt—stalled. Stalled dead center between wanting to please her and please himself. *Sometimes you have to ignore what people are going to say about you, and just do what you want.* Yah, bullshit, he thought. Do what you want as long as it doesn't interfere with what someone else wants. He picked up his coat off the bed and pulled it on. He hoped he could find his jumper cables.

NINE

THE CAMARO BUMPED THROUGH A POTHOLE, dragging bottom against the frozen slush, and pulled to a stop just inside The Dive's parking lot. Bruce Mitchell scanned the rows of pickups and cars and then let the Camaro creep forward, past the building toward the back of the lot.

"See The Beast anywhere?" he asked, looking for the familiar shape of St. John's fabled 4x4 pickup. Under the glare of the icy blue floodlights, the parking lot looked otherworldly: piles of dirty snow pushed up against the light poles, hard-edged shadows in odd places, the colors of the cars strangely altered. The Camaro's midnight-blue hood looked almost blood-red.

"There." Joanna pointed to the row of cars parked along the side of the building. Halfway down the line, the cab of The Beast rose head and shoulders above the other vehicles, dwarfing them. Bright red by day, the 4x4 looked purplish in the artificial light. It was, indeed, The Beast.

"He's been here awhile if he's that close to the building," Bruce said, feeling guilty—they were an hour-and-a-half late. "Looks like we're back in the cheap seats." He swung the Camaro around a row of cars and headed for the back row, easing into a narrow space between a beat-up Monte Carlo and a new Toyota 4x4.

"We should have come early, too, instead of going to bed, so we didn't have to hike clear across the parking lot," Joanna said as they hauled themselves out of the Camaro. "I've got two sweaters on under my coat, and I'm cold already. I must be crazy to get out of bed and go out with a couple of clowns like you two on a night like this."

"Not crazy, just adventuresome," he laughed. "It'll be fun." He gave her a tight squeeze as they made their way between the cars, the north wind hard at their backs. "We'll get some of The Dive's best antifreeze in you and you won't feel a thing." He stopped under a light to give her a warm, lingering kiss, conscious of—and pleased by—the picture the two of them made to any onlookers. Usually you did this on the way out of a bar at closing time, after you had picked someone up you didn't even know.

They hustled from the otherworldliness of the parking lot into the dimly-lit otherworldliness of The Dive. The place was already crowded. The air was heavy with smoke; the floor vibrated with the solid beat of dance music coming from the back room. A hockey game played on the television set that hung above one end of the bar, its sound lost in the music. Come play-off time, if the North Stars were in it, it would be standing-room only in The Dive as fair-weather hockey fans jammed the place, crowding around additional television sets the management brought in. But tonight only a small knot of hard-core fans sat at the bar watching the Stars struggle against the Chicago Blackhawks, bitching at the management to turn down the goddamn music.

He spotted St. John sitting in their usual corner booth with its good view of the TV. Bruce noticed a sudden frown crease his friend's unshaven face as he looked up and recognized them; but by the time they had worked their way around the knot of hockey fans to the booth, the frown was gone, replaced by St. John's customary lopsided grin. St. John stood up, broad-shouldered in his heavy quilted vest, to receive the high five that was their usual greeting. Under his vest, St. John was wearing his faded blue Minnesota Twins World Champions sweatshirt from the 1987 World Series.

"Butch," he shouted over the music. "Lose your razor?"

"Hey, Sundance." St. John smacked his palm, ignoring the dig.

"What's the score?" he jerked his head at the television set.

"Shit, don't ask." St. John dropped into his seat. "Four-zip, Hawks. Still the first period. It's about time you found your way into this ritzy place. I'm way ahead of you." He thumbed at a half-dozen empty brown beer bottles lined up along the wall. A cigarette burned in the ashtray, which was nearly full of butts. A copy of the *Pioneer Press* was on the table.

Bruce patted Joanna on the back. "Had to stop and pick up another treasure hunter," he said. "A first-timer, almost." He nudged her into the booth ahead of him.

"Hello, Dennis." Joanna smiled at St. John as she slid into the booth, but her eyes shifted up to Bruce, flickering with uncertainty.

"Hi, Jo." St. John's voice was almost lost in the beat of the music. His eyes were narrow under the visor of his Ford cap.

Feeling the two sets of eyes on him, Bruce pulled off his coat and hung it on the back of the booth, not looking at either of them. A flash of regret passed through him; Jo had said at lunch that she believed she made St. John uncomfortable, and it looked like she was right. Maybe he should have come alone.

"You hear today when you're going back to work?" he asked as he slid into the booth beside Joanna.

"Nah, not yet," St. John replied. "You guys eat?"

"Yeah," he admitted. A rush of warmth flooded over him at the memory of the two of them snuggled in Joanna's bed, eating the tuna fish sandwiches that she had gotten up to fix for them. They *must* be crazy to get out of bed and go out on a night like this.

"Well, shit, you mean I've been sittin' here starving to death, waiting for you for nothing?" St. John stood up, waved his arms wildly to catch the waitress's attention, then motioned with both hands as though he was directing a jet plane toward their booth.

It was not a jet plane that came to their booth, but Trish the Swish, one of The Dive's waitresses, who was only slightly smaller than a jet plane. Trish the Swish was so named by St. John for the swishing sound her heavy legs made rubbing together as she walked. On nights when action in the place was slow, they often joked around with her, leading her on with no real intentions, then laughing behind her back at her attempts to flirt. Her face broke into a smile as she recognized him. The smile melted away when she noticed Joanna. He suddenly felt very uncomfortable, unsure of just how much of his past life he wanted Joanna to see.

"Well, if it isn't the Sundance Kid," Trish said. "Haven't seen much of you around these parts lately." She sized up Joanna in one sweeping glance. "And now I see why."

"This is Joanna," he said stiffly. "Jo, this is Trish." The two women exchanged cool greetings, Joanna's eyes darting over Trish.

"So how you been, lover?" Trish asked intimately.

"Are you here to talk or work?" St. John interrupted.

"Your buddy, Butch, is in a lousy mood tonight," Trish said in a loud stage whisper, holding a hand up to hide her mouth. She turned to St. John, holding her pen and order tablet in mock anticipation. "What would Your Grumpiness like tonight?"

St. John ignored her playfulness. "Steak sandwich, fries, a bowl of chili with extra crackers. And another brew."

"Are we hungry tonight, Butch?" Trish teased. She turned her attention to their side of the booth. "Anything for you two?"

"You want to split an order of fries, or something?" he asked Joanna.

"Just a Diet Coke."

"Two Diet Cokes."

"The contents of the refrigerator and another beer for the Grump, and two Diet Cokes. Nice to see you again, lover." She smiled and swished off toward the kitchen.

"Lover?" Joanna asked teasingly, poking him in the side with her elbow. "Lover?"

"Don't get the wrong idea," he said. "She calls everyone that. Right, Butch?"

"She never calls me that," St. John said. "What's with the Diet Coke? You lay off the brewski and not tell me?"

Bruce patted his stomach with both hands. "Getting a spare tire."

"If you got out and *worked* for a living in a good physical job," St. John needled, grinning at him, "say *construction,* for example, you wouldn't have to worry about that."

"If I had a construction job," he shot back, "I could spend half the goddamn winter sitting around with my thumb up my ass not working." Not so much the words, but St. John's tone of voice irritated him. There was too little joke in it.

St. John said nothing. He took a final drag off his cigarette and stubbed the butt out in the ashtray.

The music stopped, and above the noisy chatter of the patrons, they could hear snatches of the hockey game. He and St. John had sat in this booth hundreds of times, it seemed, in the past ten years, watching the North Stars struggle through one season after another. Now it all seemed like wasted time. He watched the Stars blow an easy goal. The instant replay showed that the skater had tripped on his own skate, drawing a barrage of insulting remarks from the bar-side coaches gathered under the television set. Across the table from him, St. John muttered something that he couldn't hear.

A slow dance came on the speaker system, one of Joanna's favorite songs. He felt a sudden desire to be in the back room on the dance floor with her, moving among the other couples in the smoky darkness, his arms around her waist, her head on his shoulder, the two of them moving in a tight, dreamy circle. He reached under the table to stroke Joanna's leg. She looked at him, a smile twitching at her lips, lighting up her eyes. He shot a glance across the table. St. John was looking at him, frowning.

Trish returned to the table with their drinks. "One Stroh's, two Diet Cokes. Are you running a tab?"

"Nah, I'll pick up this one." Bruce pulled out his wallet, laid a five-dollar bill on the table. He left the change on the counter; St. John, he had learned from years of experience, was a notoriously poor tipper. Since meeting Joanna, a waitress herself, he had noticed a distinct improvement in his own tipping habits.

"Where do you think that medallion is, anyway?" He reached for the newspaper that St. John had brought with him and opened it to the treasure hunt clues.

"You said Como Park on the phone last night." St. John took a long pull off his beer. "You say that every year."

"Well, someday I'll be right. This is as good a year as any. Hasn't been hidden there for a few years."

"We talked about them little kiddie rides in the park last night," St. John said. "If they're still there."

"Well, let's run up after you eat and take a look."

Joanna stirred in the seat beside him. "Before you two get too far into this, I need to make a trip to the ladies' room," she said. "Where is it?"

"There ain't many ladies come to this place," St. John said, "but the cans are in the back."

Bruce stood up to let Joanna out. She gave him a low, hurt look as she slid out of the booth.

"That was an asshole thing to say," he said as he watched her disappear into the back room. "You get up on the wrong side of the bed this morning, Butch?" He dropped into his seat, and propped his elbows on the table.

"You didn't tell me you were going to bring your lady friend along," St. John said. He took a hit off his beer, then studied the tabletop intently.

"Is that a problem?"

"Where the hell have you been?" St. John exploded, looking up, his eyes blackening. "You said you'd be here around five. I've been sittin' here for two goddamn hours. Shit." His face turned hard in the dim light.

"I stopped to pick up Jo and we got . . ." He felt embarrassed, suddenly, and cornered. "We got a little sidetracked, if you know what I mean."

"Christ," St. John said hotly, "do you two do anything else?"

The accusation in St. John's voice stung. He looked across the table at his friend. St. John glared back at him. He felt his own anger ignite. "You know what they say—use it or lose it," he said, realizing too late the implication.

"Tell me about it," St. John muttered savagely. He pulled his pack of cigarettes from his vest pocket, and lit one. The cigarette tip glowed red as he inhaled deeply and blew a lungful of smoke into the air. He looked away, staring out into open, smoky space.

Bruce watched the cloud of smoke swirl and slowly dissipate in the already smoky air. His anger seemed to dissipate with the smoke. "Look, man. I'm sorry. I didn't mean it like that. I was talking about myself. It was a joke, okay?" He looked around the room, suddenly struck by what a god-awful dive The Dive really was, how he didn't want to come here anymore. "And I'm sorry about being late. But this woman— I'm just crazy about her. It's so good I just can't believe it. I'm not just talking about screwing. She's so . . . The whole thing is—"

A storm of curses erupted from the knot of hockey fans sitting at the bar. "Shit!" St. John slammed a fist on the tabletop. "Chicago just scored again. Five to nothing."

He sipped his Diet Coke, wishing it were a beer. He watched the Stars and Hawks reassemble at center ice for the face-off. Chicago controlled the puck, firing it toward the Stars' net. The Stars scrambled toward their own net, behind and off-balance.

"Well, anyway, I'm sorry," he said.

"Forget it, Sundance," St. John said after a while. "It's nice somebody's getting it."

Bruce turned his attention back to the hockey game, the rapid trips up and down the ice. He identified with the puck. Joanna appeared from the back room, and he slid over to make room for her.

St. John waited for her to sit down, then cleared his throat roughly. His eyes were fixed on the Stroh's bottle in front of him.

"Jo . . ." he began, stumbling, reaching for the words, ". . . when . . . when I told you where the bathrooms were, I didn't mean that because you were here that you weren't a lady. I'm sorry."

Her eyes narrowed slightly. She smiled ambivalently. "It's all right, Dennis," she said. "I know what you meant."

"Come on, call me Butch," St. John said, suddenly jovial. "It's Butch and Sundance, right Sundance?"

"Yeah, sure," Bruce agreed. He watched Trish come out of the kitchen and maneuver her way through the cluster of tables with St. John's order.

"I hope this food cheers you up a little, Butch," Trish said as she set the dishes in front of St. John with a thump.

"Anything else for you two, Sundance? No? Well, see you later, lover." She winked at him and swished away. He felt Joanna's elbow in his ribs.

"So," St. John said as he heavily salted his french fries, "we're talking Como Park here?" He lifted the top off the sandwich and hammered the piece of steak with salt.

"We said the clue about trains and the one about planes might refer to the kiddie rides," Bruce said.

St. John reached for the paper. "Okay. Clue 2 is about trains and Clue 4 is planes. But what does this Clue 3 about the queen and river mean? I was looking at that before you got here. *Enter with a queen, leave via river, this little clue may make you shiver.* It doesn't say what you're entering and leaving."

"Probably the park where the treasure is, don't you think?" Bruce said. He reached across the table to steal one of St. John's french fries. It tasted of salt and grease.

"Then what the hell does *enter with a queen, leave via river* mean?"

Bruce pondered the terms, tapping out the beat of the music on the table. "How do you get into the park and out of the park?" he asked.

"On a road or a street," St. John said. He took a pull off his beer. "You think queen and river mean the names of streets?"

"Could. Or it could be you drive by something related to a queen and a river."

"Like what?" St. John bit into his steak sandwich.

"Beats me. I'll recognize it when I see it. It'll be a big clue, a tip-off like on 'Murder, She Wrote' or something." He drained the last of his Diet Coke, and crumpled the can in his hand. "We'll be driving along and see it. Something will go click in my weak little brain, and I'll say 'Oh, dear god,' or some stupid-ass thing like that, and we'll go rushing off to the exact spot where the treasure is hidden."

"Right," St. John said.

"How about the new clue about running races?" Joanna asked. "How does that fit in?"

"You think runners could mean joggers around the lake?" St. John looked from his sandwich at Bruce.

"Maybe." Bruce stole another french fry. "But that's pretty far away from the carnival area. Course, we could drive up there and look firsthand if you'd hurry up and eat."

Crowded into The Beast's cab, Joanna sitting in the middle, they pulled onto Lexington Parkway and headed north toward Como Park.

"So we want to check out the kiddie rides and look for something related to queen and river," St. John said.

The pickup passed under the old cement railroad bridge, and passed the dark, snowy softball fields that hummed with games during the hot summer nights.

"What's the name of this street?" Bruce asked as St. John swung off Lexington and headed into the park.

"Horton Avenue," St. John said. "Any Queen Hortons that you know of?"

"No, and no Horton Rivers either," Bruce said.

"I'm not even sure which one of these streets leads up to the zoo," St. John said. "I ain't been up here for a long time."

"It's this one," Joanna said, pointing to a street that curved off Horton into the dark trees. "I come up to the zoo all the time in the summer."

"What's the name of the street?" Bruce said.

St. John took the turn wide and stopped, kicking the brights up to illuminate the street sign. "A-i-d-a, however that's pronounced. What do you think? It could be some queen's name."

"She was probably some Amazon queen or something," Bruce said. "Somebody we never heard of. That's what they do, pick somebody so obscure that you've never heard of 'em."

"This is the carnival right here," Joanna said, pointing off to the right into the darkness. "There's a parking lot up ahead a little ways. I don't know if it's plowed out."

"Well, if it isn't, The Beast can handle it," St. John said proudly. He dropped The Beast into second gear and drove ahead until they found the entrance into the parking lot, which was plowed after all. He pulled in and stopped.

Behind an old-fashioned split-rail fence, vague forms lay half buried in the deep, trackless snow.

"Looks pretty dark in there," St. John said. "Can't recognize a thing, can you?"

"Let's go in and look around," Bruce suggested.

"Think we should?" Joanna asked.

"Who's to know? Besides, if it's really in there, then they expect people to go in. They wouldn't hide it somewhere where they didn't want people to go. You got a flashlight, Butch?"

"Right here," St. John said, reaching under the seat. "Let's go." He opened the driver's door and bailed out to the ground. "Watch that first step—it's a lulu," he called over his shoulder.

"Ready?" Bruce asked Joanna. He felt the warmth of her breath against his face, and felt an urge to be off somewhere else with her, locked skin to skin. They had been fools to come out here when they could have stayed at Jo's.

"I wish I had drunk some coffee or something," Joanna said as they climbed down from The Beast's cab.

One by one, they slipped between the wooden rails of the fence. With the round spot of yellow light from St. John's flashlight bobbing in front of them, they slogged through the deep snow toward the nearest dark form. Under St. John's flashlight, the dark form turned into a flat, empty platform,

"Can't tell what it is," St. John said. "The cars, or whatever you call them, that you sit in are missing." He moved the beam of light over the platform, found a set of steps descending from the platform into the snow. Above the steps, an entrance arch made of pipe rose above the platform. St. John stopped his beam of light at the top of the arch on a sign that shot rays of red light into the night off its reflective red letters. "Tilt-A-Whirl," he read. He flashed the beam across the snow-covered platform again. "They must have stored the cars."

"This doesn't look good," Bruce said. "If they did that to all of the rides, we're wasting our time."

St. John led the way toward the next form. Bruce felt Joanna's mittened hand slip into his own.

The light flashed over undefined machinery. Here and there, huge gears and heavy steel wheels stuck out of the iron hulk, each wearing its own little snowcap. Six empty arms stretched up from the base toward the sky, arms that had held swings or airplanes. The hulk of snow-covered iron looked like some great machine that had been stripped of its usable parts and then abandoned.

"Can't tell what the hell that is," St. John said. "Those arms obviously held something."

They moved on to the next form and the next. More snow-covered machinery, wheels and gears, empty arms. They found the concession stand shuttered tight, battened down for the winter, a snowbank against the door.

"Can't tell what any of this stuff is," St. John said, sweeping the beam of light across the deserted grounds. "They must store the cars and stuff for the winter. Probably so shmucks like us won't vandalize 'em. Well, that shoots the hell out of the Como Park theory."

"What about that big locomotive that we talked about?" Bruce said. "The one where you could ring the bell by pulling a cord."

"That's gone," Joanna said. "That's been gone from here for years."

A gust of wind moved over the grounds, chilling their already cold faces, stirring the stiff limbs of the trees above their heads.

"Shit, let's go," St. John said.

They slipped through the fence and crawled back into The Beast. St. John started the engine and spun the 4x4 around in a tight circle toward the entrance.

"Looks like our reading of the clues wasn't too good, Sundance. I guess we'll have to start over. Maybe tomorrow there'll be a good clue that will make the rest of these make a little sense."

"Maybe," Bruce said.

The three of them fell silent as the 4x4 wound out of the trees and into the open spaces. Across the empty softball fields, above the dark line of trees and the streetlights that lit the snowy ground, the sky was bright with reflected light from the city, neither white nor black. A dark white sky. St. John had come up with that description late one winter night as the two of them rested, lying with their backs on their sleds, on top of the tallest hill of the Como golf course. Half-stoned, staring into the sky, St. John had proclaimed it dark white. Those had been the days, the days when they had sworn they would never be taken alive. And now, tonight . . . .

"Once around the lake, Sundance?" St. John said as they pulled up at the Horton-Lexington stoplight. Without waiting for an answer, he turned onto Horton and headed east to pick up the boulevard that wound its way around the east side of the lake. "We can take a look and see if old Charlie is stuck in the ice anywhere out there."

"Who?" Joanna asked.

"Charlie Pitts," St. John said.

"Who's Charlie Pitts?"

"Sundance never told you about Charlie Pitts? Well . . ." St. John slipped his arm around her. "A new audience." And he was off, in his element, recounting a tale that Bruce had heard him tell at least twenty times.

"Charlie Pitts was one of the James Gang. You've heard about Jesse James? Okay. The James Gang tried to rob the bank in Northfield in 1876. They ended up getting shot to pieces. A couple of the gang got killed in Northfield, and the rest of them got away. Somewhere after Northfield, the Younger brothers and the James brothers split up; Charlie Pitts went with the Youngers. They finally got hunted down by the posses, and old Charlie got himself killed. This doctor gets hold of the body, see, and decides to use Charlie as a skeleton in his office. So he sticks Charlie in a box and dumps the box in Como Lake to let the bones bleach white—skeletons don't automatically come in white, you understand. This little kid comes along in the dead of winter and runs across the box stuck in the ice. Buried treasure, the kid thinks. He manages to get the lid pried open and out rolls Charlie's head. The kid—can't you imagine this kid with the shit scared out of him?—runs and gets his old man, who reports it to the cops. So the word gets out about this terrible murder in St. Paul. The public is in an uproar, demanding that the criminals be caught. The cops say they have matters in hand, when they don't have the slightest idea what happened. The doctor—"

St. John coughed, cleared his throat, and coughed again. He rolled down his window and spat out into the night.

"The doctor," he continued, "who had left the area for a while, hears about it, and sends a brother or a friend to the cops to tell them the true story. And that's the story of Charlie Pitts. So when we go by the lake, we always check to see if any of Charlie got left behind."

They rounded the north end of the lake and climbed the hill where the street had recently been redirected around the newly restored pavilion.

"Well, no sign of Charlie," St. John said, as they entered the traffic circle at the south end of the pavilion's parking lot. "At least the lake is still safe for democracy."

"Still safe for democracy?" Joanna echoed. "I think I missed something."

"God, doesn't Sundance tell you anything important?" St. John said. "Sundance, you got to educate this lady on the important things of life here." He pulled over to the curb, pointed into the darkness at a cigar-shaped form running parallel to the ground, dark against the white snow. "Over there," he said. "That's a torpedo. Actually, it's a monument to the USS *Swordfish,* which sank in the Pacific in World War II. Sundance and I got it all figured out. If an enemy sub ever surfaces in Como Lake, we'll just fire this torpedo at it and sink it. We'll be heroes for saving St. Paul from the Commies or whoever. Right, Sundance?"

"Right," Bruce heard himself agree. Old jokes, boring jokes that they had laughed at hundreds of times—jokes that suddenly were not funny with Joanna around. He felt for her hand in the darkness of the cab, gave it a squeeze, a promise that they would be away from here soon, off together in each other's arms.

"You going to come in for a brewski?" St. John asked as he pulled into The Dive's parking lot again. "I hear this is a pretty ritzy place."

"I think we're gonna pass," Bruce said. "We both got classes tomorrow."

"Shit," St. John said. "The hockey game's still on. Come on in. Let's watch them get their asses kicked."

"Not tonight." He'd had enough of identifying with the puck, being slapped back and forth between goals.

"God, you're a real party pooper lately." St. John shut off The Beast's engine.

"I'll call you tomorrow," Bruce said.

"Yeah, but will you still respect me in the morning?" St. John said.

TEN

A HELL OF A NOTE, COMING HOME from work at eight-thirty at night, Keith thought as he headed down the dark, icy steps to his apartment. At the bottom of the stairs, it was so dark that he had to pull off his gloves and guide the key into the lock with his bare hands. Once inside, he turned on the lights and slammed the door on the cold. Immediately, the sharp little bark of Tiffany, the poodle from hell, cut through the apartment's dry air like the clean sweep of a sword. "Stuff it, you little shit," he muttered. God, he'd love to kill that miserable little mutt. The empty coffee can from this morning was still in the kitchen trash. All he had to do was stuff her into it, snap on the plastic lid, drive to Lake Phalen, chop a quick hole in the ice, and send her straight to the bottom.

He dumped his coat, briefcase, and the bag containing his supper on the coffee table. Opening the paper he had picked up at the SuperAmerica on his way home, he sat down on the couch to read the newest clue again. Clue 5: *In a distant place they're running races, from the treasure site you can't see the runners' faces.* What the hell did that mean? He read through the other clues again, looking for some kind of quick connection. Nothing jumped out at him. He pitched the paper on the coffee table and stared at it.

Maybe there would be room in the coffee can for General Jerry, too. When he had arrived at work just at noon, the General had promptly hauled him into his office, closed the door, and bitched him out for half an hour.

"I'm really fed up with this, Keith," Jerry had begun as soon as he was settled behind his desk. "This kind of bad communication stops right now. It can't happen again."

"But I talked to you about taking the week off," he had protested. "Like I told you on the phone this morning when you called. We stood right in the doorway here—" he had pointed over his shoulder "— and talked about it."

"And I'm telling you that saying 'I'm thinking of taking a week off' is not the same as getting the vacation form, filling it out, and getting yourself put on the schedule."

"There's only six of us in the office. It's a stupid procedure."

"That's not the point. The point is that it is the procedure and you didn't follow it. If you don't follow a simple procedure like filling out a vacation form, how am I to know that you're following important procedures, like keeping your logbook up-to-date so we can bill our clients correctly?"

"I fill out my log book," he had said.

The General had made him go through his accounts one by one, telling him where he was with each one, how many hours he had charged against them in the past week, and what was coming up during the remainder of the week. All the while, Jerry had scribbled notes down on his ever-present yellow legal pad, using the gold fountain pen he had taken to carrying.

"How about Gopher State Products?" Jerry had asked. "They need that reprogramming done so they can issue their January billing."

"I can finish it first thing Monday morning."

Jerry had looked up from his legal pad. "They need it done by Friday."

"But I'm out the rest of the week."

Jerry had capped his fountain pen then, and tucked it into his shirt pocket. "Keith, you said that you could crank that program out with, and I quote, 'no trouble.' You're already a week past our target deadline. This has to be done by Friday. I don't care how you get it done, but I expect it to be done. Is that understood? Now if you want to take some days off, fill out a vacation request. But since we didn't have a chance to make any arrangements to cover your accounts while you were off, if they need you, you'll have to come in. I expect you to call in every morning."

"That's not fair. What the hell kind of vacation is that?"

"Under the circumstances, it's plenty fair. Keith, you're in deep shit around here, in case you don't know it."

"What do you mean?"

"I mean," General Jerry had leaned over toward him, lowering his voice, "that we've been through this stuff before with you, and Wilson is sick of it. He told me this morning to dump you, and I talked him out of it. This time. But I'm through making excuses for you. The next time something like this happens will be the last time. Unless you clean up your act, fly right, or whatever you want to call it, you'll be out of here on your butt. I'm serious, Keith."

With that, General Jerry had leaned back and reached again for his frigging fountain pen. Jerry, in his big-shot white shirt and fashionable tie, writing a reminder note about Gopher State on his goddamn desk blotter calendar. He'd hated the son of a bitch for a moment, right then.

"What's with you, Jerry?" he had demanded. "We go back a long way together. We started the same day, for chrissake. You always used to tell me that rules were made to be broken. You used to tell me Wilson was full of it. But ever since you became programming manager, you've changed. Kissing up. Stupid little rules like vacation request forms. Shirt and tie. You're acting like a goddamn boss."

"I am a 'goddamn boss,'" Jerry had said. "Your goddamn boss. It's my job to see that work gets done on time."

"By threatening to shit-can one of your friends because of a stupid rule that doesn't mean anything?"

"If you weren't my friend you would have been out of here already. And it's more than that and both of us know it." Jerry capped his fountain pen and tucked it in his shirt pocket. He had leaned back in his chair, very bosslike, pressing his hands together. "You know, Keith, the sad thing about you is that you're as good a programmer as I've got, but you can't seem to get it through your head that you have to work with people instead of against them. You just don't seem to get it."

As I've got. As if he were Jerry's property or something. Angry, he'd gotten up to go then, but Jerry had held up his hand to stop him, as though he were a policeman stopping a bus.

"Two things: Gopher State has to be done by Friday. And if you pull something like this again, you're out. That clear?"

Jerry, take your job and shove it up your ass if that's the way you feel about it. I quit. Get somebody else to do this Mickey Mouse crap. That's what he should have told Jerry. Instead, he had answered by slamming Jerry's door behind him as he left his office. He had felt the eyes of the other programmers on him as he strode back to his cubicle.

The chewing out had gnawed on him all afternoon as he sat hunched over the computer's keyboard, working on the Gopher State program, which he planned to finish here at home, and then dump into Gopher State's system by sending it over his modem. Jerry had been a friend once. But now . . . Now he was an asshole. A big shot with a necktie.

He opened the bag and spread his supper out on the table: two double hamburgers, two large orders of fries, and a hot apple pie that, like the burgers and fries, no longer seemed very hot. He went into the kitchen and poured a large glass of milk.

Settled back on the couch once again, he picked up the paper and reread the clue. *In a distant place they're running races, from the treasure site you can't see the runners' faces.* Evidently you could see some sort of running track from the treasure site, and it must be some distance away, if in a place too distant to see the runners' faces. To really see a distant place, maybe the treasure site was above the running place, up on a hill or a cliff.

He went to his desk to get a yellow legal pad that he had stolen from work. With a black pen, he scratched out a list of places where runners might run races: high school tracks, junior high school tracks, grade schools, maybe, colleges most certainly. What he could do was look up all the addresses of schools and colleges and plot them on his map.

He'd have to get started on tracing his queen and river street names. It would be easy. Just take a red marker and draw in all the queen streets on the map, then take a yellow marker and draw in all the river streets. They were bound to cross or intersect with some parks somewhere. And, he bet, there would be a pink line that he had drawn yesterday nearby, marking a railroad track from Clue 2.

Popping open the paper carton of one of the hamburgers, he gathered it up, dripping, in his hands and took a bite. Too much special sauce, he thought as he chewed. The french fries proved to be only lukewarm, but extremely salty, the way he liked them.

The taste of the salt made him think suddenly of Sandy. She used to rag on him about using too much salt in his diet. "Your blood pressure will go out the top of the gauge and kill you someday," she had told him once as he had salted their order of fries at the pie shop in Roseville. She had gotten furious with him when he laughed at her.

He found himself thinking about her a lot the last couple of days, not unusual for this time of year. Somehow the treasure hunt and Sandy had always been tied together in his mind, ever since their first year together, when she had introduced him to it. This time of year, he often caught himself thinking about her as he read the clues and slogged from park to park in the cold with his shovel. What was she doing now? Who she was with? Did she still look for the treasure? How were her lousy kids doing? These days, of course, he hadn't the slightest idea where she was. She'd changed jobs and moved, that much he knew. Her home phone number was now unlisted. She'd probably found someone else, some rich lawyer or stockbroker who dressed in expensive clothes and drove a sports car.

The thought of her brought back the dream that he had had about her during treasure hunt week the year after they had split up. The dream had started with him stooping over and picking up the medallion, which was encrusted in a clear chunk of ice. Knocking the ice from it, like a diver knocking the barnacles from a Spanish doubloon found on the ocean floor, he held the freed medallion above his head in victory. As the sun glinted off the medallion, his life changed. The snow around him melted as winter turned into summer. As he walked from the treasure site toward his car, he watched it transform before his eyes from the rusted-out gold Nova with its dented fenders into a sleek, black Corvette, just like the one he and Sandy sometimes saw, and she never failed to point out, on their walks around Lake Phalen. And Sandy herself, out of his life for months, suddenly appeared, dressed in white and sporting a flawless tan. The two of them slid into the Corvette and drove away into the sunset.

He finished the hamburger and opened the second one, which was almost cold. Like the first, it had too much special sauce, making the center bun soggy. The fries, too, had gone a little soggy.

Maybe he would bump into her this year in one of the parks, trudging along in the down parka he had once bought her, a shovel resting on her shoulder. The thought of seeing her again was both exciting and scary. It would satisfy his curiosity to get a look at her, if for no other reason than to see if she had lost the weight she was always trying to lose. God, what would he say to her? She'd probably introduced her stockbroker/lawyer friend to the treasure hunt, and the two of them would be shuffling along, holding hands. It would be pretty awkward. She'd probably ignore him.

Instead of Sandy, he'd probably run into General Jerry, wearing his goddamn necktie over his parka. He should have quit today—quit right on the spot. Told old Jerry where to shove it. He could probably get Gopher State and a few of his other clients to break off from PROgrams, Inc. and go with him. He could become an independent programmer. If he found the medallion, he could use the money to get himself set up.

But he wouldn't find it sitting here gnawing away on a burger. He gathered up his supper and the paper, and moved over to his desk at the end of the room. He switched on the computer and booted up his Clue 5 file to add this year's fifth clue to it. The white characters appeared one by one on the black screen. He liked the look of them: clean, simple, and predictable.

He'd find the treasure, by god, no matter what it took. It would be great. Finding the medallion would show them all: Sandy, General

Jerry, and the rest of them at work who had stared at him as he marched back to his desk. He glanced up at his bulletin board at the little strip of cash register tape with Toni's phone number on it. He could even call up Toni as a celebrity.

ELEVEN

THE SLED SPEEDING DOWN RICKETTY HILL, runners chattering on the frozen snow, wind whistling in his face. The thrill of speed. The tree suddenly looming up before him, racing toward him. Rudy's voice, calling from the top of the hill, distant and shrill with fear: "Alfred! Alfred, roll off! Roll off! Alfred!" His own voice, a scream, rising in his throat: "No! No!"

He jolted awake at the sound of his name again, spoken gruffly by an unfamiliar voice. Darkness surrounded him. The familiar dusty smell. The bare mattress under him. Not Ricketty Hill, but Rudy's room. The hard yellow beam of a flashlight suddenly stabbed out of the darkness into his eyes, blinding him. He held his hand up in front of his face to shield his eyes, aware of movement in the darkness behind the light.

"Are you Alfred Krause?" a man's voice asked.

Alfred felt his gut tighten. He looked away from the bright light at the bedroom floor. "Who wants to know?"

"Police officers. Are you all right, Mr. Krause?"

"The light's in my eyes."

"Mr. Krause, are you all right?"

"I can't see." He threw off his coat and struggled to sit up. The beam of light shifted to the floor. The entire room was suddenly flooded with light as someone switched on the overhead light. The bright light hurt his eyes. Squinting, he saw two policemen, one holding a flashlight, the other, a heavy-set man, aiming a gun at him.

"Are you all right?" asked the policeman who held the still-shining flashlight.

"Yes, I'm all right. What do you want?"

"Your wife sent us. You didn't come home and she was worried."

"Genevieve called you?"

"She told us you left around noon and hadn't come home." The heavy-set man holstered his weapon and stepped out into the living room.

Alfred swung his legs off the side of the bed. His neck and shoulders ached from the lumpy mattress.

"I guess I must have fallen asleep," he said.

"Are you sure you're all right?"

"Yes." He stood up. "I'm fine. I fell asleep."

He recognized the policeman with the flashlight, a young man of about forty. He was one of the officers who had come the night he had found Rudy lying on the living room floor. The young man and the other policeman had stood around Rudy's body, talking nonchalantly about the upcoming Thanksgiving holiday. To them, Rudy had been just another stiff.

The heavy-set policeman came into the room again. "Place is a mess," he said. He looked bored at finding nothing more than an old man who had fallen asleep on a bare mattress.

"I'm cleaning the place out," Alfred said. "Getting ready to sell."

"Big job," said the young policeman. He clicked off his flashlight and clipped it to his belt.

"You selling this bed?" asked the heavy-set one. "Nice piece. Solid brass."

His partner threw him an annoyed look. "Mr. Krause, you were yelling something when we came in. Sounded like 'No, No!'"

The sledding dream. Years since he had had it. Years ago, when he was just a kid, he had nearly been killed sliding down Ricketty Hill, rolling off the sled in the nick of time before it crashed into the tree at the bottom of the hill. Later that same day, Ralphie Treniery had not rolled off in time, hit the tree head-on, and died. For years after seeing Ralphie's limp, bloody body lying lifeless on the snow, he had plummeted down Ricketty Hill nightly in his dreams, unable to roll off the sled as the death tree reached for him, terrifying him. Yet each time he woke up screaming, the dream had somehow reassured him that he was alive.

Ralphie had died, and he had lived. He sank down on the bed again, overwhelmed by the randomness of accidents, of chance. Or was it chance?

"Are you sure you're all right?" the young policeman pressed.

"Yes, I stood up too quick is all."

"Go home, Mr. Krause," the young policeman said. "Your wife is worried."

Genevieve was at the living room window when he swung the pickup into the driveway. She was waiting for him in the kitchen when he came in the back door.

"I suppose you're mad at *me* now," she said, her arms folded across her chest. "But it's late, and I was worried."

"I fell asleep," he said sheepishly.

"You fell asleep? All afternoon?"

"I told you we should have left the phone hooked up," he said. "You could have called then."

He hung up his coat and cap in the back room, not at all mad at her. At least she was talking to him again. The kitchen felt warm after the chilly drive home from Rudy's. The starchy smell of boiled potatoes mingled in the air with the faint odor of fried meat. A cast-iron skillet, its bottom covered with grease that had turned white, sat on the front burner of the gas stove.

"I fixed supper," Genevieve said, "except for the gravy. I didn't know when you would be home."

He glanced discreetly at her to see if she had meant anything nasty by the remark. He felt awkward, the way their makeups always made him feel. Too often, one of them said something that shattered the fragile, wordless peace treaty they had negotiated almost before it began.

"Don't need gravy," he said. "Butter'll do."

He sat down at his place and watched her set the table and dish up the plates. Fried pork chops, boiled potatoes, green beans.

He felt ravenous, realizing that he had not had a decent meal in two days. He waited politely for Genevieve to say the simple grace that she always said before meals.

"In the name of the Father, and the Son, and the Holy Spirit. Amen," she began, crossing herself. "Bless us, O Lord, and these thy gifts, which we are about to receive from thy bounty, through Christ our Lord. Amen. In the name of the Father, and the Son, and the Holy Spirit. Amen." She crossed herself again.

He cut into one of the two pork chops on his plate.

"Tastes good," he said as he chewed the first bite. "We ain't had pork chops in ages."

Over dessert of home-canned peaches—his favorite dessert—Genevieve looked squarely at him from across the kitchen table. "Alfred, why don't you want to go? We had agreed to go, and now you buck up and say you won't go."

Now he understood the change of attitude, the pork chops, the home-canned peaches. It amused him, it was so transparent, so obvious.

"You said we could never afford to go when Janet was little," Genevieve said. "Or you were too busy. You always said we would travel after you were retired. Well, you're retired now, whether you like it or not, and here you are dragging your feet. I want to go on one trip before I die. I've never been anywhere. All I've ever done is stay home and take care of you and Janet and this drafty old house. Janet's lived in Houston two years now, and I want to go see her. See our grandchildren."

"I don't think staying home and taking care of your family is doing nothing," he said.

"I didn't say it was. That's not what I meant and you know it. I'm not one of those women who thinks *housewife* is a dirty word. I've always been happy to be at home—just as happy as *you've* been to have me here. I just want to go on a vacation."

"I can't go because we need to get Rudy's house cleaned out," he said, shifting the blame onto her shoulders. "You've been on me since before Christmas about it, saying I'm too slow."

"That can wait. It's been there since Thanksgiving. If we don't get done before we go, it'll still be there when we get back."

He put down his spoon, feeling like he was losing ground. "But you've been hounding me about it. You go ahead and go. That's okay by me."

"Well, I don't think that's the real reason you don't want to go," she said, her voice as stiff as one of the starched collars on his white shirts.

They finished their dessert in silence.

He left the table and went into the living room. The afternoon edition of the *Pioneer Press* was on the ottoman. He picked it up and checked the front page. The usual tragedies grabbed the headlines: fighting in distant countries where the U.S. had no business being; a young woman found dead along the banks of the Mississippi, foul play suspected. There had been a time when murders were rare in St. Paul. Like the Ruth Munson murder back in the thirties when he was a kid. The story had occupied the front pages of the *Pioneer Press,* the *Daily News,* and the *Dispatch* for days after her burned and mutilated body was found in an empty room of the abandoned Aberdeen Hotel, up in the Ramsey Hill section. The police had never solved the case, which only made it seem all the more sensational. Now, it seemed, the police were always finding bodies around town, along the river, in alleys, in marshes. No wonder Genevieve had called the police.

The afternoon treasure hunt clue was at the bottom of the page. Clue 5: *In a distant place they're running races, from the treasure site you can't see the runners' faces.* Now what did that mean? Runners running races.

Genevieve came into the room and lowered herself into her chair. He peered around the edge of the paper at her.

"Did you read this treasure hunt clue?"

"It didn't make any more sense to me than the rest of them did," she said. She picked up her *Reader's Digest,* opened it, and turned up the dog-eared page that marked her place. "Like the one about the queen and the river. That seems like a big clue, but I can't figure out what they're talking about."

He turned to the inside of the paper. "*Enter with a queen, leave via river, this little clue may make you shiver.* I don't know about that one, either. Maybe something to do with the river. This one—*Watch planes come and watch them go, leaving far behind all this ice and snow* — has something to do with planes landing and taking off. You can see planes from where the treasure is buried, I bet. That could be Mounds Park or Harriet Island again. You can see Holman Field from either place."

"Maybe it's the other airport," Genevieve said. "Are there any parks where you can see the big planes land and take off?"

"Cherokee Park, maybe," he said. "And there's that park below the Ford plant along the river. I don't remember its name."

"*I think I can, I think I can* in that one clue must refer to trains," Genevieve said.

He lowered the paper into his lap as the same memory drifted across his mind for the second time that day. "Remember how much Janet liked that book about the Little Train That Could? We must have each read it a thousand times to her."

Genevieve put down her *Reader's Digest.* She looked for a moment like she was going to cry. "Alfred," she pleaded, "come with me. I don't want to go alone. I've never flown in an airplane before. And Janet sounded so disappointed when I told her you weren't planning on coming."

He hid behind the paper again. He didn't want to undo things, to ruin the peace they had made. Yet going up in an airplane, hoping God didn't get distracted, that he couldn't do.

"I'll think about it," he said after a moment.

TWELVE

"BUT YOU SAID," CHRIS WAS SAYING in an insistent tone as he followed his father into the living room, where Sharon sat finishing her copy of *Inc.* magazine. "You said we'd talk about the clues tonight. This morning, you said." As she knew he would, Chris looked over to her for help, a pleading look on his face.

Over the top of her magazine, she watched her husband. You handle this one, she thought. You're the one who stayed at work until almost ten o'clock.

Phil slumped onto the couch and stretched out his legs. He threw his head back, and, staring at the ceiling, let out a long sigh.

"It's too late, Chris," he said, leveling what Sharon thought of as his supervisor's gaze on his younger son, a look meant to close the conversation. "I just got home and it's almost your bedtime."

But Chris held his ground. "You said we would," he pouted, pushing his luck to the limit. He planted himself squarely in front of his father. "I did my homework right after school so I'd be ready." The son keeping the father honest.

"Okay, okay." Phil held his arms in front of his face and ducked behind them, as though dodging a blow. A gesture of surrender. "Can I at least take off my coat and tie?"

He stood up and slipped off the dark blue suit coat and draped it neatly over the back of the couch. He loosened his maroon tie, unbuttoned the cuffs of his white shirt, and rolled up his sleeves.

"Fifteen minutes," he said, "and then it's bedtime. With no arguments. Deal?"

"Deal." Chris held out his open palm to take the skin the two of them always exchanged to seal the endless deals they negotiated.

"Where's your big brother?" Phil asked as the three of them trooped out to the table.

"He's upstairs talking on the phone," Chris said as he dropped his treasure notebook on the table in front of him.

On the phone. Sharon settled into her place at the table. The girl Lisa again?

"Go call him," Phil said.

"Jeff, get your buns down here! Dad's home!" Chris hollered, his voice cracking on the last syllable.

She slapped at him affectionately with the back of her hand. "You know better than to holler like that," she said. "At least go to the foot of the stairs before you holler."

"Do you ever get the feeling life imitates art?" Phil asked after Chris had scurried out of the room. "I swear to God I saw the Beaver yell for Wally exactly like that once. We think we're leading real lives, making real decisions about real things, but all we're really doing is acting out scenes from 'Leave it to Beaver.'"

"Except that Ward never came home at ten o'clock," she said. "Why so late tonight?"

"And June never ragged on Ward when he'd had a hard day at the office," Phil retorted.

"Well, excuse me," she said. "I'll just put on my pearl necklace and go vacuum the living room."

Phil gave her a forlorn look. "I'm sorry," he said. "I didn't mean to snap at you. Just a long day, that's all." Under the harsh yellow kitchen light, he suddenly looked tired, his eyes bloodshot, a thick blue sheen of stubble darkening his face. He unbuttoned his vest, a blank look on his face.

They heard the boys stampeding down the stairs.

"Wally and the Beaver never sounded like a herd of buffalo on the stairs, either," he said. "I swear they'll go right through the steps someday."

The boys arrived in a swirl of motion, dropping into their seats as if they were trying to win a game of musical chairs. Jeff carried the street map and the afternoon paper.

"Beat ya," Chris gloated.

"So what's the new clue?" Phil asked. His voice, she noticed, carried considerably less enthusiasm than it had that morning.

Jeff spread the paper out on the table in front of him. *"In a distant place they're running races, from the treasure site you can't see the runners' faces."*

"Read it again," Chris said. Jeff ignored him.

Phil ran a hand through his hair and rubbed the back of his neck. "Now that's a strange clue. Read it again." He listened, his head cocked to one side, as Jeff reread the clue. "Runners and races," he said after Jeff had finished. "That seems to be the key. Anyone have any ideas about what that means?" He looked around the table at each of them. "Come on you guys, think," he prodded, his voice tinged with impatience.

A distant place, she thought. Now that was the real key, at least as far as Phil was concerned, anyway. Ever since his excited telephone call to her at the bookstore yesterday morning, he had been in a distant place, overexcited, preoccupied. This late night, she felt in her bones, was connected somehow to the promotion offer.

"The marathon!" Chris said suddenly. "You know, we walked up to Summit Avenue and watched it last fall. Yeah, that's it," he shouted. "The marathon!"

"Not so loud, Chris," she said. "We're all right here." A pleasant memory. It had been a sunny, chilly Sunday morning last October when they had pulled on hooded sweatshirts and walked up Cambridge Avenue to Summit to watch the marathon leaders run by. Standing on the boulevard with a cup of coffee, joining with others from the neighborhood to applaud the sweating runners as they passed, she had—after a year-long marathon of her own—felt like a St. Paulite at last.

"That's a good suggestion," Phil said. "Write it down, Chris." He pointed at Chris's notebook. "Now, let's really analyze what this clue says. Jeff, read it again. Slowly." He listened as Jeff read through the clue, weighing the importance of each word.

"In a distant place they're running races," he repeated, half to himself, *"from the treasure site you can't see the runners' faces.* So," he concluded, "standing where the treasure is, you look at the place the races are being run. And it's too far away to see the runners' faces. So the treasure can't be on the marathon route, but somewhere that you can see from the marathon route."

"I was sure it was the marathon," Chris said dejectedly. "Shoot." He drew a square in the notebook, and colored it in with his marker.

"Don't get discouraged, Chris," Phil lectured. "You let yourself get discouraged, and you never accomplish anything. Where's the map?"

Jeff slid the map across the table toward him. She noticed that he had finally gotten it folded back into its original folds. Phil unfolded it, spreading it out like a tablecloth.

"What are all these red dots here?"

"The map's got the measles," Chris said. He giggled at his own joke.

"I looked up all of the Dairy Queens I could find, and marked them on the map," Jeff said. "There were thirty."

"Good job." Phil nodded his approval.

"None of them are right next to a park," Jeff said. "The green on the map means it's a park. I don't know for sure exactly where on the street some of them are. I sorta guessed on some of them. A lot of them are out in the suburbs. I guess they could be crossed off."

"Not necessarily," Sharon said. "What does the first clue say—something about Ramsey County?"

Jeff turned to the inside of the paper and searched for the earlier clues. *"Somewhere on the ground in Ramsey County, King Boreas has hidden his royal bounty."*

"Is there part of Ramsey County that isn't in St. Paul?" she asked.

Phil studied the map for a moment. "Lots of it."

"Then I'd say that any Dairy Queen in Ramsey County is a candidate," she said. "At least for the time being."

"You're probably right." Phil glanced over the map. "We'll have to consider them all. At least for now. So back to the marathon. What was the route for the marathon last year?"

"Along the Mississippi and then down Summit Avenue," Jeff said. "It ended up by the State Capitol."

Phil traced his finger along Summit Avenue. "Not much for parks," he said. "There's green along the river, and the street itself is green, but I don't think that's where the medallion is going to be. Remember, the clue hints that the place where the races are being run isn't the same place as the treasure site."

"It could be along the river," Chris said. "There's green there. Jeff said that means a park. Maybe that ties into the river mentioned in Clue 3. It'd be neat if there was a Dairy Queen nearby."

"I'm kind of bothered by the word *races*," she said. "The marathon is only one race. The clue says *races*. They're running *races*. I think it means some place where they run more than one race."

"You know, that's a good point," Phil said, nodding in agreement. "That's a really good point." A frown bent the corners of his mouth. "What would be other places where races are run?"

"Oh, I know. A college track. Like over at Macalester." Chris's enthusiasm had returned.

"That's the idea," Phil said. "College and high school tracks, maybe health clubs, too. Boys, here's your assignment for tomorrow night: plot out the locations of high schools, colleges, and health clubs on the map. See if they're near any parks. Check them against the Dairy Queens. See if there are any tracks near a Dairy Queen that's near a park of some kind. The ones that are, we'll have to check out 'on site,' as they say. Maybe we can take a drive by them tomorrow night—weather permitting. I heard on the car radio on the way home that it's supposed to snow tomorrow—a lot.

"Now," he said, jabbing a finger at Chris, "we had a deal, Slapshot, and we're already fifteen minutes past our fifteen-minute time limit. Get yourself off to bed. Both of you."

"But—" Chris protested.

"No buts," Phil interrupted, his voice suddenly sharp. "Get going."

Chris slammed the notebook shut, gave his father a dark look that made Sharon dread their future confrontations. He stalked out into the dining room. A moment later, they heard him trudging up the stairs, the Beaver being sent to his room to think things over.

Jeff took his time folding up the street map. She could see the wheels turning in his head, cranking out the words, lining them up.

"Dad, if we go out looking tomorrow night, can I have a friend come along?"

"Sure. I guess it's okay. Tell him to dress warm and wear his boots. We'll be just like the Steger Expedition to the North Pole. Nothing will stop us."

Jeff looked for a moment as if he wished he had not brought up the subject. She smiled at him and the color rose in his face. She had guessed right. It wasn't a 'him' who would be coming along. He looked for a moment as though he wanted to say something more.

"Yes?" she said.

"Nothing. G'night."

"Good night."

"Good night, Tiger." Phil crossed his arms on the table and rested his chin on them. He watched Jeff disappear into the dining room. In the light, she saw that his hair was becoming as much salt as pepper. Lover (though not like those days of high passion at Boston U), husband, father, high-octane sales manager, with a big promotion in his pocket if he accepted it. The organizer, the planner. The man who ran the show. But none of that registered on his tired face. The lights were on, as Jeff would say, but nobody was home.

"Penny for your thoughts," she said.

"I'd have to give you change," he said, his eyes not moving. "I was just thinking about how settled we are, and how much I hate the idea of packing up and moving off somewhere to start all over."

She tried to hide her surprise. Never in her life had she expected him to say something like that.

"Then other times," he continued wanly, "it doesn't seem too awful. We did it once and lived to tell about it." His eyes flickered up toward her, then fell away. "Hell, I don't know what to do." After a moment, he sat up straight in a sudden, swift movement. "Yes, I do, too."

Here it comes, she thought. The moment of truth. She felt her stomach turn a somersault.

"I'm going to bed."

She laughed, a wave of relief washing over her. It only lasted for a moment. There would be another day, soon, when jokes could not be made about it; a day when they would have to decide. She rubbed her eyes, suddenly tired herself.

"I told Elaine today, just so it wouldn't be a complete surprise to her."

"Well, don't call the real estate agent just yet," Phil said, planting his open palms on the table and pushing himself to his feet.

"What do you mean?"

"I mean that Wally and the Beaver might have a lot more chances to pound their way through our stairs." He patted her on the shoulder as he passed by.

"Good night, June."

WEDNESDAY

ONE

Steven stood in the shower, trying to pull a melody out of the sound of the rushing water. Sometimes he found his best tunes while standing in the shower where it was all steamy and warm, hot water running across his shoulders, down his back. The only trouble was he couldn't bring his guitar into the shower with him to put notes and chords together. Lying in bed, just after the alarm clock had gone off, he'd thought of this terrific lyric about a pair of young lovers searching for treasure—some fabled lost treasure—and at the same time searching for their own happiness. The words that had popped into his head would be for the chorus:

> They were searching,
> Searching for treasure,
> Searching for the love
> They once had,
> Searching for the times
> That were glad.

It would be a story song—a long one. He could picture the lyrics on the white album sleeve, filling one column and half of the next. It would be like Harry Chapin's song "Taxi." That was such a great, great song, so melancholy and sad.

He'd tell the story of the young lovers' search for the lost treasure in the verses, and the story of their search for happiness in the chorus. The Winter Carnival treasure hunt wouldn't work as the treasure they were trying to find. The record executives would think it was too local. He'd have to come up with some really good lost treasure for them to look for—something that was famous or really symbolic. Something totally mysterious.

The bathroom door opened suddenly, and he heard the clunk of the toilet lid against the tank. Debi, the world's greatest sleeper, astoundingly, unbelievably, was up. He peered around the shower curtain at her.

"Is the bed on fire or something?"

"Do you mind?" she said, frowning at him from the toilet seat, her voice hoarse from sleep.

"Excuse me. I *was* here first," he said, pulling his head back into the shower.

The water pressure dropped at the sound of the flush, and he automatically stepped away to avoid the rush of scalding water that would quickly follow.

The lid banged down on the toilet seat. The bathroom door slammed shut. A bathroom run. She was probably burrowing in under the covers again. He stepped back under the shower stream.

They'd made up, of course—they always did. Last night after their fight, he'd gone out and tried the Honda. It had rolled over encouragingly a few times before giving off that low growl that signaled a dying battery. He had called his pal Knickerson from work, and made arrangements for him to come over tonight and give them a jump.

He would like to have given Debi a jump, too, but one thing he had learned since their marriage was that you couldn't be mad at your wife one minute and then try to seduce her the next. Since she was awake, maybe they could do it this morning before they went to work. He shut the shower off, dried himself off with a towel, and wrapped it around his waist.

Debi was not in the bedroom where he figured she would be, nor was she in the living room. The front door was open, and he heard light footsteps running up the hall stairs. A moment later, she slipped through the doorway, carrying Fitzgerald's paper. Her T-shirt barely covered her ass.

"New clue," she said, holding up the paper.

"You went out in the hall like that?" he demanded.

"It's six-thirty in the morning. Who's going to see me? You're not exactly dressed for the day yourself. Or are you planning to go to work wearing just a towel?"

"I'm not out running up and down the stairs of a public hallway."

"Some public hallway. So dark you can't see your hand in front of your face. Did you tell Fitzgerald to change the bulb?"

"A week ago."

"Well, you better tell him again." She turned on the light behind the couch and curled up against the arm, pulling her T-shirt down around her.

"Okay," she said, snapping the newspaper open. "Are you ready for this? Clue 6: *Diamonds are a girl's best friend if you're talking rings, but think of boys and see what this clue brings.*" She peered around the paper at him. "What do you think that means?" Without waiting for an answer, she disappeared behind the paper again. "God, what a stupid clue. If diamonds are—"

"It's referring to a baseball diamond, obviously," he interrupted, sliding into the big chair. She was up and running for the day. There would be no quickie this morning.

The newspaper crumpled into her lap. "That's too easy."

"What else could it be?"

"I don't know. Maybe there's a jack or king of diamonds somewhere or something. Baseball diamond is just . . . dumb."

"Why is it dumb? Because you didn't think of it first?"

"Up yours, Carpenter." She disappeared behind the paper again. "You know, this is a sexist clue," she said. "I'm not a girl, I'm a woman. And besides," she peered around the newspaper at him again, "diamonds aren't my best friend. My best friend is a well-diversified stock portfolio, with the right mix of short-term and long-term investments, high and low risk."

He ignored her. Neither feminism nor the stock market were subjects he wanted to argue about with her this morning, or any morning for that matter.

"Baseball diamonds and running tracks," he said. "It has to be near a high school or college. Or a playground of some kind. What about that list of schools you were making up last night?"

"It's on the secretary."

He pushed himself out of his chair toward the secretary. Halfway across the room, his towel came apart and fell to the floor. Debi wolf-whistled. He responded by mooning her as he bent over to pick up the towel, hoping the sight might somehow arouse her interest. But she had already disappeared behind the newspaper again.

"All right," he said, snatching the list off the secretary. "If running races refers to running tracks, and diamonds refers to baseball diamonds, then it *has* to be near a school of some kind. All we have to do is figure out which school."

"You just said that," Debi interrupted. "And we made the same conclusion last night. I still don't buy baseball diamonds completely as a clue. Why would they give essentially the same clue again—twice in a row? Last night's clue indicated a school. Why would they indicate a school again?"

"Well, all of the clues indicate the same spot," he said. "The treasure spot." But now that she had raised the question, he wasn't so sure that both clues did refer to schools. The more you questioned things, the less sure of them you became. He returned to the big chair with the list of addresses.

"Well, at least one of these clues has to refer to schools. You sure you got all of 'em down here?"

"Yes," Debi said, clearly annoyed by the question. "Let's assume that the running races clue refers to schools. We've got to start somewhere. That would mean that diamonds must be something other than baseball diamonds."

"Like what?" he said. "In relation to boys, remember."

"I don't know. I'm just trying to get some ideas out, okay? Last night, we said we were going to drive by all these schools and look for parks or something nearby where the treasure could be. Maybe something will pop out at us if we drive by them."

"What we really need to do," Steven said, "is figure out what some of these other clues mean. We sorta junked everything we talked about on that clue about the queen and river. How did that go?"

Debi turned to the inside of the paper. *"Enter with a queen, leave via river, this little clue may make you shiver.* I still think that has something to do with the *Mississippi Queen."*

"Delta Queen," he corrected.

"All *right,"* she snapped, *"Delta Queen."*

"Just for the sake of argument, what else could it mean?" He felt chilly suddenly, sitting out in the living room in just a towel. Fitzgerald had probably been jacking around with the thermostat again.

"There's the Winter Carnival queen," Debi suggested. "Maybe there's a Queen Street somewhere. Yeah, that's it! *Enter with a queen.* Then you'd leave on the river. Maybe there's a Queen Street that runs up to the river."

"You know what?" She sat up swiftly, swinging her bare legs around onto the floor. "I bet that diamonds refers to the jack or king of diamonds. That ties into royalty as a theme."

"I still think diamonds refers to baseball or softball diamonds," he said.

"God," Debi said. "You're impossible. I'm going to go take my shower." She threw the newspaper at him as she rose from the couch and headed toward the bathroom.

Carrying the list, he followed her, shutting the bathroom door behind him to keep in the warmth. Debi pulled off her T-shirt and disappeared into the shower. A moment later, he heard the patter of the water against the shower curtain. He plunked down on the john to read through the list of addresses. None of them was familiar to him—some of the streets he had never even heard of, and there was no Queen Street on the list. The tiny room started to fill up with steam. Clearly, they needed help.

"Shit, I don't know where any of these schools are," he said over the rush of the shower. "We should get Knickerson at work in on this with us. He knows St. Paul pretty well."

"Why?" The question floated over the shower curtain at him like a puff of steam. "We'd just have to split the money with him. Just pump him for everything he knows, and then we'll look ourselves."

"That's not very fair."

"Who said anything about fair? There's money involved here. You don't get rich splitting your income with somebody."

He stood up and laid the newspaper on top of the toilet tank. He wiped the steam from the mirror with a washcloth, then opened the medicine cabinet and took out his electric razor.

"Why don't you ask somebody at your office about where it might be?" he said as he plugged the razor's cord into the outlet and switched on the razor. "Pump them." The razor's head felt cold against his cheek.

"Steven, don't be ridiculous. These are professionals. Major leaguers. They don't mess around with stuff like this."

"They're not all stockbrokers. How about What's-Her-Name, you know, the one with—"

"With the big boobs, I know. You mention them every time you see her. Jackie's a clerk. I don't hang out with the other clerks."

"What's wrong with them?" The shower stopped. The curtain was shoved aside. Debi, streaming wet, reached for a towel. She buried her face in it.

"What's wrong with clerks?" he demanded, turning to face her. "I'm a clerk. And so are you."

"Nothing's wrong with clerks. But you get judged by who you hang out with. You hang around with clerks, you're perceived as a clerk." She stepped out of the shower.

"You hang around the big shots when you're a clerk, and everyone thinks that you're a brownnoser, that you're sucking up. Or fucking up." He rubbed a hand across his face in search of missed whiskers.

Debi gave him a wounded look. "That wasn't very nice," she said in a hurt tone. "That was—"

"A low blow?" he said teasingly. Satisfied that he hadn't missed any spots, he shut the razor off and turned to put it back in the medicine cabinet.

Her towel caught him squarely in the back of the head.

"Hey," he said, whirling around. "I was just talking about what other people might say, okay? I know you're not . . . you know . . ."

"Fucking up?" Debi's eyes glinted with anger.

He reached out and put his hands on her shoulders. "Look," he said. "I'm sorry." He slid his arms around her and pulled her close to him. "I really mean it. I'm sorry." She laid her wet head against his shoulder. He felt the heat of her body against his chest.

"Honest, Deb," he said, pulling back to look in her face. "I didn't mean it the way it came out."

"You're forgiven, I guess." She pecked him on the lips.

He slipped his hand around the back of her neck, and pulled her head against his shoulder. It had been days since they had shared such a tender moment, and he wished it could last longer.

"Just so you know, Steven, I'd never do that." She pulled away from him. "I'd never screw the boss to get ahead."

She picked up her hairbrush and ran it through her wet hair. "But you're not the only one with big plans. I'm not going to rot away in St. Paul forever. New York is where the financial action is. If Mr. Savage ever gets transferred there like he wants to, he might take somebody along with him. It might just as well be me."

"You mean you'd move there? You've never even been there."

"No, but you never know. Maybe Mr. Savage will take me up the ladder with him, and I'll end up with a Wall Street office and make a hundred thousand dollars a year. Live in a Manhattan penthouse and everything."

"What about me?"

"If I get a job that pays a hundred thousand a year, you can quit being a library clerk and do your music. Are you through with the sink?"

"I still have to brush my teeth."

In the bedroom, Steven threw his towel on the bed and rummaged through his top drawer for a pair of clean underwear. Debi's idea of moving to New York was news to him. She had always talked about going to law school someday. He heard the sound of the hair dryer in the bathroom. He was down to the underwear with the stretched-out elastic. He'd have to get at his laundry tonight. Debi staunchly refused to do any of his laundry. It was some kind of power thing to her. He'd written a song about running out of clean clothes and having to dig dirty ones out of the hamper. "The Hamper Diving Blues" was the sort of song Steve Goodman would write if he were still alive. Or maybe Jimmy Buffet.

He pulled on his underwear, snapping the band around his waist to at least give the illusion of snugness. From the bottom of the drawer, he pulled out two white socks with unmatching stripes at the tops, and sat down on the bed to put them on. A sinking feeling settled over him the way it did so many mornings as he got ready for work. He hated the library. Not really hated it; he just wanted to be doing something else. He'd much rather work on his treasure hunt song. He hadn't practiced his guitar for two hours last night as he had promised himself. He looked over at the guitar case in the corner. Tonight, for sure. After he and Knickerson got the Honda jump-started. Two hours. Without fail.

New York. The words spun great images in his mind: Broadway, the Empire State Building, the Statue of Liberty, Central Park—places and things he had heard about all his life. It would be fun to go there. He had fantasized about touring there someday—selling out Madison Square Garden like the big rock and roll bands did. But living there. The idea sent a shiver down his back. Maybe they could get an apartment in the Dakota Building, like John Lennon did before he was killed.

His jeans, he decided, would last another day, although he had already worn them Monday and Tuesday. They felt cold as he pulled them over his legs. He slipped on a fresh T-shirt and pulled on a white ski sweater.

A hundred thousand dollars a year. He'd have to make a really good album to keep up with her—a Top Ten, or even a Number One.

Debi charged in from the bathroom to take another run at the world record for getting dressed. She ripped off her towel and flung it at the bed.

"I'm convinced," she said as she jerked open her top dresser drawer. "I think that diamonds refers to the king or jack of diamonds." A white bra, panties, and pantyhose sailed through the air toward the bed. "That ties royalty in as a theme. Remember in the first clue—royal bounty?" Her arms and legs flashed white as she put on her undergarments. "Then there was the queen clue. Now diamonds. I'll bet there's a boat on the river that's the *Jack of Diamonds* or *King of Diamonds*. The *Delta Queen* and the *Jack of Diamonds*. Or Queen Street and the *Jack of Diamonds*. That'd mean the treasure is along the river, maybe."

She strode over to the closet, disappeared inside briefly, then reappeared with her power outfit for the day, a bright red dress with a white blazer.

"But are there any schools along the river?" He jammed his feet into his tennis shoes. "And wouldn't that be giving the same clue twice? If Delta Queen meant the river, then using Jack of Diamonds to mean the river doesn't make sense."

"All the clues point to the same spot," Debi said as she pulled the dress over her head. "Maybe running races doesn't refer to school tracks at all." She adjusted the dress around her waist and buttoned the white buttons up the front.

"If that's the case," he said as he stood up, "then we're back to square one."

"So we'll read the next clue," Debi said. She picked up a pair of red high heels. "Are you ready? Let's go."

"You eating breakfast?" he asked as they passed through the living room.

"Uh-uh. There's a meeting this morning. There'll be donuts."

Steven snorted to himself. Where he worked there were never donuts. Just work. He stepped into the kitchen to grab an apple to eat on the way to the bus. When he came out of the kitchen, Debi already had her coat and boots on, and was unlocking the front door.

"You get to lock up," she said.

He grabbed his coat out of the closet, putting it on as he went.

The hallway was still dark, though the pale beginning of daylight lit the bottom of the stairs near the front door.

Halfway down the stairs, they saw the door to Fitzgerald's apartment open. The caretaker leaned out and peered around on the floor in front of his door. Muttering to himself, he reached back inside to switch on the outside porch light, then shuffled out into the hall. He opened the front door and stuck his head out into the cold. Through the glass transom above the front door, Steven could see snowflakes swirling like flying moths in the yellow porch light.

Fitzgerald turned around, slamming the front door behind him, just as the two of them reached the bottom of the stairs.

"Mr. Fitzgerald," Steven said uneasily. "How are you this morning?"

"Terrible, just terrible," the caretaker growled, shaking his white head. "Little snot of a paper boy didn't deliver my paper. Must've been scared off by the snow."

"Is it snowing?"

"Blizzard coming," Fitzgerald said. "When I delivered papers, we didn't let the snow stop us. No sir. We was responsible for them papers, and by god, we delivered 'em."

"Maybe it's just late," Debi said.

"Kids today." Fitzgerald shook his head again. "Too soft." The caretaker shuffled back into his apartment, slamming the door behind him.

Steven felt a spasm of guilt in the pit of his stomach. "I'd better go back up and get it."

"Why?" Debi hissed. "He never even suspected us. And why didn't you remind him about changing the light bulb?"

He turned to look at her for a moment, then started back up the dark stairs.

TWO

"I GET SO DAMN SICK OF WINTER about now," Bruce said as he backed the Camaro from his parking spot behind the building into the rutted alley. When he touched the brakes, the Camaro slid backwards on the thin layer of new snow that already covered the old ice.

"Yikes! It's slick already," he said.

The Camaro's headlight beams flashed through the gray morning light, alive with swirling snowflakes. They were businesslike snowflakes, the kind that signaled a lot of snow. The rush hour traffic was creeping by on South Robert Street, headed into downtown St. Paul for the day.

"That doesn't sound like a treasure hunter's feelings about winter," Joanna said from the seat beside him. "I think the new snow is pretty, even if you don't like it. Look how it freshens everything up." She pointed at the old snow piles pushed up on the South Robert boulevard. "The snowbanks look like they just got a coat of fresh paint."

"But you don't have to shovel the sidewalk on a corner lot," he complained, easing the Camaro forward so the tires would not spin.

"You'll have to shovel to find the treasure," she teased.

"That's different," he said. "Besides, if we're going to get six or seven inches of snow, I'd just as soon get it during the night so we could skip classes and stay home. I think it would be fun to get snowed in, don't you?"

"I'm sore," Joanna said. "I don't think I can stand any more fun. Shovel snow. Get some exercise. That'll get rid of the spare tire you were complaining about last night."

He felt her fingers digging playfully into his side through his down coat.

"Hey, cut it out," he said, shying away from her. "Let's get a paper."

He waited for a semi to grind by, then pulled out onto South Robert and almost immediately ducked off to the right into the SuperAmerica parking lot.

"You want anything, Jo?" he asked.

"Another hour of sleep."

"I'll see if they have one."

He left the motor running and was back in a moment.

"So what does it say?" Joanna asked as soon as he slid into the driver's seat and slammed the door. He answered by tossing the paper into her lap.

Joanna pulled off her white mittens and opened the paper. "Clue 6: *Diamonds are a girl's best friend if you're talking rings, but think of boys and see what this clue brings.* Well, even I know what that means," she said, glancing over at him. "Baseball and softball diamonds."

"Yeah, but which one?" he said. The Camaro fishtailed on the packed snow as he punched the gas to beat the light and get back onto South Robert ahead of the traffic. They headed north toward downtown.

"There's about a million baseball diamonds in town," he continued. "Every park's got at least one." He wiped the fog off the inside of the windshield. "One of these clues is going to have to give away something major pretty soon."

He fell in behind a battered Volkswagen, its rear bumper missing. Probably in the back seat, he thought, where the rear bumper of his old VW had spent most of its time.

He looked at Joanna out of the corner of his eye. She looked so serene and quiet, half-hidden in her lavender coat, as she scanned the headlines on the front page. He, on the other hand, felt edgy and tense this morning, his stomach already sour without even a single cup of coffee.

Last night she had said it, those three little words that both thrilled and terrified him, words he had longed to hear, yet dreaded. "I love you," she'd said after they got home from The Dive and settled into bed. It was not the first time the word love had come up. Jo used the word love to mean sex. "Such nice love," she often said afterwards, as she snuggled against him, her head on his shoulder. But this was different. This was the real thing. And, in a hailstorm of confused emotions, he had uttered those four little words that he knew spoke to obligation and expectation more than to love: "I love you, too," he had mumbled uncomfortably.

The house and kids, those pleasant fantasies that had floated through his mind a couple of nights ago, materialized in the snowflakes that seemed to dart at the Camaro's front end. Two nights ago, he had longed to hear those three little words. And now that he had heard them, well . . . He stole another glance at her, disguising it as a look down a side street for oncoming traffic. He felt a current of yearning burn through him. He had come to recognize it as a different kind of yearning from that which had haunted his thoughts about other women. With other women, he felt his yearning deep in his pants. But with Joanna, it was different. Snuggled in the covers together afterwards, her head against his shoulder, drifting in the cozy afterglow, he felt a satisfaction that ran far deeper than just sex. Never had he felt that kind of satisfaction before, not even when he lived with Michelle. He found the difference both curious and a little frightening. Did he actually love Joanna?

The Camaro slid to a stop behind a string of four cars. The light changed to green, and one by one the cars spun away.

"Do we have time to stop at the Busy Bee?" he asked, as they neared Page Street.

Joanna looked at her watch. "We can't stay too long. Classes start in half an hour."

"Ten minutes," he said. "Just long enough to have a cup of coffee and a donut."

He pulled the Camaro over to the curb and parked. "Bring the paper with you."

They hurried through the whirling snowflakes toward the Busy Bee's front door. The Busy Bee Cafe was just a little neighborhood cafe, with customers in flannel shirts and baseball caps who were as unpretentious as the fake wood-grain tables and red vinyl chairs. But the portions were tasty and large, and the prices were cheap. In the grim days following his breakup with Michelle, he had eaten out a lot. He'd gotten to know the owners, Connie and Gordon, and most of the cooks and waitresses.

The cafe was nearly full. Marci, the morning waitress, smiled at him from the kitchen window, where she was picking up an order. Connie waved at him through the kitchen window.

He held up two fingers, and then formed a circle with his thumb and forefinger, his signal to Marci for two cups of coffee and two donuts. He pointed toward a just-vacated booth along the south wall.

The seats were still warm from the previous occupants. Joanna pushed the dishes to the edge of the table where they could be picked up. Marci materialized with two white coffee mugs clutched in one hand, the Pyrex coffee pot in the other.

"Morning, Bruce," she said. "Hi, Jo." Here he was just Bruce Mitchell, not the Sundance Kid. Marci poured their coffee with a practiced hand, and picked up the dirty dishes with her free hand. "Be right back with your donuts."

"So Mr. Treasure Hunter," Joanna said, smiling over the rim of her coffee mug, "Where is it?"

"Como Park has ball fields," he said. "It could still be there." The coffee tasted strong, biting at his taste buds.

"Where do you really think it is?"

"Hell, I don't know." He set his cup down and scooped up the newspaper. "There must be something in these clues that will give us some ideas."

He turned to the inside of the paper, where the earlier clues were printed. Marci returned, setting down two saucers, each holding a huge glazed donut.

"Treasure hunting today?" she asked, leaving before either of them could answer.

He took a bite of his donut, reading through the clues to himself. He paused as a snatch of conversation from another table caught his ear.

"Well?" Joanna pressed.

"Shh." He motioned with a slight nod of his head at the table.

". . . I tell you, it's gotta be over around Mounds Park somewhere . . . ."

Bruce turned toward the table. A pair of hulking men hunched over a newspaper. The speaker wore a blue quilted vest over blue insulated coveralls. His thick beard was streaked with gray. A Twins cap pushed back on his forehead revealed a receding hairline. He looked about forty.

His friend wore a camouflage vest and a bright orange hooded sweatshirt over dark green coveralls. Both wore heavy, insulated boots. Bruce knew the uniform—they were construction workers off work for the day, hanging around the coffee shops for something to do.

"Look." Big Blue pointed with a thick index finger at the paper spread out between them. "There's the railroad yards down below the park along the river bottom. That's Clue 2. And the airport's right there. You can watch planes come and go from Mounds Park. That's Clue 4. There's joggers all over the place. That's Clue 5. And the Mississippi River's right there, too. That has to tie into Clue 3 somehow."

Bruce glanced at Joanna, arching his eyebrows.

"So what's the queen refer to?" Camouflage Man demanded.

"I don't know. Maybe there's a business named queen or a street."

"You could be right," Camouflage Man conceded.

"Could be, hell! I'm right. It's over there." Big Blue slammed a fist on the table. "Sure as hell. Four thousand bucks in the bag." He drained the last of his coffee with a gigantic swallow. The white mug clunked against the tabletop. "Let's go. I got two shovels in the back of the truck."

He pulled his billfold from his hip pocket, counted out four greasy dollar bills, and tucked them under the edge of the plate.

"You comin'?" Big Blue stood up. He looked like he weighed about 250 pounds, half of it belly.

Camouflage Man pushed back his chair and stood up. He pulled a pair of chopper mitts out of his vest pockets.

"We better walk right out there and pick that sucker up, Chuck, or I'm splittin'," he said as he shoved his hands into the mitts. "If I'm going to freeze my ass off outside, I might as well go to work and get paid for it."

"Oh, quit bitching, Lindstrom. It's something to do. Shit. Let's go."

Bruce watched them work their way through the maze of tables. The door banged shut behind them. He felt the blast of winter air move over him. Big Blue: St. John in another ten years. The guilt that he had felt last night outside The Dive came back.

"What?" he said, catching the questioning look in Joanna's dark eyes.

"You look funny."

"What do you mean, I look funny?"

"You have a funny look on your face."

He took another bite from his donut, chewed slowly, debating what to say. "It's nothing."

"Come on, what?" Joanna said.

"I was just thinking about St. John. I should have gone in and had another beer with him. He probably wanted to talk about something and I shut him down." He looked across the table into Joanna's eyes, remembering the same look yesterday in the cafeteria. "But I wanted to be with you."

A look of anger flashed over her face. "Don't blame me," she said stiffly. "I'm not going to be put between you two."

"I'm not blaming you! I'm—"

"Yes you are," she interrupted, her voice rising. "Yes you are. What you're saying—" The words came in a heated rush "—is that if it wasn't for me, you'd have gone back in with him. If that's not blame, tell me what it is!"

He stared across the table at her, anger boiling in his stomach. He felt old machinery starting up, words of defense—a counterattack—forming on his lips. But he bit them off. Don't screw this up, he told himself. Don't ruin things by being an asshole. This is too good to screw up.

"I don't mean to put you in the middle," he said softly, reaching across the table to take her hand. He traced the inside of her palm, conscious of how fine and delicate her hands were. "I shouldn't have brought it up."

"Not talking about it isn't going to make it go away, Bruce."

He looked up into her eyes. "Hey, make up your mind. You just jumped on me for bringing it up."

"*I* jumped on *you*?" Joanna jerked her hand away from his.

He looked away from her, over the heads of the Busy Bee's customers. An old Dr. Pepper clock hung on the north wall, the numbers 10, 2, and 4 in large red numerals, the red Dr. Pepper logo in place of the numeral 6. A relic from another time.

"Look, I'm sorry, all right?" he said, turning back to her. "It's not your fault. I just saw those two guys sitting there, and it made me think, wow, that's just what St. John'll be like in ten years: still banging around from one construction job to the next, getting old and fat. It bothers me, you know?"

"Maybe you two should spend some time together without me, so you can talk to him." She brushed a flake of glazed sugar from her upper lip.

"I don't know. All he wants to do is the same old stuff. He wants to go out looking for love, running around, all that Butch and Sundance shit. He's always said we'll never be taken alive. Sometimes I think he really believes we're going out together in a blaze of glory, like Redford and Newman did in the movie."

"I don't remember how the movie ended," she said.

"Butch and Sundance went to Bolivia to rob banks," he said. "They tried to go straight—tried to change—but they couldn't. So they just kept robbing banks. Finally they got cornered by about half of the Bolivian army in some dumpy little town. They holed up in a barn, and finally loaded their guns, and ran out into the street and got shot to pieces."

He finished his coffee and wiped his mouth with a paper napkin. "When you're twenty-five, going down in a blaze of glory seems pretty cool. It doesn't appeal to me much anymore."

"So what do you want, Bruce?"

"I don't know. I just know I should have gone in and talked to him," he said. And before Joanna could say anything, he pushed himself out of the booth. "Let's go," he said, digging in his pocket for a wad of crumpled dollar bills. "We're going to be late."

Outside, it was snowing a little harder. The traffic had picked up. The Camaro crept along behind a van which blocked most of the view ahead. They passed under the George Street viaduct and descended between the concrete retaining walls. At the bottom of the hill, a string of cars was lined up at the Concord Street light.

Joanna stared silently out her window, watching the drab buildings of the industrial park go by. He felt uncomfortable in the silence and responsible for it.

South Robert Street curved sharply to the left. Making this curve always fascinated him. Pulling out of his alley and heading north, it seemed like north, and he knew exactly where he was going. But making this curve and heading across the bridge into downtown, the city's skyline looming up before him, also seemed like going north.

They started across the Robert Street Bridge into downtown St. Paul, the frozen Mississippi below them. To the west, the NSP smokestack was a ghostly column, its lights flashing, throwing strange flickers against the falling snow. On clear days, he could see beyond the NSP stack, past the Schmidt brewery, all the way to Ft. Snelling. To the east, the bluffs of Mounds Park hunched together, towering over the railroad yards and the great bend in the Mississippi. They heard the roar of a small passenger jet rising up over the river bottom into the snowy sky.

At the north end of the bridge, he turned left onto Kellogg Boulevard and fell in behind a lumbering MTC bus. They passed the Radisson Hotel. He gunned the Camaro through the Wabasha Street traffic light. As usual, the traffic looked backed up on the Wabasha Bridge, commuters like himself headed into downtown from the West Side.

Across the river, the low profile of the Harriet Island pavilion was barely visible in the snowy gray daylight.

"There's softball fields on Harriet Island," he said, suddenly and inexplicably remembering a softball game played on a breathless, scorching Sunday afternoon at one of Michelle's office picnics. "Maybe the medallion's hidden there."

Joanna looked at him. "Maybe," she said. "I'm sorry I snapped at you."

He reached out beside him and felt for her hand. "I love you," he said, keeping his eyes on the road ahead. He felt a little squeeze on his hand.

THREE

THE NOVA SLID SIDEWAYS ON THE PACKED SNOW as Keith headed out of Phalen Park on Johnson Parkway. The snow was coming down hard enough to keep the windshield wipers busy as the flakes melted against the warm glass. It had been a waste of time taking a swing through the park. Although he had found baseball diamonds at the Phalen Recreation Center, the closest railroad tracks, according to the pink lines he had drawn on his map, were actually up in the part of Phalen Park that lay in Maplewood. The Maplewood city officials had, of course, kicked up such a fuss about the terrible destruction by treasure hunters on two different occasions that the medallion was certainly not hidden anywhere within Maplewood's city limits. And finally, the only planes that came and went were the passenger jets in their long descent toward the Twin Cities International Airport.

He should have followed his gut feeling and skipped Phalen Park altogether. Coming out at all this morning had been something of an impulse. He should have been working on his queen and river names in Clue 3, but the need to get out and actually look had flooded over him; so he had packed up the Nova with his newspaper, map, a thermos of coffee, and a shovel, and hit the street. Others, he knew, were already out looking.

He drove through Phalen Shopping Center. Mounds Park, he thought—now *that* had possibilities. Railroad tracks were just below the bluff, according to his map, and the downtown airport was just across the river. Planes landing and taking off would be within sight of the park. There were joggers there, certainly, within season. Maybe he would spot a street name from his list of queen and river names. It all hinged on the baseball diamonds. If he found baseball diamonds, he'd start looking for a place to dig.

The Nova passed under a railroad trestle, and a minute later, he pulled up at the Seventh Street traffic light. The SA's parking lot was about half full of cars. For a moment, he was tempted to pull into the lot and run in to see if Toni Stoltz was working today, but before he could decide the light changed to green. A horn sounded behind him. He floored the accelerator, spinning through the intersection.

The tidy little houses along Johnson Parkway looked much like the houses of Silver Bay that were built in the fifties during the mining boom. His parents' house, in fact, would blend right in with any of these little bungalows. Perhaps it was for this reason that he didn't feel very much at home here, even though he had lived in one East Side apartment or another since he first came down to the Cities. While the modest houses of the newer parts of the East Side at least looked pleasant, if undistinguished, the older sections, like along Payne and Arcade Avenues, looked shabby to him, old houses shoehorned together on tiny lots. But East Siders maintained a fierce loyalty to their roots, and he had learned long ago to keep his opinions about the East Side to himself.

Johnson Parkway ended at Burns. He turned right and almost immediately veered left onto Mounds Boulevard, chugging uphill into a wooded area. A sign at the intersection of Mounds and Thorn announced his entrance into the park. Near the top of the hill, the street wandered toward the edge of the bluff. Behind the stand of trees he could sense, more than see, the great drop to the flood plain two hundred feet below.

Ahead on his left, the park shelter materialized from behind a curtain of falling snow. Clustered around it were the half-dozen Indian mounds that had given the park its name—huge white lumps rising ten or twelve feet above the ground.

He pulled into the empty parking lot, drawing up next to the curb, and killed the Nova's engine. The park was scarcely a block wide; he could look north across the snowy expanse and see the houses on the other side. A chain link backstop stood about a hundred yards away. A thrill shot through him—that satisfied Clue 6.

He hopped out of the car, unlocked his trunk, and pulled out his shovel. The snow was coming down a little harder than when he had left the apartment. An inch-and-a-half of new snow had already fallen, covering the foot or so of old snow that was on the ground.

At the backstop, he rested his forehead against the cold metal wire, and surveyed the snowy field. This was not a regulation baseball diamond. Deep right field was on higher ground than the infield, which would have killed ground balls rolling into the outfield. Deep left was dotted with small trees. The backstop had acted like a snow fence. On the north side of it, the snow was about three feet deep, swept up against the chain link wire by the north wind into a long, low snowdrift that stretched from the backstop out toward the pitcher's mound. Picking a place to dig was going to be a problem. None of the first six clues gave any hints about *where* in the park the medallion was hidden—in whatever park it was hidden. Where would he put the medallion if he were hiding it on a baseball diamond? The backstop seemed like the most likely place, probably on the front side where the snow was deepest, the work the hardest. He moved around to the end of the backstop and tested the drift with his shovel. It seemed hard as cement. This was going to be real work.

He dug out a trench about two feet back from the wire, listening for the sound of the shovel striking some object as he drove it into the snow with his foot. The medallion could be loose, or it could be glued into a candy wrapper, or hidden inside a rolled-up newspaper. He inspected each shovelful of snow for foreign objects before heaving it aside.

It took him ten minutes to dig along the length of the backstop, and he was sweating by the time he finished. Sweat dampened the hair under his stocking cap, and trickled down his ribs beneath his shirt. An ache had settled into his lower back. He straightened up slowly, and looked with disappointment at the trench he had dug. The snow was only a foot deep behind the backstop. He shoveled his way along the length of the backstop, listening, inspecting, and again came up with nothing. He leaned against the backstop to rest.

Where to look now? Staring through the wire, he noted where home plate was, then trudged around the backstop to the spot. He dug out the snow to the ground in a circle about six feet in diameter and found nothing. Next, he dug out the pitcher's mound; then first, second, and third bases. Nothing. Perhaps it wasn't on the ball diamond itself, he thought as he rested on the handle of his shovel. Maybe the diamond only marked the area, and it was hidden nearby. He crawled under each of the nearby picnic tables to see if the medallion had been fastened underneath the table or the seat. He dug through the frozen ashes of the lone charcoal grill, finding nothing.

There weren't any obvious places left to search. Maybe the clues had something hidden in them that he had missed, something that he could spot now that he was here. It was worth going back to the car to reread them. He retraced his tracks out from the car, which were nearly filled with new snow. The Nova's windshield had already begun to frost over. He unlocked the door and crawled in.

He read every clue carefully, letting each word sink in, then looked across the park, hoping some word would click, that the tumblers would suddenly fall into place.

By the time he studied the landscape for the sixth time, he was convinced he had wasted his time. The problem was where else to look. Where else—

A tap on his side window made him jump. An old face, puffy and reddened by the cold, peered at him through the frosted window. For an instant, he thought it was his old man. The same bushy eyebrows, the same thick black glasses that slightly distorted the boozy, red eyes. Keith rolled the window down about halfway.

"Didn't find it, huh?" the man yelled. His breath rolled out in a cloud. Keith half expected a blast of whiskey breath but smelled nothing.

"Find what?"

"The medallion. What do you think I'm talking about, Carver's Cave? If you find that, let me know!"

"I'm not looking for the medallion."

"And I ain't standing here freezing to death in the snow, either. I seen you digging a few minutes ago. And what do you call that stuff?" The man gestured toward the map spread out across the steering wheel.

"If you ain't looking for the medallion, then you must be one of them drug dealers I keep readin' about, meetin' up in some strange place with somebody to sell drugs. You look like you could be a drug dealer." He straightened up and surveyed the Nova with a sweeping glance, then leaned into the open space of the window again. "This ol' car looks like the sort of junker a drug dealer would drive." The man's eyes twinkled behind the thick lenses.

"All right," Keith said. "So I'm looking for the medallion. So what?"

"Knew it. You don't look like no drug dealer. I just said that to get you to admit it." The man coughed and turned away to spit.

"Well, Sonny," he said, turning back, "don't worry about me. I ain't gonna steal your ideas; they probably wouldn't do me any good, anyway. Been looking for thirty years and I ain't found it yet. Probably never will, neither." He coughed again, a long, railing cough. Bending over double, he coughed a third time and spat a gob of phlegm into the snow.

"Damn old cold keeps hangin' on. Used to look just nights, now I got all day to look, too. Retired last summer. The wife chases me out of the house, says I get underfoot. She'll change her tune when this cold turns into the pneumonia and I die from it. Mind if I get in a minute?"

Without waiting for an answer, he started around the front of the car toward the passenger side. Reluctantly, Keith leaned across to unlock the door.

". . . Worked for the railroad," the man continued as he crawled into the car, slamming the door so hard that the whole car shuddered. "And I mean the real railroad—not this pissant organization they call a railroad nowadays. What a laugh. The old robber baron would have a heart attack if he seen what they've done to his railroad. Damn glasses—"

The old man pulled off his fogged-over glasses and rummaged around in his pocket. He pulled out a red bandanna.

"Used to work in the yards all over St. Paul." He inspected the bandanna for a place clean enough to wipe his glasses. "Como, Dale Street, Jackson Street. Most of 'em are gone now. Turned into shopping centers or some such thing." He jammed the glasses back on his face, and returned the bandanna to its pocket.

"Name's O'Conner," he said, extending a thick-fingered hand. "Ralph O'Conner. St. Paul Irish. Don't know where they came up with the Ralph."

"I'm Keith."

"First name or last?"

"Just Keith."

"Where you from, Just Keith?"

"Around," Keith said, irritated by all the questions.

"You know, Just Keith, you ought to lighten up a little bit. Life's too short to walk around with a sour look on your kisser, suspicious of everything."

"Maybe you ought to mind your own business," Keith said bluntly. "Or get out."

"Well, now," O'Conner said, undaunted, "you sound just like Mabel. She's always telling me to mind my own business, every time I try to get fresh with her." The eyes twinkled again. "Maybe I'll just do that. Get the pneumonia and die. That'd show both of you."

"Well, don't die in my car," Keith said.

O'Conner laughed a loud, rattling laugh that ended in a cough. "That's more like it. So where do you think it is?"

"Where what is?"

"The medallion. Are you going back to that old game?"

"I don't know," Keith said.

"Me neither," O'Conner said. "But it ain't here. I figure it's up by Lake Phalen now."

"I don't think so," Keith said.

O'Conner gave him a mischievous look over the top of his glasses. "You wouldn't say that just to throw me off the trail, now would you, Just Keith?"

"No." The old man's frankness was so wide open that it seemed to require openness and honesty in return. "There's baseball diamonds there, but the railroad tracks are too far away."

"Well, I probably will end up waitin' for the last clue come Saturday, when they tell you right where to look, just like I do every other year," O'Conner said. "Then I'll go out there and some intelligent, eager soul with an ax will cut off my toes because he thinks I'm standing on top of the stupid thing."

He coughed violently, folding his arms over his stomach, bending over so far that his forehead nearly touched the dash.

"I better get going before I die in your car," O'Conner wheezed. "You wouldn't want that, now would you?" He opened the car door. "Good luck to you, Just Keith."

"It's Keith Reynolds."

"Well, so long, Keith Reynolds." O'Conner extended his hand. Keith hesitated a moment before extending his own. He felt his fingers being crushed by O'Conner's powerful grip.

"If I don't find it, I hope you do," Keith said.

O'Conner threw back his head and laughed. "If I don't find it, I hope nobody does." He slammed the door behind him. As he slogged away through the falling snowflakes, Keith saw him bend over and spit into the snow.

Keith reached into the back seat for his thermos. He opened it and poured coffee into the cup. The aroma filled the Nova's interior. O'Conner had crossed the park and was walking west along the street. He was a funny old coot, a real talker. Not a bit like his old man after all. His old man didn't say more than ten words a day, unless he was drunk. His old man. What a laugh, to borrow O'Conner's phrase. Stuart A. Reynolds, unemployed mechanic for the mining company, sitting around Silver Bay for the past half dozen years, drinking up his wife's meager salary while he waited in vain to be called back to work.

He hadn't been home for years, not since that Thanksgiving Day when Sandy had finally met his family. After a year of putting it off, he had finally given in to both her and his mother, and taken Sandy home to meet the family. His brother, Kevin, and sister, Karen, were there from Duluth with their families, as were assorted aunts and uncles and cousins he saw at holidays, weddings, and funerals. They were all there to meet the future Mrs. Keith Reynolds.

Most of them had been out of work for nearly a year, and the group talked of nothing else. His old man, already half in the bag before Macy's Thanksgiving Day Parade was over on television, dominated the conversation, waving his drink around at the unemployed uncles and cousins.

"If we could just get a couple of breaks, we could beat the pants off that cheap foreign steel. I know we could. Putting them foreigners out of business with good-quality American steel, now that'd be the coop-dee-grace."

"It's pronounced coo-day-graws, Dad," he had corrected, embarrassed. "Huh?"

"It's pronounced coo-day-graws."

His old man had looked into his glass for a long moment, then up at him, his red face set in that murderous look that the whole family had come to know all too well.

"You think you're pretty smart, don't you? Because you went off to college. And whose money did you spend to go? Mine. Went off to become a hot-shot biologist. The next Jonathan Sack, you said. And what happened? You quit."

"Jonas Salk, Dad," he had said. "And I finished. I worked in a lab for almost five years before I got out of it. I just wasn't into it."

"You go off to college," his father snarled, ignoring him, "on some-one else's money, and then you just throw it all away because you weren't 'into it.' You think I was into being a mechanic all these years?"

"Please, Stuart, let's not get started," his mother had pleaded.

"You go to school on someone else's money, then throw away a whole career because your weren't 'into it.' Then you got the nerve to come back here and look down your nose at the man whose money you spent."

The aunts and uncles and cousins had sat silently at first, wide-eyed and embarrassed, wishing they were somewhere else. Then, one by one, they had slipped into the kitchen or out the front door. Kevin and Karen had melted away, too, as they always did, leaving him squared off against the old man alone.

"I told you you would never amount to anything, didn't I?" his father said, refilling his glass at the makeshift bar set up on the top of the television set. "And I was right."

"Yeah, and you were going to be the next shop foreman, too," he had fired back. "Make big money. I didn't see your Cadillac parked in the garage."

"Hey, it's not my fault they laid me off."

"Why don't you go someplace else and get a different job instead of sitting around here shit-faced all the time? Other *men* are doing it."

The insults had flown like knives back and forth across the room. Sharp, piercing.

Finally, he had lost both his patience and his temper. "Hey, get off my case. Just fuck off!"

"Stop it! Stop it!" his mother had screamed, wedging herself between them. "Keith, I won't have that word used in my house. Not on Thanksgiving, not on any day."

"Yeah," his old man chimed in. "You can just get the hell out of my house until you can show some respect for your elders."

He and Sandy had left then, before dinner was served. He remembered as he headed through downtown how tired everything had looked in the house: the large brown coffee stain on the wallpaper of the dining room that wasn't there the last time he had been home; the sag in the center cushion of the couch, and its threadbare arms.

"You see why I hate going home," he had said to Sandy as they headed toward Duluth. The rest of the drive home had been almost wordless.

His phone had been ringing when they got back to St. Paul.

"He was drunk when he said that," his mother apologized, her voice tight and sad with embarrassment. "He's sorry."

"Why do you have to apologize for what he said, Ma?"

"He can't come to the phone right now."

"What's the matter?" he had said cruelly, "is he passed out on the floor?" His mother's silence had indicated he was right.

His mother's peacemaking efforts had been diligent. "He's going into treatment," she had told him in the spring following that awful Thanksgiving. "He's been sober a year," she had informed him the next year. And most recently: "Dad really misses you," she had written at the bottom of the Christmas card she had sent him last month. "He'd be glad to see you, if you just came home."

Stuart A. Reynolds. A real piece of work. His old man had completely missed the handwriting scrawled on the brick walls of the shuttered buildings along the main drag—hadn't foreseen the shutdown, hadn't recognized the end of an era. His old man had stayed in Silver Bay, withering away. Toni Stoltz and her husband had given up on Silver Bay, had moved down to the Cities, and withered away anyway. And himself: a computer programmer working for a company that climbed all over you because you forgot to fill out a goddamn vacation slip. Not exactly setting the world on fire, as Toni put it. It was a long way away from what he had started out to be. He *had* wanted to be the next Jonas Salk, to make great discoveries that benefited humanity. His dream had gone no further than a biology major in college and a few years of work in a research lab. There had been no enlightening discoveries that benefited humanity, only long hours of boring tests, and a supervisor who ragged on him for the slightest mistake, the slightest variation in procedure. After five years of frustration, he had gone home from work one day and never returned. There had been a year or so of kicking around, and then Jerry had gotten him interested in computers. A stint in programming school, and here he was, working under his friend who wore a necktie to work and acted like a boss instead of a friend.

He stared out across the park, watching the heavy snowflakes fall from the gray sky. A big man in a blue quilted vest and another in a camouflage vest and orange sweatshirt shuffled by, carrying shovels over their shoulders. They headed toward the backstop.

It would be nice to hunt for the medallion with somebody. A gray feeling of loneliness settled over him as softly as the snowflakes swirling around outside the car.

FOUR

"ELAINE, DO YOU KNOW WHERE THERE ARE any baseball diamonds?" Sharon asked over her shoulder, as she hung her coat on the little hook on the back of the bookshop's door.

Her partner answered from her place behind the elevated counter without bothering to look up. "What do you want with a baseball diamond this time of year?" The fingers of her right hand danced over the calculator, adding up dollars and cents.

"The treasure hunt," Sharon said. "Clue 6 in this morning's paper." She unzipped her boots and stepped out of them. "Didn't you read it?"

"Oh, that," Elaine said. She hit the Total key on the calculator. "I never pay any attention to it." She frowned at the total. "That doesn't look right." Her fingers danced again.

"I thought everybody in St. Paul dropped whatever they were doing during the week of the treasure hunt."

"Not this kid," Elaine said.

Sharon slipped into the tennis shoes that she kept at the store. She pulled the morning paper from the tote bag she carried in lieu of a briefcase, and spread it out on the counter.

"Diamonds are a girl's best friend if you're talking rings, but think of boys and see what this clue brings. Phil and the boys are convinced that it means baseball diamonds. At least that's what they guessed this morning at breakfast."

"When Nicholas played in Little League last summer, we must have been to every baseball diamond in town," Elaine said, "but I couldn't find a single one of them now." Her fingers continued their dance.

"We promised the boys we'd go out looking tonight if it doesn't snow too much. Come on, Elaine. You must remember how to get to *one* of them."

Elaine hit the Total key on the calculator again and looked up. "You of all people should know how I am about St. Paul geography." She wrote the total down in the ledger. "Good news. We're running almost 7 percent ahead of our projected revenues."

"Look out, chain bookstores, here we come," Sharon said. She folded the newspaper and returned it to her tote bag. She *did* know how Elaine felt about St. Paul, recalling many times that cloudy October day over a year ago when the two of them had been out scouting store locations and Elaine had gotten hopelessly lost. When she had teased her about it, Elaine had lashed back in anger: "I know how to get to the grocery store, where the boys' schools are, how to get to the Rosedale shopping center, and where the nearest movie theater is. That's all I want to know about St. Paul."

While Elaine drove around in search of a familiar landmark, she had sat speechless in the passenger seat, shocked into silence, rethinking the whole idea of a bookstore partnership with this woman who flew off the handle so easily. It turned out that they were only ten blocks from Elaine's house. Once inside the safe haven of the Murphy garage, Elaine had slumped over the steering wheel as the automatic garage door closed behind them and the interior of the garage grew dark. When she spoke, it was with a voice that was near tears.

"I'm sorry I snapped at you. I didn't . . . It's just that . . ." She had looked up then, her face lined with an expression that Sharon couldn't read. "To tell you the truth, I don't *want* to know where anything is. Before, when we moved to a new place I really threw myself into the community, you know, PTA, Junior League, all that. But now . . ." She gathered up her purse and opened the car door. "Now," she continued, in full control of herself again, "I don't want to know much about where I live. You know how soldiers in the war movies don't want to be friends with anyone because it hurts when they die? You get to know a place and it's too hard to leave."

Until two days ago, Elaine's stubborn refusal to learn anything about St. Paul had left her amused and a little puzzled. But now—thinking of her own painful adjustment to St. Paul, and the prospect that it was all for naught, all to be gone through again—she at last understood.

"Any business?" she asked Elaine.

Elaine looked down at her with her are-you-kidding look. "Loads," she said. "It's been like I-94 in here this morning . . . on Sunday. During a blizzard."

"That good, huh?"

"That good." Elaine bent over the ledger again. Her fingers tapped in the figures—the store's past, its future.

Sharon got a fresh dustcloth from the box under the counter. It was an old linen napkin from a set that she had brought from Boston. She had finished dusting the Literature section yesterday and left off halfway through the Westerns. Science Fiction, Mystery, and Romance still needed their monthly dusting—not that romances hung around long enough to collect much dust.

She found her place in the Ls, amid the tattered copies of the handful of westerns Elmore Leonard wrote before he switched to crime novels. She looked at the dustrag in her hand. The little things you remembered. She had set the table with these napkins for their first Sunday dinner in St. Paul, and Chris had spilled chocolate milk in his lap, staining this very napkin so badly that it never came out. She'd finally given up on getting it clean and consigned it to the rag drawer in the basement. Ironic that she should reach under the counter and come up with this particular napkin, on this of all days. Just the sight of it stirred painful memories.

For weeks after moving in, she felt like she and Phil and the boys were staying at someone else's house on an extended vacation, and that one day—soon, she hoped—they would pack up and fly home to Boston. But the blazing days of autumn had given way to the bitter days of winter and the vacation dragged on. And on. Now, deep in the cold heart of their second winter in St. Paul, the hope of one day packing up and going home had dimmed; but she still mourned—privately, of course— the loss of old haunts and old traditions back home in Boston. Back home.

In those first months here, she had missed the ocean like a close friend, longing for a walk along the beach, with the brooding, restless Atlantic foaming over the sand beside her. And she found herself missing a hundred little things she had once taken for granted: being able to run to the fish market for really fresh seafood, strolling through the shops on Newbury Street, afternoon tea at the Ritz Carlton. She missed dinner at the Union Oyster House, with a trip afterwards to Bailey's for a hot fudge sundae, thick fudge running over the side of the silver dish. She even missed Fanueil Hall and the Old State House, tourist traps she hadn't visited in years. Just knowing they were there to visit if she had wanted to had always been enough.

Those early months of learning how to get around: during the day when the boys were in school and Phil at work, she had taken long walks through her neighborhood; and then, map spread open on the car seat, she had taken to the streets in the Taurus, exploring in turn the West Side, the East Side, the Midway district, and Frogtown, St. Anthony, and a score of little neighborhoods without names, searching for connections, footholds in this strange little city-town. Early in her travels, she had spotted a colonial tower on the horizon that reminded her of the Old State House, and after working her way through the maze of St. Paul streets, found it to be—much to her disappointment, which then gave way to amusement—a Montgomery Ward store.

Through her journeys, she assembled her own perceptions of St. Paul, independent of the glossy picture books they bought the day they purchased the house, independent of Phil's pronouncement that it was a nice town (What did he know? He was as bad as Elaine when it came to getting around, one of the St. Paul-impaired.).

St. Paul, she observed, was remarkably clean, free of the decades of soot that had blackened the old buildings in the heart of Boston. It was also prosperous. The bad sections of the city that her elderly new neighbor warned her about ("Our kind don't drive through there, dear") were elegant when compared to Roxbury, where whites really didn't drive, or even South Boston's block after block of battered brownstones.

She preferred St. Paul to Minneapolis. St. Paul was an eastern city, conservative like Boston in embracing the postmodern world. It had a sense of history, albeit Victorian history, of which people were proud. Minneapolis, on the other hand, with its postmodern buildings and trendy attitudes, was more of a western city, eager to embrace anything new or anything that would bring in the bucks.

The St. Paul Public Library building looked vaguely like the Boston Public Library. Cass Gilbert was the St. Paul equivalent to Charles Bulfinch. The St. Paul Chamber Orchestra was neither the Boston Pops nor the Boston Symphony. And so on.

Now all that discovery, all that effort, was threatened. St. Paul wasn't Boston, but the known was certainly preferable to the unknown, to another city to be explored.

The shop door opened for the first time since she had come in. The customer was a well-dressed man about thirty-five or forty, who looked like he had stopped to kill time between appointments. He wore a blue cashmere overcoat, with a maroon scarf peeking above the black lamb's-wool collar. Without giving herself away, she watched to see what books he picked up. He ignored the romances and science fiction, working his way through the Literature section, looking in turn at a succession of books by Fitzgerald, Faulkner, and Hemingway. In the Ms, he lingered over the Larry McMurtry titles, then picked up a copy of Melville's

Moby Dick, which he carried with him. He looked at the Steinbecks and the Twains, and then went back to the Ms and slid *Moby Dick* back into its place.

The man looked over and caught her looking at him. A smile formed under his mustache. "Guess I better pass," he said apologetically. "I can't find the time to read the stuff I want to, let alone the stuff I should." He left the shop, quietly pulling the door shut behind him.

She went back to her dusting. The stuff I should read. Didn't *anyone* want to read real literature anymore?

"So has your husband said yes to the promotion and put the house up for sale, ready to uproot the family against its will, all for a bigger title and even longer hours than he has now?"

It sounded like a line right out of a television sitcom. Sharon looked around the shelf of books at Elaine, still sitting behind the counter.

"Did you rehearse that?"

"No, I've been doing it live on stages across the eastern half of the country for the past ten years. Why would I need to rehearse?" Elaine put the calculator under the counter.

"I don't know." Sharon moved around the shelf and leaned against the counter. "He didn't sound very decided last night. He told me not to call the real estate agent yet."

"Oh, don't let him fool you. That's just part of the song and dance. Dean agonized—" Elaine clenched her fists and scrunched up her face in an exaggerated expression of agony "—just *agonized* over every transfer and promotion he's ever been offered—and he's accepted every one of them."

Sharon ran the dustcloth over the top of the counter. The action made her feel like a waitress again, back at the coffee shop on the Boston U campus.

"I worry about the boys," she said. "How did your boys take the last move?"

"Nicholas seemed to do okay. As long as he can play baseball in the summer and hockey in the winter, I don't think it makes much difference where he lives. But Martin had a harder time, I think. High school's such a hard time to move. He never talks much about Westport. Or Cleveland or St. Louis, for that matter. But his grades always slipped."

"It was just the opposite with us. Jeff did okay. It was Chris who had the trouble."

"There you go," Elaine said. "Add it up— the mommy, number one son, number two son—and it all says it's hard to move, no matter what age you are. You'd think the daddies would catch on wouldn't you?"

"I just worry that they've got roots established here now, and that moving will be hard on them. Jeff has a girl friend. She lives on Summit Avenue, no less."

"Oh, boy." Elaine laughed, throwing her hands up in the air. "The next thing you have to worry about is becoming a grandmother. Every time Marty comes up to me and says, 'Ma, I gotta talk to you,' I think, oh, no, here it comes, he's gotten somebody pregnant."

A grandmother, Sharon thought. Not at forty. Please, God, don't do that to me.

"I assume one of you talked to him about the birds and the bees?" she asked.

"I did when he was twelve," Elaine said. "I can't depend on Dean to do anything like that. It's not connected to his paycheck. I don't know who was more embarrassed about it, Marty or me."

Sharon propped her elbows on the counter and rested her chin in her hands. "We were going to be so much more open with our kids about sex than our parents were with us," she mused. "What happened to us?"

Elaine propped her own elbows on the counter, in imitation, and leaned in to within an inch of her. "We grew up," she said. "Maybe our nerve atrophies with age."

Sharon let her arms collapse onto the counter. She rested her chin on her forearms. "If my kid makes me a grandmother at forty, watch my nerves disintegrate completely."

Elaine closed the ledger and put it under the counter. She glanced at her watch. "I sure don't feel like working. What do you say we lock up and play hooky the rest of the day?"

"Sure. We could go out and look for the medallion."

"That'll be the day. Have you seen the new William Hurt movie?"

"You're serious, aren't you?"

"Of course I am."

"But what if somebody comes?"

"What if they do? Who's going to tell on us? We're the bosses. That's one of the reasons I opened my own store, so I could make the rules.

And one of my rules is that on slow days when I don't feel like working, we can close up and go to the movies."

"Maybe it'll pick up this afternoon," Sharon argued. "People stocking up for the blizzard. We might miss some big sales. Maybe the Queen of Hearts is already through her stack and needs another fix of romantic porn."

"One customer in the past half hour?" Elaine said, holding up her index finger as if in verification. "So what if somebody comes and we miss a few bucks? Money isn't everything. At least that's what you're trying to convince Phil of, isn't it? You're as bad as he is, for godssake."

"Ooh, that hurts," Sharon said, clutching her heart as though wounded. An afternoon off to play, just the two of them, actually sounded like fun. It would be good to get away from dusting books, away from her expectations, away from The Decision that hung like a noose in front of her. She filled in the afternoon in her mind. A good, old-fashioned movie, coffee afterwards, maybe a little dessert thrown in for good measure. Something with chocolate. She leaned across the counter and tossed her dustrag where she thought the box should be.

"Okay," she said. "Let's go. But I'm not sure about William Hurt. He's so full of angst."

Elaine smiled. "He can keep his angst under my bed anytime he wants to."

FIVE

"Alfred."

Genevieve appeared in the bedroom doorway. "I said lunch is ready." Alfred looked up. She had pulled on Rudy's old denim jacket over her sweater to ward off the chill that still lingered in the house, despite the fact that they had turned up the heat when they arrived just before nine o'clock. The arms of the jacket hung nearly to her fingertips. He pulled open the bottom drawer of Rudy's bedside bureau.

"Alfred." He heard the edge in her voice.

"I've only got this bottom drawer left, and then this bureau is finished."

They had thought themselves nearly finished with the paper sorting, but he had discovered that the bottom drawers of the bureau here in Rudy's bedroom were filled not with clothes, but with more news-papers and magazines.

"You can finish after we eat," Genevieve said. "Come on now, before it gets cold."

"All right." He drew himself to his feet and moved around the end of the brass bed toward the kitchen. There was no point in risking the peace that they had established. This morning over a breakfast of French toast and sausage that she had fixed for them, she had been as friendly as she had been angry the morning before.

In the kitchen, Genevieve stood at the old four-legged gas stove, dishing up two bowls of vegetable beef soup. The smell of gas flame mingled with the aroma of fresh coffee.

"I know you don't like soup out of a can, but it's easier," she said. "I don't know how Rudy could cook anything on this stove. Maybe that's why he always stayed so thin."

"It's all right," he said. "I'm hungry enough to eat anything." He stepped to the kitchen window and, with a swipe of his hand, wiped from the glass the moisture that was rapidly turning to frost. "Snow's really coming down," he said, looking out into Rudy's backyard. "Must be four or five inches already."

"Won't it be nice to get out of all this snow and cold?" Genevieve set the bowls of soup on the table. "Janet says it hits seventy degrees down there some days during February."

Houston. She had taken last night's promise to think about going as an agreement to go. The promise had been more of a stall than an actual promise. He had no real intention of going, but it was better to enjoy a couple of weeks' peace and then spring it on her at the last moment. He sat down at the kitchen table in what had always been Rudy's place.

"We need to get our airplane tickets ordered," Genevieve said, as she pulled her chair up to the table. She bowed her head, crossed herself, and recited the grace.

"Janet says the earlier we order, the cheaper the tickets will be," she continued. She pushed back the sleeves of Rudy's jacket.

"We made good progress this morning," he said.

"He saved everything," Genevieve complained. "Some of those clippings! I can't for the life of me figure out why he kept them."

"Well, you know how he was. He was a little interested in just about everything." He reached for one of the bologna sandwiches on the plate between them—white bread, with one slice spread with butter, the other with mustard, the way she had always made them for his lunch bucket. The taste of the sandwich made him wish he was back at work.

"I brought the paper along," Genevieve said, pulling it from the box in which she had brought their lunch supplies. "I thought we might want to look at it again."

"As if we didn't have enough newspapers around here already," he said.

"We should have the afternoon paper," she said, "to see what the new clue is."

At breakfast, they had discussed the treasure hunt clues, making no real progress other than to conclude that Clue 6 meant baseball diamonds. Without Rudy, it hadn't been much fun. Finding the medallion without Rudy's help seemed the most remote of possibilities.

Genevieve spread the newspaper on the table beside her plate.

"If we find the medallion, we could use the money for the trip." Genevieve cautiously sipped a spoonful of hot soup. "This isn't so bad."

Alfred blew on a spoonful. It tasted bland, nothing like Genevieve's vegetable beef soup when she made it from scratch. He looked at the yellow walls around him. On this snowy, gray day, they looked even more dingy than they were. These walls would definitely have to be painted before they listed the house with the realtor. Still, he liked this room. He always had, even back in the days when he had stood by the cookstove on cold winter mornings while his mother stripped off his nightshirt and helped him get dressed. His mother and this kitchen—

"Alfred?" Genevieve's tone indicated that this was at least the second time she had said his name.

"Huh?"

"I said 'I still don't know what they mean by the clue about the queen and the river.'"

"I don't know, either."

"Do you think maybe it means the Winter Carnival queen? Maybe somewhere along the parade route? That would explain *enter with a queen,* but what would the *leave via river* part mean then?"

"I don't know. I suppose it could." He looked around the room again. It had changed little over the years. The four-legged gas stove, now itself an antique, had replaced the nickel-plated, wood-burning cookstove he remembered as a boy. A dozen or so years ago, a new refrigerator had replaced the old one that Rudy had bought before Janet was born. The enamel-topped table at which they sat had stood here in the corner of the kitchen for as long as he could remember, its wooden legs getting a fresh coat of white paint every decade or so. All comfortable changes, made slowly, almost imperceptibly over the years. Maybe that was why he liked it here: it was a good place to hide from the modern world as it raced toward the end of the century; a room where he could forget that he was retired and had nothing to do. Here he could always—

The clatter of Genevieve's spoon startled him as it bounced across the enamel tabletop and fell to the floor. Across from him, her face was blazing, her mouth puckered into a circle, her eyes narrow behind her glasses.

"All right," she fumed. "So I'm not Rudy. I'm probably no good at this compared to him. But you don't have to ignore me." She glared at him.

He looked away from her, feeling his face turning hot with embarrassment. Her spoon had landed on the linoleum about two feet from his chair. Slowly, he bent over to pick it up, feeling his half-eaten lunch backing up in his throat as he doubled over his middle. As he struggled upright again, he felt for a dizzying moment like he was going to vomit. He laid the spoon quietly on the table.

"I wasn't ignoring you," he said, still not looking at her. "I was just thinking about something else."

"What?"

"Nothing. You wouldn't be interested."

"What?" Genevieve persisted, crossing her arms over her chest. "If you're going to ignore me, you could at least tell me why."

The words fluttered to his lips before he could stop them, startling even himself.

"What would you think about moving down here?"

"Move down here?" Genevieve's eyes widened in surprise. "Why?"

Why indeed. Could he explain it? Could he explain that her movements about the old stove had reminded him of his mother? That the few vague memories he had of his parents were so strongly connected to these rooms? Could he ever describe in words the longing he felt to be close to them again, to Rudy, and even old Tantchen, the stern maiden aunt who had come to take care of Rudy and him after their parents were killed?

He said nothing.

"Why do you want to move down here?" Like a prosecuting attorney, Genevieve presented the evidence against moving. "Our house is bigger. Look at this kitchen. He never did a thing to it. The outside needs fixing up. Ours has that nice aluminum siding that's still in good shape."

Aluminum siding that had earned him six weeks of silence because he had refused to to Highland Park, he thought ruefully.

"It was just a thought," he said.

"Well, it's a silly thought. It makes no sense at all to pack up and move up here."

"You're right. It was a silly thought," he agreed. "I don't really want to move down here. I was just thinking out loud."

They finished their lunch in silence. He fixed his eyes on his soup bowl. Whatever peace they had established had been shaken. The last thing he wanted was to get on her bad side again. He got up, went to the stove, and poured coffee into two of the heavy, stained mugs that Rudy always used. He filled the mugs too full. Coffee dribbled thickly down the sides of the mugs as he carried them toward the table. Genevieve wordlessly took the mug, not looking up at him. He sat down himself. He felt heat on his palms as he cradled his hands around the mug. So many times over the years they had sat this way over their coffee, grim and silent, half-mad at one another.

She was right, of course. She wasn't Rudy when it came to the treasure hunt, but she was working on it, even if the only reason was because she wanted the money to go to Houston.

"There must be baseball diamonds all over town," he said.

"What?" Genevieve looked up at him suspiciously.

"The clue."

"Oh. I suppose there are," she said coolly.

"You don't suppose they mean the old Lexington ball park, do you?" he said. The St. Paul Saints' old ball park had once stood on the corner of Lexington Parkway and University Avenue. But like so much of his life, both the park and the Saints were long gone, victims of the modern world. The ball park was a parking lot, and the team was only a memory of old geezers like himself.

"They probably don't," he went on, "since it doesn't exist anymore. Remember how we used to go and watch the Saints play? I wonder when they tore that down. It was after the war, I remember. Or was it during the war?"

"It was still there when Janet was a baby," Genevieve volunteered.

"How do you know that?" Alfred felt both relieved and grateful for the comment.

"I remember going to a game and changing her on the floor in front of my seat."

"Now there's a ball diamond," he said, making a connection. "There must be a ball diamond at Monroe where Janet went to school. We could drive past there on the way home."

"Well, we'll never be ready to go home if we don't get back to work," Genevieve said. "I wish we were done with this job. Maybe we should hire somebody who runs estate sales to finish for us."

"What, and give them half or more of what we make?"

"You always do things the hard way," Genevieve said. She got up to clear away the dishes.

"I'm going back to work." Alfred pushed himself out of the chair and lumbered off toward Rudy's bedroom. The dining room table was covered with old china that Genevieve was sorting through. The pressed-back chairs were piled with faded linens and table cloths. The floor of the small living room was strewn with boxes full of papers to be thrown away. Maybe they should hire an estate sale company, or whatever you called them, and part with the money to get this over with.

In Rudy's bedroom, he settled himself on the floor before the bureau that stood next to the bed and pulled open the bottom drawer. It was filled to the top with the front sections of the *Pioneer Press* and *Dispatch*, laid down one by one after they were read. He worked his way down the stack, his fingers walking through the important events of the last twenty-odd years: the 25th anniversary of JFK's assassination, the Challenger disaster, the attempted assassinations of Reagan and Pope John Paul II, the return of the hostages from Iran, the election of Pope John Paul II, the death of Pope John Paul I, John Paul's election, the death of Pope Paul VI, Nixon's and Agnew's resignations, the signing of the Just and Honorable Peace in Vietnam, the moon landing.

Under the newspapers, he found a stack of news magazines. As he burrowed through the stack toward the bottom of the drawer, his heart suddenly quickened in his chest. No news magazine had ever had a cover like this: two men stripped naked, locked together, a black square blanking out the spot where their bodies joined.

He listened for Genevieve in the kitchen and heard water splashing, dishes rattling in the sink. Quickly his fingers probed to the bottom of the drawer. There were eight magazines. He pulled the top one from under the newspapers, ready to hide it at the sound of Genevieve's footsteps in the dining room. He flipped through the pages. The pictures shocked him, naked men engaged in every kind of act imaginable. There were no black squares blanking out the places where their bodies joined together. His stomach felt like it was full of quicksand. He buried the magazine under the papers again, and closed the drawer quietly. He'd have to get rid of these, somehow, without Genevieve knowing about them. He looked around the room, at the tarnished brass bed covered with newspapers and magazines, at the old family pictures in heavy wood frames that hung on the wall, at the crucifix that hung above the dresser. He looked at the closed drawer again, fully and frighteningly aware that he had stumbled on a very private, secret part of his brother's life.

SIX

KEITH PRESSED HIS HANDS AROUND THE MUG of hot chocolate, letting the heat soak through his palms and spread into his body. The dry clothes he had pulled on still held the chill from lying in the dresser next to the cold north wall of his bedroom. His wet clothes lay in a heap on the rug just inside the front door, where he had shucked them off when he came in from the morning's hunt, tired and discouraged. Last Saturday night, he hoped to have found the medallion by now, to be basking in the spotlight of notoriety, his picture in the paper and everything. Instead, he was cold, and his back and shoulders ached from digging.

The first sip from the mug made his taste buds turn somersaults as they adjusted to the sudden sweetness. Good, but not as good as his mother's. Hot chocolate was one of her specialties. On Saturday afternoons during the long Silver Bay winters, she always had hot chocolate waiting for him when he came in from sliding, red-faced and sniffling from the cold that rolled in off Lake Superior. His mother the fixer. He should call her one of these days.

What he really should do was get right back out and start searching again. You didn't find the medallion sitting around inside the house. Trouble was, he hadn't the slightest idea where to go looking, now that he had ruled out Mounds Park. And Clue 7 in the afternoon paper he had picked up on the way home wasn't much help.

He set the mug down on the arm of the couch, and reached for the newspaper on the coffee table. For the tenth time, he read the new clue: Clue 7: *Seven red hints should help you find, a dazzling treasure, one of a kind. Seven red hints,* obviously, was the important part of the clue; the rest was there only to fill out the rhyme. Red hints. What things were red? Stop signs, stoplights, fire engines, signs, cars, bricks, kid's wagons. It could be just about anything. *Seven red hints.* Did seven mean more than a number? Did it point to Seventh Street or the seven-hundred block of some other street?

The oven buzzer went off, announcing that the frozen pizza he had popped in when he first got home was ready. He hurried out to the kitchen to shut off the buzzer before Tiffany heard it. He almost made it.

The pepperoni pizza was very done. The cheese was bubbling and starting to turn dark at the edges, exactly the way he liked it. Hot chocolate and pizza. He could just hear what Sandy would say about such a combination if she were here. She'd scrunch up her face in a disapproving sneer. "You eat the worst combinations, Keith," she'd say.

He pulled a butcher knife out of the drawer. He held it over the bubbling surface, sizing the pizza up. The old familiar pain closed in on him. Pizza had been one of their battles. He liked his cut into pie-shaped pieces; Sandy liked hers in little squares. Whoever baked a pizza always cut it the wrong way for the other, touching off an argument that often ended with the two of them in separate rooms, not speaking to each other. Near the end of things, he had started to cut the pizzas he baked the way she liked them—in little squares—but it did no good. She still had locked him out that autumn night when he had driven over to her place to try to put things to right, to point out that all she had to do was lighten up on few things and everything would be all right. But instead of lightening up, she had become hysterical.

"I told you on the phone, it's over," she had yelled at him through the locked screen door. "You hit Jason, you bastard! Nobody hits one of my kids."

"I told you he's lying. I didn't hit him."

"He showed me the knot on the side of his head!"

"I didn't do that. I only thumped him. He got that knot when he banged his head against the side of the car door, trying to duck out of the way. It was an accident. I was only trying to get his attention. You're blowing this all out of proportion."

If he had really slugged the kid, he could understand. But he hadn't, even though Jason deserved it. He'd only given him a little thump on the side of the head. A thump was nothing compared to the way his old man used to knock him around when he was a kid. His old man had flattened him once with a right, and he'd needed stitches over his left eye. But Sandy had refused to listen.

"Having a twelve-year-old boy hurt himself trying to dodge a blow from a grownup is not blowing it out of proportion," she had screamed.

He'd gotten pissed then.

"He was stealing change out of the ashtray in my car. Did he tell you that? Stealing! That happens to be a crime."

"There's better ways to discipline a kid than hitting him."

"I told you," he had tried again to explain, "I didn't hit him; I only thumped him."

"I don't care what you call it, you're not getting the chance to do it again. You better get some help, before you really hurt somebody."

"You're the one who needs help," he'd yelled back. "To control your kid before he ends up in jail."

"Well, as of now, it's not your problem anymore. Just leave us alone."

He'd tried one last time to put things back to right.

"All right! Have it your way. I won't do it again, even if he robs a bank or knocks off a convenience store. Now open the door, will you?"

"You don't get it, do you?" Sandy had screamed at him. "I don't want to see you again. Ever! Now get out of here before I call the cops."

And he had left, knowing that she would call the cops if he didn't.

He cut the pizza into six pie-shaped pieces, slid three pieces onto a plate, and headed back to the living room.

He hated to admit it, but he still missed her. He longed to see her again, to lie close to her deep in the night, or sit around on Sunday mornings, drinking coffee and reading the paper. But those days were long gone. She was probably married by now to whatever stockbroker or lawyer she had found. And Jason, the little thief, was probably in the juvenile detention center by now.

He took a bite of pizza and burned the roof of his mouth. He gulped hot chocolate to cool his mouth. The heavy, sweet chocolate made a strange combination with the gooey cheese and tomato sauce.

That incident with Jason—he had always figured that she used it as an excuse to break up. She probably had a new guy all lined up, and was just looking for a way to dump him. The bitch. He was probably better off without her. He should quit thinking about her, quit letting her intrude on his life.

He picked up the paper again. The previous six clues were on page 3 of the A section. He read through them again, weighing each phrase, hoping that they would all add up to something, some collective, grand hint. They didn't.

He set the plate and paper down on the coffee table, and got up to get his treasure hunt notes on his desk. The notebook lay directly under the strip of cash register tape pinned to his bulletin board. The loose, round letters and numbers beckoned him. Toni was only a phone call away, waiting on the other end of the line, wanting to hear from him. An antidote to the loneliness that overwhelmed him every time he thought about Sandy. Maybe he'd give old Toni a call.

He settled onto the couch again, and flipped through the notebook. Toni had two kids who were probably monsters, just like Sandy's were. And what had the attendant at the convenience store said about her— that she acted like she knew everything, or something like that? Why get hooked up with someone like that? He should just forget about her and get on here with the business at hand.

He read through his notebook from beginning to end, then slammed it shut in disgust. Ten pages of notes he had jotted down since Saturday night, and there wasn't one thing in them, not one word, that really helped. As near as he could tell, the medallion was somewhere on the ground in Ramsey County near train tracks, near streets named for a queen and a river, at a place where you can see planes land and take off, and where you could see races being run in the distance. A baseball field was nearby, and something that gave *seven red hints*. What place all that added up to, he had no idea.

One of these clues had to give something away. He read them again. Clue 3, that was the biggest clue: *Enter with a queen, leave via river.* Queen and river referred to streets. If only he could figure out which queen and which river. It was really two clues in one—two different street names. Maybe one of the street names had seven letters, and was somehow connected to something red.

If seven red hints referred to stoplights or stop signs, he ought to be able to figure out how many corners it took to add up to seven lights or signs. He flipped the notebook open to a blank page, and sketched out an intersection, marking each of the streetlights with an X. A simple intersection made for four stops, figuring one light on each corner. A third intersecting street would make six corners and six lights. A fourth street that dead-ended in the intersection would make seven corners and seven lights or stop signs. Unless, of course, it was stoplights and a light was centered over the middle of the street. In that case, it would take— he sketched a new intersection and marked the lights—two streets intersecting to account for eight lights. He dropped the pencil on the notebook. Stop signs and stoplights didn't work out very well. The clue must refer to something else, lights or a sign or something.

He attacked the second slice of pizza, finishing it in half a dozen bites. What to do next? The best thing to do was not to push it. He could start tracing the queen and river names on his map. The map lay on the chair beside the front door, where he had dumped it when he came in. Under it was his briefcase, the Gopher State Products work waiting inside. He glanced over at the clock on his desk. A little before one, making him nearly an hour late for his call into the office. Might just as well call and get that over with.

Patty, the receptionist, answered, her voice bubbling like a water fountain. "PROgrams, Inc., may I help—"

"Patty," he interrupted, "it's Keith. Put me through to the General."

"It's a good thing you called." Patty's voice dropped to a confidential whisper. "Jerry's been waiting to go to lunch since twelve."

Jerry answered after the first ring. "This is Jerry, how can I help you?"

"Jerry, it's Keith."

"Keith." Jerry's tone was curt. "You were supposed to call in by noon."

"I know," Keith said quickly. "I got into this Gopher State program and I lost track of time."

"I tried calling you at noon. I didn't get an answer."

He could just see Jerry in his white shirt and trendy tie leaning forward in his chair, holding the receiver with one hand, the other clutching his gold fountain pen.

"I went out for a few minutes to get some lunch. Anyway, I've made a lot of headway on Gopher State. I should be able to finish it up by Friday with no problem. I still have to figure out how to connect inventory with accounts receivable for billing, but it shouldn't be much of a problem."

"Keith, that's right out of Programming 101. You shouldn't have to 'figure out' anything."

"Well, I didn't mean figure it out like I didn't know what to do," he retorted. "I know just what to do."

"Well, be sure you're finished doing it by Friday. You should probably be around on Friday in case they have any problems."

That was on the next to the last day of the treasure hunt, and no way, Jose, was he going to come in unless he had already found it.

"Don't worry, there won't be any problems," he said. "I've got this thing licked."

"Well, nothing else has come up that we can't handle," Jerry said. "But don't forget to call in tomorrow . . ." There was a slight pause. "On time."

"I won't." He hung up. "Fuck you, asshole."

God, he had to get out of there and get off on his own, where he could work at his own pace, with no white shirt and tie telling him what to do, fathering him. Jerry was such an asshole. *If you weren't my friend you would have been out of here already.* Apparently, Jerry still considered the two of them as friends. But real friends didn't pull the kind of white shirt and tie shit that Jerry was pulling on him lately. He'd talk to the Gopher State people and see if they were interested in splitting away from PROgrams—he could work for them cheaper by himself.

He spread the map out on the coffee table. The map still smelled faintly of the pink magic marker. He flipped the notebook open to the page listing his queen and river names. He could mark the queen streets on the map in red, and the river streets in yellow. Somewhere, in one place only he hoped, red, yellow, and pink lines would converge on or near a patch of green, and that would be the spot. He counted the number of streets there were to plot: thirty-six queen streets and twenty-three river streets. It would take at least a couple of hours to locate each street on the map and trace its length on the map, find each street's twists and turns and sometimes its total disappearance, and reappearance ten blocks farther north or south. The inexplicable logic of the St. Paul street system.

He should add the clues to his computer data base of old clues to see if he could uncover anything that way. He should go back out to hunt. Maybe if he drove around he would spot something that clicked into place. The idea wasn't very appealing. The drive home from Mounds Park had been slippery, the steadily falling snow packed down by the traffic into a glaze of ice. The paper's headline had predicted a total of up to twelve inches, not the kind of weather you wanted to be in with a ten-year-old car with a bad battery.

He drained the last of his hot chocolate, and carried the empty plate and mug back to the kitchen. On the counter, the remaining half of the pizza had grown cold, the cheese turned into a solid yellow mass. Maybe instead of stoplights, *seven red hints* was a big sign, like the towering red "1st" sign that perched atop the First Bank Building in downtown, blinking away through the long winter nights.

Maybe he should finish off Gopher State this afternoon, before the treasure hunt got to Thursday and Friday, days he couldn't afford to be distracted. He paused at the kitchen doorway and looked around the living room. What he really should do was clean up this place. It looked like hell: clothes draped over the backs of chairs, newspapers all over the carpet, a fast-food bag here and there. It got that way often without . . . without someone around to keep after him to pick up things. He gathered up his wet clothes off the floor, and carried them into the bathroom. He hung the socks on the towel rack, and his pants and shirt on the shower curtain rod. Maybe he could keep things on the light side with Toni. Stay in control. A movie now and then. An occasional dinner, even get laid if she was agreeable to it. Maybe he'd give her a call later after all.

In the hallway on the way back to the living room, he suddenly clapped his hands together. Blinking away in the night. Christ, that was it! He spelled the word in his head, ticking off the letters on his fingers. Seven. *Seven red hints.* That was it. That was *it.* He grabbed the phone book off the desk, and rustled through the pages to the S section in search of the address. He snatched up the map, traced a finger along West Seventh Street, heading out toward the airport. The airport. Jesus. *Watch planes come and watch them go.* This was it! The nearest green was Cherokee Park, across the Mississippi River on the West Side. Perfect. You could stand on the high bluff and look right down on the Schmidt brewery sign, blinking away in the night. His heart pounded in his chest, a hammer against an anvil. His stomach felt like he had just taken the long plunge on the roller coaster at Valley Fair. This was it! Frantically he checked out the names of the streets that bordered the park. Annapolis was the south border, Chippewa made up part of the east border. Queen Anne and the Chippewa River. *Enter with a queen, leave via river.* This was it. *This was it!*

He started to haul on his boots. It would all have to wait: Gopher State, General Jerry, housecleaning, Toni. It would have to wait. On the back burner. He was heading out to Cherokee Park, blizzard or no blizzard. The medallion was there; he *knew* it, felt it in every cell of tissue and bone in his body. And by god, he was going to find it!

SEVEN

"STEVEN CARPENTER, TELEPHONE!"

Carleen barked the announcement from the back of the room, where the processing room's one telephone hung on the yellow wall directly behind her desk.

He jumped up at the sound of his name, wondering who it was. He seldom received calls at work. Carleen, the processing staff's designated telephone receptionist due to her proximity to the telephone, threw him a sour look as she returned to her desk. He glanced up at the clock. Ten minutes until three-o'clock break. Ten more minutes, Carleen, he thought, and you can go have a cigarette. Around here, everyone lived for three o'clock, especially the smokers. A hollow feeling formed in his stomach as he grabbed the receiver that hung upside down on its twisted cord. Maybe someone was hurt or sick . . . .

"Hello?"

"Listen to this." It was Debi's voice, eager as a magazine salesman's. *"Seven red hints should help you find, a dazzling treasure, one of a kind."*

"What is it?"

"Clue 7," she said impatiently. "I went out after the stock market closed and bought the paper. What do you think it means?"

"You shouldn't call me at work," he said in a low voice, "unless it's an emergency."

"This *is* an emergency. There's four thousand bucks at stake."

"Read it again." He turned his face toward the wall, directing his voice at the yellow paint. *Seven red hints*, that was the key. "I don't know," he said. "Stop signs?"

"That, or stoplights maybe?" The line hummed for a moment. "I wish they'd give a decent clue. What else besides stoplights and stop signs are red?"

Red. He said the first things that came to mind: "Blood; the Red Cross; red tape."

"None of those are physical things that you can see in a park," Debi said.

"Maybe the number seven is what's important; more important than red, I mean. What could seven mean?"

"Seventh Street? Are there any parks on Seventh Street? But that doesn't make sense. Why would they say red hints if red wasn't important?"

"You're right," he conceded. In the back of his mind, he could see Debi sitting at her desk in her bright red dress and white blazer, a sea of computer printouts around her.

"Does it tie in with any of the other clues?" he asked.

"Not that I can see. Unless *seven red hints* ties in with jack or king of diamonds, like we were talking about this morning. Here, you listen to 'em and see if you can make any connections: '*Somewhere on the ground in Ramsey County*—'"

"Listen," he interrupted, "we're not supposed to tie up the line with personal calls. We can talk about it more tonight."

"Let's try and drive around tonight, okay? Is your friend still coming over to jump the car?"

"I don't know, I haven't talked to him about it today. Maybe he won't want to now with the snow." He looked out the window. Across Rice Park, the turrets and gables of the Landmark Center were nearly invisible behind the curtain of falling snow. "It's coming down pretty hard."

"Steven, if there's a snow emergency and we don't get it started we'll get a ticket. Maybe even towed away."

He thought of asking her if she was serious about New York, but decided to wait until they got home.

"I gotta go. See you tonight." He hung up the phone and started down the aisle toward his desk.

"Here, take these." Carleen pushed a cart filled with compact discs at him. "They're ready for pockets."

He wheeled the cart back to his desk. Compact discs. A boring job. Type the artist's name and the album title on a pocket, and pass it over to Knickerson to be glued onto the back of the plastic cover. Since the library's purchasing process often took several months, the albums usually had fallen off the charts by the time they reached this cart.

Knickerson was killing off the last minutes before break by sketching a couple making love on the back of a discarded pocket. The male had the same hair drawn back into a fashionable ponytail, the same earring, as the artist.

"That's pretty good. You should blow this place and go to art school."

Knickerson gave him a mischievous look. "Let me guess. That was the new clerk downstairs calling to say she wanted my body, but was too shy to ask, so she wanted you to set something up between us?"

"You wish." Steven rolled the cart around to the right side of his desk. He slid into his chair, then looked at the clock. Seven minutes to three.

"Actually, it was Deb. And she doesn't want your body, just your jumper cables. You still coming over to jump the car tonight?"

"No way," Knickerson said. "You seen the snow? When I get home, I'm planting my sweet ass on the couch."

"Come on," Steven pleaded. "If there's a snow emergency and we don't get it started, I'll probably get a ticket. Or towed away."

"No way, Jose." Knickerson shook his head, his ponytail bobbing back and forth behind him. "I'll come tomorrow, after it stops. Besides, they won't declare a snow emergency before tonight, and then you've got a fifty-fifty chance that it'll be for the north-south streets instead of the east-west, and that'll give you an extra day."

Steven inserted a pocket into the typewriter. He couldn't blame Knickerson for saying no. He looked up at the clock. Five minutes to three. Around him, he could feel the restlessness in the room's dry air. "Then you're not going out to look for the medallion tonight?"

"You kidding? You'd have to be crazy to go out and search in weather like this."

"Deb called with the new clue. *Seven red hints*, whatever that means. I said stop signs, Deb said stoplights. Any ideas?"

"Those are too easy. It's probably a sign of some kind, with red letters that spell out the name of the park, maybe. Which parks have seven letters in the name?"

"Do I look like I have a map?" He looked at the clock. Four minutes to three. "Where do you think it is?"

"Somewhere near a baseball diamond." Knickerson slipped the drawing into the pencil drawer of his desk. "And somewhere near the airport."

"In other words, you have no idea."

"In other words," Knickerson said, grinning at him, "I have no idea."

Three minutes to three. He thumbed through the CDs on the cart. This was the most pathetic bunch yet. He spotted the most recent Fogelberg album, which he had picked up several months ago, and the millionth Dylan album. But the majority of them were dance music, heavy metal or rap, music he didn't like very much.

He pulled out one of the albums and stared at it in disgust. *Exotic Fruits and Vegetables* by Metallurgy. On the front cover, a naked woman with a wild mane of platinum hair sat waist-deep in a pile of fruits and vegetables. She clutched a pair of cantaloupe halves over her breasts, seeds and juice dripping down her flat belly. He turned to the back and read the song titles: "Tooling Along Cherry Lane," "Fuzz on Your Peach," "A Fine Pear," "Cucumber Nights, Cauliflower Ears."

"Knickerson, check out the titles on this." He held the CD across the space between their desks.

"I already got it," Knickerson said. "Check out the babe on the cover. She looks like that new clerk downstairs. I'd like to check out the fuzz on her peach."

Steven snatched the CD back. "You're hopeless." Knickerson, the swinging bachelor who still lived at home with his mother. And a moron when it came to music.

He studied the CD again, reading the credits. How did this kind of stuff ever get released? He knew he could do better. He'd never write songs with titles this blatant, this tasteless. He'd be more like Steve Goodman. Goodman had recorded a great song about vegetables, "The Barnyard Dance." He knew he was going it alone, liking the kind of music he did. Almost everyone liked Dylan, but Dan Fogelberg got kicked around by the music critics and his friends alike—Knickerson, the metal head, loathed him. And almost everyone had forgotten about Steve Goodman and Harry Chapin. Some musicians got more famous after they died, but Goodman and Chapin had just sort of faded away. One day, maybe he could credit them as influences, just the way the Stones or the Beatles admitted they had been influenced by Chuck Berry or Bo Diddley or Elvis.

But to do that, he would have to get out there and make a name for himself. He slid the CD back into the stack. Tonight he would practice for two hours, no matter what. Maybe he could get his big chance in New York if he and Debi moved there. Her mention of it had come as a complete surprise this morning, but the idea had seized him. Dylan had done it, getting his start in local clubs, then going to the Big Apple and breaking into the club scene there. And Dylan had become a superstar, a legend, even with a voice that could barely carry a tune, a fact he took comfort in whenever he listened to his own voice on tape.

He heard the sudden bump and commotion of chairs being rolled back, of people moving up the aisle on their way to the break room across the hall. Three o'clock. Carleen brushed by him, a cigarette between her dry, red lips, lighter in hand. He looked across the aisle. Knickerson was already gone, hoping to get a seat near the new clerk from downstairs. He shut off his typewriter and hurried out behind them.

EIGHT

"THAT IT?" ASKED THE CASHIER, a new face that Bruce hadn't seen before.

Bruce scanned the grocery list Joanna had printed neatly on the back of an NSP envelope: spaghetti, spaghetti sauce, lettuce, French bread or rolls. The store didn't have any fresh tomatoes or cucumbers.

"I'll take a paper, too." He grabbed the afternoon *Pioneer Press* from the rack on the floor and dropped it on the counter. The headline blared a warning: Heavy Snow Moving In.

"Looks like we're really getting it tonight," the clerk said, glancing at the headline and then out the window into the snowy parking lot. He was about thirty, slender under the maroon University of Minnesota hooded sweatshirt he wore.

"Looks like."

The clerk snapped open a paper bag, shoved the rolls in the bottom, and piled the spaghetti, sauce, lettuce, and newspaper on top. He punched up the total.

"Seven dollars, fifty-one cents."

Bruce fumbled in his back pocket for his billfold. The total killed off his last ten-spot. Tomorrow, he'd have to go to the bank and draw against his savings, which were going faster than he had anticipated.

"You following the treasure hunt?" The clerk counted out the change and held it out to him.

"Sort of."

"I think it's in Mounds Park."

"What makes you say that?"

"I always say Mounds Park." The clerk pushed the grocery bag across the counter. "Sooner or later, I've got to be right."

Bruce laughed. "I think it's in Como, for the same reason."

"I hope I can make it home tonight," the clerk fretted. He glanced out the window again.

"Where do you live?"

"West St. Paul, by Marthaler Park. How about you?"

"Across the alley."

Marthaler Park. The treasure had been hidden there once, one of the first years he and St. John had looked together. Until the very last clue was printed, neither of them had ever heard of Marthaler Park.

He picked up the grocery bag. "Well, I hope you don't get snowed in."

"Me, too," the clerk said.

Bruce stepped out into the falling snow. The sky was dark white, filled with reflected light thrown up from the snowy hills. A halo of snowflakes whirled around each streetlight. He didn't care if it snowed ten feet tonight. In truth, he liked heavy snow. Snow treated everyone equally, dumping on tech school students, grocery store clerks, and millionaires alike, making everyone friendlier.

And tonight the snow was even more welcome. Joanna had volunteered to cook spaghetti if he went to the store and bought the ingredients. After dinner, they would watch whatever was on cable, or maybe listen to some music. The idea of being snowed in tomorrow was very appealing. Sitting around drinking coffee, and just doing whatever came naturally. Lots of naturally, he hoped. Those three little words he had uttered unprompted this morning in the car had popped out of his mouth again this afternoon. They had returned home, Joanna had put her arms around him, leaned her head against his chest, and squeezed him in a fierce embrace. "I love you," he had said without a single doubt. Holding her, he had felt his heart soaring like a kite on the spring breeze. And then he had felt the wetness of her tears, all the way through his flannel shirt. "I love you, too," she had said, pulling back to look squarely into his eyes, a dark, sweet smile on her face. "Don't hurt me now that we've said it."

South Robert Street was nearly deserted. Rush hour had been early today as businesses closed up before dark and sent people home. A few cars still straggled toward home, their headlights casting beams of white light through the falling snowflakes.

He turned into the alley and stopped short in his tracks. Parked between the Camaro and Jo's dilapidated Oldsmobile, sticking head and shoulders above them, was The Beast.

Damn. Shit. He moved up the slippery outside staircase with lead in his feet.

"Hi ya, Sundance." St. John, enormous in insulated coveralls and a heavy, quilted coat, stood on the rug inside the kitchen door, snow melting under his boots. A nervous version of his lopsided grin stretched across his unshaven face. Across the kitchen, Joanna leaned against the sink, gripping the edge of the counter top behind her. A newly opened can of Diet Coke sat on the counter next to her.

"Well, look what the cat dragged in." Bruce kicked off his boots. He smiled apologetically at Joanna. "I leave the house for ten minutes and you let any old riff-raff in off the street?"

"He had a gun," Joanna said.

Bruce turned to St. John. "Are you crazy? Out running around in weather like this when you don't have to?"

"Yeah, probably," St. John said. "Come on, get your treasure hunting clothes on. I got it all figured out."

"You *are* crazy, if you think I'm going out in this shit." Bruce set the grocery sack on the kitchen table. "They didn't have any tomatoes or cucumbers," he told Joanna.

"Come on," St. John said again. "Let's go. I know right where to look."

Bruce slipped out of his coat and started to hang it on the back of one of the chairs. Glancing at Joanna, he instead hung it on its proper hook.

"You mean it's not in Como Park?"

"No," St. John said. "And it never was."

"So where is it?"

"Harriet Island."

"We were just going to eat supper. Wanna eat with us? Jo's making her famous spaghetti." He slipped his arms around her from behind as she started to unpack the groceries. "At least I think it's famous." He parted the hair on the back of her neck and bent to kiss her. She stepped away from him. She was pissed. He could feel it in the way she moved.

"I don't know." St. John fidgeted with the zipper on his coat. "I was kind of hot to get right out and start looking."

"Well, I'm not going anywhere on an empty stomach, that's for sure," Bruce said. "I'm not going anywhere, in fact."

"Cinnamon rolls!" Joanna exclaimed. She held up the squashed package accusingly, a look of amazement on her face. "You bought cinnamon rolls?"

"You said if they didn't have any French bread to get some rolls."

"I meant *dinner* rolls." She tossed the package of rolls on the table with a shake of her head. "Men." She dug into the bag again. "Well, at least you got the lettuce. Do you have any salad dressing?"

"There may be something in the fridge." He opened the package and pulled a roll loose. He pushed the package across the table toward St. John.

"You want one of these?"

"Sure, why not?" St. John helped himself.

Bruce opened the refrigerator and found the last two cans of Coors. He tossed one across the room. St. John caught it with one hand. He left the door open for Joanna. She rummaged around in the back, where the leftovers always collected, and pulled out a nearly empty bottle of bleu cheese dressing, unscrewed the cap, and sniffed.

"Yech! How long has this been in here?" she said, making a face. She screwed the cap back on and tossed the bottle into the trash. "I don't suppose you have any vinegar?"

"Yes." He ducked into the back room and came out with a plastic gallon jug that was still half-full. "I bought this last summer." He glanced at St. John. "Somebody told me it worked great to clean car interiors. About all it did was make the interior smell like a dinner salad." He sat down at the kitchen table.

"I said it worked good on leather," St. John said. "You're the one who tried it on upholstery." He dropped onto a chair and flashed his lopsided grin. "I wouldn't *hoodwink* you on something as important as that. Cars. Somebody say go."

Pun derby. Bruce glanced at Joanna. She stood at the sink, filling a pan with water, her back toward him, trying not to be there, it seemed. Screw the pun derby, he thought.

But St. John was already off and running. "That was the *signal*," he quipped. "How's that for *starters*? Here, let me *dash* off another one. I'm coming up with a real *bumper* crop of puns, a real—" He stopped in mid-pun. "Come on, man, I'm killing you."

"I give. You win," Bruce conceded without looking up. The thick, white icing of the cinnamon roll tasted sickeningly sweet. Beer and cinnamon rolls were about as good a combination as beer and Oreos.

"Never seen you give up without a fight before," St. John said. He punctuated the remark with a swig of Coors.

Bruce opened the paper and read the new clue. "How do you know it's on Harriet Island?"

"*Seven red hints*," St. John said. "That's the Schmidt brewery sign. Gotta be. It's either there or up in Cherokee Park. I think queen and river puts it on the river instead of on the bluff."

"Can you see the Schmidt sign from Harriet Island?"

"Don't know. Let's go see."

"What if you can't see that far for the snow?"

"Won't know for sure unless we go look," St. John argued. "If we wait, somebody else crazier than us'll get to it first."

"The snow's pretty deep. The last fuckin' thing I want to do is get stuck." Bruce glanced over at Jo, and instantly regretted using the four-letter word. She never said anything worse than damn.

"We won't get stuck," St. John assured him, looking offended by the remark. "I drove right over here in The Beast. I've never been stuck yet with it.

"Come on," he prodded, standing up suddenly. "What's gotten into you? Don't be such a chicken shit. If you open the paper tomorrow and read that somebody found it in the middle of the night while you were sound asleep, you'll shit. That is," he added, a hard tone in his voice, "if you ever get to sleep."

Bruce looked up at his friend, felt acid anger rising in his throat. "Hey, man, that's out of line," he said in a low voice. He stood up himself. "I'm staying put tonight, okay?" He glanced at Joanna standing at the sink, washing the head of lettuce. "Come on and have supper with us."

St. John's eyes narrowed. Behind his stubble, his jaw was tight. He drained the last of his beer, crumpled the empty Coors can in his hand, and left it rocking on the table.

"Well, you two can sit in here and play house if you want, but I'm going out and look. If I find it, I'll give you a call from the Caribbean." The door slammed behind him.

Bruce looked at the crushed Coors can. It reminded him of a metallic apple core. His spirits suddenly felt like the can looked.

"Well," he said, "I guess you could say Butch is pissed. And I don't think he's staying for supper." Joanna moved about the sink, keeping her back to him. "But that's okay," he added quickly. "That means there'll be that much more for us. I can't wait. I'm starved." He watched her work. Or was she working?

"Jo?"

No answer.

He moved across the room toward her, his feet silent on the kitchen carpet.

"Hey," he said softly, touching her on the shoulder. She started and shrugged him away. With angry movements, she shook the water out of the freshly cored lettuce head.

"Jo?" He grasped her by the shoulders and slowly turned her around to face him. Her lips were pressed tightly together, silent. The tears glistening in the corners of her dark eyes told him everything she had to say.

"Hey," he said gently, touching her under the chin. "It's not your fault. He was way out of line tonight. Making that crack about not getting to sleep." He cupped his hands around her face and kissed her lightly on the forehead. Her pale skin felt hot under his lips. "Let's eat supper like we planned and see what's on TV, okay? I'll talk to him tomorrow."

Joanna drew away from him.

"Yes," she said, turning back to the sink, "but you'll brood about it all night."

NINE

"I'M DONE WITH MY HOMEWORK," Chris announced from his place at the kitchen table. With a flick of his wrist, he flipped the English book shut, then stacked his other books one by one on top of it, slamming each book down. He gave Sharon his version of his father's restless, impatient look.

She sighed as she bent to open the oven door. He always announced himself with such flourish, such salesmanship. His father's genes.

"I wish Dad would hurry up and get home so we could go out and drive around," Chris said.

"I don't think we'll be going anywhere tonight, if he ever gets home," she said, giving the pot roast a final poke with her fork.

"But I did my homework early," he countered.

"Well, then you've got it out of the way for the night, haven't you?" She laid the fork on top of the stove, and reached for a pair of potholders. "We may as well eat before this dries out completely. Your father can have whatever is left over."

"He promised."

She straightened up and set the roaster on top of the stove. "Well, he didn't know it was going to snow all day when he promised." She closed the oven door and switched the oven off.

"Somebody'll find the treasure before long."

"No one is going to go out in this weather unless they're crazy. Now let it go. Go call your brother—and don't yell."

Chris gave her the dirty look he had been perfecting lately as he passed by her.

She shared his irritation. Phil's coming home late from work was hardly unusual—they had eaten hundreds of dinners without him. But this was not a night to be slaving away at the office long after the rest of the working world had plowed their way home through the drifts. She went to the window, and pressed her face against it, shielding her eyes from the kitchen light with her hand. It was still snowing. The six o'clock news had claimed nine inches so far, reporting travel difficult on all freeways and city streets. She felt a growing uneasiness. Could he be stranded somewhere?

Travel had already been slow when she dropped Elaine off at her car after the matinee. They had finally settled on *Family Portrait*, the new Alan Alda movie, which had been billed as a comedy. If William Hurt was too full of angst, then Alan Alda's comedies were becoming so wry, and his dramas so soapy, that she could hardly tell the difference between them anymore. Still, she had appreciated the time spent suspended in the travails of the bickering Berelli family as they gathered together for a formal portrait, forgetting for a while the travails of her own life. The feeling that settled over her as she and Elaine waited for the theater's lights to darken was the same guilty pleasure she had felt whenever she skipped classes in college. She had gotten home early enough to fix a good dinner, something she did too seldom these days, and to think about what Elaine had said at the shop before they closed up. *Oh, don't let him fool you. That's just part of the song and dance.* It couldn't be true. Elaine had lost her objectivity on the subject of men and their careers, and she had good reason to. But not all men were like Dean Murphy, who worked fourteen hours a day, seven days a week, letting his boys learn about sex and life the hard way. Phil couldn't be putting on an act. She'd seen the look on his face last night as he sat at the kitchen table, and heard the doubt in the tired edge in his voice. He wasn't like Dean. He'd been there, taking the boys to hockey games, putting in the effort to get Chris's grades back on track after the move. *After the move.* If they hadn't moved, Chris's grades probably wouldn't have derailed in the first place. The way this thing went round and round.

She set the table for the four of them, and started to dish up the pot roast and vegetables. The back door opened suddenly and Phil blew into the entryway in a blast of snowy wind, slamming the door behind him. He stamped the snow off his shoes and looked up at her.

"Hi, Babe. Should have worn my boots. Smells good. What is it?"

"Pot roast." Her words came out like a watermelon seed spit off the back step. At the sight of him, home all safe and sound, she felt her irritation welling up again.

"Hot damn. My favorite." Phil gave up on wiping his feet. He kicked off his wing tips. If he had caught the tone in her voice, he ignored it. He draped his overcoat over the back of a kitchen chair, pulled down his tie, and unbuttoned the top button of his shirt. "Ahhh. The moment I live for."

"Why so la—" Her words were drowned out by feet thundering down the stairs, a herd of buffalo stampeded by the slam of the back door.

Phil looked at her and winced. "He's going to go right through the stairs one of these days, I swear."

In a moment, Chris was in the kitchen, breathless. "Are we going out to look for the treasure? This morning you said we would."

Phil jabbed a finger into Chris's chest. "Take it easy on those stairs, Buster. They're the only ones we got."

"Sorry. Are we going out?"

Phil looked him up and down. "Have you and Jeff figured out where we should go look?"

Chris looked at the floor. "Not for sure," he mumbled.

"Well, first things first." Phil used his supervisor's voice. "You figure out where to look first, and *then* we'll see about going out." He turned to her again. "You were saying?"

Before she could answer, she heard Jeff's quick footsteps on the carpeted stairs. His step had grown heavier in the past few months, more like his father's than his brother's. He entered the kitchen, a hungry look on his face.

"You could have called," she answered a bit stiffly, not looking at her husband.

"I tried to," Phil said, holding up three fingers. "Three times. But the line was busy. Somebody—" his eyes followed hers as she glanced at Jeff "—was tying up the line. What were you doing, boy, plotting to overthrow the government?"

Jeff shrugged in answer.

Close, she thought, as she carried the platter into the dining room. Plotting with Lisa of Summit Avenue to sneak off together and make her a grandmother. She would have to remind Phil to have a talk with both of the boys about responsibility and diseases. About babies.

"So . . ." Phil said as they settled into their places at the dining room table . ". . . Some weather today, huh?" His eyes flashed in her direction. "Invigorating, I'd say. Did you have much traffic at the store today?"

"We closed up about noon and went to the movies."

"What did you see?"

"The new Alan Alda movie."

"Damn," Phil snapped his fingers in disappointment. "I wanted to see that."

She passed him the platter. "We haven't gone to a movie theater together since we moved here."

"Oh, come on," he said, taking the platter from her. "It hasn't been that long. We all saw that Spielberg movie—the one where Burt Lancaster plays the ghost of Wyatt Earp wandering around in the present, and he walks into a modern-day reenactment of the gunfight at the OK Corral."

"*Now Playing at the OK Corral.* We saw that at the Beacon Hill before we moved."

Phil filled his plate from the platter. "Time flies when you're having fun," he muttered.

"Can we work on the clues?" Chris pleaded. "I already got my homework done."

"Let's eat first," Phil said. "I don't know about you guys, but I'm starved."

The pot roast was not her best. Too dry, as she had feared. But it disappeared quickly as Phil and the boys engaged, between mouthfuls, in the usual topics of dinner conversation: the weather, the North Stars and Timberwolves, Phil quizzing the boys about their days at school. Easy, safe topics. No mention of the promotion offer. Would he bring it up himself, or would one of them have to do it? In Boston, he had called them all into the living room, sat them down on the couch, and made the grand announcement. *I've been transferred. We're moving to St. Paul. That's in Minnesota.* A done deal. At least this time he was taking their feelings into consideration.

"Okay." Phil pushed his plate away. He clapped his hands together, then rubbed them vigorously. "Let's get started. Where's the newspaper and our notebook? Go get 'em." He watched the boys troop out of the dining room. "You're sure quiet tonight." He smiled at her, and leaned over and stroked her forearm. His fingers were cold on her wrist.

"Your hands are cold."

The smile left his face. He pulled his hand away. "We'll go to a movie together soon," he said. "Just the two of us, I promise."

"So what did we decide this morning?" He turned quickly toward the boys as they returned.

"That diamonds means baseball diamonds," Chris said. "That the treasure is on a baseball diamond." His voice cracked on the last word. Whether it was excitement or puberty, she couldn't tell.

"Or at least near a baseball diamond," Jeff corrected.

"I bet it's buried under the pitcher's mound," Chris declared.

"Home plate," Jeff argued. "They wouldn't want you to dig up the pitcher's mound."

"They take home plate up in the winter, dummy," Chris fired back.

"They do not." Jeff's tone was edged with contempt.

"Knock it off, you two," their father interrupted. "Team members don't fight, they work together. We'll look under the pitcher's mound and home plate." He gave first Chris and then Jeff a hard look. "And first, second, and third, if, and I emphasize if, the way you two are acting, we ever find the right baseball diamond. Now let's move on. What's the new clue?"

The boys glared at each other. There was no doubt in their minds this time that they had been jerked back into line.

Jeff unfolded the paper. "Clue 7: *Seven red hints should help you find, a dazzling treasure, one of a kind.*" His words were clipped.

"And what does that mean?" Phil propped his elbows on the table. The proper questions, soliciting the proper answers. Falling back on his management skills. He could do this in his sleep, Sharon thought. The boys, on the other hand . . .

The suggestions accumulated slowly. She only half listened. Stop signs, stoplights, a sign with seven letters on it. Something along Seventh Street. A piece of playground equipment or seven red park shelters. Chris scribbled each suggestion in the notebook.

"I don't know." Phil rubbed his face with his open hands. He suddenly looked tired. "Those are all good suggestions, but something, I don't know what, tells me that this is something special, completely unique to the treasure site. Have we figured out which Dairy Queens are close to parks? Come to think of it, the Dairy Queen sign is red."

"I checked, and there's only one," Jeff said. He pushed his plate aside and spread the map out on the table. "By Phalen Park. You can't tell how close it is on the map. We'll have to drive by it."

Chris gave a pleading look.

His father shook his head. "Not tonight, Slapshot. I could barely get the car in the garage. Let's look at the clues in terms of Phalen Park. Jeff, read each of them, and Chris, check your notes."

Jeff turned to the inside of the paper for the previous clues. "Clue 1: *Somewhere on the ground in Ramsey County, King Boreas has hidden his royal bounty.*"

"Is Phalen Park in Ramsey County?" Phil asked.

Jeff checked the map. "Yes."

"Good. Next clue."

"Clue 2: *'I think I can, I think I can,' might be a clue that has just the right meaning for you.*"

"And what did we say that referred to?"

Chris checked the notebook. "That it meant railroad tracks."

"Any railroad tracks nearby?"

Jeff looked at the map. "There's some, and they look like they're pretty close to the Dairy Queen."

"Good. We're two-for-two. Let's keep going. Next clue." He nodded at Jeff.

"Clue 3: *Enter with a queen, leave via river, this little clue may make you shiver.*"

"We said that referred to Dairy Queen," Phil said. "Now—"

"That's only part of the clue, though," Sharon said. "What about the river part? We never did come up with any ideas about what that meant."

"Well, how about the obvious?" Phil turned to Jeff. "Any rivers near the railroad tracks and the Dairy Queen?"

"No."

"I'm not even convinced that Dairy Queen is the right interpretation of queen," she said. "Maybe queen refers to something else."

"Maybe," Phil said. "Let's come back to that. Let's finish up this Phalen Park idea before we start something else, okay? That way we won't leave anything hanging. What's the next clue?"

"Clue 4: *Watch planes come and watch them go, leaving far behind all this ice and snow.*"

"We said that referred to planes coming and going," Chris said, looking up from the notebook.

"Any airports close by?" Phil waited for Jeff to check the map, then frowned when he shook his head. "No? Well, that doesn't look good. Maybe that clue means something else, too. How about the next one?"

"Clue 5: *In a distant place they're running races, from the treasure site you can't see the runners' faces.*"

"And we decided that means . . . ?" he turned to Chris for the answer.

Chris rustled the pages of the notebook. "I got marathon, jogging, and college and high school tracks written down."

"Oh, yes," Phil nodded. "College or high school tracks near a park. You boys were going to look up the addresses of schools and colleges. Do you have them? No? Well, then let's go on."

"Clue 6: *Diamonds are a girl's best friend—*"

The baseball clue," Phil interrupted. "Any baseball diamonds in our Phalen Park?"

"There's no way to tell on the map," Jeff said.

"There must be some kind of baseball diamond there," Sharon said. "What's a park without a baseball diamond?"

"Good point." Phil nodded his agreement. "Let's assume there's one there. That brings us up to *seven red hints* again."

"Can we go over and look tomorrow?" Chris begged.

"Well, let's summarize what we got here. For Phalen Park, we got the fact that it's in Ramsey County, that train tracks are nearby, there's a Dairy Queen—" he looked at her squarely "—which may or may not be the right interpretation of the clue; but no river." He shifted in his chair. "There's no airport nearby for planes to come and go, and we don't know at this time if there are any high school or college running tracks nearby, although the clue could refer to jogging paths, I suppose. That phrase running races just bothers me. Joggers don't run races. And we're assuming that there's a baseball diamond nearby. Finally, none of us has come up with a suitable interpretation of what *seven red hints* refers to."

He looked at each of them in turn. "I don't know, boys. Looks pretty skinny to me. If I were a betting man, I wouldn't put my money down on Phalen Park. At least not yet."

"Maybe there's something there that we could spot if we drove around," Chris said.

"Maybe," Phil said.

"Let's go tomorrow," Chris said.

"You'll be in school," Sharon reminded him, "or did you forget you were a student?"

"School tomorrow?" Chris gave her a knowing look. "No way. Snow day. All the kids said so."

"There'll be a new clue in the morning," Jeff reminded them. "That might help us."

"That's true." Phil looked at each of the boys in turn. "Let's hold off on going out until we see tomorrow's clue. If we can come up with a good location, we'll try and drive around tomorrow night, if . . ." he held up his hand for emphasis ". . . if the weather permits." He slapped the table with the open palm of his hand. "We're adjourned."

"Wait."

Jeff's request was barely audible. His face had changed. The enthusiasm of the treasure hunt had drained out of his eyes. He looked deadly serious, almost fearful. "Dad?"

"What?"

Jeff fingered the city map. "Have you decided whether or not we're moving yet?"

The dreaded subject dragged out into the open at last. A pointed, direct question, which had weighed heavily on everyone's mind for the past two days. Sharon looked over the island of dirty dishes at her husband. She felt her stomach lurch. How would he answer?

Phil pushed his chair back and stretched his legs out in front of him. He crossed his arms over his chest.

"It's not all my decision," he said gravely. "I asked you boys to think about what moving meant to you and let me know. So far, I haven't heard anything."

His face was set with the Challenge Look. "So what do you think?"

TEN

STEVEN CARPENTER ROLLED ONTO HIS BACK and clasped his hands behind his head. Somewhere in the darkness above him was the bedroom ceiling, with its water stain shaped like the little clouds he had drawn in pictures as a kid. Little clouds adrift in the colorless paper sky. He felt comfortably adrift himself, the tension that had twisted his guts for the past few days gone, replaced by a peaceful feeling. He inhaled deeply, drawing in the heavy scent of sex that surrounded them. It was surprising the way good sex could turn things around, and this was the best it had been in weeks. Maybe all their fighting this week had been because they had missed their Sunday-nighter.

"You know, this is the one time I wish I smoked," Debi said, breaking the silence. She shinnied up against the headboard, pulling the sheet up around her. "Don't you just feel like a cigarette afterwards?"

"Or a joint." Rolling over, he rested his head against Debi's stomach. He felt her fingers caress the back of his neck. "Peaceful Easy Feeling." He hadn't played that old Eagles tune in a long time. The thought of the song stirred the dust off a pleasant memory.

"Remember the time we laid out all night on the top row of the stadium with Hutch and Jody? Man, I don't think I ever got so mellow in my life. I thought I had gone to heaven."

"I remember being too scared to climb down again," Debi said. "You know that dope mostly makes me scared. And you two singing that awful song at the top of your lungs."

"It wasn't an awful song." He raised his head to look at her.

"Okay, so it wasn't awful. It was . . . old."

They remembered the same things so differently. Hutcherson, his sophomore roommate, had also been a seventies music fan, leaning toward country rock. A big Eagles fan, Hutch had bought used copies of all of the band's old albums, which he played endlessly. Hutch was also a lousy guitar player, the one person he felt comfortable playing in front of. One warm spring night they had sat on their beds in their dorm room, listening to a scratchy, slightly warped copy of "Peaceful Easy Feeling" over and over again, picking out the different guitar parts. When they got the song down, they had celebrated by putting their guitars back in their cases, collecting Debi and Jody, and heading off to the top of the stadium to get stoned.

"Up so high," he said, picturing the night again in his mind. "Literally and figuratively. It was so clear that night, I could almost reach out and touch the stars."

"How poetic," Debi said. "You should write songs."

The remark stung like the sudden smack of a wet towel on bare skin. He started to sit up, but he felt Debi's hand on his shoulder pushing him back down.

"Steven, I'm sorry." Her fingers were warm on his neck. "I shouldn't have said that."

He let it go, in deference to the moment. Tonight had come as a complete surprise. They had caught the same bus home, standing on opposite ends of the packed aisle as the driver plowed his way through the snow. Once home, Debi had immediately attacked the treasure hunt clues, interpreting and reinterpreting them as she paced around the living room, the skirt of her red dress swirling around her legs. She got nowhere. Suddenly she had collapsed into the blue chair, tossing the *Pioneer Press* on the floor.

"I hate to say this," she had said, "but I think you're right about the diamond clue. It must mean ball fields. Jack of Diamonds is just too big a stretch."

"Why do you hate to say it?" he had asked.

She had answered him with a teasing look. "Because I have a reputation to protect."

She had used that very line on him four years earlier, on the night he first tried to sleep with her. But she had changed her mind before the night was over.

He had taken both the look and the remark as a signal. "What do you say we damage your reputation a little bit, right now?"

Without a word, she had risen from the blue chair, ripped off her white jacket, threw it in the air behind her, and headed toward the bedroom.

Now, lying here with his head gently rising and falling on her belly, the peaceful feeling slipping away despite his efforts to hang onto it, he thought about signals. A couple of years ago, they hadn't depended on signals; they just did it, not bothering to worry about one another's needs, because their needs were exactly the same. Somehow, everything had become so complicated. Now, both of them had to be in the right mood at the same time, something that lately occurred with decreasing frequency. And they had to *have* time. They couldn't just skip work to mess around like they had skipped class.

Still, when it worked, everything seemed possible. Even New York. He sat up beside her, and pressed his bare back against the headboard.

"So were you serious this morning about moving to New York someday?"

"Sure I was. You think I'm going to be satisfied forever with St. Paul? The real financial careers are on Wall Street, not in the St. Paul skyway. I mean, St. Paul is a step up from Mankato, but it's still small-town. Just think what New York would be like. Wall Street. Central Park. And Broadway, all the theaters. It would be the coolest place."

"So when are you planning to move?"

"Oh, Steven, I don't know. It's just a dream, okay?"

"Maybe if we found the treasure medallion we could use the money for New York."

"Sure. I could get a job in an investment firm on Wall Street and you could play your music."

"I'll play in the coffeehouses in Greenwich Village, just like Dylan did."

"Do they even have coffeehouses in Greenwich Village anymore? They're probably all sports bars or gay bars by now. You'll have to go straight to Carnegie Hall."

"Carnegie Hall. Right."

"Steven, you've got to think big if you want to go places."

"Madison Square Garden, then. That's where the big rock and roll concerts are." Thinking big. Just coming to St. Paul had been one hell of a big step from the North Dakota Plains. He had felt swallowed up by all the concrete and glass. Most of the time he had stayed on campus, which had a kind of small-town atmosphere to it. When he did venture off campus to downtown, the skyline had looked so imposing, from a distance as tall and mystical as the Emerald City in *The Wizard of Oz.* But New York and the Garden! Jeez.

"I need a shower," Debi said, fanning the air in front of her nose. "And I'm hungry. It's your turn to cook."

"I was just thinking about practicing a little."

"Okay," Debi said agreeably. "You practice, and I'll make supper. But you owe me one." Foregoing her underwear, she pulled on pink sweat pants, pausing to sniff and frown before she pulled the band up around her waist. "It's a good thing we're not going anywhere tonight." She rummaged in the dresser for a sweatshirt. "Hot dogs or Campbell's soup?"

"How about both?"

"Why don't you serenade me while I cook?"

"Maybe. I've got to tune up first."

"You're good at tuning things up," she said with a raise of her eyebrows. "Dogs in five minutes."

He pulled the covers up around him, too comfortable to move. Going to New York and making it big. It was exciting to think about. How did people do it? How did they get from one place to another? How did Dylan get from Hibbing to New York and superstardom? How did Prince go from North Minneapolis to international fame? Hutch had graduated with highest honors, and was now deep into his first year of an MBA program out East. And himself? He was a library clerk. And Deb was a clerk in a brokerage firm, the bottom rung of the ladder, maybe even the ground under the ladder. What made the difference?

One thing for sure, he wasn't going to get anywhere lying naked in bed this early in the evening. He rolled off the bed and reached for his guitar case leaning in the corner of the room. He sat cross-legged in the middle of the bed to tune up. He reeked a little himself.

Trying to recall the tune he had heard in the patter of the shower that morning, he strummed a three-chord pattern. Good old G, C, and D. A lot of fine songs had been written with these chords, some of Dylan's best tunes. He closed his eyes, and put an aching tone into his delivery of the lyrics.

> They were searching
> Searching for treasure,
> Searching for the love
> They once had,
> Searching for the times
> That were glad . . .

ELEVEN

ALFRED LOOKED UP FROM THE DRIVEWAY toward the street. Although he had been shoveling steadily for thirty minutes, he was less than halfway from the garage to the curb. The muscles in his lower back screamed in protest as he slowly straightened up. He leaned on the shovel handle and rested his limp arms. The neighborhood was bathed in orange light thrown up by the city at the snow-filled clouds hanging just above the bare trees and reflected back down to the snowy lots, only to be thrown up at the clouds again. Light reflected back and forth to infinity, like barbershop mirrors. Snowflakes still fluttered out of the sky. The familiar old neighborhood looked peaceful in the snowy light. But everything was somehow askew and strange at the same time, pulled out of shape by heavy, rounded snowcaps. Across the street, the young couple's rusty green Dodge sat next to the curb, shapeless beneath a blanket of snow. The bushes in front of their house were flat under the weight of snow.

He flexed his tired arms and rotated his shoulders in their joints. He often complained to Genevieve about snow shoveling, but tonight he was grateful for the task. He needed to be busy. He needed to be alone so he could think. He bent again to his shoveling, the ache in his heart as heavy as the ache in his back and arms. Rudy. Such a shocking, frightening secret he had found in the bottom of that dresser drawer. *Why? Why? WHY?*

He felt in his bones the scrape of the shovel across the cement driveway. The scraping sound echoed off the side of the house next door. He felt the sweat trickling down his back, his legs. The snowflakes cooled his face. The soft whump each shovelful of snow made as it hit the snowy ground sounded just like his spirits felt.

The magazines had been quickly disposed of, without Genevieve catching him. On purpose, he had left his gloves in the house, and once they had locked up and crawled into the pickup to go home, he had pronounced them missing and gone back in to get them. Inside, he had stuffed the magazines in the bottom of a plastic trash bag, quickly filled the bag with other newspapers and slipped out the back door to the trash can. Genevieve had not even complained about how long he had been gone.

But the shock, the sick feeling he had felt in his stomach, was still with him. Could it possibly be true? Could Rudy be like the men in the pictures?

He stopped again and leaned on his shovel. "How come you never married?"

Rudy's answer floated to him from out of the night.

"Never found anyone who could put up with me."

"That's a lie," Alfred said into the night. "I know better. I found magazines. How come you never told me?"

"How come you never asked?"

They had never talked about it. And he had never really thought much about Rudy in that regard, as a man with needs. His own needs had been . . . well . . . put aside years ago. Rudy's needs had never really been . . . specified. There had been one woman in Rudy's life that he knew about, Marie, between World War II and Korea, at the same time he had been courting Genevieve. The four of them had had good times together, catching the streetcar downtown to go to a movie at the Strand or the Tower Theater. Marie had loved Rudy, he knew, for she told Genevieve so many times in their visits to the ladies' room, which, of course, Genevieve had later passed on to him. The four of them had even talked about a double wedding. But something had gone wrong—exactly what, Rudy was never very clear about—and Marie suddenly married another man, a butcher, and moved over to the East Side. After Marie there had been no one. *Never found anyone who could put up with me.* For years, that had been Rudy's stock reply, delivered with a chuckle, whenever the subject of marriage had come up. A lie and the truth at the same time.

"Well, what in the hell am I supposed to think about you now?"

No answer. Talking to himself. He pushed the shovel into the snowdrift. What *was* he supposed to think about Rudy now?

After their folks were killed, it was Rudy who had kept them together. Barely fourteen, Rudy had argued that he was big enough to take care of his own brother. At the wake, when relatives and strangers ignored him and continued to discuss what to do with them as though they weren't even there, Rudy had quietly motioned him outside. In the backyard, Rudy had stuffed him in the cob box and ordered him to stay there until he came for him. Rudy had refused to tell anyone where he was until they promised not to separate them. The family elders had finally decided that Tantchen, their father's elderly maiden aunt, would live in their house and take care of them. When she died, Rudy, at sixteen, had dropped out of school and gone to work for the railroad. For the next fifty years he worked in the Jackson Street yards bumping cars, work that took him around and around the yard, but never out on the line. He had been born, lived, and died in the same house, leaving behind only a houseful of newspaper clippings and a drawer containing magazines with pictures of men doing disgraceful things to one another. And one brother who was shocked, heartsick, and . . . confused.

He stopped and leaned on his shovel. So many things made sense now: the fact that Rudy had never married; the fact that he had never much gone in for dirty jokes and stories; why Rudy had been so silent when Genevieve had clucked about AIDS as God's punishment for those who sinned. Genevieve. She would never, *never* know. But he himself! How could he not have known? Could Rudy have kept this such a secret for so long, if he, Alfred, hadn't closed his eyes to it, hadn't wanted to know?

The front door of the house opened, and Genevieve's gray head poked out.

"Alfred," she called. He tried to ignore her by looking down at his work. She pushed the door open, and stepped out onto the porch.

"Alfred! You come in and rest. You'll give yourself a heart attack. Why don't you get a snowblower like everyone else?"

"I'm almost done." He shoveled faster. "It's not that bad."

"You should have waited until it stopped snowing. You'll be right back out here tomorrow shoveling again."

"It's easier to shovel twice when it ain't so deep than to shovel once after it quits. Go back inside before you catch cold."

The door slammed shut. He leaned on his shovel. What did it all add up to, Rudy's life? Had he ever been happy? Had there been some-one—a man, maybe even many of them—after Marie? People Rudy was too private about or too ashamed of to introduce to him? He thought of the crucifix hanging on the wall above the dresser in Rudy's bedroom. No, he didn't think there were people in Rudy's life that he didn't know about. He had never really thought of Rudy as a religious person— he seldom went to Mass except on holidays. But there had always been a quiet dignity about the way Rudy lived his life. He didn't talk about his beliefs; he just lived them. Rudy never strayed very far from what the Bible told him to do.

He pushed his shovel into the snow again. Whatever he decided about Rudy, he would have to decide alone. Rudy was gone. He couldn't go to him and demand to know what he was doing with the magazines, couldn't confirm if what he suddenly feared was true. Not that it would have done much good to go to Rudy anyway. There were certain things you just didn't talk about with Rudy. He had his boundaries set up like a barb-wire fence. He gave off a signal of some kind that it wasn't a subject for conversation. If Rudy never brought it up, neither did you.

He reached the end of the driveway, pushing the last of the snow out into the street. All that was left was to shovel the walk up to the front door. He turned to face the house. He had stood in this spot so many times, after shoveling out the driveway. Through the years, he had worn out a half-dozen shovels. What did it all mean, anyway?

The front door opened again, and Genevieve poked her head out.

"I'm coming," he said before she could open her mouth. He shouldered the shovel and headed up the cleared driveway toward the back door. The front sidewalk could wait until tomorrow.

TWELVE

BRUCE AWOKE IN THE DARKNESS WITH A JERK, an image from the now-familiar dream still visible in his mind, fading away like a movie screen going dark. It was the same dream every time. From a distance, he saw himself as a diver in brief white trunks, standing on a platform. With a bend of his knees and then a sudden push of his legs, he leaped off the platform into the air, in the same movement sweeping his pointed toes gracefully up above his head and touching them with his fingertips, arching his back just as he reached the full height of his leap. Then he was falling backward headfirst, the diving platform whizzing by him in a blur, every muscle in his body moving into place as he glanced down and saw the surface of the water rushing up to him, and down below that, the blue cement of the pool's bottom. This time, just as he saw himself slide straight as an arrow into the clear, bluish water with no splash whatsoever, he was suddenly awake, as if the cold shock of his entry had yanked him out of the dream.

A strange dream, since he had never been a diver. And stranger still that he had now experienced this same dream several times recently. On other nights he had remained asleep, plunging to the bottom of the pool in a watery cloud of air bubbles, planting his feet on the blue bottom, and pushing off toward the surface. Then the welcome burst through the surface, a breath of air, a shake of his head, and a check for the score as the crowd began to applaud. A nine-point-nine out of ten.

He pulled the covers up under his chin. He felt the comfortable, snug presence of the deep snow all around the house. He glanced at the clock. Past midnight. They had been asleep for only a few minutes. When he was troubled about something, he often dozed off and then woke up and tossed and turned for another hour before going back to sleep. What this dream meant, he didn't know for sure. Jo loved to interpret people's dreams, but he hadn't told her about it yet. He knew it had something to do with where he was at right now, the way he saw his life since he had met her. Something wonderful, filled with a simple grace and beauty. He rolled onto his right side, pressed himself like a spoon against Joanna's back. He lay his head on his upper right arm and wrapped his left arm around Jo's waist.

Something wonderful—but not quite perfect. He rolled onto his back again, crossed his hands behind his head. One thing for sure stood between him and a perfect ten-point dive. *You'll brood about it all night.* Jo had been right, but he had done his best not to show it. He rolled to his side and looked at the clock again. So what if it was past midnight? Most likely, St. John would still be up. If he was sacked out already, too bad. St. John had rousted *him* from a dead sleep a million times with a late-night phone call. What was the guy's problem anyway? It had to be something more than his own refusal to go out in the middle of a blizzard to look for a stupid medallion. He looked at the clock again. *Do it. Get it over with, find out what was really bugging him.*

Moving slowly so he would not wake Joanna, he eased out of bed. At the bedroom window, he saw that the snow was starting to taper off. South Robert was quiet. A pair of tracks ran in each direction through the snow. He pulled on his jeans and felt around on the floor for his flannel shirt.

In the kitchen, he dialed St. John's number. He counted the rings. Three, four, five. St. John was a solid sleeper. He imagined St. John rolling around blindly in the dark, his head full of feathers, not knowing whether to reach for the phone, shut off the alarm clock, or get up and answer the doorbell. Ten rings, twelve, fifteen. Even if he were dead, he should have heard the rings and answered by now. Maybe he was still out treasure hunting, slogging around in the snowdrifts on Harriet Island, his shovel over his shoulder. Twenty rings, twenty-one. That, or he was sitting there on his living room couch in a cloud of cigarette smoke, counting the rings himself as they echoed through the smoky air, knowing who it was and refusing to answer because he was so pissed off. The son of a bitch. On the thirtieth ring, he hung up.

Back in the bedroom, he shucked off his pants and sat down on the edge of the bed to unbutton his shirt.

"Didn't answer, huh?"

Startled, he stopped with his shirt halfway off his shoulders. He felt the mattress sink as Jo rolled over. He dropped the shirt on the floor. He slid into the warmth of the covers, felt for her, and pulled her head against his shoulder.

"No," he said after a long moment. "He didn't."

THURSDAY

ONE

THE WARM AIR INSIDE THE SUPERAMERICA felt good on his face. Keith looked around for the newspapers, but before he spotted them, the whole interior of the store disappeared as his glasses fogged up. He yanked them off and rubbed away the fog with his thumb. The place looked empty.

"Hello?"

The clerk came out of the back. He was about twenty-five, blond, with a diamond earring gleaming in his left earlobe.

"You got the Thursday morning *Pioneer Press* yet?" Keith asked as he pushed his glasses on again.

The clerk shook his head. "Not for another three or four hours. You're about the tenth guy in here asking. Try the newsstand downtown, corner of Seventh and Wabasha. Don't go to the *Pioneer Press* office. They don't have 'em there much earlier than we get 'em."

He knew the place. He had bought early papers there in other years. The newsstand sold the first papers in town, and during the treasure hunt they went fast. He pulled back his sleeve to check his watch. A little before one. The middle of the night, but he would be lucky if there were any left by the time he got downtown. This was one time he wished he worked with someone. Treasure hunters who worked in pairs often sent one guy to wait in line for a paper, while the other guy waited next to his CB radio in some park. As soon as the first guy got a paper, he read the clue to the other guy over the CB.

"You looking in Cherokee?" the clerk asked.

Keith nodded. "Me and about two million other people."

"I'd be out lookin' if I wasn't here on the graveyard shift," the clerk said. "But I wouldn't be wasting my time in Cherokee. I'd be down on Harriet Island. Closer to the river. You know, *enter with a queen, leave with a river,* or something like that."

"You might be right," Keith said. He didn't want to discuss clues with anybody right now. He just wanted to get the chill out of his bones. He was cold, hungry, and tired in that order. He went to the refrigerated display case to look at the sandwiches. There wasn't much from which to choose. He selected two precooked cheeseburgers sealed in plastic. The coffee pot was nearly full, which could be either a good or a bad sign.

"How old is this coffee?"

"A lot fresher'n those gut bombs," the clerk said. "It's pretty fresh, actually. Sold a lot of the stuff tonight. Treasure hunters like you comin' in to warm up."

"These and a large coffee," Keith told the clerk. While the cheeseburgers warmed in the microwave, he poured himself a cup of coffee and capped it with a plastic lid.

"Anything else?"

"You could make it quit snowing," Keith said. He reached for his wallet.

"I hear you." The clerk punched up the total. "I'll be shoveling snow all day tomorrow. First my place, and then my old lady's. Three-seventy-one altogether." He took Keith's five, made change, and held it out to drop in Keith's hand. "Happy hunting."

Back in the car, he started the engine and let it run for a minute. Carefully he pried the plastic top off the coffee cup. The steam rose up like a wisp of smoke. He opened the car door and poured the top inch of coffee into the snow. He blew over the edge of the cup and took a sip. It tasted surprisingly good, but it was too hot to drink. He capped the coffee again and slid the cup into the plastic holder that clipped onto the passenger's door.

He tore away the plastic from one of the cheeseburgers and bit into it. For a moment, he thought he had mistakenly bit into the plastic, but then he picked up the faint taste of cheese and dill pickle. The burger shops were bad enough sometimes, but this stuff! Just as well eat the plastic and pitch the burgers. They were probably both made at the same place, on parallel assembly lines.

Driving with one hand, he turned onto Smith Avenue. The best way to get downtown from here was to head right down Smith, over the High Bridge to West Seventh, and make a right. The second bite of the cheeseburger was little better than the first, but he was hungry enough to eat anything, and he finished it in three bites. It had been a long afternoon and evening. He had been disappointed to find several dozen treasure hunters already wandering around the park when he arrived. Through the afternoon and evening, the number of treasure hunters had continued to grow. When he had finally frozen out and headed toward the car, the whole north end of the park was swarming with treasure hunters digging away in the fresh snow.

But there was something about Cherokee Park that was beginning to bother him. The north end was close to the blinking Schmidt sign, all right, but it was too far away from the baseball backstop, which was at the other end of the park. If you were close to the backstop, you couldn't see the sign at all. Maybe the sign just located the park, and the backstop located the spot within the park. The new clue, he hoped, would give a hint that Cherokee was the right park, or else describe something within the park that he could easily identify.

Coming onto the south end of the High Bridge, he felt like he was in an airplane coming in for a landing. On the sides of the bridge, a row of fuzzy streetlights guided his descent toward the other bank. Ahead on the left, the red warning lights of the NSP smokestack were spots of pink through the falling snow. Behind NSP, the Schmidt sign was barely visible, a pink smudge in the snowy sky. Across the river above the empty black space of the rugged riverbank, the line of streetlights along Cliff Road burned dimly through the snow. Somewhere in the distance behind them, lost in the orange glow of falling snow and city light, was Cathedral Hill. Normally you could see the unlighted Cathedral from here, a brooding silhouette against the night sky, and beyond that the gleaming white State Capitol, stately and impressive even from this distance. But not tonight.

West Seventh Street had been plowed. He turned right without bothering to stop for the red light. Downtown was deserted, the sidewalks white and trackless. He cut onto Fifth Street to get to Wabasha. Downtown St. Paul. Surely the only place in the world where Seventh Street cut *across* Fifth and Sixth, and then turned into a mall.

Wabasha had not been plowed, but plenty of Winter Carnival traffic had kept the street open. A well-traveled track cut over to the little newsstand. A car was just pulling away. He hoped the stand still had some papers left. He pulled in behind the departing car and rolled down his window.

"Morning paper?"

The attendant nodded his head. Keith hopped out of the car, and slogged over to the stand. He dug in his pocket for the change.

"Just about out," the attendant said. "Would have run out an hour or more ago if the weather wasn't so rotten."

He crawled back into the car and left the door slightly ajar so he could read the clue under the dome light. Clue 8: *Midway between two trees lies the treasure, pretty as you please. But which two trees, we confess, is up to you to guess.* This did not help much. It was an inside-the-park location clue, and not a very helpful one at that. There must be a thousand trees in the park. He read the clue again. A horn sounded behind him.

"Yeah, yeah," he muttered. He dropped the paper in the seat beside him and slipped the car into gear. Out of the way, he stopped again to decide what to do. Since the clue didn't give him any reason to believe it wasn't still in Cherokee Park, he might as well go back there and search some more. You didn't find the medallion unless you were out there looking for it. And Cherokee was still as good a place as any to look. The trick was going to be walking through the park and spotting two trees that somehow stood out. In the last hour or two, he had noticed a lot of treasure hunters just walking around with their shovels over their shoulders, and now he understood what they were doing. They were looking for the right trees. He felt like he was at a disadvantage. Maybe someone had already found the right two trees, picked up the medallion, and gone home. If that were the case, the word would get out quick enough, and the park would empty fast. That had happened to him a couple of times. It was a lousy feeling.

Driving with one hand, he ate the other cheeseburger on the way back to Cherokee Park. Going upgrade on the High Bridge this time, the Nova's wheels spun in the deep snow. He passed the SuperAmerica again and wondered if Toni would be working this late at her store.

At the south end of the park, he pulled the Nova over near the baseball backstop. A horde of treasure hunters was digging away on both sides of the wire backstop and all over the infield. They were wasting their time. It wasn't there—no trees to go midway between. Maybe he still had a leg up on a few people. He uncapped his coffee and tried it again. Perfect. He leaned back in the seat and closed his eyes. His body ached from dig-

ging all afternoon and evening, and from carrying the weight of extra
clothes. It would be nice to stand in a hot shower and steam away his
aches and pains, then crawl into bed and fall asleep next to someone.
Old Toni. If he found the treasure medallion, he'd give her a call.

TWO

"NO *WAY*, JOSE," JEFF SNORTED.

Still wearing her bathrobe, Sharon turned from the counter with
her refilled coffee mug just in time to see him make a lunge across the
kitchen table for his younger brother's treasure hunt notebook. Treasure
hunting was considerably looser and more spirited when Phil was ab-
sent.

"Quit it." Chris yanked the notebook up against his chest. "I'm writin'
it down, anyway. You gotta keep open to all the options. Dad says
that—"

"'Hall trees' is *stupid*," Jeff interrupted, feigning another grab for the
notebook and instead grabbing Chris's pen off the table. He flipped the
pen into the air like a juggler's Indian club, then caught it as it came som-
ersaulting down. "Have you ever seen a hall tree outside? The treasure
is *outside*, pinhead. Don't try to read a bunch of crap into every clue like
Dad does. What the hell does he know about it? It means tree trees, like
oaks or maples. Trees are trees. It's buried midway between two trees in
some park, period." He flipped the pen into the air again.

"Give it back!" Chris grabbed for it, but Jeff jerked it out of the air,
simultaneously making another lunge for the notebook.

Chris pushed his chair back out of range and lowered the notebook
into his lap. "Hall trees isn't stupid. 'Trees are trees.' Now *that's* stupid."

"All right, you two, back to your corners," Sharon said. "And
you," she pointed a finger at Jeff, "watch your language, mister. Give him
back his pen."

"'Trees are trees,'" Chris mimicked. "How stupid can you get?"

"Sit on it, Squirrel Face." Jeff threw the pen on the table.

"You sit on it."

"Enough, I said." She set her mug down on the table with a
thump and sat down between them. "I don't know if I can put up with

playing referee to you two all day. Both of you are acting like four-year-olds. I think I'll give you each five bucks and send you to the movies for the day."

"Better make it ten, if you do, Ma," Chris said, as he scooted his chair up to the table again. "Then we can have popcorn, too." He dropped the notebook on the counter.

"I don't know if either of you is worth popcorn." Then, seeing the hurt look cross his face, she reached out and gave him a little tweak on the ear to take some of the sting out of her words. "Just kidding." She let her hand rest on his shoulder. With her free hand, she reached out and tugged the long strand of hair at the back of Jeff's neck, half expecting him to jerk away. Instead, he leaned over the table, crossed his arms, and rested his chin on them. She patted him on the back between his shoulder blades.

They all seemed a little testy this morning, despite the free snow day that stretched out before them. Especially Jeff. *Don't try to read a bunch of crap into every clue like Dad does. What the hell does he know about it?* What was that outburst all about? Some unspoken animosity toward his father left over from last night's discussion about moving? He had been unusually quiet this morning, even greeting with silence WCCO's announcement that St. Paul public schools were closed for the day.

Chris, of course, had given her a know-it-all look. "I told you last night we wouldn't have school today," he had gloated.

A brief telephone conference with Elaine had produced the decision to close the bookstore for the day. Only Phil had carried on as usual. He was already dressed for work when WCCO's school closing announcement interrupted the morning's discussion of the new treasure hunt clue.

"Nobody put an announcement on the radio that I could stay home," he had whined, milking the situation for all it was worth. "I guess I'll just go down to the office and *slave away* while you guys spend the day playing in the snow."

"Just call in and tell them you're staying home," Chris had suggested. "Then we can all go out looking for the treasure."

"I wish I could, Slapshot, but I can't today," Phil had answered. Then he had excused himself to catch the Grand Avenue bus instead of fighting the snowy streets himself. Unsure of the fare, he had taken enough change to ride halfway back to Boston.

The treasure hunt discussion had gone on, quickly degenerating into bickering between the two boys. What was it, Sharon wondered, typical sibling rivalry or delayed reaction to the lack of a decision about The Decision? Last night, the boys had wilted under their father's Challenge Look, saying nothing more than they liked it here. To her, that had been enough; but Phil had continued to lobby ever so gently for the move, reminding them that his raise—after taxes—would pay for the first year of college for Jeff, which was right around the corner. And, Phil had continued, you never advance in life if you hang back and stay with what's comfortable. If you want to be successful, it means taking risks. The sooner they understood that, the bigger advantage they would have over the rest of the world.

She had put the issue into a motion then and called for a vote. How many are in favor? Raise your hands. But Phil had refused to vote, claiming he still hadn't made up his mind, and didn't have to until next Monday. "It's not the sort of decision I'm going to let myself be rushed into," he'd said. And in the end, no one had voted, leaving the issue officially undecided. She and Phil had argued about it again after the boys went upstairs.

"They don't want to go," she had told Phil as she made the coffee and set the pot's timer for morning.

"Come off it! They didn't say that," Phil retorted. "They only said they like it here."

"The fact that Jeff brought it up at all is indication enough that he doesn't want to go," she had argued.

"Or that he's just curious about what the rest of us think. Stop poisoning everything with your own feelings."

"Poisoning everything? How can you expect them to be honest when you pump them full of garbage about how much more money you'll make and how important it is to take risks?"

"That's not garbage; it happens to be true. Look," he had said, his face suddenly drawn and his voice low, "I know this isn't easy for anybody. I certainly don't know for sure what's the best thing to do. And no matter what we decide, there are going to be misgivings and regrets. I want this to be a family decision as much as possible. We don't have to decide until this weekend, so let's give it a rest, okay?" And with that, he had picked up his wing tips from the floor in the entryway, plucked his overcoat by the collar off the back of the kitchen chair, and headed toward the front hall closet.

Now with Phil gone off to work, the three of them had the whole day to talk about it, unchallenged. She moved her hands up to squeeze each of them by the nape of the neck.

"Listen," she said. "I have something to ask you. Tell me the truth. What do you guys really think about moving? Jeff, you brought it up last night—you must have some feelings about it. Or were you just curious about what the rest of us think?" Phil's words burned on her tongue.

"I don't know. I like it here and everything," he said, staring at the city map. "It'd be sorta interesting to go, too." He shrugged. "I don't know."

"Well, if you had to say yes or no right now, what would you say?"

"No, I guess."

There. A no vote. On the record. "Why?" she asked.

"I don't know."

"Come on," she prodded.

"I don't buy that line of Dad's about taking risks all the time. It's comfortable here, you know? If you like what you've got, why change it?

"I mean," he continued, straightening up, "sometimes I wonder if Dad is ever satisfied with anything, you know?"

"Well, he has a lot of ambitions, I'll grant you that." She turned to Chris. "And what about you, Popcorn Eater?"

"I think it would be cool to go to California. Except that the Padres and the Chargers stink." He drew a little red square on the notebook page with the pen and colored it in.

"All right," she said. "What if we went to Denver instead?"

Chris shrugged. "I guess that'd be okay, too."

"So you vote to go?"

"I guess so. Why not?"

"What if we stayed here?"

He shrugged.

A split vote. Phil, for all his lobbying, had been right about one thing. No matter what they decided to do, there would be misgivings and regrets.

"What do you think we should do, Ma?" Jeff asked. The question she dreaded, one she'd asked herself a hundred times these past three days. She looked across the room, focusing on the clock above the sink. Seven-thirty. She felt their eyes on her.

"I see both sides, too," she heard herself say. "But I'm like you; I feel pretty comfortable here. I've got the store started. I'd hate to leave." There. Officially on the record herself, in front of witnesses.

"They probably don't have winter carnival treasure hunts in San Diego or Denver," Chris said.

"Probably not. At least not in San Diego. I don't know about Denver. So if we're going to find a treasure medallion, we'll have to do it here."

"Can we go out and look someplace, today?" Chris begged. "Pleeeeasse?"

His tone was playful, but he wore his father's look of restlessness and ambition, a look that had begun to worry her. She looked at Jeff, wondering if she should suggest that he call Lisa and ask her along. No, better to let him bring that up himself.

"All right." She reached for the newspaper. "But if we're going out in all this snow, we'd better have a place in mind. We pretty much ruled out Phalen Park last night because it didn't fit enough of the clues. Clue 1, we said, meant on the ground. Clue 2 had to do with trains. Clue 3 was *Enter with a queen, leave via river.* Clue 4 was *watch planes come and watch them go.* Clue 5 was runners running races; Clue 6 referred to baseball diamonds. Clue 7 was *seven red hints,* and Clue 8, *midway between two trees.*

"You know," she said, looking up, "I still think the most important clue is number three. *Enter with a queen, leave via river, this little clue may make you shiver.*"

"We said that meant the Dairy Queen," Chris said.

"I know, but we never came up with a meaning for river. I mentioned the other night that river could be a street named for a river."

"So you drive into the park past a Dairy Queen, and out of the park on a street named for a river," Jeff said.

"Or," she said, "how about entering on a *street* named for a queen and exiting on a street named for a river?"

"Hey, cool," Chris said.

"Let's make a list of names of queens and rivers."

"I already got some queens wrote down." Chris flipped the notebook back a few pages. "Elizabeth, Izabeela—"

"Isabella," she corrected.

"—Mary, Mary, Queen of Scots." He looked up.

"Anyone got any others?"

"Queen Victoria," Jeff added.

"Queen Anne," she said, remembering Richard Burton and Genevieve Bujold in *Anne of the Thousand Days*. Who were the rest of Henry VIII's queens? There were a couple of Catherines at least. The rest of them had slipped away from her. "Try Catherine. How about rivers?"

"The Mississippi, obviously," Jeff said.

"Obviously. I mentioned the Charles River the other day. Did we get that one down?"

Chris thumbed through the pages for a moment, then wrote the name down. She felt a flicker of irritation that he had ignored it the other day as unimportant. "What else? This could mean rivers that are really well known or rivers that are really obscure."

She watched Chris scribble the suggestions as they came up: the Ohio, the Missouri, the Nile, the Amazon. She recited the Massachusetts rivers that came immediately to mind: the Muddy, the Connecticut, the Ipswich, the Merrimack, and the Concord.

"Okay," she continued after they ran out of names, "what's our next step?"

"Easy," Jeff said. "Check the queen names against the street map index, then look up the streets on the map and see if any of the river names we thought of are nearby."

"No, wait," Chris said excitedly. "Check the queen names *first* to see if any go into a park. Then see if they have a river name close to them."

"Good idea." She shoved the map toward him. "Hop to it." She pushed herself up from the table.

"Aren't you going to help?" Chris demanded

"I'm going to take a shower and get dressed. You two can certainly read a map and make a list. Just try not to kill each other while you do it."

She turned on the shower and adjusted the water temperature until it was comfortably hot, then sat down on the toilet seat to let the hot water warm up the shower stall's chilly air. Never again would she move into a house with the shower against the north wall. When the steam rose up in the room, she shed her bathrobe and nightgown, and climbed into the shower, sliding the glass door shut behind her.

The hot water cascaded over her, its heat soaking into her muscles. *I feel pretty comfortable here.* For all her complaints about leaving Boston, she *did* feel comfortable here in St. Paul—in a way she had not felt since dropping out of her master's program in architecture at Boston U when Jeff was born. She had never kept her promise to herself and gone back. There simply wasn't enough time to take care of babies and study architecture, too. Watching the boys grow up had been worth the sacrifice, but she had always felt incomplete. A part-time job at an architectural bookstore after Chris started school had helped diminish the feeling. Working around the crisp, beautiful books at least made her feel connected to architecture again. Leaving the store to come to St. Paul had been hard. But the job had taught her the fundamentals of the book business, preparing her for that chance meeting with Elaine Murphy at one of Chris's hockey games. The two of them had hit if off immediately, and soon took to sitting together to cheer their boys on. By season's end, they had stopped paying attention to the game, instead discussing business ideas that eventually led to the Paperback Library.

Now with sales running ahead of projections and research underway for a second store in one of the strip malls, she hated the idea of giving it all up, making yet another sacrifice for someone else. How could she make Phil understand? Wasn't it about time someone else made the sacrifice?

She adjusted the water temperature to make it a little hotter. *I feel pretty comfortable here.* Maybe she would just spend the day standing here in the shower, letting the hot water pour over her.

She heard Chris's feet pounding up the stairs. A moment later, his impatient fist banged on the bathroom door.

"Ma! We figured it out. Hurry up."

THREE

STEVEN CARPENTER DROPPED onto the couch, letting Fitzgerald's newspaper fall to the coffee table in front of him, and glanced across the room at Debi curled up in the blue chair, her white legs sticking out from under her long T-shirt. He pushed the sleeves of his sweatshirt back toward his elbows in exaggerated movements, laced his fingers together, and stretched out his arms in front of him, palms first.

"All right, let's try this once more," he said. "You *enter with a queen, leave via river*. It's on the ground, near train tracks, somewhere near where planes fly, within sight of where people run races, near a baseball diamond, between two trees. There's *seven red hints* of some kind nearby."

He stood up, made a lap around the living room, and settled down on the arm of Debi's chair.

"Train tracks, planes, races, baseball diamonds, and trees could be in any park," he said. "But *enter with a queen* and *seven red hints* have to locate a specific park, don't you think? Those are the two clues we need to crack."

"Crack?" Debi echoed rolling her eyes. "You sound like a TV detective. Rockford or Columbo."

"Or Magnum," he said. "Don't you see the resemblance?" He gave her a quick profile. "Yeah, Magnum. He's always behind the eight ball, gets beat up, and then gets stiffed for the fee."

"I wish they'd put Magnum reruns on at night again," Debi said. "I liked that show. I liked Magnum's Ferarri."

"Maybe we should buy one with the treasure hunt money," he said. "I'm sure we could afford the gas cap."

"Uh-uh! No frivolous purchases," Debi said, wagging her finger at him. "That money's for New York."

He glanced over at the couch, recalled their fight on Sunday night, and laughed.

"What?"

"Nothing."

"What?" She grabbed a fistful of the front of his sweatshirt, and cocked her other fist in mock anger. "What?" she growled.

"Not while you're ready to pop me one in the kisser."

She let go of his sweatshirt, dropped her hands into her lap, straightened her posture, and tilted her head slightly. "What?" she asked primly.

"Promise not to hit me?"

"Maybe. What?"

"You preaching the doctrine of frugality. It just strikes me funny, that's all. I've never considered frugality as one of your virtues." He looked at her warily, half expecting her to double up her fist again and slug him for real.

But she only shrugged. "Considering that I grew up poor as a church mouse, I know how to be frugal when I want to. I'd just rather spend money."

"The country mouse turned city mouse?" he teased.

"New York City mouse." She hopped out of the chair, and moved around the coffee table to sit on the couch. She bent over the newspaper.

He slid off the arm into the seat of the chair. Everything felt loose and comfortable this morning, a carryover from last night. When they went to bed, they had done it again. Afterwards, when she had rolled away and curled up into a ball to go to sleep, her back to him and the cold bottoms of her feet against the calf of his left leg, her words had floated softly over her shoulder. "Love you."

"Me, too," he had replied.

Now, the night's snowstorm had given them the gift of a free day. He had slipped downstairs earlier to steal Fitzgerald's paper for the new treasure hunt clue. But the new clue didn't tell them what park to look in, only to look midway between two trees. So it was "back to basics," as Debi put it.

"Okay, *enter with a queen, leave via river,*" she said, picking up where he had left off. "We said maybe that refers to a Queen Street that runs into a park, and you leave on the river, meaning, of course, the Mississippi. But we couldn't find a Queen Street on the map last night. What if it wasn't a Queen Street, but a street named for a queen?"

"Could be." He nodded in agreement.

"Okay, so what are the names of some queens?" She jumped up, got the list of high school addresses and a pencil off the secretary, and carried them back to the coffee table. "Fire away."

"Queen Elizabeth," he began. "Queen Mary. Queen Victoria." He laughed. "Queen Ida."

"Who?"

"Queen Ida. She's a cajun musician. From New Orleans, I think."

"Please." Debi rolled her eyes again. "Be serious."

"I am. I think there's even an Ida Street. I've seen it somewhere. Maybe over on the East Side."

"Speaking of the East Side—"

"I'll call Knickerson in a little bit. Believe me, he's not going anywhere. He's still dead to the world. He told me once he would sleep all day and stay up all night if he could. Besides, they've got to get the streets plowed before he'll go anywhere."

"We better find out about the snow emergency so we don't get a ticket."

"They'll do the major routes first. Portland'll be safe until tonight, at least."

"Which of these queen streets do we want to check out first?" She read through the list, leaving off Ida.

"Let's try old Queen Elizabeth." He reached for the map. "Gorgeous woman, old Elizabeth. She could run in the derby, she's such a horse. I don't know why this country is so gaga about her. The whole Royal Family is—"

A knock on the door interrupted him. Debi gave him a puzzled look, then padded into the hallway to answer it.

"Mr. Fitzgerald." Her voice betrayed her surprise.

Shit, Steven thought. He stood up, holding his breath.

"You two got my paper?" Fitzgerald demanded. He sounded out of breath from the long flight of stairs.

"Oh . . ." Debi's voice dripped with apology. "Yes, we do. We just borrowed it for a moment. One of Steven's aunts died, and we were looking to see if the obituary was in the paper."

Aunt died? Where the hell did she come up with *that*, he wondered. He sat down again and listened to Debi spin the story, hardly believing his ears.

"We were going to bring it right back. I know we should have asked first. But we didn't want to wake you, if you were still asleep. We were sure you wouldn't mind. I'm really sorry."

"Aunt died, huh?" Fitzgerald wheezed. "Too bad. Tell your husband my condolences."

"Cancer," Debi said gravely. "It's a blessing, really. Steven," she called. "It's Mr. Fitzgerald. He's come for his paper. I said we were just ready to bring it down."

Sheepishly he carried the paper into the hallway. Aunt died. What balls Debi had. He was appalled by her inventiveness, and envious of it at the same time. Fitzgerald stood in the outer hall, a shadow.

"You can take it if it's there," Fitzgerald said.

"What?" he asked.

"The obituary. You can take it if it's there."

"Oh. It wasn't here. Maybe it'll be in this afternoon's." He held out the newspaper.

Fitzgerald took the paper, then shook hands with him formally. "My condolences. I'll save tomorrow's paper for you."

"Oh, that's not necessary," Debi said. "Please don't go to any trouble for us. We can buy our own."

Steven saw the gleam come into her eye.

"Maybe we could just look at it quick in the morning to see if it's there?" she asked hesitantly. "If it isn't in the afternoon paper, that is."

"Help yourself," Fitzgerald said. "Just put it back when you're done. Nice to see young people pay attention to family matters. Most kids are too busy to care these days."

"Ah . . . Mr. Fitzgerald?" Debi smiled at him apologetically. "The light bulb . . ." She pointed toward the ceiling above him. "It seems to have burned out."

"Oh. Sure thing," Fitzgerald said. "Get to it today."

She closed the door, leaned against it, and pretended to faint.

"Why did it have to be *my* aunt?" he demanded.

"I said the first thing that came into my head, okay?" Debi said. "I'm sorry. I apologize to all of your aunts, living and dead. But, you'll notice," she said as they headed back toward the living room, "that I also cleared the way for us to get the paper tomorrow. And got in a request for a new light bulb."

She sat down in the big chair. "If I can turn petty theft into condolences, a free paper, and a replaced light bulb, just think what I can do in New York."

"See what you can do with this treasure hunt first," he said.

FOUR

ALFRED TURNED HIS BACK on the Mississippi and, squinting in the brilliant sunlight, looked south across Cherokee Park. The clouds had cleared away, leaving the midmorning sky a deep blue. The winter sun was blinding on the fresh snow. He shaded his eyes with his gloved hand. He couldn't believe the number of treasure hunters that were swarm-ing around the park's trees, digging and hacking away in the deep snow. There were hundreds of them, maybe thousands.

He was probably wasting his time; but since he was here, he might as well give it a try. He glanced down at the newspaper in his other hand. Well, the ground was certainly somewhere underneath all the snow. That took care of Clue 1. Behind him, a railroad track ran between the riverbank and the foot of the bluff, satisfying Clue 2. There had been nothing along the edge of the park as he drove by that obviously relat-ed to the queen or river of Clue 3; but at least the Mississippi was be-hind him, and maybe queen referred to one of the riverboats, as Genevieve had suggested last night. From here, you could see planes com-ing and going from both airports, which took care of Clue 4. A couple of minutes ago, a small jet had taken off from the downtown airport, its deafening roar nearly splitting the cold blue sky wide open. He could see nothing for sure related to running races as described in Clue 5, but he had spotted a baseball backstop at the other end of the park, when he had first pulled into the parking space being vacated by a battered gold Nova. That satisfied Clue 6. The *seven red hints* in Clue 7 was the Schmidt sign, easily visible from here, and still blinking away every night, even though the brewery was closed. Given his con-nection to that sign, he felt embarrassed that he hadn't figured it out the moment he read the clue.

The only problem now was figuring out which two trees to look be-tween. Clue 8 said it was up to him to guess, and he hadn't the slight-est idea. There didn't seem to be a single tree that hadn't already been dug out all the way to the frozen ground.

He refolded the newspaper, jammed it into his coat pocket, and leaned over to pick up his shovel, which had fallen over. The snow had been trampled as hard as cement under his feet. How many hundreds of trea-sure hunters had stood here already, paper in hand, matching clues against the park geography?

Turning around, he looked across the river. Using familiar landmarks, he located his neighborhood, and imagined that he could pinpoint his own rooftop. Home was one place he was glad to leave behind today. Last night, Genevieve had hovered around him like a hummingbird at the feeder in their backyard, alternately beating her wings about the trea-sure hunt and the trip to Houston. He had only half listened to her go on and on about the clues, until he realized that he didn't have any better ideas himself. It was she, in fact, who had concluded that Cherokee Park was the best place to look. But this morning, she had fussed around him, clucking her disapproval as he pulled on his treasure-hunting clothes. "You should rest before you go. All this shoveling. You'll kill yourself. First, you shovel last night. And then again this morning. Now you're going out to dig in the snow some more, aren't you?"

"Well, maybe the treasure medallion will jump out of the snow like a frog and hop in my pocket, but I doubt it," he had told her.

"You be careful," she directed as he went out the back door. "You find a park bench and rest once in a while!"

He felt grateful to have something to do that got him away from Genevieve, and at the same time gave him an excuse not to go down to Rudy's. Rudy's, where eight magazines rested out in the garbage can at this very moment, along with the rest of the trash. Deep in the night, he had briefly considered going down there and burning the whole place down. This morning, he had decided to stay away, fearful that he might actually do it.

But coming out here, he realized, hadn't worked after all. He missed Rudy. Rudy should be here, too, squinting at the treasure hunt clues in the newspaper and gesturing at the landmarks with his hand, his engineer's cap pushed back slightly on his forehead. But what would he say to Rudy, mad as he was at him? Course, if Rudy were here, then he, Alfred, wouldn't know anything about what he had found in the bureau drawer yesterday, and everything would be normal.

Normal. Now that was a laugh. You could hardly call what he had found in Rudy's drawer normal. What did those magazines make Rudy? Surely Rudy didn't think it was normal, or he wouldn't have kept it such a secret. Gays, they were called now. To him, being gay had always meant being happy. He had always ignored the whole issue, skipping the stories about them in the newspaper. Their problems were of no consequence to him. Until now. His own brother, his own flesh and blood. Damn him, anyway. The tears welled up in his eyes, and he threw down his shovel, dabbing at his eyes with the back of his fuzzy yellow glove. Damn him. "You bastard," he muttered to himself. "You son of a bitch."

A pair of treasure hunters squeaked toward him on the packed snow, shovels dragging behind them. " . . . no place left to dig . . ."

He turned his face away from them, blinking back his tears. Sticking a toe underneath the shovel handle, he kicked it up, and grabbed it with his hand. He moved a few steps west to a park bench, realizing as he settled onto the cold wood that he had unconsciously followed Genevieve's orders. He would have to remember to tell her. He rested the shovel against his knee. From where he sat, he could see almost the entire length of the West Seventh Street neighborhood, stretching from downtown out toward old Ft. Snelling. Smoke curled out of a thousand chimneys.

It wasn't what Rudy was or wasn't that made him so mad. Rudy was his *brother*, for heaven's sake. He still would have loved him no matter what he was, or what he did. Even if he had killed somebody. But to keep such a secret from him was unforgivable. Why couldn't Rudy have talked to him about it?

What could Rudy have said? How could he have broken the news? *Alfred, sit down a minute. I need to tell you something. I'm not normal. I don't like women.* He winced at the harshness of the words. No wonder Rudy had kept it to himself. How could you tell someone something like that? How had Rudy known? How *long* had he known—all the way back to when their parents were alive? Had he ever told anybody? Maybe he had told old Tantchen, and the shock of it was what had killed her. Old Tantchen. He chuckled to himself. The things they had pulled behind her back. It was a wonder she hadn't had them thrown in the hoosegow.

What did this thing mean? Until now, he had always believed that Rudy had lived the most ordinary of lives. Fifty-odd years with the railroad. Born and died in the same house. No wife and kids left behind to carry on the family name, just a houseful of junk, and a little money in the bank. What did it all add up to, Rudy's life? Did all that add up to success or failure? What was success, anyway? A big, flashy job? A lot of money? A bunch of friends? If that was success, Rudy never achieved it.

And what about himself? What kind of success was he? He gathered up his shovel and pushed himself to his feet. He strode off into the park, hoping he had left the question behind, left it sitting on the cold wood of the park bench.

FIVE

BRUCE MITCHELL HUNG UP AFTER a dozen rings. Jeez, St. John was being stubborn. He ought to drive over there and give him hell for being such an asshole. He refilled his coffee cup, killing off the last of the pot Jo had brewed when they first got up. The coffee smelled too strong to drink by itself. He rummaged through the cupboards for something to help improve its flavor. Next to the Rice Krispies, he spotted the half bag of Oreo cookies left over from the other night. The cup was too full and he had to walk slowly into the living room to avoid slopping hot coffee on his hand.

"Not home?" Jo said.

"Didn't answer, but he's there." He sank onto the couch beside her, and offered her the Oreos first. "St. John's not the kind of guy who goes out and does stuff alone. He just won't answer the phone because he's pissed at me."

"That's pretty childish, if you ask me," Jo said. She took an Oreo, twisted it apart, and turned her attention back to the television set. She licked at the white frosting. *Dirty Dancing* was on cable this morning. It was her favorite movie, one that they had already watched several times since they met.

He popped an entire Oreo into his mouth and sipped at the coffee. The combination tasted a lot better than beer and Oreos had the other night. Jo was right about St. John, of course, but it still bothered him to hear her say it. It wasn't the criticism that bothered him so much as the fact that St. John was being such an asshole, which made the criticism possible.

"Since there's no classes today because of the snow, I could go out hunting with him if the turkey would just answer the telephone." He polished off another Oreo and retrieved the morning newspaper from the floor. "He might be right about Harriet Island. This newest clue sure as hell doesn't tell you which park to look in, just to look midway between two trees. Harriet Island is as good a place to look as anything I can come up with. When it comes to figuring out clues, he's usually the brains of this outfit." He looked over at Joanna, who was lost in the movie. "Am I talking to myself here?"

"Hmmh? Sorry."

Jo drew her knees up, planting her bare heels on the edge of the cushion. She rested her chin on her knee, and continued to lick the frosting from the Oreo. On the television set, Baby, wearing a plain dress that still made her look sexy and a lot older than sixteen or whatever she was, came out of her room and walked the length of the porch to where her father sat alone, staring off into space.

"How many times have you seen this?" He fished in the bag for another Oreo.

"How many times have you seen *Butch Cassidy?*" she said without looking at him. "Shhhhh."

On the screen, Baby confronted her father, first apologizing for lying to him about her relationship with Johnny, the dance instructor, then accusing her father of lying to her about the value of sticking up for someone. Jo's face was expressionless as Baby spoke her piece, and then sadly turned and walked away.

Jo turned to him. "So it's a dumb movie. I like it, okay?"

"I like this movie." He gave her his Groucho Marx eyebrows. "Especially the part where Patrick Swayze jumps her bones out in the woods."

"You jerk." She grabbed the pillow from the end of the couch and hit him on the side of the head with it, causing coffee to slop on the back of his hand.

"Hey," he protested, switching the cup to his other hand. He wiped the back of his scalded hand on his pant leg, then shook it in the air. Two of his knuckles were turning red. He blew on them, staring at her over his fingers, not sure if she was being playful, or if she was actually mad at him. Comments about jumping someone's bones usually drew a friendlier response.

"I'm sorry." She took his hand by the fingertips and looked at the back of it. "It doesn't look too bad." She gave the reddened knuckles a light kiss, avoiding his eyes.

"Did I say something wrong?"

Jo shook her head. She reached for another Oreo, twisted it apart, and studied the two halves, one black, the other white. She watched the screen for a few moments.

"I talked to my mother yesterday," she said. "She called when I went home for a while after classes." She pressed the Oreo halves together again and set the cookie on the arm of the couch.

So that was it. Her parents again. He rubbed his knuckles against his pant leg.

"What did she say?"

"She called to tell me about this article she read about computers, and how graphics were all being done on computers. According to this article, graphics designers will become obsolete. Everyone will be able to do their own designs on computers. She said I should have gone into computers, instead of graphics."

She watched the screen as Baby sat alone in her room. "So as usual, I'm messing up my life." She looked up at him. "Did you ever disappoint your parents?"

"Sure. All the time," he said. "Kids always disappoint their parents. It's our job." In truth, he had never really thought much about it. His parents lived a few miles away. He talked to them about once a month, saw them on holidays or when his old man needed an extra hand on the landscaping crew.

"No, I mean *really* disappoint them. Like Baby did." She nodded toward the television. "Nothing I ever do seems to please my mother. According to her, I'm always screwing up my life. I shouldn't have dropped out of college, even though I hated it and was wasting their money. I shouldn't have called off my wedding because the guy was going to be a lawyer. It was fine that I went back to school, but now she's decided I'm studying the wrong thing. I'm always doing *something* wrong, but I never know what it is until it's too late."

She motioned toward the television. "Baby, at least, gets it all worked out with her father in the end. But real life isn't the movies."

Her voice broke off, and he knew she was going to cry. He set his coffee cup down on the floor, and tugged at her shoulder until she turned around and lay her head in his lap. Gently he stroked her shoulder, then burrowed his fingers into her hair to caress the back of her neck. So that was why she liked this movie so much. A happy ending to her own problem.

"I don't think Mother understands that I'm just not a big person," she said in a low, sad voice. "I don't want a lot. I just want someone who'll be there for me and treat me nice. Daddy's like that, but she doesn't appreciate it." She wiped at her eyes with her fingertips.

"I'm here," he said.

She rested the open palm of her hand on his kneecap, and gave it a little hug. "I know."

"What do you think your mother would say if she knew you were sleeping with an unemployed, ex-construction worker with another woman's name tattooed on his arm?"

She turned her head to look up at him, smiling at him more with her eyes than her mouth. "She'd probably think I was still screwing up my life. A lawyer wouldn't have anyone's name tattooed on his arm. But I don't care what she thinks." She raised up and gave him a kiss that tasted of Oreo frosting, then dropped her head into his lap again.

"But you do care," he said softly. She buried her face in his lap and started to sob. Suddenly she rolled off the couch, knocking the cookie off the arm, and ran into the bedroom. The door slammed behind her.

He leaned over and picked up the fallen Oreo. He placed it on the arm of the couch, so it would be there when she returned. He had learned in their short time together that there were no words of comfort when these strange little moods suddenly overcame her. Outburst, retreat, and return. That was the pattern in these one-sided, fruitless fights she had with her mother. His job was to be here when she came out. Once he had figured that out, it was a task he was happy to perform. After all, some relationships worked and some didn't. But numerous times as he sat alone waiting for her to put herself back together, he had considered going over to her parents' house alone someday, introducing himself, and telling Jo's mother what a total zero she was for treating her the way they did.

The bedroom door opened and Joanna came out. She had dried her face and combed her hair, but her eyes were still red. She slid into his lap, put her arms around him, and laid her head against his chest.

"I'm sorry," she said.

"It's all right. You okay?" He felt her nod.

He ran his hand lightly up and down her back. On the television set, Patrick Swayze was making his speech about the type of man he wanted to be, a person who was there for other people. Next he would put on a record, and everyone in the audience would end up dancing. Baby and her father would patch up their problems, Patrick would finally earn Daddy's respect, and everybody would live happily ever after.

Patrick Swayze, however, didn't have the problem of being there for his girl friend and his best friend at the same time.

"So you going to go out treasure hunting with us if I can ever get ahold of that turkey?"

Jo moved off his lap onto the cushion next to him. "You guys go. I don't want to get stuck in the middle any more than I already am. You guys go find it, and then you can take me someplace where it's warm with your half of the money."

"We could go over to your parents, and you can introduce me to them. I'll flash a little cash under your mother's nose. Think that'll impress her?" he asked.

Joanna reached for the cookie on the arm of the couch. She twisted it open and popped the white half into her mouth. She held the other half out for him, and he opened his mouth to receive it.

"Just don't show her your tattoo," she said.

SIX

GENERAL JERRY ANSWERED THE PHONE in his boss's voice.

"Jerry, it's Keith. Calling in like you said. Everything is going okay on Gopher State. I'm going through the program for bugs now. I already called the office manager and told her I'd dump the program into their computer tonight, and then be on call tomorrow in case they have any problems. But there shouldn't be any."

"Good," Jerry said. "Everything needs to go well tomorrow. Make sure you're available all day if they need you. I'll give you an extra day off if they tie you up all day."

"I don't foresee any problems."

"Great. I guess there's nothing here that we need you for. How's the rest of your vacation going?"

"It's okay. Not doing anything special, just kicking back a little. Might take in a movie tonight if they get the roads plowed."

"Go see the new Alan Alda movie. I saw it a couple nights ago. Classic Alan Alda. Well, here comes Patty, I better go. Keep me posted on how it's going at Gopher tomorrow."

"Okay."

He hung up the receiver, heard his quarter click through the tumblers, and dug into the coin return with his finger to see if it had accidentally been released. The return was empty. He let it snap back into place, and headed back toward the booth where his lunch awaited him. It had gone smooth as silk. Maureen Naylor, Gopher State's office manager, had been a pushover on the phone, and for all his big-shot attitudes, old General Jerry was pretty easy to fool.

For a lunch hour, the burger shop was quiet. A few treasure hunters, their coats unzipped, snow melting off their boots, stood in line waiting to order. Most of the seats were empty. Outside, a white MTC bus rattled by on West Seventh Street, headed toward downtown. West Seventh had long since been plowed. Despite the official tally of thirteen inches of snow, the city was already returning to normal. With many of the snow emergency routes already plowed, the treasure hunters who had stayed at home because of the roads would soon be out in force. That meant more competition.

He took off his parka, tossed it into the opposite seat, and slid into the booth. Twenty-four hours of treasure hunting was taking its toll on him. His back and shoulders burned under his sweaty clothes. The chill had eaten into the marrow of his bones. A long, hot shower followed by a good nap would feel pretty good right now.

He surveyed the tray holding his lunch. All morning he had been starving, but now he felt almost too tired to eat. Fast food was taking its toll on him, too. After the plastic cheeseburgers he had eaten in the middle of the night, he couldn't face another burger. Instead, he had ordered a twenty-piece box of chicken nuggets, a garden salad, and more coffee. He was about coffeed out, but he needed it to help him warm up and stay awake. But he would pay for it later; in two hours he would have to piss out in the middle of the park in broad daylight, with a million treasure hunters milling around him.

He opened the see-through salad container, tore the top off the French dressing package, and squeezed the thick orange contents over the lettuce. He opened the box of chicken nuggets and peeled back the tops of two packages of hot mustard sauce.

The salad dressing was tart on his taste buds, the lettuce crisp. It was pretty good for a fast-food salad.

He opened the afternoon paper to the front page and read Clue 9 again with disbelief. *A hint to get you out of your seats, the queen and river refer to streets.* Christ. He had left Cherokee Park at midmorning to wait in line for the first edition of the afternoon paper for this? He already knew that queen and river referred to streets; had since Monday.

But which streets? He read the article that accompanied the clue. "Treasure Hunt Continues," the headline read. A photograph, probably taken yesterday afternoon, showed a trio of treasure hunters, heavily bundled against the falling snow, shoveling through a snowdrift in Mounds Park. According to the reporter, as of early this morning people were still searching in parks all over the city—Cherokee, Mounds, Highland, Harriet Island, Linwood, St. Anthony, and Hidden Falls. Usually by now the hunt had narrowed down to one or two places. This new clue would send people scrambling to their street maps to look for streets named after queens and rivers, just like this morning's clue had set them to attacking every tree in sight. Cherokee Park, with its Annapolis and Chippewa Streets, would fill up with even more treasure hunters, if that was possible.

Still, he wondered as he worked his way through his salad, was Cherokee the right park? He read again the list of parks where people were searching. How many of them had streets that matched the queen and river clue? He had not bothered to check out his entire list of queen and river names, because Cherokee had fit so many of the clues. He had been anxious to get out and dig. The list was back home on his desk, but there was a street map out in the Nova's glove compartment. He could look at streets around the parks mentioned in the newspaper article. But the map was out in the car, he was in here where it was nice and warm, and his ass was dragging.

He finished the salad and moved on to the chicken nuggets. They weren't bad either, but the hot mustard sauce was not as spicy as he liked. He ate about half of them and closed the box. He would eat the rest later. Even stone-cold, they would taste better than plastic cheeseburgers.

He sipped his coffee, wondering what he should do with his afternoon. He had to get Gopher State finished up pretty quick. It was supposed to be done by tomorrow. On the telephone, he had laid the right groundwork for tomorrow in case he or someone else hadn't found the medallion by then; but if it came to that he would have to play it carefully. Jerry wasn't a complete idiot, and if he ever wanted to get Gopher to split away from PROgrams, he would have to stay on Maureen Naylor's good side. He *could* go home and work on it until Friday morning's clue came out around eleven o'clock tonight. But you didn't find the medallion sitting around inside writing a stupid computer program.

He yawned and sipped at his coffee. He was getting tired of Jerry and PROgrams. He had to get out of there and go off on his own. Or maybe he should quit computer programming altogether and find something that wasn't full of routine bullshit. Kiss civilization good-bye and head up to the Boundary Waters and live in a cabin. He could work as a fishing guide during the season.

He opened the Express section of the paper to the comics page. He read "The Wizard of Id," his favorite, first. Today's episode featured the stable hands discussing the finer points of stable life. By the final frame, the cartoonists had gotten off another life-is-shit gag, and one of the stable hands was staring right out of the page at him, a bewildered, victimized look on his face. A look he identified with, a feeling he understood.

"More coffee, sir?"

Startled, he looked up. A young woman stood next to him holding a coffee pot, an artificial smile on her face. She had blond hair tucked under a paper hat. He could tell that behind the unbuttoned brown sweater she wore over her restaurant uniform, she was stacked.

"'Scuse me?"

"More coffee?" She raised the pot slightly.

More coffee? Sure, if you'll sit down and have some with me. What are you doing for the rest of your life? I'm packing it in, moving to the Boundary Waters. Want to go with me?

"Ah, sure."

"Usually it's too busy for us to come around," she said as she refilled his cup. "Enjoy." She smiled again.

He twisted around in his seat to watch her as she moved away from him toward the next occupied booth. She was a bit heavy through the hips, which he liked.

He turned back to the funnies. He read "Doonesbury" and "Zippy," "The Far Side," "Duffy," "Momma," and "Sylvia." As usual, "Sylvia" made no sense to him. He only read it because Patty at the office claimed it really explained how women thought. Having read it intermittently for more than a year now, he still hadn't gained any new insight that helped him in the romance department.

The coffee girl passed by him again, her coffee pot nearly empty. He watched her as she raised a portion of the counter, stepped behind it, and lowered it again. If he squinted at her, she looked a lot like Toni, only about fifteen years younger. She set the pot on the burner and disappeared into the kitchen.

Old Toni. What should he do about her? She, at least, seemed interested in him, which was nice for a change. But maybe that meant she was pushy. The guy at the SuperAmerica where she worked had indicated that. And she had kids that would probably hate him. Maybe he should just forget about her.

He checked his watch. A little before one. He had killed more than an hour here. Time to get rolling. He opened the front section of the paper to the previous treasure hunt clues. He still had to figure out if he should keep looking in Cherokee, or if he should look someplace else. That, and hit the can before he went back out into the snow and cold.

SEVEN

"I'M GOING TO TRY BACKING UP," Sharon hollered out the open driver's window. She shifted into reverse and stepped on the accelerator. The Taurus's engine raced as the front wheels spun. The boys scurried around to the front. Through the windshield, she could see them lean into the job with their shoulders, pushing with all their might. She felt the front end of the car digging down into the snow.

"No good! Let's try ahead again." The boys hustled around to the rear bumper. She shifted into drive, and tried to ease the car forward. The car rocked forward for an instant, then the front wheels started to spin again and the car sank deeper. She threw the car into park.

"That's it," she announced, as the boys came up to stand by the driver's window. "I don't know how I let you two talk me into this." She popped the trunk lid so the boys could get at the shovels. "You made the agreement. If I drove, you guys would dig us out if we got stuck. Well, we're stuck. So start digging."

Jeff grinned at her from beneath his stocking cap. "You having fun, Ma?"

"The most fun I've had since I had my wisdom teeth pulled," she said. "Dig so we can get out of here."

Chris stared off across the railroad tracks at the thicket of trees that separated them from Como Park. He was wearing an old pair of his father's gloves, which made his hands look overly large for his body.

"It shoulda been here," he groused.

"Come on," she said. "Dig us out so we can go somewhere else."

She ran the window up and turned up the Taurus's heater. Actually, she *was* having fun. She couldn't recall the last time the three of them had spent a whole day out knocking around together. With so many school events and hockey and basketball games, it happened too rarely these days.

They were just south of Como Lake, mired in a long, diagonal snowdrift on the corner of Victoria and something, brought here by a remarkable series of clue interpretations.

She had come downstairs after her shower to find the boys hunched over the street map on the kitchen table, their earlier bickering apparently forgotten.

"Ma!" Chris had greeted her, "Victoria Street goes right into a whole bunch of parks."

Jeff had taken a red pen and traced Victoria's route from south to north, all the way to Ramsey County's northern border. Along the street's broken route through the county, there were six possible treasure sites: Linwood Park, Como Park, Lake Owasso, Snail Lake, Island Lake, and Turtle Lake.

At first, no one could identify a street named for a river. They were almost ready to begin tracing the next queen name when Jeff made the connection. Avon Street. Shakespeare, the Globe Theater, and Stratford-on-Avon. All from sophomore English, a class he claimed to hate. Avon Street followed an even more broken route than Victoria, but on the map at least, Avon butted into or exited Linwood Park, Como Park, and Lake Owasso. All three locations had railroad tracks nearby. They had decided to check out Como Park and Lake Owasso first because each had a school close to Victoria, which could satisfy the clues about running races and baseball diamonds. They had hoped that they would spot seven red hints on the school grounds.

And so, with visions of riches dancing in their heads, they had ripped the clues out of the morning paper, dressed in enough heavy clothes to survive an expedition to the North Pole, gotten the snow shovels from the garage, and headed off to seek their fortune.

She squinted out the window into the brilliant sunlight. It was all here. They were stuck on a street named for a queen. Off to their left, was an elementary school, its playground a trackless white—unoccupied today, but surely the site of children running races when school was in session. A baseball backstop stood close enough to the car to hit with a snowball. Straight ahead were railroad tracks that Victoria didn't cross. Two blocks down to the east was Avon Street, bearing the name of a river. On the map, it had all fit together, the perfect treasure hunt solution. Almost. The only thing that proved to be missing, once they arrived here in person, was park land to dig in. Instead of finding the expanse of park indicated by the green on the map, they had found only railroad right-of-way, the school yard, and private property. She had gotten stuck trying to turn the corner.

Jeff rapped on the driver's window. She pushed the window button and felt the cold air move in as the window went down. "Try backing up," he said.

She waited for the boys to assume their pushing positions at the front bumper, then shifted into reverse and gunned the engine. The Taurus hesitated for a moment, then suddenly rocketed backward as the spinning wheels found traction. She hit the brakes and the car slid to a stop. Through the windshield, she watched the boys pick themselves up out of the snow and brush off their clothes. They shouldered their shovels and trotted toward her. She followed her incoming tracks for a hundred feet, then backed into a private driveway that had already been shoveled to turn around. She popped the trunk lid again.

The boys threw their shovels in and slammed the lid. They piled into the car, Jeff in front, Chris in the back.

"Sorry 'bout that, guys."

"Have you ever thought of taking up drag racing, Ma?" Jeff said. "You could be the next Shirley Muldowney."

"Shoot," Chris said. He kicked the back of the front seat with a heavy boot. "I thought for sure this was the right place."

"Life isn't always what it looks like." The familiar tone of the statement made her wince. She glanced into the rearview mirror, and saw the boys give each other a look. They had caught it, too. "Good lord," she conceded as she goosed the car out into the street, "I sound just like your father, don't I?"

They headed south on Victoria. At Front Street, Victoria dead-ended into a cemetery and she stopped. She stared a moment at the gray and brown headstones, cold and silent under heavy caps of new snow. "Give me the map," she said. She spread it across the steering wheel, marking Como Park with a finger.

"Where we going next, Ma—Lake Owasso?" Chris asked, his enthusiasm already returning.

"I've had doubts about Lake Owasso all along," she said. "Seeing how this turned out, I don't think it's worth it. There isn't any green at all around Owasso on the map. It could be a toxic waste dump, for all we know."

"A toxic waste dump, by a lake, next to a school?" Jeff said. "Come on, Ma."

She waved the remark away. "Figure of speech, okay? Let's try Linwood Park." She turned back to the map. Victoria did not look like it went all the way through. She scouted a parallel route. Front Street west to Lexington, south on Lexington to St. Clair, and then east on St. Clair to Victoria and a right turn into Linwood Park. That would do it. She handed the map back to Jeff. She felt a grin forming on her mouth. "Here, fold this up."

"Gee, thanks."

She signaled a right turn and headed west on Front. The street hadn't been plowed, but the traffic had worn away the snow, opening a narrow track down to the pavement. She hated driving in snow. She would rather just go home, and curl up next to the radiator with a good cup of coffee. But if they went home, the magic, the fun of the day would be lost. Once home, each would disappear into a different part of the house, and the day would dissolve into one like every other.

She could really get out of the snow if Phil accepted the San Diego job. On days like this, warm-weather climates were worth just about any price. Hadn't she been griping at Phil about the cold just last Sunday morning? She must have been crazy not to have jumped at the chance to get out of this climate. But there had to be a better reason for moving than just escaping the weather. So the weather would be better in San Diego. How long would it take for them to feel comfortable there, or in Denver?

Comfortable. Jeff had hit it right on the head this morning. Somewhere along the line, without her ever realizing it, St. Paul had ceased being a small town out in the middle of the cornfields, populated by nice but bland people. It was more than just comfortable. It was home—even on this snowy day, as she crept along Front Street, fingers crossed that they wouldn't get hung up if she accidentally strayed out of the track, the snowcapped headstones slipping by out of the corner of her eye. So what if they did get stuck? All they had to do was get out and shovel. And sooner or later, the snow would melt.

She turned south on Lexington and fell in behind a city dump truck that was sanding the street. The sand rattled in the Taurus's fender wells, sounding like rain on a windowpane.

If you like what you've got, why change it? Jeff was right. She liked it here. She liked the store, and Elaine, and the fact that the boys were settled again. Why change, indeed? Why take a risk that paid off in dollars and cents, but robbed them of what was familiar and comfortable? Was it a crime to be satisfied with comfortable? Apparently it was to Phil, the great risk-taker, the man who was always willing to pull up his tent stakes in pursuit of the corporate grail. Phil, who seemed most at home bragging about the last sales quota he had shattered.

They passed over I-94, approaching the Summit Avenue intersection from the north. Familiar territory. A block later, as she crossed Grand Avenue, she looked east toward the bookstore. Grand was already plowed curb to curb. Maybe they should have opened today and picked up business from people who hadn't gone to work because of the snow.

The store's income would be lost if they moved. Had Phil thought about that? Given a good year and a successful expansion, it could generate the money necessary for Jeff's college expenses, nullifying Phil's argument that the move would put them in a better financial position.

At St. Clair, she turned left, negotiating the Taurus around a high ridge of snow left by the plow, and headed east. Although the street had been plowed, the homeowners were still busy shoveling out. A snowblower roared on the south sidewalk, spewing a plume of snow into the air. Its operator, plastered with snow, looked like a walking snowman.

"The park should be up here a ways on the right," she said. "We must be getting close."

"Here's Victoria," Jeff said, as she pulled up at a stop sign. He let out a low whistle and pointed out to the southeast. "Wow, look at the people!"

To their right, Victoria zigzagged into Linwood Park and curved around to the east along the brow of the bluff. The driveway was filled with parked cars. She let the Taurus roll through the intersection as they looked the park over. It was a small, wide-open space about the size of a city block. A stand of small evergreens and tall, leafless elms stood between the curved driveway and the edge of the bluff. Around every tree, treasure hunters were digging away in the deep snow.

"Doesn't look like we're the only ones who thought of this, does it?" she said.

"Man," Jeff said in disbelief, "there must be a couple hundred people here. I never thought about having to compete with other people. I sorta pictured us out here all alone."

"Somebody probably already found it," Chris spoke up from the back.

"If they had, everyone would have left by now," Jeff said.

"But how do you know when it's been found?" she said, glancing ahead for oncoming traffic as the car crept along St. Clair. "Chris has a point. If I found it, I sure wouldn't jump up and down and celebrate. I'd slip it quietly into my pocket and head for the car, so no one would be tempted to mug me."

"*Then* you would jump up and down and celebrate," Chris said.

"Then I would jump up and down and celebrate."

The narrow driveway came out of the park, crossed St. Clair and became Avon Street.

"Well, that's definitely *enter with a queen, leave via river,*" she said. She turned left on Avon and pulled over at the first available parking spot. Before she had even shut off the ignition, Chris and Jeff had hopped out of the car and headed around toward the trunk to get the shovels. She popped the trunk lid. With her hands resting on the steering wheel, she leaned forward, letting her forehead rest on the top of the wheel. It was a lot of effort, this treasure hunting and deciding.

A tap on the window startled her. She jerked up and saw Jeff peering in at her. His face was solemn, concerned. She opened the door a crack.

"You okay, Ma?"

She nodded, reached for the treasure hunt clues that lay on the console beside her, and stuffed them into her coat pocket.

"Let's go," she said.

They made a tour of the park on foot, following the driveway as it made a sweeping arc along the bluff. To the east, they could see downtown St. Paul, its modest skyscrapers gleaming in the early afternoon sun. Across the valley on the other side of the Mississippi, the sunlight warmed the wooded bluffs.

She pulled the clues from her coat pocket. "This is obviously Ramsey County, so that takes care of Clue 1," she said as they dodged around a trio of treasure hunters. "Clue 2 is trains."

"According to the map, the railroad track is down there somewhere," Jeff said pointing over the edge of the bluff.

"Clue 3 is queen and river. We're okay on that," she said. "Clue 4 is *Watch planes come and watch them go.*"

They searched the sky east to west for planes, shielding their eyes with gloved hands. The sky was an empty blue; no clouds and no planes.

"Well, the airport is out that way," she said pointing to the southwest. "Maybe you can see planes landing and taking off from here."

"We said there were two airports," Chris said. "Where's the other one?"

"By downtown." Jeff turned and pointed back toward the east.

"Well, let's say that we'll be able to see planes landing or taking off from one airport or the other," she said. "That brings us to Clue 5, running races."

They had walked about halfway around the open space of the park. The driveway widened into a small parking lot of a dozen spaces filled with cars and pickup trucks. A few feet from the bumpers, the bluff ended with a drop of a hundred feet or more to the valley floor. She was struck by the panorama. The wooded bluffs in the distance and the neat houses below them, smoke curling from their chimneys, looked familiar, though she had never before stood in this spot. This was a view she would have to remember. A place to come to ponder the great problems of the world.

"There's the railroad tracks," Jeff said. He pointed below them at the foot of the bluff. "And look over there." He pointed across a freeway that paralleled the foot of the bluff. A good quarter of a mile away stood an old red brick school building, adjoining an empty white space that looked like a football field.

"At Quincy in Boston, our football field had a track around it," Jeff said. "Maybe there's a track around that. You sure wouldn't see runners' faces from here."

"You could barely see the *runners* from here," Chris said. "They'd look like ants."

"All right, then," she said. "We're okay on Clue 5. Clue 6 is base-ball diamonds." She looked the field over. "There's probably a diamond down there, too. That brings us to Clue 7's *seven red hints*. We said it could be a sign or lights. See anything like that?"

They studied the valley, saw nothing, then turned around to the north to the park itself.

"I don't see anything," Jeff said.

"Then we must be missing it," she said. "Too many clues fit for this not to be the right place." She looked at the clues a final time and stuck them back into her pocket. "Clue 8 is *Midway between two trees*." She glanced around the park. Jeff may have underestimated the size of the crowd. "There's plenty of trees here. But they do seem to be occupied, don't they?"

"What do we do, Ma?" Chris said.

"Pick your trees," she said, "and elbow your way in."

EIGHT

THE HONDA'S ENGINE SPUTTERED, coughed, and start-ed to die. Steven raced the engine a couple of times, flooring the accelerator. He watched Knickerson slam the hood on the Honda, then disconnect the jumper cables from the Chevy's battery and bang down its hood. Knickerson came around to the Honda's open window, looping the jumper cables into a black circle as he walked.

"That would have cost you twenty-five big ones if I'd been a tow truck," Knickerson said. "Those tow truck guys'll be ordering new Cadillacs by the end of the day."

Money. He hadn't thought about paying Knickerson anything, but now he felt obligated to at least offer him something. Trouble was, how much?

"How about taking ten bucks for this?" he asked, not looking Knickerson directly in the eye.

Knickerson laughed and shook his head. "Nah, don't worry about it. Just set me up with that new chick who works downstairs."

"I'll tell her you're good at jump starts."

"And back rubs, too." Knickerson grinned and looped the cables a final time. "Better let her run for a half hour to forty-five minutes to recharge the battery. If it's not a really old battery, that should do her."

"Hey, thanks, man."

"See you tomorrow, Slick."

Debi came out the front door of the building just as Knickerson's Chevy roared away. She was dragging a pair of snow shovels and carrying the street map. He leaned over and unlocked the passenger door. She opened the door, stuck the shovels behind the seat, and piled in, slamming the door hard enough to make the whole car shudder.

"That didn't take long," she said.

"Did you ask Fitzgerald for those shovels, or just swipe them?"

She gave him a wounded look. "I'm *deeply* hurt that you would insinuate that I am dishonest," she said, touching a pink-mittened hand to her heart. "Of course I asked him." Her eyebrows danced. "I promised him you'd shovel the walk when we get back in return for the loan."

"Bullshit," he said. "If you promised, *you* shovel."

"But you're going to shovel snow when we're digging for the medallion," she argued, grinning at him.

"That's different and you know it. There's a ton of money at stake," he said.

"Maybe the medallion is hidden on our sidewalk," Debi suggested.

"Clues don't match up." He pulled out of the parking spot, bumping into the track made by the passing cars, and headed east on Portland. He turned to look at her.

"You didn't really promise him, did you?"

She gave him an exasperated look that told him no. "Where to first?" she asked.

"Let's drive over to the funeral home and visit my dear dead aunt's remains." He braced himself for the punch in the shoulder he knew was coming. It was only a playful poke.

"I'm not dressed for a funeral home," she said. "I've got so many pairs of long underwear and jeans on, I'll have to reintroduce my thighs to one another tonight."

"I'll take care of the introductions personally," he said. She punched him again. "Let's get the afternoon paper at the SA on Grand. Maybe the latest clue will help."

"I still say Cherokee Park," Debi said. "Queen Elizabeth and the Delaware River. We couldn't find any river to match Victoria Street. So let's go to Cherokee Park. We can walk around and match the rest of the clues when we get there."

He made a U-turn at Milton and headed west again on Portland. At Chatsworth, he made a left, crossed Summit Avenue, and made another left on Grand. The SuperAmerica was at the end of the block. He pulled into the parking lot and Debi ran in for the paper. She was back in a moment.

"Big help," she said, slamming the car door behind her. "Clue 9: *A hint to get you out of your seats, the queen and river refer to streets.* We already know queen and river refer to streets. We want to know which streets."

She frowned at him.

"Well, let's head for Cherokee Park, then," he said. He backed the Honda around to pull out of the parking lot. "How do we get there?"

Debi studied the map for a minute. "Down Grand to Smith, then over the Mississippi. On the other side of the river, Smith intersects with Elizabeth, and we make a right. Elizabeth and Delaware intersect right on the edge of the park, according to the map."

He waited for a car to go by, then pulled out and headed east on Grand. What a day. No work. The sun was out and it wasn't too cold. The car was finally running. He'd been laid twice in twenty-four hours. And with a little luck, they would soon be off on a major-league adventure.

"So, New York City mouse," he said, "are we going to go out and pick that little sucker right up when we get there?"

"Absolutely," Debi said. "First stop, Cherokee Park. Second stop, Portland Avenue to pack, and then it's off to the Big Apple."

"Start spreading the news," he sang, deepening his voice to faintly suggest Sinatra, "la la la la la . . ." Debi chimed in, Liza Minnelli with laryngitis. They faked the lyrics until they hit a line they both knew. "These little town bluesssss, are . . ." They stumbled, unable to get a handle on the lyrics, "la la la la . . . I'll la la la la la la la la, in old New York . . ."

The song trailed off in laughter. It was hard to have a big finish when you didn't know the words.

"That was pretty terrible," Debi said. "I don't think Frank and Liza have a thing to worry about."

"Not yet, anyway," he agreed. He would have to write his own song about New York.

NINE

ALFRED SWITCHED OFF THE PICKUP'S ENGINE and shut down the heater. The afternoon sun was already low in the western sky. Its rays suddenly slanted under the tinted strip along the top of the windshield, catching him in the eyes. He reached up and flipped the sun visor down, briefly catching sight of his weathered face in the visor's little mirror. Now that he was warm again, he felt almost drowsy. On the radio, the woman announcer was interviewing an author he had never heard of about her book on raising teenagers. The woman sounded nervous and kept answering in one- or two-word sentences, and the announcer was working hard to draw her out.

A group of treasure hunters, shovels resting on their shoulders like rifles, marched single file in front of the pickup, heading out of Cherokee Park. Since he had climbed into the pickup to warm up, the trickle of discouraged and shivering treasure hunters had increased to a steady stream. But the park was still filled with treasure hunters methodically digging away through the deep snow. He had spent the better part of his day out there with the rest of them, wandering around the park from tree to tree, digging through snow that had already been dug up and sifted through at least a dozen times.

And digging through his own life, sifting through things he had not let himself think about for years. So many things to measure success by. Which ones did you pay attention to? The house you owned? The car you drove? The money you had in the bank? The job you had? No matter how he measured it, he didn't add up to much. If Rudy hadn't been much of a success, *he* sure as hell hadn't set the world on fire, either. Some exciting, successful life he had lived. Worked and lived his whole life in the same neighborhood, settling early into a groove. A job, a wife, a house, and a child—everything his generation was supposed to have—by the time he was twenty-five. Was that an early success, as he had once told Genevieve in one of their arguments, or simply falling into a rut, as she had so bluntly accused him of doing?

Strange how some people could just pick up everything and go, while others couldn't. Janet's husband Dan had packed up the family, and moved the whole kit and caboodle down to Houston for his career. Dan had enthusiastically laid it all out before him the night he and Janet had announced their plans. *It's a dream job, the career opportunity of a lifetime. The savings-and-loan crisis and the ups and downs of the oil industry make Houston a perfect place to practice bankruptcy law. My old law school roommate will bring me into the firm as a partner. Gross an easy two hundred fifty thousand a year.* A strange city in a different state on the other end of the country, all for a job. *He* hadn't been able to move three miles to a newer house in Highland Park, while keeping the very same job.

Career opportunity of a lifetime. Kids these days went about everything so deliberately. You could hardly call the day he walked into the Schmidt brewery asking for a job looking for a career opportunity. He had just been grateful to get a job at eighteen. He had never planned to stay at the Schmidt. Bottling beer wasn't the kind of job that you bragged about in the barber chair on Saturday mornings. But he had never really planned to move on to something better, either. The years had simply rolled by, piling up into decades, until all of a sudden, it had been thirty-seven years. And then one day the company had closed the place down and he was suddenly retired.

Dan had talked about Houston as being a dream job. He, Alfred, had had his own dream once. He remembered the pride and sense of accomplishment he felt the day he had moved his box of clothes and a few pieces of furniture from Rudy's down to the Martin house on Goodrich. A wife, a house of his own. Later, a daughter. He had never looked beyond that.

Now what did it all add up to? He was nothing but an old man, with an old wife, living in an even older house, gussied up with fake siding. A parent to a grown daughter with her own family who lived so far away that you had to fly in an airplane just to get there. Someday, soon enough, someone—probably Janet—would be cleaning out his things, just like he was doing now down at Rudy's. His mark on the world would be his name carved in the gray granite of a headstone.

The air in the cab had chilled. He started the engine and switched the heater on again. The heat rolled out from under the dash, warming his toes. After a few minutes, he shut off the engine. On the radio, the announcer had finished her interview with the author and was now talking about inexpensive winter vacations in Mexico.

Why had he settled for so little? Why hadn't he wanted more, tried harder? Why had he always been so . . . so *grateful* for what everyone else seemed to take for granted as the minimum that life owed them?

He watched a trio of treasure hunters march single file past the front of the pickup. So many had given up and left that a path was forming in the snow on the boulevard.

Why had he settled for so little? Because he had learned very early not to expect much from life, and then there would be fewer disappointments.

Genevieve had wanted more of everything, and she had been continually disappointed, as she so frequently pointed out. She had wanted more children. Soon after Janet was born, she had become pregnant again, but miscarried the baby, a little boy. After that, try as they might, there had been no more babies. She had wanted to move up to Highland Park, away from West Seventh, but he had refused to move in the end, a decision for which she had never forgiven him.

A white Honda went by and swung into the empty parking space two spots in front of him. A young couple got out. The girl, wearing pink mittens, pulled a pair of snow shovels out of the back, and the two of them hurried through the snow into the park.

What would he do differently if he had any or all of it to do over again? Try harder? Take risks he hadn't taken? Move up to Highland? What difference did it make to even think about it? It was too late. He was too old to try. His day in the sun was over, and he had wasted it.

You measure a good day's work by the feeling you have about yourself at the end of the day. Rudy had said that once, years ago, when they had spent one whole Saturday afternoon fixing a tiny leak under the kitchen sink while Genevieve paced about, demanding to know when she could wash dishes. He looked up into the sun visor's little mirror. His own eyes stared back at him, gray and sad. If you measured success that way—the feeling you had about yourself when you got to the end of things— he had struck out again, going down on three straight pitches.

There was little he could do about it now except go home, as he had done every day of his life. Home to where Genevieve waited for him, the way she had most every day of *her* life. He started the pickup again, checked the rearview mirror for traffic, and pulled out onto Annapolis, feeling every inch a failure.

TEN

Bruce Mitchell spotted the beast as he turned off Pierce Butler into the parking lot behind St. John's building. It was parked in its usual spot at the far end of the lot, sealed in behind a ridge of snow left by the snowplow. So the turkey had been here all day, just like he figured. He parked the Camaro in an empty spot and killed the engine.

Inside, he loped up the steps to the second floor. At the top of the stairs, he could hear the Robert Cray Band cranking out the blues from St. John's end of the hallway. Jesus, he wondered as he headed down the hall, why weren't the neighbors complaining? He rang St. John's doorbell, waited a moment, then rang it again.

"Keep your shirt on!" St. John's voice was terse and surly behind the door. He heard the rattle of a chain, a lock being turned, and the door was jerked open. Over his gray sweatshirt, St. John was wearing an unzipped, blue quilted vest. His Ford cap was pushed back on his forehead. His eyes widened in surprise, and his jaw hardened behind the stubble of beard.

"You stop answering your telephone?" Bruce greeted him, raising his voice to be heard over the stereo.

"I answer it when I feel like talking to somebody." St. John turned and stalked away, leaving the door half open.

He followed St. John in, giving the door a shove behind him. "I've been calling you since last night."

The living room was a mess. The air smelled of smoke and a garbage can that needed to be emptied. A stack of newspapers and magazines spilled off the coffee table onto the carpet. Two days worth of dishes were stacked on the floor around the big chair. Oprah was on the television set.

"Jesus, did the maid quit or something?"

"Fired her. She wouldn't wear one of those skimpy black outfits." St. John stubbed out his cigarette in an ashtray filled with butts that had been smoked down to the bitter end. Immediately he lit another, took a deep drag, and moved over to stare out the window. A cloud of smoke surrounded him as he exhaled.

Bruce turned down the stereo. "Why didn't you answer your phone, man?"

St. John turned around to face him. His eyes were solid. "I figured it was just some asshole trying to sell me a bunch of shit I didn't need."

"What the hell is that supposed to mean?"

"Forget it." St. John moved over and plunked himself on the couch. He stared into the carpet.

"You all right, man?"

"What the fuck do you care?" St. John said in a hard tone without looking up.

"I came over here because I was worried about you."

"I'm surprised you could roust your pansy ass out of the house. You sure couldn't last night."

"Hey, give me a break. It was snowing like hell last night. Did you go out digging around last night?"

"I drove over there, didn't I? Ready to go out and look. You're the one who crapped out! You didn't use to act that way."

Bruce bent over and picked up a magazine that lay face down on the floor. He turned it over, saw that it was a recent issue of *Penthouse*.

"I know you're pissed at me about last night," he said quietly. "I'm sorry, all right? I came over here to tell you that, since you're too god-damn stubborn to answer the phone, and to see if you wanted to go out searching for the medallion this afternoon."

He swept the hand that held the *Penthouse* around the room. "But I didn't expect to come over here and find the place looking like the city dump, and you sitting here whacking off with this—" he held the magazine up, then pitched it on the coffee table "—and feeling sorry for yourself. Come on, Dennis, get back in the ball game, for shitsake. You can't just sit here feeling—"

"What's this Dennis shit?" St. John interrupted, glaring up at him. "You haven't called me Dennis in ten years."

Bruce unzipped his parka and rubbed the back of his neck. He hadn't come over here intending to get into all of this, but it seemed too late now to avoid it. He sat down on the couch next to St. John, and rested his elbows on his knees.

"Look," he said after a long pause, "the Butch and Sundance days are over." Yet another line out of the movie, one they had never used before. "Things change. You gotta go with the flow. It's time to move on, you know?"

St. John launched himself off the couch and moved over to the window again. He stared out into the parking lot for a moment, then wheeled around.

"Yeah, well some of us don't have much to move on to," he said bitterly. He took a drag from the cigarette and blew an angry cloud of smoke into the air. "Some of us ain't so lucky. Some of us ain't lined up with some slinky new babe."

The air in the room suddenly felt charged and brittle, as if lightning had struck nearby.

"So that's it, huh?" Bruce said, leaning forward on the couch. "I've got someone and you don't?" He looked around the room. "Well, you're never going to find anyone sitting here in this dump feeling sorry for yourself. All you've done lately is piss and moan about everything."

"And all *you've* done lately is brag about your girl friend," St. John said hotly. "Life's been fucking me over, only you seem too fucking busy having fun to notice." He took a final drag from the cigarette and crushed it out savagely in the ashtray. "Let me tell you, I'm sick of it, man," he continued in a deadly tone. "I'm sick of hearing about your hotshot career plans, and I'm fuckin' sick to death of hearin' about how many times you've nailed your girlfriend."

He was on his feet in a split second. He grabbed at St. John's arm and missed.

"Hey, goddamn it," he exploded, "don't you lay that shit on me. Up yours! I've been where you're at. I know how you feel. But something good has finally happened to me, and goddamn it, you won't even let me mention it! For the past month, every time I open my mouth about her, you cut me off right at the knees and change the subject. Don't think I haven't noticed."

"Why the fuck should I have to sit and listen to that happy shit all the time?"

"Because you're my friend, goddamn it! That's what friends are for. To listen. I listen to you, don't I?"

"Hey, fuck you!" St. John yelled. He kicked a stack of dishes. Glass shattered as plates and glasses flew everywhere, rolling around the carpet in crazy circles. "I can't believe you've got the balls to say something like that. 'I listen to you, don't I?' What kind of shit is that? I'm sitting here run over by the goddamn eight ball, and you're pissed at me because I don't want to listen to you talk about humping your girl friend! Man, I can't *believe* this shit."

Bruce felt his fists clench, felt the urge to swing twitching down the length of his right arm. "Listen," he said, taking a step toward his friend, "you lay off about her. You knock her one more time, and you'll be picking your teeth up off the carpet."

St. John snorted. He opened his arms in a gesture of invitation. "Have at it," he said scornfully. "I hope you brought your goddamn lunch with you." He snorted again. "Or do you have to run home and eat with your chickee, and then hop in the sack with her?"

His punch caught St. John squarely under the left eye. The connection made a smack like a baseball into a mitt. He felt hard bone against his knuckles, then an explosion of pain. The punch snapped St. John's head back. Arms flailing, he reeled backward, falling on top of the coffee table. The spindle legs snapped with a loud crack, and the coffee table collapsed under his weight. He rolled off the shattered table onto the carpet, scattering newspapers and magazines everywhere. For a long moment, St. John didn't move. Then his hand slowly moved up to his wounded face.

Bruce stared at St. John's prostrate form, horror-struck. His insides turned to water. This wasn't why he had come over here. He felt a blur of pain in his hand and looked down. His knuckles were skinned and oozing blood.

St. John suddenly loomed up in front of him, a broken leg from the coffee table clutched in his right hand. An angry red mouse was already forming over his cheekbone. The skin was split open, and blood was starting to trickle down the side of his unshaven face. He raised the broken table leg above his head. His eyes were glazed with rage.

Bruce instinctively planted his feet and raised his arm to protect his face. In the split second before St. John advanced, he knew he would have to take the blow on his forearm, which was protected by the sleeve of his heavy coat. St. John took a step toward him and raised the table leg a little higher. He waited for St. John to lunge.

Instead, St. John stopped. He lowered the table leg. He glared at him. The blood had trickled all the way down his face.

"Get out!" he shouted.

Bruce didn't move.

"Get out!" St. John raised his weapon again. "Go home and play house with your girl friend! Become the president of fucking General Motors if you want to. Just get out of here before I kill you!"

Bruce yanked the door open and slammed it shut behind him. He heard the crack of wood against wood as St. John threw the table leg at the closed door. He listened for a moment, heard nothing, and then turned away. Halfway down the hall, he heard Robert Cray wail the blues as St. John turned up the volume on the stereo again.

ELEVEN

K EITH STOOD IN THE SHOWER, hot water cascading over his aching shoulders. God, was he tired. He hadn't worked this hard since last year's treasure hunt, and all for nothing. It just didn't add up right. Cherokee was the wrong park. He could feel it in his bones as surely as he felt the warmth of the rushing water spreading through him. Sure, the clues all fit, but not naturally enough; more like pieces of a puzzle that you banged together with your fist. He had been too eager to get out there and dig. Should have gone through the queen and river names one by one, checking them out on the street map. The medallion was probably in some dinky little park nobody had ever heard of, and a horde of treasure hunters was tearing apart that park right now. Maybe someone was bending over this very moment to pick up a piece of garbage that held the medallion inside it. He would never figure out which park it was standing in here. He shut off the water and reached around the shower curtain for a towel. The whole bathroom was full of steam. Quickly, he toweled himself off and slipped on his bathrobe.

The air in the bedroom felt ten degrees cooler. It would feel good to slide right into bed, pull up the covers, and go to sleep, but he could sleep later. First, he had to make those phone calls, and then get out his map and go to work on those street names. He checked the clock on his nightstand. Twenty before five, just about the right time to call Gopher State. Maureen would be anxious to go home by now, and not likely to ask a bunch of questions.

He picked up the receiver and dialed the number.

"Gopher State Products." The receptionist's voice had that end-of-the-day tiredness.

"Maureen, please."

"One moment."

"Maureen Naylor, may I help you?"

"Maureen, this is Keith from PROgrams, Inc. You're still there. I'm glad I caught you."

"Still here, but just about to head for home, and not a moment too soon. You're calling to remind me to leave the computer on tonight. Beat you to it—I remembered."

"I'm afraid that's not why I'm calling." He put a bit more urgency into his voice. "A problem's come up. I'm working on your program at home today. I was basically done and just checking it over to see if I could find any bugs, and we had a power failure. My landlady upstairs must have plugged in too many appliances and blew a fuse or something. Anyway, I lost my power and when I booted up again, I could only find about half of your program. I'm still not exactly sure what happened. I lost some of my own stuff, too, but that's not important."

"Oh, no," she said. "What about your backup?"

Backup. Old Maureen had more on the ball than he gave her credit for.

"Well, this part I hadn't backed up yet. I was just about to do that when the power went."

"I thought you had surge protectors to prevent things like this from happening."

"We do, but they don't always work. Friend of mine says that about half of the ones you buy don't really work. Guess he's right."

"So what does this mean?"

"It means that I'll have to go back and rewrite the parts of the program that were lost. I'm not going to be able to dump this in tonight like I had originally planned. I hope this won't cause you major problems."

There was a pause as she evaluated the situation.

"Well, I suppose it would be okay if you had it ready to go on Monday. But no later," she added.

He relaxed. Monday was the word he wanted to hear. "Are you sure that won't be a problem? If I worked through the night, I could probably be done around midmorning tomorrow if that would help."

"No, there's no point in you working all night. We've got until next Wednesday before we start running our payroll. But we've got to run on Wednesday, or we'll have a revolt among our employees."

"That shouldn't be any problem. I'm really sorry this happened."

"Well, it's not a major problem as long as we've got it Monday. You better get yourself a surge protector that works, though."

"I should," he agreed. "Leave your computer on Friday night, and I'll dump in the file over the weekend."

"It will be ready on Monday morning then?" Maureen asked.

"Monday morning, no problem," he said.

"All right then, talk to you Monday. Bye."

"Bye."

He hung up the phone. That had gone all right, but not quite as well as he had hoped. If Maureen asked about backup files and surge protectors, he would have to sharpen his story before he called his own office. General Jerry would ask tougher questions. But with a little polishing here and there, he could still make it work. He had time to think about it. It was still too early to call his office—Jerry would still be there.

He dug through his dresser for clean jeans, long underwear, socks, and a sweatshirt. He sat down on the bed to pull on his socks. He could say that he was backing up Gopher State when the power went, and that he'd lost stuff off his hard drive and backup disk at the same time. He would have to add that he had lost a lot of stuff of his own, too—milk the situation a little. Jerry would fall for that. He liked giving old Jerry the snow job. Snowing old Jer paid him back for all the shit he turned around and dumped back on *him*. You really had to watch what you said around Jerry, because he was so good at turning it against you. Like telling Jerry Gopher State was no problem. He'd meant only that he knew how to do what needed to be done, but Jerry had turned it around so that "no problem" meant he was supposed to crank out the Gopher program in a couple of hours and was way behind.

He pulled on his long underwear. Jerry was a lot like his old man in that respect. You had to watch what you said around both of them; not give them anything to use against you. Jerry, at least, didn't turn the tables on you and then use it to justify beating your ass off, like his old man used to do. Jerry just made you feel like a piece of shit.

Pulling on his sweatshirt as he went, he headed for the living room. At his desk, he rifled through the papers for the list of queen and river names. He counted the names again: thirty-four queens, twenty-four rivers; fifty-eight names altogether. This was going to take awhile.

He unfolded his street map and looked up the first queen name, Ann Street, on the map index. He flipped the map over and located section M-18. It took him several scans of the section to spot Ann Street—a tiny, three-block-long street that ran into West Seventh. The name of the street was printed in tiny black letters, with bigger numbers in red printed over them. There were no parks anywhere near the street. At this rate, he would be there all night checking out fifty-eight names.

He got up and went out to the kitchen to make himself a cup of hot chocolate. Why did he bother with this stupid treasure hunt anyway? Why didn't he just bag it, drink his hot chocolate, and go to bed and get some sleep? He could get up around midnight or so, crank out the Gopher program, call Maureen in the morning, and still hit the original deadline. After tonight's call, she'd be impressed that he had worked all night, and more likely to split off from PROgrams and go with him.

It hit him halfway back to his desk, hot chocolate in hand. There was a better way to go about this, a way to cut the list down to a few queen and river names. *Seven red hints* had to be the Schmidt brewery, and *Watch planes come and watch them go* had to mean one of the two airports. All he had to do was see which parks fit those two clues, and then look at the streets surrounding each of those parks for queen and river names.

He set his cup down and took up the map again. He located the brewery at the corner of West Seventh and Jefferson. Anything near there that was green was a possibility. Besides Cherokee Park, there were five green spaces on the map that looked close enough to be in sight of the Schmidt sign and close enough to one or the other airport: Highland Park, Linwood Park, and three little green spaces with no names. He scouted the streets around Highland first. Eleanor was a possibility for queen. He checked his queen list. Bingo. One down, one to go. He looked for a river name, reading through the surrounding street names twice. Nothing. Highland wasn't it.

The three little parks were easy to check. Each had only four streets, one on each side. He found nothing that even remotely could be interpreted as a queen or river name. That left Linwood. He studied the map. There was Victoria Street. As in Queen Victoria. That satisfied the queen part of the clue. He looked for a river name. St. Clair, probably not. Linwood, probably not. Pleasant, no. Avon, no. Grotto, no. Hold it. Avon. Stratford-on-Avon. That was it! Enter Linwood Park off Victoria, exit onto Avon. There was even the pink line of a railroad that he had marked the other day, running along the southern border of the park. This had to be it. Why hadn't he done this the other day? The place was probably crawling with treasure hunters already. He could be there in twenty minutes.

He checked his watch. It was past five. Everyone would be gone from the office by now, so it would be okay to call. As soon as he got this call over with, he would put on his pants and get going. He picked up the receiver and dialed the office number. No one would get his message until morning, and by then he would be back home from Linwood, the medallion in hand. Three rings, four rings, and then Patty's taped voice, formal and stilted. "Thank you for calling PROgrams, Inc. Our office hours are 8:30-5:00, Monday through Friday. If you would like to leave a message, please wait for the sound of the tone."

He took a deep breath, poised and ready. The tone beeped in his ear. "Jerry, it's Keith. I guess I shouldn't have been so smug about Gopher State when I talked to you this noon. We've got a problem. I've already talked to Gopher about this and they're okay with it, but I thought you should know . . ."

TWELVE

THEY WOULD HAVE PIZZA TONIGHT, Sharon decided, closing the refrigerator door. As soon as Phil got home, she would call the Green Mill and order the deep-dish special with extra cheese. By the time it was delivered, the boys would be home, too.

She sat down at the kitchen table, and sipped at the morning coffee she had reheated in the microwave. A pleasant day, all in all, not counting the boys' battle at the table this morning. She and the boys had proved themselves dedicated, if unsuccessful, treasure hunters. By four-thirty, they had searched the whole west side of Linwood Park, even finding a baseball backstop on the park's lower side, west of the Victoria entrance, which tied into Clue 6. Chilled and tired, they had finally decided to call it quits for the day. But on the way to the car, Chris had spotted the red neon letters S-c-h-m-i-d-t winking on one by one in the dusk to the east, and connected them with *seven red hints*. A hurried conference had followed. The medallion was most likely to be on the east side of the park, Jeff insisted, in sight of the Schmidt sign. Suddenly refreshed and recharged, the boys had stayed to search the east side of the park. They had orders to take the St. Clair bus home at six-thirty, whether the medallion was found or not. After supper, Phil could take them back to the park if they wanted to go. She would curl up next to the radiator and let the heat work the chill and the ache out of her muscles.

The sudden ring of the telephone startled her. She stood up and leaned across the peninsula to pick up the receiver. It was probably Phil calling to say he was running late.

"Hello."

"Charles Flannary. Is Phil there?"

The voice, clipped and authoritative, immediately put her on edge. Charles Flannary was always all business. Never a hello or good-bye. She might as well be an answering machine.

"He's not home yet," she said. "I expect him any minute. I'm surprised he's not home already."

"Have him call me. I'm still at the office." Not a request, but a directive.

"I'll give him the message soon as he gets home." It was hard to keep the edge out of her voice. She started to hang up, but Flannary's voice— a different, slightly warmer tone than before—jumped across the widening space between the telephone receiver and her ear. Her hand froze in midair.

". . . should offer my congratulations . . ."

What? She jerked the receiver back to her ear. Congratulations? The word tripped an alarm inside of her, sent a clanging signal to her brain that made her catch her breath.

"It's a plum job for Phil . . ." Flannary's voice became a buzz in her ear. "I'll bet you won't miss this lousy Minnesota weather, huh? Could use some of that San Diego sunshine myself . . ." Plum job? San Diego sunshine? Sirens and whistles started wailing somewhere in the back of her head, nearly drowning out Flannary's voice. ". . . wasn't rooted in so deep here, I'd have taken that job myself and left Antarctica behind for Phil or some other poor devil . . . told Phil last Monday when he accepted the promotion how lucky he was to have a good corporate wife like you taking care of the home front . . . ."

She managed to croak out a thank-you and a good-bye and hang up. The sirens and whistles—red and blue warning lights flashing—arrived in the very front of her head and stopped, so loud and shrill she thought her head would split open. San Diego. She felt behind her for her chair and sank onto it. Everything moved in slow motion, as though she were under water. San Diego. The kitchen cabinets swam in front of her eyes, then dissolved into a brown blur as it all started to sink in. He'd taken the promotion! Without telling her he was going to. He'd taken it. Last Monday. Flannary's words rained on her like falling debris. He had accepted it *last Monday*, the same day it was offered. She pressed her hands against the sides of her head, tried to silence the sirens and whistles, the pounding in her brain.

She went to the sink and turned on the cold-water faucet. Bending over, she splashed her face, rubbing the cool liquid over her closed eyes. She massaged her temples. She shut off the faucet and, eyes still closed, fumbled on the towel rack for the hand towel to dry her face. The towel smelled of orange juice, cleansers, coffee, things spilled and wiped up.

She sat down again at the table, her heart stunned, thrown out of rhythm. She drew in a ragged breath. It had all been a masquerade these last four days, all this indecision and concern for their feelings. A sleight of hand. Why had he bothered with this charade, this ridiculous tap dance? Why hadn't he just come home Monday night, all revved up, and made the grand announcement, the way he had about the move to St. Paul? The excited tone in his voice when he had called at the store on Monday—he had probably already accepted the job when he called, and just couldn't keep it all to himself.

She looked around the kitchen. The walls were closing in on her. She had planned to paint this coming spring, when the weather warmed up and she could open the windows to kill the smell of fresh paint. Get rid of this fire engine-red woodwork and repaint it white or a light blue. Maybe even replace the cabinets. A final project that would make this house completely her own. Well, not now. The kitchen would be a project for the next occupant.

She sipped at the coffee again. It tasted bitter and oily. A family decision, Phil had said. The liar. How could he have faced her and the boys, lying to them the way he had last night? How would he spring it on them so it looked legitimate, like a decision reached only after painful deliberation over the weekend? He would probably call them all together in the living room on Sunday night, poll them one by one, and then, wearing that solemn look on his face, speak his piece. *I know we're settled here and it will be hard to leave, but in the long run the move will be good for the family. Otherwise I wouldn't even consider it.* The dirty, lying bastard. She got up and poured her coffee into the sink. Indeed, how *would* he play it? She had said nothing to Flannary to give away her surprise, nothing that would cause him to mention their conversation to Phil. She had half a mind to just sit on this and see what—

She heard the front door open and bang shut. Her heart started to race in her chest. Let it be the boys, she prayed. Please let it be the boys. But it was Phil's voice that called out from the front hallway.

"Hi, Babe! How was your snow day?"

THIRTEEN

"YOU WANT TO GO BACK AFTER SUPPER?" Steven Carpenter asked as they approached the High Bridge.

"I don't know if there's any place left to look," Debi said. "The whole park has been turned upside down. Let's go home and eat supper first, and then decide. And, by the way, it's your turn to cook tonight, for sure. I cooked last night when it was your turn, remember?"

He looked out beyond the railing into the darkness as they started across the bridge. Beneath them, the frozen Mississippi wound like a dark ribbon through the city's lights. A large yellow moon had risen over the river bluffs to the east, lighting up the night sky. Downtown's lights twinkled through the cold air; the red neon "1st" sign atop the First Bank Building winked on, then off.

The thought of going home to their apartment and cooking supper after a long afternoon digging in Cherokee Park was not very appealing. He glanced at Debi out of the corner of his eye. She was a vague form in the darkness.

"Why don't we eat out tonight?"

"Oh, let's eat at home and save our money," Debi answered tiredly.

"Come on," he pleaded, "let's eat out. Are you on some big economy kick or something? We can afford to. We don't have to go anywhere expensive, for pete's sake. What have you got against going to some cheap place and getting a burger or a pizza? Or tacos, even. Anything, I'm not fussy."

"I'm just tired, that's all," Debi said. "And my back is killing me." She moved around in her seat. "I never realized how big a park was until I tried to dig it up. I'm going to be sore all over tomorrow."

"I never expected to see so many people," he said. "There were more people in that park than in my whole hometown."

"Yeah, and every one of them seemed to be standing right on top of me," Debi said. "A couple of times my shovel actually collided with someone else's. I get the creeps when there are so many people that close to me."

He felt tired himself. It had been fun at the beginning. Surveying the landscape, trying to match up two trees to dig midway between that no one else already had. For the first hour, they had made the snow fly like a couple of snowblowers. But as the afternoon sun sank in the west and darkness crept in from the east, treasure hunting had ceased being fun and settled into work. Hard work. Sifting through snow that had already been sifted through who knew how many times, back muscles screaming when he straighted up to rest.

"You think it's really there?" he asked as they reached the north end of the bridge.

"You tell me and then we'll both know." Debi yawned. She rubbed her face with her hands. "Where else could it be?" She yawned again. "I'm so tired. I can't stop yawning."

"You suppose somebody found it already?" he said. Even in the dark he could feel her glare at him, as though the mere thought of spending all afternoon digging for nothing was almost more than she could contemplate.

"Come on, let's eat out," he said. "I don't feel like going home yet."

"I feel too grubby to go into a restaurant and sit down," Debi said. "Let's drive down Summit Avenue and window-peep instead. Go through downtown and up Kellogg Boulevard so we can start at the beginning."

"Make a deal with you," he offered. "We'll drive down Summit, and then stop and pick up some Chinese food to take home. I'll buy."

"Okay, deal." She leaned back in her seat, feigning sleep. "Wake me up when we get to the Cathedral."

He turned right onto West Seventh Street, and drove past the closed-up shops and businesses toward downtown. What a deal he had cut! Not only had he gotten out of cooking, but he had done it by agreeing to drive down Summit Avenue, one of his favorite pastimes. Ever since his American Studies professor had introduced him to the avenue during a course on the Gilded Age, he had been fascinated with the humongous old houses and the people who built them. He'd done his final paper on Summit Avenue as an example of the Gilded Age, and aced the course. Debi had gone on some of his trips up and down the street when he was doing his research and had gotten hooked, too. Together, they had driven down the street many times. The fact that their apartment was only a block off Summit was the main reason they took it, and was probably its best feature.

At the edge of downtown, he made a left on Kellogg Boulevard, and followed it over the ornate I-35E bridge and up the hill to where it curved around to the west. To their right, the State Capitol gleamed white in the night, as though it had been lit for a movie shot. When he stopped at the John Ireland traffic light, Debi sat up in her seat. She looked up toward the spot where John Ireland ran into Summit Avenue.

"Do you ever feel like Summit Avenue doesn't belong in a place like St. Paul?" she said. "I mean, I've never been out East, but it seems like it belongs on Long Island or in Europe to me."

"I know what you mean," he said as he waited for the light to change. "It seems bigger than the rest of St. Paul somehow. Especially at night."

As they turned into Summit Avenue, the cathedral, immense and brooding like they imagined the cathedrals of Europe to be, rose up out of the hill like an ancient stone formation. Above the cascade of front steps, Jesus amidst his apostles gazed down upon them benevolently, his face etched with shadows thrown by the harsh floodlights. The cathedral inaugurated Summit Avenue. After it came the great Richardsonian mansion built by James J. Hill, the railroad robber baron, and now owned by the Minnesota Historical Society, followed by a half mile of delightfully pretentious stone houses put up in the Gay Nineties. Most of these drafty, expensive old barns had been subdivided over the years into apartments, or one by one willed to unsuspecting foundations, cultural societies, or other nonprofit organizations. Few people really knew who owned them now; they were still identified by the original family's name, and those private owners who could afford the house payments and the heating bills lived in anonymity.

But it was still fun to stare in through the leaded glass windows at the first-floor rooms and marvel at grand staircases, intricately carved woodwork, great crystal chandeliers, and beamed ceilings, wondering what it would be like to have the money and the power to live there.

The continuity of homes was broken by a small park, a triangle of grass where Nathan Hale stood ten feet tall, his hands bound behind his back with green cord, staring eastward toward the old part of Summit Avenue, wondering, perhaps—given the gilded view—if he could have his one life back. Summit Avenue ran along the bluff, but neither faced it nor, to the casual observer, seemed aware of it, for all the houses fronted inward toward the street. However, the original owners, as he had learned in his research, had long ago exercised their wealth and power, defeating plans to run the street along the bluff so the common citizens of St. Paul also could enjoy the splendid view of the Mississippi Valley. That view the wealthy had reserved for themselves.

At the University Club, the street turned away from the bluff, running due west toward the Mississippi River. The houses were smaller but no less pretentious in their show of wealth and prosperity; window-peeping was just as much fun. To their right stood the wooden Victorian jewel, one of their favorites. Interspersed with the older houses of stucco, brick, and granite were new town houses, built by court order to resemble their nineteenth-century counterparts; combining elements of old and new architecture with modern building materials, and achieving mixed results.

But even these self-conscious hybrids of the old and new were far more pleasing to the eye than the occasional modern one- and two-story boxes done up in pink or green—simple servant girls among the faded beauty queens and dowagers.

Just before Dale Street, they passed the soot-darkened brownstone row houses where F. Scott Fitzgerald had lived while he worked on his first novel. Passing this brownstone always gave him hope. If Fitzgerald could make good from St. Paul, perhaps he could, too.

They passed the law school, its new library blazing with light. Beyond Lexington Avenue, the roofs lowered suddenly, the lots narrowed, the houses shrank up in size and shaded off into bungalows, small for this street, but lavish and extravagant anywhere else. These "bungalows" held the street for the last two miles, past the colleges of Macalester and St. Thomas to the bend in the river. None of them really stood out from the rest. Many were smaller versions of houses on the older part of Summit Avenue, built in the teens and twenties with new money, their owners eager for the recognition and prestige that a Summit Avenue address carried. The avenue terminated with a pair of fifties ramblers—one turquoise, the other white brick—that more properly belonged in the suburbs.

They turned around on East River Road, which ran along the bluff of the Mississippi. Steven paused to stare at the war memorial honoring those who died so that others might build great houses. It looked like a religious monument of some kind; perfectly appropriate, he thought. The religion of money. There had to be a song somewhere in all of this.

"I just love driving down this street," Debi said, breaking the long silence. "It fills me with ambition."

"The best-preserved Victorian boulevard in America," he replied, quoting an article he had read during his research. As he accelerated up the gentle hill past St. Thomas's lower campus, a sinking feeling came over him. Summit Avenue filled him with hope, but it also gave him a premature sense of failure.

They were almost to Snelling Avenue on their way back, peering into the windows of houses on the south side of the street, when Debi suddenly sat bolt upright in her seat.

"God, are we stupid!" she blurted out. "You know what street is a block east of Victoria? Avon! As in Stratford-on-Avon. Victoria goes into that little park south of us, and Avon goes out. We saw that on the map this morning. How could you take so many literature courses and not make a connection like that?"

"It was American literature," he said defensively. "You didn't think of it either until now."

She pounded the dash with a pink fist. "I can't believe we didn't think of it. That park is practically under our noses. You could walk to it from our apartment in about ten minutes. Drive down there so we can look around."

"Let's eat supper first," he said.

"The heck with supper. We can eat later. If this is the right place, there's probably just as many people digging there as at Cherokee."

"But I'm hungry," he protested. "And I thought you were tired."

"Tired, shmired." She waved a pink fist under his nose. "If we don't go right down there, you're going to be a lot worse off than hungry. You're going to be dead."

FOURTEEN

"ALFRED . . ."

He looked up from the evening paper across the little table that separated his chair from Genevieve's, and squinted around the cone of light thrown from the reading lamp.

Genevieve sat forward in her chair with her hands in her lap—the usual manner that indicated she had something to discuss. Behind her glasses, her eyes studied him nervously, then looked away.

"Alfred," she began again, "there's something I want to talk to you about."

He was ready for her. On the way home from Cherokee Park, he had figured it all out. He closed the newspaper and left it in his lap.

"I know, I know," he said. "We need to order the tickets to Houston. Well, I've been thinking about that, too. Instead of flying down there, why don't we drive?"

"Drive?" Genevieve wrinkled her nose.

"Why not?" he asked. "It'd be a lot cheaper than flying, and we'd get to see part of the country. We could drive through Iowa and Missouri and Kansas and Oklahoma on the way down. We've never been to any of those states. You always complain we never took any trips when Janet was home. Well, you can't see the countryside from a plane. You're up too high. This time of year, it'll just look like a big black-and-white quilt."

She sat back, speechless for a moment. The suggestion had taken her by surprise, as he had hoped it would.

"I don't know if I could sit all day in the truck," she said finally.

"Well, think about it, and let me know," he said. He opened the newspaper again. That would put things off for another day or two. She would refuse to drive, he was sure of that. But the offer would give him more ammunition for the future. *I did too offer to go. I wanted to drive, but you turned that down flat.* He found his place in the article that he had been reading, but before he could continue, Genevieve spoke again.

"There's something else I want to discuss." Genevieve spread her fingers across her knees. "While we're down there in Houston . . ." She looked away from him toward the fan-shaped window of the old front door. ". . . I want us to look into moving down there."

It was his turn to be speechless. He looked up at her from the newspaper. He hadn't expected *this* at all. He heard her take a deep breath.

"Janet says Dan is really settled in now with his firm. She says they're happy down there and plan to stay. We aren't getting any younger, Alfred—" Her chin quivered and she broke off. Tears formed around the edges of her gray eyes. "I want to spend some time with our grandchildren before I die."

"You aren't going to die," he said. "Where'd you get that idea, anyway?"

She ignored him, plunging on in a tone that sounded like she had practiced while he was gone. "And you shouldn't be out in the cold in the wintertime. All the snow shoveling and car starting. You complain about it yourself. Think what it would be like down there, nice weather year round!"

What it would be like down there was some strange place full of strange people. Nothing familiar and comfortable around him at all.

"But we've always lived here," he said.

"I knew you would look at it that way," she said, an accusatory tone creeping into her voice. "But think about it. Rudy was our only close relative here. With him gone, there's really nothing to hold us here. We should be where our family is."

Nothing to hold us here? How could she say that? There was plenty to hold them here. St. Paul, this neighborhood, was . . . was home, so much so that he scarcely ever thought about it. It just was. The only problem was that they kept changing everything on him. They tore down this, and built that. They closed down his company. People kept big secrets from him. People kept dying or moving away.

"We've always lived here," he said again. He felt an ache creeping into his muscles.

"Well, you think about it some," Genevieve said. She leaned over and patted his knee. "We don't have to decide about it now. Let's just look around while we're there." She hoisted herself to her feet. "I'm going to have some ice cream. You want some?"

He shook his head. He stared at the newspaper. The columns of words blurred under the headlines. He could hear Genevieve moving around in the kitchen. The cupboard door opened and closed, followed by the silverware drawer. He heard the door to the freezer open and bang shut. Familiar, comfortable sounds he had heard every day for most of his life. So this was what she had been building up to. Ever since he had come home from the park, she had fussed around him. Did he have any luck? Were there lots of treasure hunters there? Was he cold? Did he want anything, coffee or maybe a hot bath? What did he want for supper? Move to Houston. She had probably been chewing on this for days, since the weather had turned so wretchedly cold a week or so back. No wonder she had been so adamant yesterday about not wanting to move down to Rudy's house.

Genevieve returned carrying a sauce dish filled with vanilla ice cream topped with chocolate syrup and chopped nuts.

"I read that new treasure hunt clue," she said as she settled into her chair again. "Clue 9. *Queen and river refer to streets.* We never thought of that, did we?"

He made his escape to the basement, passing the wooden cat doorstop standing guard at the basement door. She wouldn't bother him down here. Except to wash clothes, Genevieve rarely came down to the basement.

He threw on the workshop light, and sat down on one of the carpentry horses. The workbench was still covered with old tools and odds and ends brought down from Rudy's: an old drawing knife with a blade so dull it would scarcely cut butter; an ancient brace and bit frozen in position by rust; old crosscut and ripsaws, their wooden handles splitting apart.

The ache had settled into his bones. He felt brittle and dry, like fireplace kindling. He looked at the neat rows of his own tools hanging on the white wall. Many times he had come down here to stare at these ordered rows to restore some kind of order to his life.

He wasn't going. That was that. If he went, she would just nag him about moving once they got there, and he wouldn't have a minute's peace. Wanted to see their grandchildren grow up, did she? Well, so did he, but he wasn't the one who up and moved a thousand miles away. If Janet,

Dan, and the kids wanted to see him, they could just come home. They were the ones who ran off to Houston and left Genevieve and him behind. Let *them* come home.

He picked up the drawing knife and ran his thumb along the blunt, nicked edge. He felt blunt and nicked himself. Everything had changed. These old tools had been replaced by power tools and table saws. Changes and changes all the time. He laid the drawing knife down again. Well, moving to Houston was one change he damn sure wasn't going to make.

FIFTEEN

Bruce Mitchell pulled over to the right side of the street, but did not even bother to shut off the Camaro's engine. Even in the darkness, he could tell that Harriet Island was nearly deserted. In the circles of light cast by the streetlights, he could see where snow had been piled up by treasure hunters earlier in the day; but only a handful of die-hard searchers remained, moving between pairs of trees like black ghosts against the snow. St. John, the son of a bitch, was wrong in concluding that the medallion was buried here. Far to the west, past the NSP smokestack, he could see the Schmidt sign light up in the night. At least St. John had been right about that.

He watched a pair of treasure hunters shoulder their shovels and start off across the snow, apparently headed toward a van parked a few yards down the road. Giving up for the night. The sight of the two figures walking together gave him a hollow feeling. This wasn't the way he had envisioned treasure hunting earlier today, out here all by himself. Jo had begged off on this scouting trip, confessing that one night of treasure hunting in the snow and cold had been more than enough. As for St. John, well, *screw* him. As of this afternoon, not only were the Butch and Sundance days officially over, but the Dennis St. John and Bruce Mitchell days as well.

It had taken awhile for that realization to soak in. The fight had replayed itself over and over in the back of his mind as he drove across town toward home. He had pulled into his parking place behind his apartment with the image of St. John holding the broken coffee table leg above his head still sharp in his mind, the menacing words still ringing in his ears. *Just get out of here before I kill you!* For several minutes, he had remained in the car, waiting for his insides to quit shaking. When he finally went inside, Jo had noticed his bleeding knuckles immediately, and taken up his hand in both of hers.

"What happened?"

"Nothing," he had replied, pulling it back.

"You got in a fight! You went over there to talk to him, and got into a fight?"

"It wasn't much of a fight. I only hit him once. He threatened me with a club and I left."

"He threatened you with a club?" Jo shook her head in disbelief. "What were you fighting about?"

He had shrugged, wanting neither to lie nor tell the truth. "I told him the Butch and Sundance days were over. He took issue with me."

A look he couldn't read had flashed over Joanna's face. He had immediately thought of their argument at the Busy Bee.

"Don't worry. It's not your fault. Like I told you the other day, it's been coming on for a long time. Long before I met you."

She had made him sit on the couch while she got a warm washcloth from the bathroom and carefully washed the raw, exposed flesh over his knuckles. The gentle movement of the washcloth had burned his injured flesh, temporarily blocking out the throb of bruised bone and muscle.

"You should have this x-rayed," she had advised.

"It'll be all right," he had insisted. He had flexed his fingers and closed his hand into a fist. "If it was broken, I wouldn't be able to bend it."

"You need to travel in safer company," she had said, pressing her lips lightly against the back of his wrist. "First, I make you spill hot coffee all over yourself this morning, then your best friend attacks you with his chin."

"It wasn't his chin," he had replied. "It was his cheek. And after today, he's not my best friend. The bastard can drop dead, for all I care." At that moment, he had suddenly realized that the punch had done more than bruise his knuckles and maybe break St. John's face. It had shattered their ten-year friendship.

Pain shot through his hand when he gripped the Camaro's gearshift lever and shifted into reverse to execute a jackknife turn in the middle of the road. He spun the steering wheel and eased the car into a backward ninety-degree turn. The pain shot through his hand again when he shifted into first gear. Nothing is broken, he told himself; it's just going to be sore for a few days.

He let the Camaro creep along. It *had* been coming on for a long time, for months really. What had gone wrong, anyway? Through years of knocking around from one construction project to the next, through years of looking for love, through those rotten months he'd spent with Michelle, even through all the bad shit that went down between St. John and Karen, they had remained friends, celebrating the good times, toughing out the bad. Butch and Sundance, taking on the whole Bolivian army. It had gotten all screwed up about the time he had signed up for classes at Tech. He and St. John had talked about going back to school for a couple of years. Night after night, they had driven the streets together and planned new futures. They wouldn't end up laborers like their fathers. They would give up construction work and learn a trade, make something of themselves. Then one day he had told St. John that he was signing up for fall classes. St. John had given him an odd look, mumbled an "all right," and delivered a half-hearted high five. After he started classes, things had never really been the same. And then, a couple of months ago, he had met Jo. Since the day he had first introduced her to St. John, the S.O.B. had been almost hostile. It wasn't fair, St. John cutting him off every time he even so much as mentioned her name, just because he was lucky enough to have someone come into his life. But he had held his tongue until today. *Or do you have to run home and eat with your chickee, and then hop in the sack with her?* The fucking son of a bitch. He had really asked for it. He hoped he'd broken his goddamn face with that punch. It would serve St. John right if he had.

Across the Mississippi, the downtown skyline rose up into the night sky. From down here on the flat, it was a respectable-looking skyline. Straight across from him, the West Publishing building seemed to rise up out of the river ice, a shadowy mass of dark brick. Next to it stood the county jail. Above them on the bluff, he could see City Hall and the telephone company's buildings. To the east, over columns of lighted windows that seemed anchorless in the dark, the Radisson sign glowed red, and behind that, the great neon "1st" sign winked on, then off. He could see Kellogg Square, the post office building, and the buildings that made up Lowertown.

He accelerated toward Wabasha Street. One potential treasure site down, and two to go. Assuming that *seven red hints* did refer to the Schmidt sign, he and Jo had studied the map and concluded that Harriet Island, Cherokee Park, and Linwood Park were the most likely places where the medallion could be hidden. He had come out alone to scout the parks, mostly for the fresh air. And to think. He did his best thinking at night, out driving around. He had St. John to thank—or blame—for that. The two of them often tooled around the city into the wee hours, listening to tapes and trying to work out solutions to life's great problems. Over the years, they had probably logged enough miles to go around the world a couple of times.

At Wabasha, he waited for a car to pass and then turned right, heading south. So what did he think? The bastard had actually threatened to kill him with a club, just like he had threatened Karen's boyfriend. What the hell did that mean? Was he serious, or was it just a bunch of words? It didn't matter, because he was through with the son of a bitch. As far as he was concerned, St. John could sit in his dump of a living room until the garbage got so deep that it caved in and smothered him. Or he could open his *Penthouse* and beat his bone until it fell off. Or Karen could call him every day, and twice on Sunday.

At Plato, he made a right. Off to his left, the dark bluffs of the West Side loomed over him. He veered off Plato onto Ohio Street. The Camaro chugged up the steep grade, past houses with living rooms and bedrooms lit with blue television light. People catching the ten o'clock news. He turned the steering wheel hard to the left to make the hairpin corner near the top of the bluff.

Cherokee Park was bustling. Ahead in the Camaro's headlights, he could see people crossing the street into the park without bothering to look for cars, shovels, picks, and choppers resting on their shoulders. Deep in the park, beyond the endless line of cars parked along the curb, he could see beams of light from lanterns and flashlights cutting through the darkness, casting long ellipses of bright light over the white snow. Around the silhouettes of evergreens and leafless oaks and maples, he could see clusters of treasure hunters digging away.

He let the Camaro inch along as he watched them dig. He had a shovel in the trunk in case he wanted to get out and do a little digging himself. After a few moments, he eased the Camaro up to speed again. Not tonight. He didn't feel like getting out there in the dark and cold.

He would drive up into the ritzy part of town and try to find Linwood
Park instead. He cut over to Smith Avenue, and headed north toward
the High Bridge.

He groped in the dark for a tape, opening the little plastic box with
his uninjured left hand. He shoved the tape into the deck. The pounding opening of Bruce Springsteen's "No Surrender" filled the car. Great.
Of all the tapes to pull out in the dark. St. John had owned a different
pickup the year this tape came out. They had cruised all over the city,
the windows rolled down, Bruce Springsteen expressing their feelings
about the world to all within range of the truck's speakers. And this song
had been their theme song. No retreat, no surrender, they had agreed.

He reached out and pushed the stop button. Enough of that shit.
He surrendered, already.

FRIDAY

ONE

THE NOVA SKIDDED TO A HALT at the Victoria Street stop sign. Keith looked across the dark expanse of Linwood Park. Just like he figured. The place was swarming with treasure hunters, black forms moving like ants over the white snow. Flashlights winked in the dark like giant fireflies. He turned north on Victoria and drove for almost two blocks before he found a spot to park. The street had not been plowed, and he didn't know which streets were being plowed first during the snow emergency, but the hell with it. If the city ticketed him, so what? He'd pay it out of his treasure hunt money.

He jumped out of the car and slammed the door behind him, not stopping to lock it. Quickly he opened the trunk and grabbed his snow shovel. He felt around in the corner of the trunk where he kept his two-cell flashlight. He found it with the switch already in the on position. He clicked it on and off a couple of times. Dead. He must have accidentally left it on earlier, and the batteries had run down. He shook it, then banged it against the lip of the trunk. He clicked it on again. Still dead. Shit. He threw it down and slammed the trunk lid. Damn it to hell, anyway. Why had he let himself fall asleep? Of all the rotten, lousy luck. After he had called the office and left his message, he had gone back to the bedroom to put on his pants. He remembered sitting down on the edge of the bed and pulling them up to his knees. He must have laid back on the bed for just a second, his feet still on the floor. He vaguely remembered looking up at the ceiling. A moment later, it seemed, it was pitch black all around him, the green numbers of his digital clock glowing in the darkness: 11:30. He had jumped up, his mouth dry as cotton from hanging open, took one step—and fell flat on his face in the dark. His pants were still around his knees. Thrashing around trying to get up, he had kicked over the little brown trash can next to his bed, knocking it against the closet door. An empty pop can had tumbled out and clattered across the tile floor. The commotion had sent Tiffany into a barking frenzy upstairs.

Now, as he hurried down the middle of Victoria Street toward the park, it was long past midnight, and he had lost six hours of valuable digging time. The wooden handle of his shovel bounced on his shoulder as he ran. Snow crunched under the treads of his Sorels. No one seemed to be leaving the park. That meant no one had found it yet. Or at least the word hadn't spread that someone had found it. Maybe he still had a chance.

He reached St. Clair, jogged up the sidewalk for half a block, then started across the street toward the park. A horn suddenly blared to his right. He looked up, saw a pickup truck bearing down on him. He dropped the shovel and dove back toward the curb. The driver laid on the horn as he swept by. The snow broke his fall, and he was on his feet in a split second.

"Asshole!"

He gave the retreating pickup the finger. His heart started to pound under his ribs. Christ, he'd almost bought it right there, not paying attention to things. He'd have to settle down, concentrate. He brushed the snow off his clothes. He was wet already, and he had not even moved a shovelful of snow. His shovel. He looked around for it. It lay in the middle of the street, its handle broken in two. He picked up the pieces and examined them. Shit. There was no repairing this. He threw the broken handle toward the curb. The shovel end still had a few inches of handle. It would have to do.

Safely on the curb, he stopped and studied the park. He had never searched here before. It was mostly open space. Clue 8 had stated that the treasure was midway between two trees. What few trees there were stood around the edges of the park, each surrounded by a crowd of treasure hunters. He could hear a hum of voices, the sound of shovels against snow. Flashlights bobbed in the darkness. Well, which two trees should he pick? Probably best to walk the park once to see if any pair of trees really stood out, or really *didn't* stand out. He'd start on the other side, next to the bluff. From there, he would be able to see the Schmidt sign, not that that would mean anything.

The open area of the park was trampled with footprints, like a school playground after recess. No use looking out here in the open where there were no trees. Halfway across, he felt something underfoot. He bent over and fumbled in the snow under the toe of his boot. A metal object, flat and hard. He held it up, turned it this way and that. A Coke can squashed flat. Left last fall by some litterbug of a kid and covered up by the snow. He threw the can over his shoulder.

At the east end of the park, he spotted a pair of tall elms. Beyond the brush that rimmed the bluff, the Schmidt sign suddenly lit up in full and then flashed off. The letters started to wink on, one by one. This looked like as good a place as any. He elbowed his way into the crowd of searchers, ignoring them. He bent down and scooped up a shovelful of snow. Shaking the shovel from side to side, he let the snow sift over the edges until the shovel was empty. He scooped up another shovel and sifted, then another. Another. And another. He felt the familiar ache start to creep into his lower back again. This was going to be tough with a broken shovel. He dropped to his knees and kept shoveling.

TWO

"BUT SOMEBODY'LL FIND IT during the day, and tonight'll be too late," Chris argued. He drew an angry red square in the treasure hunt notebook and colored it in with heavy, punishing strokes of his red pen. "If they didn't already find it during the night. We should have stayed later than ten o'clock," he added.

He isn't going to give up on this, Sharon thought as she watched him draw and color in another square. Jeff had already read the new treasure hunt clue in the morning paper, pleaded his case, and conceded, leaving the breakfast table to go upstairs to get ready for school. But Chris had stayed behind to argue the appeal.

"Missing one day of school to look won't hurt anything," he insisted. He gave them each a pleading look, first his father and then her. "I'm all caught up on everything. And I'm doing okay. You saw my last report card." He stuck out his thirteen-year-old chin and delivered a final jab, his voice tinged with resentment. "If it was just Jeff that was asking, you wouldn't be making such a big deal about it."

"Jeff's grades didn't take up residence in the basement," Phil said curtly without looking up from the business section of the paper. He had seemed distant and distracted during the discussion of the new clue, his mind obviously on more important subjects than treasure medallions. Like how to keep his ridiculous charade going another two days. Last night, in the seconds between the time he called out from the front entryway and when he entered the kitchen, she had made her decision: wait him out, see how he plays it. She had been civil, if not exactly warm and friendly, for the rest of the evening. If Phil had felt her coolness toward him, he had done a good job of hiding it. Roaming about the kitchen, nibbling on leftovers, he had bantered with the boys, who arrived shortly after he did. When the pizza finally arrived, they had demolished it in ten minutes, then all three of them had gone to Linwood Park to search for the medallion, leaving her alone.

She had given in and called Elaine, the only person she could turn to. Elaine's response had been both predictable and profane.

"Oh, that lying bastard," Elaine had fumed. "Does he know you know?"

"No, not yet."

"What are you going to do?" Elaine asked.

"I don't know," she had answered.

"I'd divorce him if I were you. I swear I'd divorce Dean if he ever did that to me."

This morning, she still did not know what she was going to do, other than wait to see what he did. She watched the little father-and-son drama continue in front of her.

"Come on," Chris pleaded, "just this once."

Phil had looked up from his newspaper, and then across the kitchen table at her for a final ruling, as she knew he would. The concerned, loving parent.

"What do you think?" he asked.

"Let him go," she said, looking away. She heard the frost in her voice.

"All right, then," Phil said, "you can miss school this once—" he held up an index finger for emphasis "—and look for the treasure medallion. But this is a special occasion and you are not, I repeat, *not* to mistake this as our approval to skip school whenever you want to. Are we clear?"

"Clear."

Chris bolted out of the kitchen toward the stairway. His voice echoed throughout the downstairs, cracking with excitement. "Hey, Jeff! Dad says we can skip school and go back to the park again. Move your big butt. Let's go!" His feet pounded up the stairs.

Dad says. She makes the ruling, he makes the announcement and gets all the credit. She got up to refill her coffee mug.

She heard Phil sigh behind her. "You wonder, sometimes, what he's going to be like when he grows up, don't you?"

She snorted to herself as she reached for the coffee pot. She didn't have to wonder, she knew. He was growing up to be just like his father. One day he, too, might come home, look his family right in the eye, and lie through his teeth. She was surprised, in a way, that Phil had agreed to let them skip. Probably getting on their good side, softening them up for the big announcement.

Phil swallowed the last of his coffee. He rose to his feet, rinsed out his mug, and set it in the sink. "Well, I need to move my big butt, too, or I'm going to be late. What do you say to dinner out tonight, all of us?"

"Fine."

"Someplace with decent seafood. You want to scout and make reservations for us?"

"Sure," she said to his back as he disappeared into the dining room. Seafood. He knew how much they all missed good seafood. He must be worried that they were going to resist when he finally made the grand announcement. Whenever he made it. She should start a pool and sell chances. Date and time for a dollar. She and the boys and Elaine could all get in on the action. She'd put her money on Sunday night, right after supper.

Phil reappeared in the kitchen doorway, buttoning his overcoat. A scarf hung loosely around his neck.

"See you tonight, Babe." His departing kiss seared her cheek.

After the back door slammed, she rubbed the kiss away. Business as usual for him. Well, he wouldn't think it was business as usual if he knew what she had thought about last night while he snored blissfully beside her. She had dissected her marriage and finally figured out what kind of person Phil really was, had always been. Everything was all tied together, like colored silk scarves knotted together at the corners and pulled from a magician's hat. She had pulled and pulled on the train of scarves,

all the way back to their beginning. It had always been this way; she holding the career ladder steady for him while he ascended. A good corporate wife taking care of the home front, Flannary had called it. Well, she
would call it something else. Taking a back seat came to mind. Or being
a second-class citizen. She had dropped out of her masters program in
architecture at Boston U when Jeff was born because Phil had been adamant
that he not be raised by strangers. One of them would have to stay home,
he had insisted. Telephone equipment sales paid their bills, while grad-
uate school in architecture did not. Phil had promised her that she could
go back after Jeff was older. And she had bought it. But then Chris had
come along and needed a full-time parent, and she had bought the whole
argument all over again. And so her plans to become an architect had
been permanently shelved. They could have worked out some kind of
plan that included grad school, if Phil had only been willing.

The move out here to St. Paul was another example. She had been
forced to give up her job at the architectural bookstore, which had finally just gone to full-time. The owners had suggested that she could
eventually work into management. Another career opportunity torpedoed,
and Phil had been the one who pushed the button.

Each time it had happened, she had convinced herself that her sacrifice was for the good of the family. But now . . . now that she had
been so blatantly lied to, now that she saw how Phil had *manipulat-
ed* her . . .

She got up and started to load the dishwasher. She stared at the red
woodwork, hating that she wasn't going to get to paint it.

Elaine's question rattled around in her mind. What *was* she going
to do? One thing for sure, she wasn't going to subject herself to Elaine's
wrath today. She reached for the phone and punched the bookstore's number. Her own voice answered via the answering machine: "You've reached
the Paperback Library. Our hours are nine A.M. to five P.M., Monday
through Friday, ten to four Saturday, and noon to five on Sunday. To leave
a message, please wait for the tone. Thank you, and keep reading."

"Elaine," she said, "it's me. Can you handle things today? I'm not
up to coming in. I'll call you later." She hung up the receiver.

The boys came downstairs, dressed in old stone-washed jeans and
heavy gray sweatshirts.

". . . look at that last clue again . . ." Jeff pulled the paper out from
under the treasure hunt notebook. "Clue 10: *A bluff figures in the hunt,*

but high or low, we'll have to punt." He studied the clue for a moment, working the corners of his mouth. She noticed the shadow of mustache that made his upper lip look dirty. God, he's so grown up. He ought to have some say in what happens to him.

". . . bluff has to be the key word," he was saying. "The only other word that could mean anything is punt."

"You punt in football," Chris suggested. "On the fourth down. Maybe they mean that you could play football in that wide-open place."

"Na." Jeff shook his head. "Football's got nothing to do with it. Punt is just in there because it rhymes with hunt. It just means it's hidden near a bluff, but they ain't saying whether it's at the top or at the bottom. Aren't saying," he corrected himself. "It's at Linwood. Gotta be."

She sat down at the table again and took up her coffee mug. She should tell the boys. Tell them that their father was a liar, a manipulator. Push him off his pedestal and send him crashing to the ground. It would serve him right.

"Sit down, guys," she said. "I've got something to tell you."

The boys dropped obediently into their chairs. She brought her hands together and rubbed her nose, trying to figure out where to begin. How did you tell two boys something that would probably make them hate their father?

"Ma," Chris said, "before you start, can you drop us off at the park on the way to the store?"

She looked into Chris's eyes and knew she couldn't tell them. At least not now. She pushed her chair back and stood up. It was time to quit feeling sorry for herself.

"Better than that," she said. "I was just about to tell you that I'm playing hooky today, too. Let's get saddled up and go find that medallion."

THREE

S TEVEN CARPENTER STRAIGHTENED UP SLOWLY, planting his palms on the end of the shovel handle to help pull himself upright. The muscles in his back felt like rope stretched too tight, the strands fraying and breaking one by one. He leaned on his shovel handle, and surveyed the area around him. He had dug through the snow midway between these two trees twice. He and about twenty-five other treasure hunters. The medallion wasn't here.

He pulled off his gloves and blew on his hands to warm them. Nor was it midway between the endless other pairs of trees he had dug between since they had arrived here last night. The fun had long since gone out of treasure hunting. He was cold. His feet felt as though they were made of wood. He was soaked to the skin, and he needed to take a leak. Bad. He looked around for Debi. They had split up an hour ago to double the amount of ground they covered. He spotted her about a hundred and fifty feet away, midway between two other trees, leaning on her shovel like a government worker. She was talking to a woman wearing a purple ski jacket and a white hat.

He glared at her and poked the snow with his shovel. What a slave driver. They never had eaten supper last night. Instead, she had kept them out here almost all night. They had gone home at dawn, just long enough to eat a quick breakfast, change into dry clothes, and call in sick to work. If she was going to insist they be out here around the clock, the least she could do was keep digging.

A ripple of cheers suddenly passed through the crowd of treasure hunters, like a wave at the Metrodome that couldn't quite get started. He saw heads turn toward the east, gloved hands pointing. Shit, someone must have found it. His eyes followed the pointing fingers, expecting to see a happy treasure hunter dancing around in celebration. Instead, he saw that everyone was pointing at a van from one of the television stations that had just pulled into the park. The van rolled up the curved driveway and parked in the little parking lot that faced the bluff. The doors opened and a man and woman climbed out. He recognized the woman as a reporter, but he couldn't remember her name. The driver walked around to the passenger side and opened the van's side door. He hoisted a camera to his shoulder. The woman gathered up a microphone and cord, and slammed the door shut. They scanned the park, and then the woman pointed in his direction. The two of them started across the snow toward him, dodging around treasure hunters. He turned away and tried to disappear. If anyone at work saw him on the six o'clock news after he had called in sick, he'd probably be fired.

As the news team approached, he could hear the reporter outlining the shot. ". . . set up so that you catch me just in front of the crowd, and have the panorama in background. I'll do my opening. Then zoom in on some shovels for a few seconds. Get a couple of cold faces, zoom in on shovels again, and then cut back to me for a finish. Let's get this bullshit over with and get back downtown, before something breaks . . ."

They had moved right past him as though he were a tree or a trash can. He followed them. Around him, he could feel others being drawn along. A crowd started to form around the cameraman.

The reporter selected a spot in front of Debi and the woman in purple and a dozen or so other treasure hunters. She motioned the cameraman around in front of her.

Debi better move out of the shot, he thought, or she would be on the six o'clock news for God and everybody to see. Including her boss.

"Deb!" he called and pointed at the camera.

The reporter looked over her shoulder to get an idea of the shot. "Keep digging," she instructed the treasure hunters. "Don't look at the camera and don't wave." She turned to the cameraman, took a deep breath, and nodded.

Debi still hadn't moved. She was only about twenty feet behind the reporter. If she was going to get out of the shot, she would have to move now.

"Hey, Deb!" he hissed in a loud whisper.

The reporter lowered the microphone. "Come on, fella, give us a break, will ya?"

His face burning, he melted back into the crowd.

The reporter raised her microphone again and drew another deep breath.

"The search for the Winter Carnival treasure medallion is reaching a fever pitch here in St. Paul's Linwood Park, as searchers dig through the snow in search of the little medallion that could earn them up to four thousand dollars. One of the more recent clues says the medallion is hidden midway between two trees, and as you can see—" the reporter gestured behind her "—most treasure hunters are searching between two trees. The question, of course, is which two trees are the right ones?"

The reporter lowered the microphone. "That's a keeper, Russ. Okay, now for the wrap-up. You guys are doing great," she called over her shoulder. "Just keep digging." She raised the microphone again.

"Only one of the hundreds of people searching here will be lucky enough to find the medallion. For most treasure hunters, it will be 'just wait until next year,' but for some lucky treasure hunter, it will be a dream come true. For the six o'clock news, I'm Ellen MacKenzie, along with cameraman Russell Graham, here in St. Paul's Linwood Park."

Ellen MacKenzie looped the microphone cord as she moved toward her cameraman.

"Shoot some footage of boots, shovels, and cold faces," she said. "Maybe do a sweep of the park, and zoom in on a group of searchers. We can edit back at the station, and I'll do some voice-over if we need it. Hurry up and let's get out of here."

Steven gave the news team a wide berth as he moved toward Debi. She was talking again to the woman wearing the purple ski jacket.

". . . we live in an apartment that overlooks Summit Avenue," Debi was saying. She glanced up at him.

He grimaced. Overlooks Summit. That was a good one. Their apartment faced Summit, all right—from a block away.

"We live down by Macalester," the woman said. "In Tangletown. My boys are around here somewhere." She scanned the crowd, and pointed toward a knot of treasure hunters digging around a small evergreen. "Over there. The one wearing the green army jacket and red stocking cap, and the younger one right next to him in the blue coat and Vikings stocking cap."

"It's really a beautiful apartment," Debi said, "but we won't be here much longer. We're moving to New York for our careers."

"Oh?"

"We've gone about as far as we can go here," Debi said. "My husband—" she nodded at him "—is a musician. He's working on songs for an album, and has a better chance to break in there."

"What do you do?" the woman asked.

"I work in investments. My supervisor is planning to move to New York, and he'll take me along as his assistant."

The woman turned toward him. "What instrument do you play?"

"Guitar," he said. He felt his face turning red.

"And you're going to make a record?"

"Well, someday." His face burned with embarrassment.

"Well, you better let your wife have her career, too, if you want to stay married to her," the woman said. "My husband just accepted a job in San Diego without even telling me. He doesn't know I know. I'm still trying to decide whether I'm going to go with him, divorce him, or hire someone to kill him and collect his life insurance."

He exchanged glances with Debi. The woman gave them an odd look, then suddenly shouldered her shovel and headed in the direction of her boys.

"Geez," he said when she was out of earshot, "what's with her?"

"I don't know," Debi laughed, "but somebody better warn her husband about her."

"I've never said you couldn't have your own career," he said. "Whatever gave her that notion?"

"Nothing I said," Debi insisted. "All I said was we were moving to New York. And then she pounced on you, and said she was thinking about having her husband killed."

"Well, that's his problem," Steven said. "You've got your own problem. What are you going to do if your boss sees you on the six o'clock news after you called in sick?"

Debi shrugged. "Oh, he probably won't see it. There're three television stations in town."

"But what if he does?"

"If he does, I'll just tell him I felt better. It's no big deal."

No big deal. If it were he who had been caught by the television camera, he'd be sweating it out.

Debi twirled the shovel handle in her pink-mittened hands. "So where should we look next?"

"I don't suppose you'd be willing to take a break, warm up, and get something to eat?"

She cast a look around the park, looked up at the mid-morning sun. "One of us could go get something for both of us. But somebody needs to keep looking."

"I'll go," he said. "I need to go to the bathroom."

"Bring me some dry mittens," she said. "My green ones are in the hall closet."

He headed across the snow toward the north side of the park. The Honda was parked almost halfway home, facing south on Victoria Street. Coming back from breakfast at dawn, they had taken the first parking space they found, knowing there would be nothing closer to the park.

A musician. Debi had actually introduced him as a musician. She had said it right out loud, as if it were really true. He had never called himself a musician before, but he guessed that was what he was now. When he played, that is. He had not played a single chord since Wednesday. They had been too busy with the treasure hunt for him to practice. He would have to practice three or four hours a day over the weekend to make up for lost time.

A musician and an investment broker living in New York. It sounded nice out loud, even if it was a little crazy.

FOUR

ALFRED SAW SOMETHING SLIDE OFF the end of his shovel. With effort, he leaned over to pick it up. His heavy clothes bunched up around his middle, making it hard to bend over. He grunted with the effort, and as he straightened up, he had to take a step sideways to steady himself. The object was a large paper cup, like young kids bought at the convenience stores. It had been smashed flat and folded up in an unnatural shape. The layers were frozen tightly together and encased in a sheath of ice. He shook the cup, listening for a rattle, then held it up to the sunlight, looking for the dark, round shadow of the medallion. He saw a round shape near one end. His heart bounded in his chest. *This could be it.*

He turned the shovel over and banged the cup hard against the curved bottom several times. The ice splintered like glass. He dropped the shovel and shucked off his gloves, letting them fall to the ground. The splinters of ice bit into his fingertips as he pried them away, hot and cold at the same time. The cup came apart at the creases, layer by frozen layer. He let the pieces drop to the ground as he peeled them off. The ice and the excitement sent shivers running through him. When he got to the round shape, he saw that it was nothing more than the cup's round bottom, turned inward and covered up.

In disgust, he threw down the remaining pieces. Using his shovel as a cane, he stooped again to pick up his gloves, steadying himself as he straightened up. He slapped the snow off the gloves and pulled them on, feeling disappointment creeping over him as his fingers touched the matted lamb's wool. He felt snow melting on his wrists. His heart settled back into its normal rhythm. He should have known better than to have gotten his hopes up.

He looked up and saw that he was being watched from twenty feet away by a young man dressed in heavy, insulated coveralls and a blue hooded sweatshirt, the hood pulled up over a tight-fitting stocking cap. He was paused in midshovel, as though where he deposited the shovelful of snow depended upon what the paper cup had held. The young man immediately realized he had been spotted, and let both his gaze and his shovel fall to the ground. Then he looked up again. A half smile spread across his reddened cheeks.

"Thought you'd found her there for a second," the young man said.

"Me, too," Alfred said, embarrassment overwhelming him. He must have been a silly sight, tearing into the paper cup like a five-year-old opening a Christmas present. He poked at the ground with his shovel. "Should have known better, though. I ain't lucky enough to find things."

The young man crossed the ten steps between them. "I've been looking since daybreak," he said. I thought for a second it was going to be 'wait till next year,' like they keep saying about the Vikings."

The young man's dark Fu Manchu mustache glistened with ice. From under his gray stocking cap, a matching shock of dark hair whipped in a sudden gust of wind.

"Cold enough for you?" Alfred asked.

"This week isn't so bad except for this snow," the young man said. "Last week sure was a bitch, though."

"Sure was," Alfred agreed.

The young man held his bare hand over his mouth to melt the ice that clung to his mustache. "What made you decide that it's buried here?" he asked from behind his hand. His knuckles were scabbed over as if he had been in a fight, or a wrench had suddenly slipped.

"That clue about the queen and river," Alfred said. "Queen Victoria and the Avon River in England. You can see the Schmidt brewery from here—that's the seven red hints. Least that's how I read 'em."

In truth, it had been Genevieve who, after reading the clue in the evening paper again, had come up with the name Victoria, looked it up on the map, and then looked up Avon in the dictionary they had bought for Janet when she started high school. She had come downstairs to the basement with the news, interrupting his solitude. Armed with her information, he had left the house right after breakfast, before Genevieve got around to talking about plane tickets.

"That's the way I figure it, too," the young man said. "But where do you look once you get here? That's what I'd like to know." He gestured around the park. "Midway between two trees, one of the clues says. There's plenty of pairs of trees here, and they've all been dug around a hundred times. I'm surprised somebody hasn't found it by now."

"Somebody will today," Alfred predicted. He leaned on his shovel handle. It actually felt good to talk to someone. He hadn't talked to anyone except Genevieve for days, and all she wanted to talk about was going to Houston. But what was this guy doing out here in the middle of the day, when he should be at work? Unless he was one of those slackers who lived off the government on unemployment.

"You workin'?" he asked.

The young man shook his head. "Worked in construction, but I quit last fall. I'm going to tech school. Skipped classes today to see if I could get lucky and strike it rich." He laughed as though he had made a joke. "I'm studying web printing."

"How's that?"

"Printing. You know—newspapers, magazines, books, stuff like that."

"Oh," Alfred said. "Sure. I get you now." Everybody, it seemed, was reaching out to grab at something more than what they had. "How'd you pick that?"

The young man leaned on his shovel. "Couldn't see myself pushing a wheelbarrow filled with cement when I was fifty-five or sixty. I mean, there's nothing wrong with hard work. As long as somebody else is doing it."

Alfred laughed.

"I wanted something that had a good future and was indoors, so I wouldn't have to be outside in the winter. Something where I didn't have to use my back all the time." He pushed the shock of hair up under his stocking cap. "How about you?"

"Retired," Alfred said. "Used to work at the brewery." He nodded toward the east. "Worked there thirty-seven years, then they closed the place up on us. I was too old to go anywhere else. So I'm retired."

The young man let out a low whistle. "Thirty-seven years. That's a long time. What are you doing these days?"

"Not much. Just sitting around. Planned on doing some fishing with my brother, but he up and died. Don't care now whether I go fishing or not."

"That's too bad."

"Healthy as a horse one day, dead the next. Sitting there in his easy chair, drinking a cup of coffee just before Thanksgiving, and bang, a heart attack hit him. Keeled right over onto the floor, dead. We'd started building an ice fishing shack and everything. A deluxe model."

"What a shame."

"We used to hunt for the treasure together. Almost found it one year— saw somebody pick it up. It's no fun out here alone. I don't even know why I'm here."

The words had tumbled out of his mouth. The good old days. Before Rudy died; before yesterday's discovery in the bottom drawer of Rudy's bureau.

"What a shame," the young man said again.

"The wife, she wants us to move to Houston now, where our daughter lives, but shit, I can't do that. I grew up here." He pointed below the bluff at the steep-sloped roofs and chimneys. "Right down there. My whole life's been right here. I'm too old to go off and start something else."

"I don't know, it might be nice to get out of this weather," the young man said.

"I don't want to go off to some big city and have to get used to a bunch of strangers," Alfred said. "I'd rather stay here and put up with the cold."

Why couldn't he be as honest with Genevieve as he was with this young fella he didn't even know? Because he would never see this guy again, and it didn't make a damn bit of difference to him what this young fella thought or said about him later. But Genevieve. He had to live with her every day.

"My daughter, she up and moves away because her husband could make a fortune down there, and now we're the ones supposed to come visit. People ought to be satisfied with what they got. The whole world'd be in a lot better shape if people would just stop thinking they had to have everything."

The young man suddenly poked the ground with his shovel and backed up a step. "Well, guess we better keep searching. Won't find it standing here shooting the shit."

"Probably won't anyway," Alfred said.

"Well, you never know," the young man said as he moved away. "Somebody's got to find it."

Alfred went back to his own shoveling, settling into the familiar rhythm: fill the shovel with snow, sift it out, fill it again.

He had talked too much, blurted out his whole life story to the kid. Once started, it had all come tumbling out of him: the brewery, Rudy, Genevieve's wanting to move. Rudy. It was the first time he had spoken to anyone about him since that dreadful discovery in Rudy's bottom drawer. The shock and the hurt still lingered, but he had realized in the wee, sleepless hours of the night that, in the end, what Rudy was or was not didn't make any difference. Rudy was who he was, whether or not anyone knew his secret. Rudy hadn't changed. It was his own knowledge about Rudy that had changed so suddenly. No, it was more the realization that things never stayed the same—even the things that seemed permanent, the things that you were sure of—that's what bothered him so. Everything kept changing all the time, making him leave behind what was familiar and comfortable, forcing him to confront new things that required thought and evaluation and decisions.

If only things would stop changing. If he could just grab hold of the pendulum with both hands and make time stop today—no, the day before Rudy died—and not have any more changes to deal with. But that was impossible; time just kept racing along, throwing more and more changes in his face. Now with the year 2000 roaring down on him, the century racing toward its frightening end, he didn't know if he was up to making any more changes. He'd much rather be back in some earlier time, surrounded by Rudy, his parents, even old Tantchen.

His shovel struck something hard, giving off a scraping sound. He leaned over and brushed the snow away with his gloved hand. It was a rock about the size of a baseball. No way could they hide a medallion in that. He pitched the rock off to the side.

Straightening up, he leaned on his shovel again. The young man in the coveralls and blue sweatshirt had moved about a hundred feet away, but somehow seemed much farther away than that. He felt as though he were peering at the young man through the wrong end of a telescope. On either side of him, a dozen or more treasure hunters were busy digging away, ignoring him. He felt invisible.

Alfred stopped to rest. There was a way to get away from all of this. His dream the other night had shown it to him. At first, seeing all those dead faces again had frightened and confused him. Afterwards, sitting alone at the kitchen table with his brandy, his stomach twisted into knots, he had not understood what he saw. But now he did. There was nothing to fear. The look on Rudy's face was not threatening, but welcoming. The sound of Rudy's voice as he extended his hand had been joyful.

It would solve everything.

FIVE

BRUCE MITCHELL TURNED HIS BACK to the bluff, and looked north across Linwood Park. For the umpteenth time, he read through the list of clues he had cut out of the morning paper and stuck in the breast pocket of his coveralls. There was no question that the medallion was here somewhere. All the clues fit. Train tracks, streets named for a queen and a river, the Schmidt sign, airplanes coming and going, a bluff, a baseball diamond, everything. Only trouble was, *where* in the park? Clue 8 said the treasure was midway between two trees. But, like he had asked the old geezer awhile ago, which two trees? Every tree in the park had been paired up with another and the space between them dug out, all the way down to the frozen ground. And no one had found it; at least, no word had gone out that it had been found. And now the hordes of treasure hunters were hacking away at the withered grass, digging up chunks of frozen earth. Come spring when the frost went out of the ground, the place would look like hell.

He stuffed the clues back into the pocket of his coveralls. A hundred feet away, the old geezer was still digging between the same two trees, a rumpled figure in his brown coat and billed cap. Strange old bird. He had seemed all right at first, even friendly; then all of a sudden he'd started cutting up his family, and ranting and raving about how the world would be a better place if people would just be satisfied with what they had. That's when he'd gotten the hell out of there. He'd heard enough of that garbage around construction sites.

It was obvious, though, that the old man missed his dead brother. He could relate to that, on this of all days. Digging in the snow alone all morning—your clothes soaking wet and your toes turning numb—wasn't any fun in itself. Shooting the shit with someone, swapping jokes and puns, running down the foreman at work, and passing a pint back and forth—that was the fun part about treasure hunting.

No chance of doing that this year. Despite his coaxing, Jo had politely but firmly refused to skip class and come out here with him. And even if she had come, it wouldn't have been the same. What was really fun about the treasure hunt was hunting with St. John. But there would be no treasure hunting with St. John.

He grabbed the tip of the index finger of his glove with his teeth and pulled out his hand. He wiggled his fingers and formed a fist. Much of the bruised feeling had gone away during the night, but his knuckles were puffy and red, the exposed flesh now covered by purplish scabs. He pulled on the glove again. The fleece scraped against the scabs, setting off the damaged nerve endings. Pain danced across the back of his hand.

Yeah, but you should see the other guy. What did St. John's face look like this morning? He had thrown the punch so quickly that St. John hadn't had a chance to duck, and had taken the full force of the blow right on the cheekbone. He'd opened his cheek up enough to bleed, that much he remembered.

Throughout the night, St. John had haunted his sleep. As he tossed and turned, the image of St. John brandishing the broken coffee table leg had turned grainy and dark, dissolving into a picture of him lying prostrate on the floor, bringing his hand up to his bloodied cheek with agonizing slowness. St. John's angry voice had remained, but behind the anger he had heard the pain. *I'm sick of hearing about your hotshot career plans, and I'm fuckin' sick to death of hearing about how many times you've nailed your girl friend.*

He jabbed his shovel into the ground, crossed his palms over the dull point of the handle, and rested his chin on the backs of his hands, ignoring the screech of pain in his knuckles. Across the park, the St. Clair bus rolled to a stop and let off two heavily bundled figures carrying snow shovels. More competition. The figures waded through the snow and paused in the middle of the park, trying to figure out where to go.

Maybe St. John was right. Would he want to hear St. John brag about his sex life if he were in St. John's shoes? Probably not. Talking yourself up to someone who was down was a shitty thing to do. The Sundance Kid would never treat Butch Cassidy that way.

But, goddamn it, he was tired of being the Sundance Kid, tired of playing outlaw. You couldn't be satisfied forever with the same old stuff. Things changed. You moved with the flow. You decided what you wanted out of life and worked for it, despite what that old geezer had said. That was why he had gone back to school. That's what had put this park and the houses across the street—this whole city—on the map. He winced at how corny it all sounded.

The thing of it was, you had to balance what you wanted with what you already had. And sometimes something had to give. But St. John couldn't see it that way. He always held on to things too long, always looked on the gloomy side of things. *Some of us ain't so lucky.* St. John was a hell of a lot luckier than he gave himself credit for, he was just in a bad spot right now. The guy had a good place to live, decent transportation, and a job. And until yesterday, he had had a good friend.

The point of the shovel handle was sharp against his palms under the weight of his chin. He flexed his hands inside his gloves. He should have let St. John blow off steam, and then set him down and told him that he had a good foundation to build on. Should have told him that the weather would warm up and he would go back to work. Should have told him that all this shit with Karen would eventually blow over. That he'd meet somebody new and things would get better. That's what he should have said. And he should have figured out some way to draw St. John out on why he wouldn't sign up for school, the way they had always planned. But instead of being a friend, he had flipped his own cork, accusing St. John of not listening to him brag about his good luck, building himself up in his own eyes after being behind the eight ball himself for so long.

He felt a gust of wind through his damp clothes and shivered. Enough of this, he told himself. Forget about it. What's done is done. Get back to work before you freeze to death standing here.

He inspected another shovelful of snow, and then stopped. There was no medallion here. The clue said midway between two trees. He surveyed the park again, looking for two trees that somehow stood out. At opposite ends of the park, two very tall trees stood like bookends. They were directly opposite each other, and about the same size, a set of sorts. Midway between them would be about dead-center in the wide-open space of the park. The snow was crisscrossed with the tracks of treasure hunters heading in and out of the park, but no one was really searching out there. Hell, what did he have to lose? He walked through the snow until he was midway between the two trees. It felt a little silly out here in the middle all by himself, a hundred and fifty feet from the nearest tree.

The snow was only about eight inches deep. He jabbed the shovel into the snow and lifted out a shovelful. He tilted the shovel sideways to let the snow sift out. He turned over another shovelful, then another, settling into a steady rhythm.

Ripping into St. John like that was probably a lousy thing for him to do, but damn it, St. John had let him down, too. He had every right to ask St. John to listen to his good fortune and be happy for him. Friends weren't supposed to be there just for the heavy stuff; they were supposed to be there all the time. St. John shouldn't have been cutting him off all this time whenever he mentioned Jo. He should have said he was glad for both of them. But St. John hadn't done any of that. He'd just been an asshole. From St. John's point of view, maybe Jo threw a wrench into everything. Maybe that was why he was so hostile toward her. Not so much that he was simply jealous that he didn't have a woman of his own, but that Jo took away from their time together.

So the Butch and Sundance days were over. No trip to Bolivia, no going out together in a blaze of glory. Their movie had ended with the Sundance Kid, in his own eagerness to quit the outlaw business, failing to come through for his partner, his all-time best friend, instead punching Butch's lights out because Butch had goaded him. He wished he could take that punch back, but it was too late. St. John's cheek would soon heal, but his pride was another matter. Hell, St. John wouldn't even answer the goddamn telephone after he had refused to go out treasure hunting with him the other night. No amount of apology would convince St. John to put getting punched out behind him, to let bygones be bygones.

He had Jo to be with, but what the hell would St. John do? He would go back to work when the weather straightened up. One construction season would melt into the next, and pretty soon ten years would slip by. St. John would be fat and forty, like that guy at the Busy Bee.

He stopped digging and leaned again on his shovel. He searched the clusters of treasure hunters, hoping to catch sight of the familiar quilted vest and Ford cap, knowing he would not. Like he had told Jo, St.

John was not a doer, the kind of guy who would cut loose and go out and do things alone.

He felt the dampness of his wet clothes against his arms and legs. A good swig of brandy would taste really good right now. But it had been St. John who always brought the pint they passed back and forth, and St. John was probably sitting in his dump of a living room, listening to the blues, and giving himself goddamn lung cancer with those lousy cigarettes he chain-smoked.

He jabbed his shovel into the snow and pried back on the handle. Shit, he should just quit and go home, spend the rest of the day watching the tube. But the digging at least gave him something to do. He drove his shovel into the snow again. He was going to miss the ornery son of a bitch.

SIX

THIS WAS POINTLESS, KEITH DECIDED. He was bone weary. His back ached from bending over so far to accommodate the broken shovel handle. And when he dropped to his knees to save his back, the snow soaked through his clothes, turning his knees numb. He rose to his feet and slapped the caked snow off his knees. Either he could keep wandering around, aimlessly digging between this tree and that, or he could give up and go get a newspaper containing the newest clue; it had probably been out for a couple of hours by now. Clue 11 might give some further indication where in the park the medallion was hidden. As long as he didn't know what it said, he'd be at a disadvantage. He'd only held off going after it because he would have to leave the park. It would take him a half hour to leave, find a newspaper box, and get back. A long time to be gone. Still, it was probably worth it for even the slightest edge it would give him. The final clue, published late tonight, would give the precise location of the treasure. The moment that clue came out, everybody would be jammed into the same spot, tripping over each other, and his chances of finding the medallion would dwindle to almost nothing. He could probably find a newspaper box up on Grand Avenue. Unless . . . Shading his eyes from the sun, he scanned the trea-

sure hunters, and spotted two men studying a newspaper about twenty yards away. He trudged toward them.

"Over that way, you think?" one was saying, pointing toward the
northeast. He looked burly in blue insulated coveralls and a quilted
vest. His heavy, untrimmed beard was streaked with gray. He wore a
Twins cap pulled down over his eyes to cut the glare. He looked
vaguely familiar.

"'Scuse me," Keith said. "Is that the latest clue?" The two men looked
at him.

"Yeah, Clue 11," said the one holding the newspaper. He wore a
camouflage vest over an orange hooded sweatshirt and dark green insulated coveralls.

"You mind if I have a look at it?" The two men looked at each other.

"Sure," said the man in camouflage. He held the newspaper
out. "Go ahead. What can it hurt? We're probably not going to find
it anyway."

Keith took the paper and turned so that the sun was behind him
and the shadow of his head fell over the blinding white of the page. Clue
11: *In a classic can the treasure hides. This little clue may help you turn the
tides.*

"In a can between two trees," he said aloud.

The two men nodded. "Yeah, but which two trees?" the man in camouflage asked. "We were just saying that maybe it's closer to St. Clair."

"What makes you think that?" Keith asked.

"Most people are digging around by the bluff," said the bearded man,
gesturing to the south. "And no one has found it yet, least not that's been
announced. If it was over there, someone would've found it by now. So
it must be over here, where fewer people are looking. Stands to reason,
don't it?"

"What kind of can do you think they mean?" the camouflage
man asked. "Classic Coke can?"

"Your guess is as good as mine," Keith said. He handed the newspaper back to the bearded man and started to turn away.

"Hey, you're welcome," the camouflage man said.

"Thanks," Keith said over his shoulder. He put some distance between himself and the two men. They were probably right that it was
in a Classic Coke can. The name even matched. Had classic been spelled
with a capital C in the clue, or put in quotes? That would have in-

dicated a brand name. He wished he could take another look at the clue. He glanced at the two men, now headed toward the north side of the park. Better not. Maybe Classic Coke can was too obvious. Maybe classic simply meant familiar, and it was in something like a Campbell's soup can, or a Folger's coffee can. But those cans would be out of their natural environment here in the park, and would stand out. It was probably hidden in a pop can or a beer can, something common to the park, like someone had drunk its contents and then tossed it aside as junk.

Tossed aside as junk. Holy shit! He'd stepped on a Coke can earlier! God, when? He felt his heart take off in his chest, the blood suddenly run hot in his body. It had been dark. He'd been walking, felt it underfoot, and bent over to pick it up. That meant he must have been on his way into the park. He'd picked it up, identified it as a can, and then thrown it aside. Goddamn, that had probably been it! A smashed Classic Coke can. That was exactly the sort of thing they would hide the medallion in. Jesus, he should have thought of that, should have looked at it closer. Why hadn't he? He'd just missed getting creamed by that pickup. He was rattled and not thinking clearly like he usually did. If that truck hadn't come by and knocked his senses out of kilter for a moment, it would have clicked that a smashed can was a good hiding place. He would have inspected it more closely. And right now he would be sitting home, four thousand dollars richer.

Where the hell was it he had picked up that can? He hurried through the snow to the curb to look for his tracks. Everything looked different in the daylight. His tracks had long ago been obliterated by the countless comings and goings of eager treasure hunters. He'd jogged partway up the block on the north side of St. Clair before he had started across the street; he remembered that. Then he had heard the pickup horn, looked up, and saw headlights bearing down on him. The memory sent a chill through him. It had all happened so fast. He'd dived for the curb, gotten up, and found that the pickup had run over his shovel. The shovel handle. Look for the shovel handle. He crossed the street. He searched the piles of snow thrown against the curb by the snowplow until he found the broken shovel handle sticking out of the snow. He picked it up. All right; this had been about where he had crossed the street and entered the park.

He spun around and recrossed the street. Now to re-create his walk through the park. He'd walked partway across the open space in the middle, then moved off toward the southeast. When had he stumbled onto the can—before or after he'd changed directions? Before. Then it would be on this side of the middle. He'd thrown the can over his shoulder; he remembered the whirring sound it had made in the night air as it flew. He tried to recall the force of the throw. Had he just tossed it, or really fired it off into the night?

A few people were already milling around out in the middle of the park. A guy in tan coveralls and a blue sweatshirt was digging in a businesslike manner, like he'd figured it out. Well, he still held an advantage over the rest of them. He *knew* there was a can out there somewhere. No way to be casual and inconspicuous about this. Just get out there and get at it.

He retraced, as best he could remember, the route he had taken in the dark. He stopped about halfway out to the middle. It could have been here that he'd stepped on it. Or fifty feet farther on. There was a lot of middle out here, and it could be anywhere—like the proverbial needle in the haystack. And maybe it had been picked up and tossed aside again. And again. He remembered reading about one year when the medallion had been hidden in a ball of ice and tossed into a snowbank. When it was found, it was yards away from where it had been placed, transported there by a long succession of eager but careless shovels. The finder had found it lying in the snow like a quarter that had been dropped accidentally, the surrounding ball of ice chipped away from it. God knew how many times during the week someone had picked up that Classic Coke can and thrown it aside, just as he had. It was anybody's guess how far from its original location the can was by now, or what shape it was in.

The guy in the tan coveralls glanced at him, and then went on with his digging. It wouldn't take long before more people would start wandering out here to dig, too.

Keith dropped to his knees and pushed his shovel into the snow. His heart was pounding in his chest, his fatigue had vanished. He was closer to finding it than ever before. All he had to do was keep looking, but he was running out of time.

SEVEN

———

"I THINK WE'VE JUST RUN OUT OF PARK." Sharon turned around and looked to the south. Over the last two hours, they had worked from tree to tree all the way from the bluff to the point where Victoria Street entered the park. Now, standing at the park entrance, a decision on what to do next was in order.

"I'm hungry," Chris said. "Can we go and get something to eat?"

"Not if we want to find it." Jeff's eyes moved around the park, plotting their next move. He had taken today's treasure hunt very seriously, directing their search operation with the iron hand of a field general.

"But we've looked everywhere twice," Chris complained.

"Then we look again." Jeff's tone was surprisingly grim, filled with resolution. "Quit complaining."

Chris stepped behind his brother's back and stuck out his tongue. His eyes met hers, and a smile played at the corners of his mouth as he pulled in his tongue. So grown-up, and yet such a little boy at the same time.

"Are you getting discouraged?" she asked.

"I'm not discouraged," Chris insisted. "I'm *hungry.*"

"People are looking out in the middle," Jeff said, pointing. "Let's look out there."

"Can we go get something to eat first?" Chris begged. "I'm starving."

"Chris, quit acting like a damn wuss," Jeff snapped. "Or else just go home."

"I'm not a wuss," Chris fired back. "You're a slave driver."

"Come on, you two, that's enough," she said. "I think we're all getting a little hungry and cold." She pulled back the arm of her coat to check her watch. "It's two o'clock. Let's look for another hour. If we don't find it by then, or someone else doesn't, then we'll get something to eat."

She herded them toward the middle of the park. A couple dozen treasure hunters had staked out small territories and were methodically turning over one shovelful of snow after another. She noticed the young couple she had talked to that morning and steered the boys away from them. *I'm still trying to decide whether I'm going to go with him, divorce him, or hire someone to kill him and collect his life insurance.* No sooner had the words left her mouth than she regretted them. They had hung thickly in the air, like smoky breath. The boy and girl had stared at each other with puzzled expressions, and she had moved quickly away to avoid having to say anything more. The girl was now wearing green mittens instead of pink. She was leaning on her shovel handle, apparently directing her husband's digging efforts. What did it matter what they thought of her? She would never see them again anyway. But what about herself? Was it just a flip remark, or a Freudian slip of deeper, murderous thoughts? Should Phil start sleeping with one eye open, or hire someone to taste his food before he ate? So atypical of her—threatening to hire a hit man was much more in keeping with Elaine's temperament. Maybe Elaine was rubbing off on her.

What had possessed her to say such a thing in the first place? It was the girl's remark about moving to improve her husband's chances of making a record. That's what had set her off. Too close to home. Where was it they were going? New York, of course. So full of themselves, the girl especially. The girl reminded her of Phil, not so much in what she said, but in the tone she used. Somewhere in the edge of the girl's voice, you could almost hear the stone mason's chisel, etching her words into granite. Maybe the girl did have enough chutzpah to get all the way to New York, but the boy had just stood there.

She gave the couple a final look, then turned back to her digging. She herself would never want to be that age again; but if she were, she would do a few things differently.

"Ma!" Chris's voice, cracking with excitement, interrupted her digging. She turned around, half expecting to see him holding up the treasure medallion. Instead, he was pointing through the knot of treasure hunters.

"Look!"

A blue and red fast-food truck had pulled into the same little parking lot that the television van had parked in earlier. A line of hungry treasure hunters was already forming as the attendants raised the windows to open up for business.

"Can we get something?" Chris asked. "Somebody could get in line, and the other two could keep digging."

"Did 'somebody' happen to bring any money with him?" she asked. Chris's face fell.

"All right," she said. "I'll buy if you fly." She unzipped her coat pocket, and dug down along the bottom of the lining for the ten-dollar bill she had put there before they left the house.

"Get me a hot dog or two," she said. "Mustard and relish if they've got it." She turned to Jeff. "How about you?"

He shrugged. "Whatever."

Chris plucked the bill out of her hand. She watched him run toward the truck, dodging and weaving between the treasure hunters. He would make a good running back someday.

"Now." She reached out, grabbed Jeff by the sleeve of his army jacket, and turned him around to face her. "What's bothering you today?"

"Nothing," he said.

"Don't tell me 'nothing.' You've been kicking Chris's behind all over the park today. Now what is it? I want to know."

He avoided her eyes as he spoke. "I just think it sucks that we get all settled here, and then Dad gets this big promotion offer." His eyes came up and met her own. "I mean, I've thought about it the last couple of days. I really don't want to go through all of that crap again. I felt like a geek here for the first year. Just because my grades didn't go down like Chris's, Dad acts like moving here was a breeze for me. You do, too. Well, it really sucked! Now I've finally made some friends, and Dad's wants to move again."

She stared at him, stricken. An accusation she had not expected. But it was true. She and Phil had put their efforts into healing what damage they could see: Chris's low grades. Why had it never occurred to her until this instant that Jeff must have struggled too? Both boys had been put through the same experience, uprooted and transplanted here in this strange midwestern soil. He had never complained about it. Everything looked fine from the outside. The cardinal sin of parenting: assumption. Nothing showed, so no problem existed.

"I guess . . ." She reached out and rested her hand on his shoulder. He was stiff under her touch. "You're right. We just—"

"And then Dad puts the pressure on *us* to decide whether we want to move or not. What if we don't want to, and he turns the offer down because of us? I mean, it's a big opportunity and everything. What if he says no, and they never make him another offer?"

She closed her eyes to escape from the look on Jeff's face. Damn Phil, anyway. Not only had he outright lied to all of them, entrusting them with false power, he had also managed to instill in them a sense of guilt. They, not he, would be responsible for stalling his career advancement. She should tell Jeff right now—no, both of them—that the decision was already made—a done deal, as Phil would say—and that they should quit worrying about it, for whatever they thought wouldn't make a bit of difference in the end.

Her mouth opened, but the words didn't come out. Better to wait until the big meeting, until Phil herded them all into the dining room and took The Vote. Give him the benefit of the doubt, on the outside chance that she had misunderstood what Flannary said, or that Phil might, at the last minute, snap to his senses and change his mind.

But waiting until the big meeting would do nothing for Jeff. He glared owlishly at her, his head scrunched down into his shoulders.

"Do you want to move?" she asked.

His eyes darkened. "No."

"Then that's what you should tell him when he asks. You're responsible only for your feelings, not his."

He went back to his digging. She watched the treasure hunters hacking away at the snow. They used shovels of all descriptions, as well as ice choppers, picks, and garden trowels.

What would Phil do if she refused to go? Tell Flannary that he had reconsidered and changed his mind, or go to San Diego without her? And if it came to that, what would become of the boys? Which one of them would the boys view as the villain if it came down to separation? Would it ever come to that? Did she have the strength to survive Phil's sales pitch, his unrelenting torrent of logic?

Chris returned, clutching a row of five hot dogs against his chest, munching away on the sixth.

"No relish," he said, his mouth full. "Just mustard." He passed out two hot dogs each to her and Jeff.

She unwrapped one and took a bite. It was almost cold. Chris had overdone it on the mustard, squirting a wide strip down both sides of the hot dog. She wrapped the hot dog up again, and stuck both of them in her pocket. She would be good and hungry by dinner. Dinner. She hadn't done her homework yet, hadn't hunted up a good seafood restaurant and made reservations so Phil could soften her up for the big announcement. Well, the hell with that; it was like asking a prisoner to make his own noose for the hanging. They could go to one of the restaurants on Grand Avenue. Phil could have a seafood salad.

Noose. All of these death images creeping into her thoughts. Maybe Phil had better be on the lookout after all.

EIGHT

As HE DUG THROUGH THE SNOW, Steven Carpenter let his mind wander out to New York. He'd play the little clubs at first. He would have to find out where the record executives hung out, and try to get on the bill in those places. Then one night he would be putting his guitar in its case after a show, and an executive would come backstage and introduce himself. He'd be on his way.

He was ready to head for New York as soon as they got the money together. It would be so sweet to say good-bye to his job at the library, although he would miss Knickerson. It all depended on Debi's boss. Or finding the medallion. Every minute it wasn't found either increased or decreased their chances of finding it, he wasn't sure which.

"Deb!" He turned to where she was digging a few feet away. "If we find this little sucker and win the money, we wouldn't need to wait until your boss gets transferred. We wouldn't be able to afford the Dakota, but maybe we could get an apartment near Broadway, or in Greenwich Village, or near Central Park."

"Uh-uh," Debi said. She leaned on the end of her shovel, too. "Not an apartment. A loft."

"Hey, yeah." Lofts always looked cool in TV shows and movies. They could rent a huge one with a high ceiling. One end could be the kitchen, the other end their bedroom, and the living room in between. A bathroom off in the corner, curtained off. Or just the john curtained off. The tub could be right out in the open. An image of the two of them doing it in an old claw-foot tub, bathed in a beam of sunlight from a skylight, flashed through his mind. He had never gotten her to do it in the bathtub before, or anywhere out of the ordinary, for that matter. When it came to locations and positions for having sex, Debi was right out of the nineteenth century. Maybe the location of the tub would change her habits.

"What are you smiling about?" Debi asked.

"Nothing."

"You've got that sneaky look I don't like," she said. "What is it? Tell me."

"I was just thinking about what kind of bathroom a loft would have, that's all."

"One of those old water closet jobbies with the tank overhead and the chain, maybe," Debi offered.

"It'd have to be a place close enough to work for you," he said. "Where's Wall Street from Greenwich Village or Central Park?"

"I don't know. Can't be too far."

"Within walking distance?"

Debi gave him a disgusted look. "No way do you walk in New York. You take the subway."

He set back to work, a warm feeling in his belly. So that would be their life. Debi would take the subway to work on Wall Street, and he would stay in their loft and practice his guitar and write songs all day. He would even fix supper for them, which would be ready when she got home. And then late at night, he would go out and play, eventually getting discovered and signed to a record deal.

"I'm cold," Debi complained. She pulled her coat collar up higher with a green-mittened hand. "I wish there was a place to warm up around here."

"They must have coffee or hot chocolate on that food truck. I could go for a cup of hot stuff myself."

"I drink anything hot out here and the next thing I'd need is the bathroom truck," Debi said.

He stared at the truck window. An old guy was turning away, a white cup in one hand, a hot dog in the other. "Nobody in line," he said. "Now'd be the time to go."

"You got any money?"

"How come I always get to be the bank?"

"I didn't bring my purse, okay?" she said irritably. "I didn't think I could carry it and dig, too."

He reached under his coat for the wallet in his back pocket. Debi snatched the five-dollar bill he held out for her.

"Coffee or hot chocolate?"

"Coffee. Hot." He watched her stride off toward the truck.

A loft in New York. A record deal. It all sounded so cool, so exciting. So impossible. His record, if he ever got to record it, would actually be a compact disc, or a cassette tape, of course—vinyl records were nearly a thing of the past. He knew just the style of lettering he wanted for the title, *American Dreamer*. Heavy red, white, and blue letters with stars and bars worked in. Real Fourth-of-July, mom-and-apple-pie stuff. The cover photo would show him sitting at the wheel of an old junked car, a Caddy convertible, its headlights and windshield broken out, weeds growing up around it. Or better yet, have him standing in front of it, holding a beat-up old suitcase, his back to the camera and his thumb sticking out, like he was trying to hitch a ride. Yeah, that would look cool. It would make a really deep comment on the state of the American Dream, like Springsteen's *Born in the USA* had.

The idea sent a current of energy through him, and he went back to digging. He'd write songs that told one long story, about a relationship between a man and a woman and their version of the American Dream. "Buried Treasure" could be about the greed that had gripped the country during the Reagan Years. But that song wasn't going very well. He'd been too busy with the treasure hunt, and couldn't seem to get started on the verses. At this point, all he had was the chorus, the couple's search for their lost love for each other. "I Wish I Knew Why" could be the last song on the album, about the end of everything—the couple's relationship, and the American Dream.

To make a whole album, he'd have to write a lot of really good songs. If the one-long-story concept didn't work out, maybe he could do a couple of cover songs, like Dylan's "Tangled Up in Blue," if he could master it well enough. He could do Springsteen's "Meeting Across the River." Or pay tribute to Steve Goodman or Harry Chapin, like the Stones and the Beatles had paid tribute to their influences.

A white object fell off the front of his shovel. He leaned over and picked up a rolled-up White Castle bag smashed flat by the weight of the snow. He had noticed other treasure hunters picking apart pieces of trash. He unrolled the bag, and inside found four White Castle boxes, three of which still housed hamburgers, glittering with frost. He looked in the bottom of the sack, saw nothing. One by one, he took the hamburgers out of their boxes. Nothing again. If the medallion were here, it had to be frozen inside one of the hamburgers. He stuck two of the burgers back into the sack and tucked the sack under his arm. With his bare hands he started to work apart the frozen bun on the remaining burger.

"Save your time." Debi, carrying two cups with covered lids, was hurrying toward him. She handed one to him. "While I was paying for the coffee, I overheard someone say it was hidden in a Classic Coke can, according to the newest clue in the newspaper."

"So? That doesn't tell us where to look."

"No, but at least we know what to look for, stupid."

Stupid. The word cut. He held out the frozen White Castle. "Want a hamburger to go with your coffee?" he asked.

NINE

ALFRED SANK ONTO A PARK BENCH that faced the bluff overlooking the West End neighborhood. He rested his shovel against his knee. The chill of the wooden seat sent a shiver through him as it ate its way through the layers of clothing. Behind him, he could hear the sound of shovels scraping through snow, the hum of voices as the treasure hunters feverishly continued to search. So let them hunt. He needed to rest a bit. He let out a long sigh. He was tired of shoveling snow. Tired of everything.

The daylight was fading fast. Immediately below him, the houses and streets and snowy yards were already gray with shadows as the orange sun sank into the hills of Highland Park. A stream of cars, headlights on in the gathering dusk, traveled in each direction on the gray strip of I-35E Parkway. He had never gotten used to this freeway—this wound—that cut through the neighborhood. He located West Seventh Street and followed it through the extending shadows to where Rudy's house should be. So much had happened in that house. There was still much to happen. He watched as the gray shadows raced toward the east, sweeping over the blinking Schmidt sign, over the neighborhood where his own house stood, and on toward downtown and Dayton's Bluff, toward infinity. Soon the pinkish sunlight lit only the tops of the wooded bluffs of Cherokee Heights, across the valley on the other side of the great Mississippi. The gray shadow crept further up the bluffs with each passing minute. A world in transition from daylight to dark.

So it was decided then. Such an easy decision, really, when he got right down to it. He had been foolish to fight the idea for so long. It would solve everything. Put a stop to this nonsense about Houston. It would solve the problem of what to do with the rest of his life. And there would be no more changes assaulting him, demanding adjustment, acceptance.

He felt the knots in his stomach loosen. It felt good to know. For months, the future had stretched out in front of him, full of unknown changes, yet so empty at the same time. A puff of wind traveled over the neighborhood below him, bending the plumes of chimney smoke that rose from the old houses. The shadow had crept up and over the wooded bluffs across the river. Everything seemed so quiet and peaceful here, despite the noises of the treasure hunters behind him.

Genevieve, no doubt, would be stunned when she found out. But she would finally be free of him to do whatever she wanted. She had always been unhappy. God knows she'd told him so enough times, in a thousand small ways. If he could go back and do one thing differently, he would make her happy. She deserved that. God knows he'd tried through all the years, done his best. But it wasn't enough.

It might have all turned out differently had his parents lived. Maybe he wouldn't have always been satisfied with whatever life chose to give him. Maybe they could have taught him something that would have made him more ambitious, more willing to take risks. But it was too late. He was who he was, and this was what it had led him to. Everyone would scratch their heads and ask why. Well, why not? If they could only understand how he felt, they would see it was a good decision, the right decision.

It would be nice to see everyone again, to take his own place at that banquet table. He hated to leave here, but he hated the idea of staying even more. He had missed them all so much, for so long. Still, it was a long way from here to there. And there was the matter of when he would leave, a final decision to make.

In the distance behind him, he heard a sudden burst of raspy laughter. He turned on the bench so he could look into the park again. The treasure hunters were still digging through the snow, solitary figures, groups of twos and threes. Most of them had abandoned the rim of the park where all the trees stood, and moved out into the open space in the center. It had been so much fun in the old days, out here with Rudy, digging away with everyone else. He gathered himself up and pushed himself to his feet. He shuffled through the snow toward the center of the park, threading his way through the crowd. Finish what you start, Rudy always said. The day he and Rudy had made the doorstop, he had wanted to quit, but Rudy wouldn't let him. *Finish what you start.* He'd started this year's treasure hunt as a memorial to Rudy. He'd stick it out here until the medallion was found and then go on home.

He pushed his shovel into the snow and raised it up. He tilted the shovel sideways and watched the snow trickle out. He brought up another shovelful and another. Hard work for a tired old man. After a while, he stopped to rest. He happened to look up. A few feet away, he noticed the young man in the tan coveralls he had talked to that morning suddenly bend over and reach into the snow.

TEN

BRUCE'S HAND CLOSED ON A COLD, jagged object. He straightened up, and saw in the fading light that it was an aluminum can smashed flat from top to bottom. Whoever had stamped this can flat had put some effort into it. But along the telescoped side, he saw the familiar red color, part of the unmistakable white Coca-Cola script. His heart jumped. He shook the can, imagining he heard a rattle. He looked through the pop-top hole, saw nothing. He jerked off his gloves, letting them fall to the ground. It took a moment for his bare fingers to twist the cold metal apart. He saw where a slit had been cut just below the top lip of the can. He twisted and pulled at the can, prying its ends apart. He shook the can again and heard a distinct, coinlike rattle. He stuck his little finger in the pop-top hole and felt something solid and flat move. He peered into the pop-top hole again, and saw the curved edge of a coin, the raised letters SURE MEDA. Treasure medallion.

"Yeeesssss!"

The word shot out of him like a roman candle. He leaped into the air, realizing in a split second that he had made a mistake, had given himself away completely. By the time his feet hit the ground, the world around him had stopped. Everyone stood frozen in place, startled by his cry. In one heartbeat, he was struck by the things he saw, how clear the world was. The old geezer from this morning was standing ten feet away. A boy in a green army jacket and another wearing a blue coat and Vikings stocking cap. A woman wearing green mittens. A man holding a broken shovel, a look of disbelief spreading across his reddened face. Behind them, he saw treasure hunters moving rapidly toward him from all directions. Quickly he turned away. This was no place to celebrate. Gripping the can so tightly that the cold metal cut into his palm, he shoved his hand as deep into his coverall pocket as he could. He shouldered his shovel and moved quickly through the gathering crowd, leaving his gloves lying in the snow.

In two minutes he had crossed St. Clair Avenue, and raced the two blocks north to where the Camaro was parked. He dropped the shovel, dug out his key, unlocked the driver's door, and crawled inside in a single, fluid motion. He locked the door again. For a moment he sat there, his heart pounding in his chest, his breath coming out in gasps. The fatigue that had settled over him in the afternoon had vanished. He felt wide awake, totally alive.

When he was sure no one had followed him, he got out again and unlocked the Camaro's trunk. He put his snow shovel away. Then he opened the toolbox and looked for a screwdriver. It took a few moments for him to tear open the can enough to release the medallion. He tossed the screwdriver back into the toolbox, closed it, and shut the Camaro's trunk. He turned around, leaned against the trunk, and studied the medallion, holding it up toward the streetlight.

It was about the size of a silver dollar. In the center was a crest guarded by two roaring lions. Above the crest, in a downward arc around the edge of the medallion, were the words KING BOREAS in raised capital letters; below the crest, the words TREASURE MEDALLION in larger, all capital letters arced upward around the curved edge. On either side of the crest were two raised snowflakes. He turned the medallion over and studied the other side for a moment. He squinted to read the raised type. Instructions for turning in the medallion and claiming the prize. Well, that answered that question. With a flick of his thumb, he flipped the medallion into the air like a quarter, then caught it in a sweeping grasp. He leaned back against the trunk, and looked up through the limbs of a leafless elm into the sky, letting it all soak in for a moment. Damn. He had finally found the little sucker. After ten years. He threw back his head and let out a yell.

"Whoooooooeeeeeeee!"

It felt so good, he did it again. The yell echoed off the houses around him. On the other side of the street, a porch light went on. A moment later, the front door opened and a man stepped into the lit doorway, his shadow stretching down the shoveled sidewalk. From down the street, he heard the buzz of voices. People were already leaving the park. Word had gotten out fast. He better get out of here before someone found him and mugged him.

He slipped the medallion into the breast pocket of his coveralls and buttoned the brass button to secure it. The wind stirred the tree limbs above his head, cooling his sweaty face. Around him, the sequined snow lay deep on the ground. To the west, between the steep roofs of the great old houses, behind the stiff black limbs of the boulevard trees, the sky was a deep orange that was fading to a purplish red before his eyes. Off to the east, the sky had turned a metallic blue, the first stars already twinkling down on him. He opened the driver's door of the Camaro, and stood for a moment before he got in. He felt his heart, big as a football, beating a slow, solid rhythm deep in his chest.

He looked up again at the stars. It was going to be a fine night.

ELEVEN

KEITH WATCHED THE TREASURE HUNTERS file out of the park. The word that someone had found the medallion had spread quickly through the crowd, passing from one person to the next on puffs of steamy breath. Treasure hunters, dragging their shovels, picks, and choppers behind them, had started filing out of the park within a couple of minutes, heading for their cars and pickup trucks. He heard weary snatches of conversations as the people streamed by him. ". . . Ma, let's order a pizza again tonight, okay?" ". . . your father wants to eat out tonight . . ." ". . . ought to stop off somewhere and get a snort. I'm so cold I won't get thawed out until spring . . ." ". . . worst bunch of clues I've ever seen. Never told you where the hell to look once you got here . . ." ". . . hope the old lady has supper on the stove; I could eat a horse . . ." ". . . next year, goddamn it. Just wait till next year . . ."

Next year, indeed. He should go home. He was exhausted, cold, and wet. Hungry. And disappointed. Shit. He'd been *so damn close*. Again.

Ten fucking feet away. The guy's yell had gone through him like a sword. A girl had pointed at the guy as he left, and loudly claimed it was just an act and they should keep searching. But he knew better. That yell was too excited, too real and spontaneous to be an act. It hadn't taken the girl and her boyfriend very long to give up and head out with everyone else. He shivered inside his clothes. Christ. He had actually held the damn thing in his hand and then thrown it over his shoulder as junk. That stinking pickup. If it hadn't practically run him down, he would have entered the park clearheaded. Then he would have realized that a crushed Classic Coke can was the ideal place to hide a medallion—he seemed to remember that they had actually done that once before; he'd check his notes when he got home. Or if that lousy Clue 11 had come out earlier, like it should have, he'd have been on the lookout for the can. The guy from earlier this afternoon was right. The clues never told you where to look except midway between two trees. Now, from where he stood in the middle of the empty park, he could see the two tall trees guarding opposite ends of the open space of the park. Just the kind of match he had kept looking for, but they were too damn far apart to be easily spotted. That was perfect, he had to admit. The rest of the tree pairs were too obvious. Below his feet, the snow was as fine as powdered sugar. It was that way throughout the park, he knew. Every ounce of snow had been dug up, inspected, sifted through by a hundred or more people. With the number of people who had been here looking for it, it was amazing that the medallion hadn't been found earlier. Against the white of the snow, he could see bits and pieces of trash. Lost gloves and hats. Shovels left behind. In the daylight, the place would look like the state fairgrounds after the last day: crushed paper cups, rolled-up hot dog wrappers, and empty pint bottles everywhere. The clean-up crews would have plenty of work to do come Monday. They did every year.

He should go home. Take a hot shower. Eat something and get some sleep. He had plenty to do tomorrow himself. The shovel felt heavy as a cement block in his hand. He held it up. Maybe he could put a new handle in it. *Fuck it.* He tossed the shovel on the ground with the rest of the trash, and started off across the snow, trying to remember where the Nova was parked.

TWELVE

"SO WHERE ARE WE GOING TO EAT, MA?" Chris asked
for the second time as they trudged up Avon Street, pushed along by the
crush of treasure hunters leaving the park. The crowd had spread out,
filling the street and both sidewalks, like baseball fans exiting the
Metrodome after a loss. No shouts of happiness, of victory. Just tired,
cold people in a hurry to get home. Up and down the street, car doors
were slamming, engines were firing up, headlights flashing on. Behind
them, a horn sounded to move them out of the way.

"Ma?" Chris pressed as they stepped in behind a parked 4x4 to let
the car go by.

"I don't know, Chris," Sharon snapped. "I haven't given it any thought."
A lapse in home front duty that she, the good little corporate wife, un-
doubtedly would pay for in some small way. Well, fine. The corporate
migrant worker had a few lapses of his own she would be happy to bring
up. Like making unilateral decisions that affected the whole family. Like
lying.

"Not some place really swanky," Chris said.

"No," she agreed. "Not some place really swanky. Wherever your
father wants to go, as long as we don't have to get dressed up or sit and
wait."

Take-out chicken would be fine with her. Or burgers. Wherever they
could get the fastest food and get it over with. She would much rather
just go home, eat a quick sandwich, and disappear somewhere in the house
so she wouldn't have to look at him, wouldn't have to listen to his small
talk, wouldn't have to watch him cutting up with the boys. Or better
yet, she'd like to disappear into the crowd and hide until this weekend
was over.

The Taurus sat under a streetlight, its silver-blue color a flat gray
in the copper light. She felt along the bottom of her coat for her keys,
which had slipped through the hole in her pocket and were now somewhere deep in the lining. Digging them out, she unlocked the trunk, and
tossed her shovel into the empty space. The boys did the same. She slammed
down the lid with a force that rocked the whole car, surprising her. A
frustrating business, being out in the cold all day long, alone in the cold
knowledge of Phil's week-long deception. She should have gone down

to the bookstore today after all and listened to Elaine's tirade. At least with Elaine she would have a sympathetic ear, if she could get a word in edgewise. And she would not have been forced to keep up this deception. Keeping Phil's secret from the boys made her feel equally guilty, an accomplice to high crimes against the family.

They piled into the car, Jeff in front, Chris in the back. Their breaths immediately fogged the windshield. She started the engine and switched on the defroster to clear the fog. The Taurus was penned in by a large silver and black Suburban. Cars and pickups sat bumper to bumper as far north as she could see, and as far behind them as she could see in the side mirror. She adjusted the mirror so the headlight glare from behind did not catch her in the eye. She switched on her turn signal and edged out as far as she could, ready to take advantage of a break in the traffic.

Jeff had slid down in his seat, hands shoved deep in his pockets, his head back against the headrest. His eyes were closed.

"You're sure quiet," she said. "You haven't said 'boo' since we left the park."

He shrugged. "We were just so close, that's all," he said after a moment. He pulled off his red stocking cap. In the light from the headlights of a passing car, she saw that his brown hair was plastered to his forehead with perspiration. "I mean, we actually saw that man find it."

"Did you see the way that guy took outta there?" Chris spoke up from the back seat. "Just like you said you would, Ma. Only he whooped once and gave himself away. Some guy probably followed him, beat the snot out of him, and stole it."

"I looked *right* where he picked it up just a minute or two earlier." Jeff's voice was barely audible with disappointment. "I should have found it."

"Well, you win some, you lose some," she said, and immediately winced. A hollow, glib cliche, more befitting Phil than herself. The kid deserved better than that. It was more than not finding the medallion that was bothering him, she knew. *I just think it sucks that we get all settled in here, and then Dad gets this big promotion offer.* He was right. It sucked. Which made her cliche all the more hollow, cruel even. You win some, you lose some. If Jeff only knew how big they all had lost. She strained for something meaningful and reassuring to say.

"We did pretty well for the new kids in town, I think." She reached through the darkness and patted him on the shoulder. "We were right there at the end. That's more than a lot of people can say. Don't beat yourself up about it, just because you missed it." Some comfort on one level, at least.

"Next year!" Chris's confident voice floated out of the darkness behind them. "We'll find it next year, for sure."

"There won't *be* a next year." Jeff's voice was bitter. "Dad'll take that job, and this time next year, we'll either be living in Denver or San Diego."

"Not if we tell Dad we don't want to move," Chris replied. "He said."

Jeff answered by closing his eyes again.

A pickup truck stopped to let her pull out into the traffic lane. She waved a thank-you. She inched the Taurus along with the traffic, grateful for the silence. She was too tired to get into it. It would all come out over the weekend anyway. Everything would hit the fan altogether too soon. The bitterness in Jeff's voice hung in the air around them. What would he think when—if—he found out that he really had no part in the decision? That it was all a big lie. What would that do to him, and to Chris, too?

She glanced in the rearview mirror. Chris had disappeared, apparently stretched out in the back seat. She wondered how he really felt. He was too closed off, too glib, like his father. Two years ago, he had acted excited about the move to St. Paul. But when they got here, his grades had nose-dived. And poor Jeff. No visible signs of difficulty in making the adjustment and they had stupidly assumed everything was fine.

As they approached Grand Avenue, she signaled a left-hand turn.

"Go down Summit, would you?" Jeff said, breaking the long silence.

"What for?"

"Just do it. Please?"

Dutifully, she shut off the signal and drove another block before turning. To their right, the law school buildings were ablaze with light. But Jeff's attention was drawn to the other side of the street. He sat up, and discreetly watched out of the corner of his eye as they passed a brick house of no particular style. A big house, but not gigantic. A perfect evergreen frosted with heavy snow stood sentry in the front yard. Why such interest in this house? *She lives on Summit Avenue, down by the law school.* Of course. Lisa of Summit Avenue. This was her house.

Jeff slid back into his original position. She considered saying
something, then thought better of it. There would be other girl friends
to talk about, wonder about, whether they moved or stayed here. She
felt her anger rising up inside her like floodwaters. But the choice of
breaking up with a girl should be his, not his father's. Damn Phil, anyway. Damn him.

Chris's voice sounded weary as it came from the back seat. "We could
go to that place down on Randolph for pizza, Ma. I could just about eat
a whole pizza by myself."

THIRTEEN

BY THE TIME THEY HAD WALKED the two blocks up
Victoria to the Honda, Debi was ranting.

"I can't believe it," she said for what seemed to Steven like the hundredth time. He unlocked the trunk and threw their shovels in.

"I actually saw the guy bend over and pick it up," Debi continued
as she moved around to her side of the car. He unlocked the driver's door,
slid into his seat, and leaned across the car to unlock the passenger door.

"That close!" Debi's green mitten nearly bumped him in the nose
as she thrust her hand in his face. She measured zero distance with her
thumb and collected fingers. "We were that close. I mean, if we had been
ten feet over, one or the other of us could have just as easily turned up
the shovelful of snow with the can in it as he did. Why was he lucky and
not us?"

He started the car and bumped out of the parking lane into the track
cut in the icy street by the cars. He wished Debi would just shut up.
He was disappointed, too. They had been close, couldn't have been any
closer. But the other guy had been the lucky one. Always the other guy.
Now it was over, and all he wanted to do was get something to eat and
warm up.

"Ten feet," Debi started up again. "Just ten feet."

"Give it a rest, would you, Deb?"

"Give it a rest? We just barely miss out on collecting four thousand
dollars and you want me to give it a rest? We should have found it."

"But we didn't."

He stopped for the red light on Grand Avenue. Victoria Crossing was bustling with the Friday night crowd. The parking lot was full, a half-dozen cars prowling the driveways, waiting for someone to come out and leave. A knot of pedestrians stood on every corner of the intersection, waiting for the lights to change.

"Well, we should have," Debi insisted. He felt the accusation behind the statement.

"Well, we didn't. So just lay off." Just a few more blocks and they'd be home. He'd get a magazine and go sit in the can by himself for a while. The light changed to green and he spun the wheels as he started up.

"They should have published the clue about the classic can earlier," Debi said. "That way, we would have known what to look for at least, since we didn't know where—"

"Jesus, Deb!" He turned his head toward her as they started through the Summit intersection. "I'm tired of—"

"Steven, look out!" Debi shrieked.

From the west, a hulking white Buick LeSabre was bearing down on the red light at thirty miles an hour, obviously with no intention of stopping. He slammed hard on the brakes. The Honda's wheels locked, and the car skidded like a sled into the intersection. He felt the steering wheel freeze in his hands, and the brake pedal die under his foot as the engine stalled. The insipid red warning lights in the dash flashed on. Desperately he pumped the brakes as the LeSabre grew larger. He braced himself for the crash.

The LeSabre slid to a stop directly in front of them, its front door less than a foot from the Honda's bumper. Steven shook his fist at the driver, who simply gave him the finger and floored the accelerator.

"The dirty bastard!" He threw open the door. "Up yours, asshole!" he screamed. "Learn how to drive!"

A horn sounded behind him. He started the car and eased forward, trembling. Debi was silent beside him.

"Well," he said, struggling to calm himself, "there's the ten feet we didn't get at the park. If we had gotten our ten feet there instead of here, we'd have just gotten creamed."

FOURTEEN

A<small>LFRED SLOWED THE PICKUP TO A CRAWL</small> as he passed his house on Goodrich Avenue. The living room lights glowed softly through the pulled drapes. In the side yard, an oblong splash of bright light fell out into the driveway from the kitchen window. Genevieve was probably making supper, or else sitting in her chair in the living room, feet up on the ottoman, her *Reader's Digest* in her lap, waiting for him to come home, as she had for most of her life. He closed his eyes and pictured her as she had looked that morning: blue housedress, a gray sweater buttoned over her plump middle. This whole thing must have been hiding in the back of his mind early this morning, for he had taken extra pains to say goodbye to her, instead of announcing his departure by slamming the back door as he usually did. He had known for sure at the park later in the morning, the instant he had asked himself what he was going to do with the rest of his life. The answer had been so simple.

It would be tough for Genevieve, afterwards. But the house was paid off; his pension and social security would take care of her. She would probably sell the place and move down to Houston anyway, so she could be close to Janet. He gave the house a final look. He should never have put that ugly siding on; it always made the house look like it was trying to act younger than it was. But maybe it would help the house sell.

He drove down to the corner, turned right, and headed out West Seventh. The pickup hummed along past the businesses and houses he knew so well. So many times he had traveled this route. He passed the Schmidt brewery for the last time. The Schmidt sign blinked on letter by letter, went dark, then blinked on again in full. Waiting for the Randolph light to change to green, he felt the anticipation in his bones, a feeling that he was headed home.

He left the pickup parked in front of Rudy's house. Someone would spot it soon enough, but by then it would be too late.

Inside, he turned on the light in the living room. His breath rolled out in front of him. The room was still in disarray. Genevieve could pay some estate company to come in and clean the place out. It was what she had wanted to do all along.

He sat down in the rocking chair and rocked for a bit. The squeak made a comfortable sound against the silence. So many of his family had come and gone in this house. Tantchen had died in the cramped bedroom upstairs. And his parents. They had been brought here right after the streetcar accident, then taken to the undertaker's parlor. His eyes fell on the irregular coffee stain in the rug. And Rudy, of course, right here in this very room, his secret left behind for him to find. There was just one final detail to attend to, and he could join everyone at that table. He would tell Rudy when he got there that it didn't matter, that he didn't care. But why had he kept it a secret all those years? His hands clenched into fists.

Everyone, Genevieve especially, would want to know why. Some people left a note. He rose from the rocking chair and went to Rudy's secretary. He rummaged through the drawers until he found a simple white tablet and a yellow pencil that needed sharpening. It would do. Who should he address it to?—Genevieve? The police? Maybe no one. How could he explain it without going into a lot of details that no one would understand? He licked the end of the pencil. The words appeared on the page, naked and alone. *It's better for everyone this way.* Should he sign it? No need; they would know it was from him. He pulled the sheet loose and put the tablet and pencil back in the drawer. He folded the note and put it in the bib pocket of his overalls.

He looked around the room. Where? Not here, in the middle of all this junk. Not in the dining room or the kitchen. Not upstairs, or in the basement. Rudy's room. That was the place. It had been his parents' room originally. The old bed and matching bureaus had been wedding gifts from Grandpa and Grandma Krause. He himself had been born in that room, in that bed. It was proper that he die in it.

He got up and moved through the dining room into the kitchen. He opened the basement door, snapped on the light, and made his way down the rickety wooden steps. This basement was even more of a hole in the ground than his own. It had limestone walls and musty, damp air that chilled the bones winter and summer alike. He opened the doors of the old wooden wardrobe pushed in under the staircase. The shotgun lay in its case on the top shelf, pushed all the way to the back, out of sight. The brown cloth case was covered with cobwebs when he drew it out. God only knew when the gun was last fired. He pulled the string to loosen the knot and opened the flap. Slowly he drew the shotgun out of the case. The metalwork was brown with a thin coating of rust, the finish on the scarred wooden stock and barrel grip blackened and cracked.

He broke the shotgun open, held the barrel up to the bare light bulb, and sighted down its inside. More rust, but it would probably get the job done if the shells would still fire. Holding the broken gun over one arm, he stood on his toes and fumbled on the shelf with his free hand. He found the box in the far corner.

The flapped lid on the square box was damp and tore off at its hinge when he opened it. The flap slipped out of his grasp and fell to the floor. They were old shells, the metal jackets green with age. He hoped they were still good.

He carried the gun and shells upstairs to Rudy's room. He laid them on the bed, then took off his coat and hung it on the brass end post at the head of the bed. He had heard how it was done. Load the shell, cock the hammer. Set the barrel under the chin, pointed back toward the head, then reach down and pull the trigger. It would be over in a flash and he would be free. Free from a world that couldn't be satisfied with itself, a world that kept changing and changing. Free from the rest of his life. Free from himself. Free from—

He reached for a shell. A din of voices rose inside his head, people crying out to him from two worlds. Rudy. His parents. Genevieve. Janet. His grandsons. And then, over all of them, his own voice. In fear. In anger. No. "NO!"

Abruptly he snapped the shotgun shut. What was he doing, anyway? He couldn't do this. Couldn't. No matter how bad things were. This wasn't the way, blowing your brains onto the ceiling above. He couldn't do this to Genevieve. To Janet and the boys. To himself.

Trembling, he slid the shotgun back into its case, closed the flap, and tied the string in a knot like a shoelace. He carried the gun and shells at arm's length to the basement. He laid the shotgun on the top shelf of the wardrobe again and pushed it toward the back. When he bent over to pick up the flap that had fallen to the floor earlier, he vomited, a slick, heavy mucus. He laid the lid on top of the box and tucked the rounded flap down as best he could, then returned the box to its place in the corner.

Upstairs, he sank into the rocking chair again. Rocking helped to settle his stomach, helped to slow down his heart. His breath hung in the air in front of him. The chill of the room felt colder than his whole day out in the park. Caught between worlds, he was—totally lost. The answer to everything suddenly no answer at all. What was he going to do with the rest of his life? Continue to do what he had done every other day? Go through the motions, absorb the knocks, the changes as best he could while he waited to be called? Biding his time. That was no answer, either.

He pulled the note from his pocket, read it, then tore it into many pieces and put them in a box of trash. He pulled back the sleeve of his shirt to check his watch. A quarter to seven. With effort, he pushed himself out of the rocking chair. It was getting late and he was expected home.

SATURDAY

ONE

STILL WEARING HIS BATHROBE, Keith tiptoed on bare feet
halfway up the cement stairs from his apartment door to retrieve the Saturday
edition of the *Pioneer Press*. Lousy paper boy. Could never get the
paper down by the door where it belonged. Shivering, he hurried back
inside and slammed the door behind him. From upstairs came Tiffany's
immediate, protective bark. The little mutt. One of these days, poodle
from hell. One of these days.

He sank onto the couch, the paper in his lap. He leaned back and
closed his eyes. His body felt like one big ache this morning. Even his
hair hurt. All that digging for nothing. All that work, just to watch some
other guy pick it up and run off. He yawned and looked at the clock again.
Seven-twenty. Too early to get up on a Saturday, especially after a week
like he'd had. He should go back to bed and sleep off his exhaustion. The
newspaper felt cold in his lap. He would look at the treasure hunt story
and then go back to bed.

He located the story on the bottom of the front page of the Metro
section, under a hokey headline: "'Classic' Clues Lead to Treasure." He
studied the man in the color photograph. Thirtyish, Fu Manchu mustache. That was the guy, all right. The longish hair had been covered up
by his stocking cap and the hood of his sweatshirt. The lucky bastard.
He read the caption under the photograph: "Bruce Mitchell, who lives
on St. Paul's West Side, followed 'classic' clues to find the King Boreas
Treasure Medallion in Linwood Park. Clues explained, page 2."

As he turned the page, he heard a familiar knock on the front door.
Shave and a haircut, two bits. Oh, no. Not that old bag this morning.
That was the last thing he needed. The knock came again, sharper. The
hell with it, he wouldn't answer it. When the knock came a third time,

he threw the paper to the floor, jumped to his feet, and stalked across the room.

He jerked open the door. Mrs. Wright had turned away and was starting up the stairs, one hand on the railing.

"Mrs. Wright."

She turned around, and her wrinkled face broke into a smile.

"Well, good morning, Keith. I heard you get your paper, and wanted to run down and tell you something before you got away. But you took so long to answer, I thought you had gone back to bed."

"I just woke up." He indicated his bathrobe. "I'm not moving too fast yet."

"Well," Mrs. Wright began as she brushed past him to go inside, "I just came to tell you that your phone rang and rang all day yesterday. I thought you should know. It must have been important. No one is sick in your family, I hope. I always worry so when the phone rings and rings."

"You didn't need to come down. You could have just called," he said.

"Oh, I know. I invent excuses to make myself go outside in the winter and get the stink blown off me, like my Maynard used to say. Otherwise, I wouldn't go out at all."

"Besides," she continued, "I wanted to bring you these." From inside her coat, she produced an aluminum foil package. "Tiffany and I couldn't sleep. So we baked cinnamon rolls first thing this morning. They're still warm. They'll go good with your morning coffee."

"Where is old Tiffany?"

"She stayed upstairs. She felt it was too cold to be out this morning. I would stay and visit, but I must get back upstairs. She gets into such terrible mischief by herself, you know."

Mrs. Wright paused with her hand on the doorknob. She shook a mindful finger at him.

"Now you must let me know about dinner. Swiss steak, remember?"

"I will." He closed the door. Her shadow crossed the living room window. "When hell freezes over."

He went into the kitchen and laid the cinnamon rolls on the counter. The floor tiles were cold on his bare feet. He turned on the oven and opened the door a few inches. He should have told Mrs. Wright to turn up the heat while she was here. The nosy old biddy. Keeping track of his phone calls. Coming down here when she could have called. Asking prying questions about his family. If she was so all-fired worried, why didn't she come down last night after he got home? At least she didn't bring her mutt this time.

He filled the glass pot from his Mr. Coffee with water and poured it into the reservoir. He dumped the old grounds into the trash, then replaced the filter and added three scoops of coffee. He pressed the "on" switch. The pot made a gurgling sound.

Who would want to talk to him badly enough to call again and again? General Jerry? In the thick of the treasure hunt yesterday, he had forgotten to call the office like he was supposed to. No problem, he could explain that. He'd tell old Jer that he had just forgotten to call because he was so wrapped up in Gopher State. And he had taken the phone off the hook so he wouldn't be interrupted. That would explain why he hadn't called, and why no one could call him. Everything covered. He looked at the aluminum foil package and decided to wait until the coffee was ready. It was probably just some telemarketer anyway, wanting money to help save the whales. Or else it was that aluminum siding guy that called all the time.

He returned to the living room and gathered up the newspaper again, settling onto the couch. Maybe it was his mother, calling to tell him that his old man was sick, or had finally wrapped the car around a light pole on his way home from a bar and frozen to death. Well, good riddance. He would break a bottle of beer over the casket, give the old bastard a good send-off. His eyes traveled to the bulletin board above his desk to the strip of cash register tape pinned there. It might have been good old Toni. It had been a week since he had bumped into her. She had sounded pretty interested. Maybe she had given up waiting for him to call and decided to call him. Dialing his number would be a way to kill time between customers. He opened the paper. She had kids, a big drawback. He would have to think about that before he did anything about her.

The clue explanations were at the end of the article, after the finder had said how lucky he was, and that he was still deciding what he was going to do with the money.

Clue 1
Somewhere on the ground
    in Ramsey County

King Boreas has hidden
    his royal bounty.
*This means that the treasure is hidden on the ground somewhere in Ramsey
County.*

Clue 2
"I think I can, I think I can,"
    might be a clue
That has just the right
    meaning for you.
*"I think I can, I think I can" is what the Little Engine That Could said,
indicating there are train tracks near the treasure site. A train track runs
at the foot of the bluff below Linwood Park.*

Clue 3
Enter with a queen,
    leave via river,
This little clue
    may make you shiver.
*Refers to Victoria and Avon Streets, named, respectively, after Queen
Victoria and the Avon River, associated with William Shakespeare's birth-
place, which is Stratford. One can enter Linwood park off Victoria and
exit the park onto Avon.*

Clue 4
Watch planes come and
    watch them go,
Leaving far behind
    all this ice and snow.
*From Linwood Park, planes can be seen landing and taking off at both
St. Paul's Downtown Airport and Minneapolis-St. Paul International
Airport.*

Clue 5
In a distant place
    they're running races,
From the treasure site you can't
    see the runners' faces.

From Linwood Park, the old running track of Monroe Junior High School can be seen. Monroe is located below the bluff, several blocks from the park.

Clue 6

Diamonds are a girl's best friend
    if you're talking rings,
But think of boys and see
    what this clue brings.
Diamonds refers to the baseball diamonds at the west end of Linwood Park, near the recreation center.

Clue 7

Seven red hints should
    help you find
A dazzling treasure,
    one of a kind.
The seven red neon letters of the Schmidt brewery sign are visible at night from Linwood Park.

Clue 8

Midway between two trees,
    lies the treasure, pretty as you please.
But which two trees, we confess,
    is up to you to guess.
Establishes that the treasure is hidden midway between two trees.

Clue 9

A hint to get you out
    of your seats
The queen and river
    refer to streets.
Establishes that queen and river in Clue 3 refer to street names.

Clue 10

A bluff figures
    in the hunt,

But high or low,
    we'll have to punt.
Indicates that the treasure is hidden near a bluff. Linwood Park is situated on a bluff that overlooks the West End of the city.

Clue 11
In a classic can
    the treasure hides,
This little clue may help
    you turn the tides.
Clearly indicates that the treasure is hidden in a can. The word "classic" is a hint that it is a Classic Coke can.

Clue 12
Linwood Park's the place
    to find the treasure.
There's more riches there
    than you can ever measure.
Line up trees, one east, one west.
    Near dead center in the park is best.
Names Linwood Park as the correct park, and provides the exact location within the park to find the King Boreas Treasure Medallion.

He had interpreted all the clues correctly. The last clue, of course, had never been published because lucky What's-His-Name had found the medallion on Friday night. He read the clues again. A lousy bunch of clues this year. None of them gave any real indication of where to look within the park. Usually, at least a couple of clues mentioned picnic tables, or tennis courts—something that really gave you an anchor point. Only the clue about the trees gave any indication of a place, and trees dotted much of the park. They should have dropped the one about running races and put in something about park fixtures.

He let the paper fall into his lap and yawned. He was tired. He'd catch up on his sleep today, then this evening get started on Gopher State. If he started on it tonight, he could probably be done sometime tomorrow, in plenty of time for dumping it in Monday morning. He wasn't looking forward to going back to work on Monday. After a week's vacation, there would be plenty to do.

The telephone rang. He tossed the paper on the coffee table and crossed the room to his desk to answer it.

"Hello?"

"Keith? It's Jerry. Where have you been? I've been calling you since yesterday morning."

Jerry. Shit. He hadn't thought old Jerry would try to call this morning.

"I've been right here. I had my phone off the hook yesterday."

"That's not true," Jerry said. "I checked with the telephone company, and they said nothing was wrong."

"Well, I was here," he insisted. "Are you sure you were calling the right number? Maybe my phone was out of order. I've been having some trouble with it lately."

"Something's out of order, that's for sure. How come you didn't finish up Gopher State yesterday like you said you would?"

"I had a power failure, like I said in my message. I had to rewrite some of the program. That's why the phone was off the hook. Look, it's under control. I said in my message that I'd talked to Maureen about it, and Monday's fine with them."

"Maureen called here yesterday with a question because she couldn't get you. Now she feels like she's getting the run-around. I can't say that I blame her."

"I told her what happened."

"Listen, Keith, if that program doesn't dump this weekend, the shit is going to hit the fan." There was a deadly pause on the line. "In fact, it's hit the fan already. I want to see your entry records on Monday. Print 'em out in hard copy, and bring the printout in with you."

"That isn't necessary. Everything'll be done."

"Bring that printout with you on Monday, or don't bother coming in." The receiver banged in his ear.

He hung up the phone. The asshole. His entry records would show that he hadn't worked on Gopher all week. Old Jerry would have him by the balls. He went into the bedroom to get dressed. He had his work cut out for him. There had to be a way to alter those dates. All he had to do was figure it out.

TWO

"WHERE ARE WALLY AND THE BEAVER?" Phil, wearing sweat pants and a T-shirt, mug of coffee in hand, settled himself at the kitchen table across from her. He was the last one up this morning.

Sharon turned the page of the *Pioneer Press* without looking up. A rare moment, the two of them alone in the house this early on a Saturday morning. Chris had gone to play hockey at the ungodly hour of seven-thirty. Jeff had driven him up to the ice arena in the Taurus, and was due home any minute. She sipped at her coffee, keeping her eyes focused on the newsprint. A rare moment, indeed, one she would have latched onto any other Saturday morning.

"Yoo-hoo?" Phil knocked on the wooden tabletop with his knuckles, as though it were the front door. "Anybody home there? I asked where the boys are."

"Jeff drove Chris up to play hockey."

Phil blew on his coffee. "So what's up for the day?"

"I have to go down to the bookstore today."

"I thought it was Elaine's Saturday!"

She glared at him. "It is, but since I didn't go down yesterday, I owe her."

She watched him take a sip of coffee. He looked a little haggard this morning. He ran a hand through his hair.

"I think I need to run down to the office for a little while," he said. "I hope that won't create a problem."

She shrugged. "Fine with me."

"Shouldn't be gone too long. No later than one or two."

"Fine."

"Can I have a section of that?"

She pushed the rest of the morning paper across the table. Phil located the Business section and opened it.

"We really should go out to eat somewhere that's nice this weekend," he said. "All four of us. If not tonight, then tomorrow for sure."

A mild, indirect reprimand at last for not following through on dinner reservations last night. In the end, they had gone to the Vietnamese place on Grand Avenue.

"It doesn't have to be seafood," he added.

She looked up at him. "Is this a directive for me to make reservations?"

"If you want to. Otherwise, I can make them."

"No problem." More words spilled out before she could stop them. "I'm just a good little corporate wife taking care of the home front." She saw movement in Phil's face, a slight widening of those dark brown eyes, and then an instant recovery. His eyebrows furrowed, an exaggerated, puzzled look that would play to the back row of a theater audience.

"You can stop your little charade," she said. "I know."

"Know what?" His face had closed over, the shock and surprise pushed back out of sight, replaced with a cartoon-like look of complete innocence. She was almost surprised he didn't bat his eyes at her. "I don't know what you're talking about."

It wasn't the actual lie, the spoken words, but that stupid, puppy-dog look that did it.

"Oh, you liar," she erupted. "You know damn well what I'm talking about. When Flannary called on Thursday night, he accidentally spilled the beans. He assumed that I knew! He congratulated me for something I didn't even know about. Something that I had no part in deciding!"

She watched his face go slack. His eyes went flat. This time there was no recovery, only a cornered look. A deer caught in the headlights.

"Babe, listen—"

"Don't you 'babe' me!" In an instant, she felt the sandbags she had erected inside herself the past two days giving way, floodwaters raging out of control, sweeping away everything. "How could you come in here for the past week and lie right to our faces?"

"Sharon, you don't understand. It was—"

"Don't understand! You *lied* to us, Phil! You accepted a transfer without even talking to me. Then you cooked up this charade. Like what we think really *meant* something to you. You looked us all right in the eye and lied! Monday, Tuesday, Wednesday—" she ticked off the days on her fingers "—Thursday, Friday! *Every day* you came home and lied! What don't I understand? You just tell me! *What don't I understand?*"

The sudden silence in the room was deafening. Sharon felt her throat closing up. Phil slowly and deliberately folded the Business section and pushed it aside.

"All right," he said in a clipped voice. "You want to know why? I'll tell you. Because I knew all of you would drag your feet, and piss and moan about how hard it would be to move, just like you did when we came here to St. Paul. I knew if I put it to a vote we wouldn't go. Everyone would sit back and take the easy way. Which means you never get ahead, never go any farther. No one in this family but me is willing to take a risk. I knew this was a good move. *Any* hesitation on my part wouldn't have looked good; Flannary made that clear when he first talked to me, before the honchos called me in. So I accepted. I didn't have any choice."

"No choice! How can you even say that? What about—"

"Just button it!" His voice rose in anger. "You wanted the truth and, goddamn it, you're going to get it. You've punished me for the last *two years* for accepting this job out here."

"Punished?"

"Yes, punished. You've *never* let me forget how much you hated moving out here. You knock the restaurants, you bitch about the weather, about this house. I didn't want to go through two more years of punishment, having you throw St. Paul up in my face every goddamn day, like you've done with Boston. This 'little charade,' as you call it, is the only solution I could come up with that covered everything. It gave you a chance to have some input, and it didn't show any hesitation to the big honchos. So everybody could be happy. Except for me, of course."

"Now wait a minute," she interrupted. "Listen here—"

"No, you listen!" Phil was on his feet, his voice boiling over. "Do you think it's easy for me to keep starting over? It's no damn piece of chocolate cake for me, either. I don't like big changes any more than you do. But my responsibility is to bring home the family bacon. I don't really want the damn job. But it's the only way I can bring in the bucks we'll need when it comes time to pay tuition and . . . and buy cars for the boys." He turned away from her, hands clamped on the counter top that edged the sink.

"You seem to have conveniently forgotten my store's income—" she snapped.

"Your store," he interrupted, his back still to her, "broke even last year. It may even make a profit this year, but only because you and Elaine didn't even pay yourself salaries. There's no reason why it won't be profitable in the future, but it's not happening right now."

He turned around, crossed his arms over his chest. Behind the bluish sheen of beard, his face was as cold as granite.

"No, it's all up to me to put the food on the table. So I suck in my gut and put my ass on the line every day for this family. I go up against assholes like Flannary day after day so there's a roof over our heads. So the boys can have a decent education and not have to work three jobs just to afford tuition, like I did."

She noticed that he was trembling. His hand shook as he reached up to rub the bridge of his nose.

"I'd have rather stayed in Boston," he continued. "Christ, I had that job licked! I could have cruised along for years with my feet up. I was scared shitless to come out here. But I took this job because it paid better. Every move I've ever made has been for the benefit of you and the boys."

"Oh, bullshit," she said bitterly. "You're doing it for yourself and you know it."

"You can believe that if you want to," he said, sitting down at the table again. "I can't stop you. But it isn't true."

They sat on opposite sides of the table. Nothing and everything to say to each other at the same time. Deep in the bowels of the house, she heard the quiet whoosh of the furnace as it kicked on. Water started to move through the radiators. The sound made her feel cold. She shivered inside her robe.

"What have you told the boys?" Phil's voice was toneless.

"I haven't told them anything," she retorted. "Your little charade is still intact."

"What are you *going* to tell them?"

"What am *I* going to tell them? What are *you* going to tell them? It's up to you."

"All right," he said after a moment. "So I shouldn't have accepted without talking to you."

"You don't get it, do you? You didn't just make a unilateral decision. You lied about it, too."

"Okay," he said. "You're right. I was wrong. *I'm sorry.* I was only trying to do what was best for this family, despite what you think."

"Well, sorry don't feed the bulldog, as they say. You're going to have to come up with something better than that before . . ." She stopped, unable to go on.

"Before what?"

"I don't know," she said.

"I screwed up," he said quietly. "I was wrong. You're right. I'm really sorry. What can I do to make it right?"

"You think you can just apologize and that's the end of it?" she demanded. But there was little anger left in her words. She felt the floodwaters draining away. Everything felt swept clean, rearranged. Just venting her anger had helped. With everything out in the open now, maybe they could . . . Wait. No. No way. This was a salesman she was talking to. Many times he had reminded her of the time-honored, golden rule of salesmanship: *The customer is always right.* He had just said that she was right. Did he mean it, or was this just another sales pitch? She would never know for sure, and worse yet, she would never again be able to trust him.

"You can't ever make this right," she said coldly. "But you can try by calling them back and telling them no."

"But I've already accepted," he said. "The paperwork's already done."

"You accepted for yourself," she said.

"What the hell's that supposed to mean?"

The garage door slammed before she could speak. Jeff. In a moment, he would come bursting in the back door, carried into the kitchen on a blast of February air.

"What the hell it means," she said, "is that I haven't made up *my* mind yet, and I don't have to right now. It's not the sort of decision I'm going to let myself be rushed into."

She got up, poured her coffee into the sink, and left the kitchen, touching the red enamel door frame as she stepped into the dining room.

THREE

STEVEN CARPENTER WOKE TO THE SOUND of voices coming from the living room. His mouth was dry and filmy. He swallowed hard and opened his eyes. With considerable effort, he managed to raise his head off the pillow. Debi's side of the bed was empty, the covers flung back. Voices again. She must be in the living room watching the tube. Looney Tunes, judging by the music. Bugs Bunny planting a big, wet smacker on old Elmer Fudd. Or Wile E. Coyote getting a boul-

der dropped on him in another of his endless schemes to get the Road
Runner. Slowly he rolled over onto his back. Every muscle in his body
ached from yesterday's shoveling. An image of poor Wile E. crumpled
under a rock, white flag raised in defeat, materialized in his head. This
morning, he could relate.

He swallowed again and looked over at the clock on the dresser. A
couple minutes after nine. He should get up, but what the hell, it was
Saturday and he felt like shit and it was so cozy here under the covers.
He pulled the covers up tight under his chin and crossed his arms at the
wrists over his chest. The mummy of Portland Avenue.

Above him on the ceiling, the water stain seemed to drift like a cloud
across the colorless sky. He wished he still had some dope. Then he could
drift away with the cloud, off to some place where it was warm and the
grass was green, someplace where dreams really came true. They had come
close, all right, but not close enough. Debi had been surly all night. He
had gone to bed early just to get away from her.

Out of the corner of his eye, he saw his guitar case leaning against
the wall. He should get up and practice, work on his "Buried Treasure"
song. Songs for his album would never get written if he spent the day
in bed. His album. Who did he think he was kidding? He was no musician, despite the fact that Debi had introduced him as one yesterday
in the park. Writing a couple of lousy songs and calling himself a musician—what a joke. He played like he had ten thumbs, and he couldn't
carry a tune for shit. And moving out to New York. A stupid idea. Storybook
stuff. They would starve if they went. Instead of playing in the clubs and
getting discovered, he would probably end up playing in the dirty,
crowded streets, his guitar case lying open on the sidewalk for tips. With
no club jobs, instead of living in a neat old loft in the Village, he and
Debi would wind up in some filthy dump overrun with rats and cock-
roaches. Or else homeless, sleeping in a cardboard box under a freeway
bridge. Two more worms feeding off the rotten Big Apple.

He looked at his guitar case again. The hell with it. He should just
sell it. Or take it out and drive the Honda over it, throw it off the Lake
Street Bridge, anything to get rid of it. Settle in at the library and become a lifer there, like Knickerson. Stay there and catalog other people's
books and albums until they carried him out feet first.

"You going to sleep all day?" Debi, wearing a pink T-shirt that hung
to her knees, stood in the bedroom doorway, hands on her hips.

"Maybe."

"I've been up nearly an hour already."

"Congratulations. I'm delighted for you."

She crossed the room and sat down on the edge of the bed.

"You're in a good mood this morning," she said. "Did you forget to take your happy pill?"

He rolled away from her to face the wall. His guitar case stared back at him from the corner. He closed his eyes.

"Come on, Lazy Bones, get up." He felt her fingers pinch him lightly on the butt through the covers.

"Cut it out," he said, jerking away from her. "I'm stiff and sore this morning."

"Sore, maybe, but not stiff as far as I can see. Come on. Get up and get dressed. Let's go out for breakfast."

He felt movement on the mattress as Debi stood up. He rolled over and looked at her. Her back was to him. She pulled the T-shirt over her head, wadded it into a ball, then turned and stuck it under her pillow. She bent over and tugged open her dresser drawer, pulled out underwear, socks, and a bra, mooning him in the process. He watched her, not the slightest bit aroused. Maybe breakfast out would be nice. A really good cup of coffee. An omelette, perhaps, and some hashbrowns.

"Where do you want to go?"

She shrugged. "Anywhere. I'm not fussy." She dropped her clothes on the bed, except for her underwear.

"All right." He threw the covers back and swung his legs to the floor.

"While we're out," Debi said, "let's stop at the furniture store. I'm curious to see if they've dropped the price on that couch and chair any lower."

So that was the reason for suggesting they go out for breakfast. Breakfast was just a ruse to get him out of the house. The furniture store was her real mission for the day. The attempted deception angered him almost as much as her dragging up the couch and chair all over again.

"We've already decided about that. We aren't buying it."

"Who said anything about buying? I just want to stop and look. There's no harm in just looking."

"You never 'just look.' We'll get out there, and if it's marked down another ten cents, you'll want to buy it."

"Well, what's wrong with wanting something nice?"

"What happened to saving money for New York?"

"Steven, don't you think it's a little early for us to be thinking about moving to New York?"

"What are you trying to do, weasel out of going?"

"No, it just takes some planning is all."

"If you don't want to go, why don't you just say so?"

"I didn't say I didn't want to go! All I said was that we needed to make some plans instead of just pulling up stakes and going out there. What's the matter with you, anyway?"

"You don't really want to go. I can tell. Otherwise, you wouldn't keep wanting to waste a lot of money on a *stupid* couch. Fine! If you don't want to go to New York, then we can just stay here and rot. But it'll be your fault."

Her underwear caught him right in the face.

"Up yours, Carpenter!" She slammed the bedroom door behind her so hard that the Dylan poster bounced off its hook and crashed to the floor.

FOUR

"MORE COFFEE?" STANDING AT THE kitchen counter, Genevieve held up the Pyrex coffee pot. Alfred shook his head. She refilled her own cup and came back toward the kitchen table to sit down.

He pushed away the remains of his half-eaten pancakes and link sausage. His stomach was still in no shape for food this morning.

"Did you get enough?" Genevieve asked.

"Couldn't hold another bite."

"I was worried about you last night," she said. "Coming home so late, and then not even eating your supper."

"I was tired," he said.

"And then not getting up this morning at your usual time."

"I'm fine," he said. "I'm still tired, that's all."

"Well, you shouldn't have stayed out in the cold all day," Genevieve said. "You're getting too old for that kind of nonsense."

"I said I was fine." But he wasn't. He had come home from Rudy's still trembling, announced he was too tired to eat, and gone upstairs to bed. Still awake when Genevieve came up after the ten o'clock news, he had feigned sleep until he heard her begin to snore. Too exhausted to get up, he had simply lain in bed, trying to figure things out. Trying to understand. For so many years, he had cruised along comfortably; then everything had changed with sudden, brutal force. His life shattered last Thanksgiving when Rudy died, shattered again when he had discovered Rudy's secret. Piece by shattered piece, he had been forced to reevaluate everything as he tried to put things back together. Rudy's life. His own. But no matter how hard he tried, the pieces went back together differently, making a completely different picture. The past, where everything seemed so comfortable, wasn't what he thought it was. Rudy's secret had shown him that. What had felt comfortable for so many years, he now understood to be complacency, laziness. Success had turned into failure. He had had one job that, in the end, was taken away from him; an old house inherited from Genevieve's father; a wife he always seemed at odds with; a daughter grown up and moved away; and a dead brother with a secret life.

This morning he had stayed in bed, unable to get up, watching the sunbeams creep up the wallpaper until Genevieve had tiptoed into the bedroom to check on him.

Everything had changed, and yet nothing had changed. Once he got up and came downstairs to the kitchen, Genevieve had fussed over him in a way that told him she was leading up to something. As she fixed his breakfast, she had asked all about the treasure hunt in Linwood Park. When he told her how he had seen the young man bend over and pick up the Coke can in the snow, she had been too full of sympathy.

And now as she settled herself at the table again, he knew that the small talk was over. He knew what was on her mind, knew that no matter how much he wanted the Houston trip to just go away, the moment of reckoning had arrived. It was only a question of how she would bring it up.

"You were so close," she said. "It's too bad you didn't find it. We could have used the money for plane tickets."

"I still think we should drive," he said. "It's too expensive for both of us to fly all the way down there. And I ain't going to move to Houston, I'll tell you that right now. So you can just forget that idea."

He watched the expression on her face change. All traces of sympathy drained away. Her eyes narrowed behind her glasses.

"I don't want to drive, Alfred," she said. "I can't stand sitting in the truck all day. And don't you tell me we can't afford to fly, because I know we can."

"I didn't say we couldn't afford to fly, I said it's too expensive. I don't want to give the airlines that much money when we could drive down there and back for less than half what it would cost one of us to fly."

"If we can afford it, and we want to go, how can it be too expensive? You just don't want to go."

"I never said I didn't want to go. I just offered to drive down there, didn't I?"

Genevieve studied the backs of her hands for a moment. She rested her arms on the table and leaned toward him.

"All right, then," she said. "Let's drive. When do you want to leave?"

Her reversal stunned him. He felt cornered.

"We wouldn't be able to go for a while," he said. "Not until we get Rudy's house cleaned out and on the market."

"When will that be?" Genevieve pressed.

"I don't know. There's a lot to do yet."

"Well let's go down there and get busy. We won't finish up sitting here."

"I'm too tired this morning," he said.

"You just don't want to go," she exploded. "Why don't you just admit it, instead of making up excuses? Why don't you want to go?"

A reasonable question. Why didn't he want to go? Why couldn't he do this one thing for her? There was no reason he could put into words. It wasn't just the fear of dying in a plane crash, for he was a man who only last night had stood ready to blow himself into the Hereafter. It wasn't just because he was angry at Janet for moving away. He didn't know why, knew only that there was something wrong, something hanging in the air that sapped his strength, his will. Something that seized the very energy it took to go to Houston, to even get up this morning.

"I don't know," he said.

"I don't know," Genevieve mocked. "I'll just bet you don't know."

He had never spoken truer words to her, but how could he convince her? She was not someone to confide in, but someone to whom you had to defend every statement, justify every idea. He looked across the table at her. She glared back at him, her eyes cold with anger. It had been that way as far back as he could remember. Disagreements. Argument and counterargument. What had happened to them? If only it were different, for there was so much he wanted to tell her, needed to tell somebody, now that Rudy was gone. Things about Rudy. Things about himself. How tired he was. How afraid. And how lucky she was. For she had nearly lost him last night, as he stood in Rudy's room, the shotgun broken open across his arm, an aged shell in his hand. But he had closed the shotgun and put it away. For her. For now.

She sat across the table from him, stone-faced, waiting for him to say something. Something she could pounce on and turn against him. She would not understand, could not understand.

"I'm not lying," he said. "I don't know why, but I just can't go right now. I just can't." He felt tears forming in the corners of his eyes.

Genevieve pushed herself out of the chair. "Then you can just stay here! I'll go by myself if I have to!" She stomped out of the kitchen. A few moments later, he heard her feet on the stairway. The slam of the bedroom door sent a shudder throughout the house.

Alfred sat alone in the kitchen.

FIVE

B RUCE MITCHELL SHUT OFF the Camaro's engine, leaving the radio on. Eric Clapton's "Crossroads" was playing, and he leaned back in the seat to listen, grateful for the excuse to postpone for even a couple of minutes what he was about to do.

I went down to the crossroads . . .

So much had happened since that shining moment last night in Linwood Park that he still could hardly believe it. After he left the park, he had driven straight to the newspaper office to turn in the medallion. His arrival had generated a flurry of activity, a string of questions. Who was he? When did he find it? What was it hidden in? Did he have a registered Winter Carnival button? No? Well, he would still receive two thousand dollars. The check would be cut and mailed to him. When was he available for an interview?

From the newspaper office, he had driven over to Joanna's apartment, his mind racing with plans. She had not believed him at first.

"You found it? You're kidding! You *are* kidding! It's a joke, right?"

"It's no joke," he had reassured her. "Get your coat. I'm taking you out to dinner. But first, we have to go home. The paper is sending a reporter out to interview me. They're going to take my picture and everything. After they make me famous, I'm taking you out for the best steak I can buy."

It was nine o'clock before they were settled at a table in the Cherokee Sirloin Room. He waited until the waiter had taken their orders and brought their salads, looking for the right opportunity.

"So what are you going to do with the money?" Jo had asked him over their salads.

"You said I was supposed to take you someplace warm," he said. "How about a cruise in the Caribbean?"

"I'm yours," she said. "When do we leave?"

"Let's go during spring break," he said. Then his mouth had gone dry, and his voice nearly disappeared as he croaked out the important words. "What do you say we make it our honeymoon?"

Jo's fork had stopped halfway to her mouth. "What?"

"Let's get married," he whispered, struggling to bring his voice under control.

"Are you serious?"

Unable to talk, he had only nodded.

Jo put down her fork. The look on her face made him stare into his salad. Panic rising in him, he had leaped to fill the silence.

"I love you."

"I love *you*," she said.

Her hand moved across the table to meet his own. They sat in silence for a few moments, their fingers intertwined. He wondered what she was thinking behind those lovely, dark eyes. For a moment he wished he had waited until later to bring this up—afterwards, when she lay against him with her head on his shoulder. And then a realization had clicked firmly into place. Out here, away from their passion, was where those words counted most, where they were really proven.

"Well?" he had prodded gently. Her hand had tightened on his.

"I hate to say this," she began and stopped.

"I hate it when people say 'I hate to say this.' It means they're about to say something bad."

"No, it's nothing bad. At least, I hope it's not bad." She massaged his hand tenderly. "It's just that . . . I have some things to straighten out first. I'm still trying to decide who I am. I'm still defining myself in terms of someone else. You know who you are. Sometimes I think I know who I am. Like when I'm with you. But I need to know who I am when I'm by myself, too. Does this make any sense?"

He could only nod. Yes. Oh, yes. All the sense in the world.

"I just want to go along like we are for a while," Jo said. "Can we just take our time?"

"Take all the time you need," he had said, struggling to hide his disappointment. "I'm here when you're ready. Tattoo and all."

"You're on the record," she had said, smiling. "I'm not about to let you off the hook."

Finally at midnight, too keyed up to sleep, he had sat alone on the couch. A hollow feeling settled over him. All the excitement seemed off-key, manufactured, without St. John around to celebrate with. But he and St. John were kaput. St. John had antagonized him, pushed him to choose. And he had made his choice, punctuating it with a right hand.

Deep in the still hours of the night, as Joanna slept beside him, her words from the restaurant had come back to him. *You know who you are.* As the clocked ticked toward morning, he had changed his mind, made a new choice. He wanted them both, needed them both in his life.

And now, sitting in the Camaro in St. John's parking lot next to The Beast, he finally had organized things into some kind of perspective. The poor old geezer in the park; he understood the old man's tirade about changes, but he was wrong. Times changed, and you moved on. It was as simple as that. You moved on, sometimes by choice, sometimes because you had to. But whether by choice or necessity, when you packed for the future, you took what was important along with you. And this was important. For there was something to be said about friendship, however flawed it was. You let each other down once in a while, but you picked things up again and kept on trucking. You either accepted what people could give you, or you didn't. St. John would always be Butch Cassidy, and at least in St. John's eyes, he, Bruce Mitchell, would always be the Sundance Kid. Well, he could be Sundance, *and* whatever Jo needed him to be, because it was all part of being himself.

But it wasn't all up to him. Not entirely. It was best to go on in and get it over with, one way or another. He opened the car door and climbed out into the chill air. A few lazy snowflakes swirled in the air around him. He planned his strategy as he negotiated the icy sidewalk. Ring the doorbell, speak his piece the instant the door opened, before St. John had a chance to react. *Look, I'm sorry I hit you. You were right and I was wrong. I should have been more supportive lately.* Or something to that effect. There would be time later to talk about the rest of it. Or else it wouldn't matter.

Inside the apartment building, he took the carpeted steps two at a time, arriving at the top with his heart thumping from the sudden exertion. At the far end of the hall, Clapton's "Crossroads" poured out into the hallway. A wonder that St. John and his neighbors weren't all stone-deaf. He felt his stomach tightening as he moved down the hall, passing the welcome mats that lay in front of the wooden doors. St. John's doorway, he noticed, had no welcome mat in front of it.

He reached for the doorbell, then pulled his hand back. The ornery S.O.B. had threatened him with a club. He should just turn around and go home. St. John knew his phone number. He could call if he ever wanted to talk to him again.

He drew in a deep breath. Settle it now, one way or another. With effort, he pushed the button with his index finger. No answer. He rang the buzzer again just as he heard the volume cut on Clapton's guitar solo.

"Keep your shirt on!" St. John's voice was terse and surly behind the door. He heard the rattle of a chain, the sound of the lock being turned, and the door jerked opened. St. John, wearing his blue quilted vest over a flannel shirt, filled the doorway.

"Yeah, what?" He was clean-shaven. His left cheek was swollen and discolored, a bluish purple that extended up and around his eye. A glorious shiner. His face showed surprise, then went flat under his Ford cap. Behind him, Bruce could see that the living room had been cleaned and vacuumed. His eyes locked on St. John's, and all the things he had intended to say jammed up and stuck in his throat.

"What d'ya say, Butch?" he croaked.

His friend's face softened at the sound of the familiar name. In an instant, Bruce knew that St. John understood everything that he had intended to say and now couldn't, knew what it all meant, knew that such words, between friends, were seldom necessary.

St. John's customary, lopsided grin seemed even more lopsided under his swollen cheek.

"Hey, Sundance," he said, and stepped back to let him inside.

EPILOGUE

THE SCHMIDT BREWERY REOPENED with a new name and under new management, but the famous Schmidt sign shines no more over the West Seventh Street neighborhood. Linwood Park was redesigned the summer after the treasure medallion was found there. The *Saint Paul Pioneer Press* ceased publication of its afternoon edition. The King Boreas Treasure Medallion Hunt now stretches out over twelve days.

Keith Reynolds was fired from his programming job, and now works as a programmer for a temporary services agency. When he finally called Toni Benson, he found that she had moved back to Silver Bay.

Phil Prescott is district sales manager for the telephone company in San Diego, California. Sharon Prescott lives in St. Paul with her sons. She owns and operates Horatio Alger's, a bookstore specializing in secondhand educational books and the classics.

A month after the treasure hunt, Genevieve Krause flew alone to Houston to visit her daughter. While she was gone, Alfred Krause shot himself in the head with his brother's shotgun. He died in the room in which he was born.

The Carpenters did not move to New York. Debi Carpenter charged a new couch and chair on the couple's credit card. Steven Carpenter wrote a song called "Credit Card Queen."

Dennis St. John and Bruce Mitchell, a.k.a. Butch Cassidy and the Sundance Kid, remain best friends.

ABOUT THE AUTHOR

Roger Barr has lived in St. Paul since 1969. He is the author of *The Vietnam War* and *The Importance of Richard M. Nixon*, published by Lucent Books in San Diego. His fiction has appeared in several regional magazines and anthologies. He has never found the King Boreas Treasure Medallion.